The King's Con

Enjoy
Morgan C. Lee

By

Morgan C. Lee

This is a work of fiction. All the characters and events portrayed are either fictitious or are used fictitiously.

Library of Congress Catalog Number: 2003114979
ISBN 1-930052-16-2

Cherokee Books
P.O. Box 463
Little Creek, DE 19961
FAX: 302-734-3198
www.cherokeebooks.com

CHAPTER 1   **1967**

THE CLASH

MEMPHIS, TENNESSEE

The coolness of the morning was wiped away as if by an invisible hand as the sun rose above the hills that surround Memphis. Slivers of amber sunlight penetrating the darkness of the jungle room reflected off the bald, white head of a ceramic monkey and spotlighted one of the pair of collared cheetahs, standing alert on a garish, acrylic orange plain. The room was quiet, except for the whirr of three window air conditioners and the soft gurgling of the fountain.

A maid, sweater clad against the arctic coldness, worked quietly, standing on the seat of the seven-foot tall, hand carved, island goddess throne, dusting its pine surface with a rag sprayed with lemon scented Pledge.

"This is the only hard part of the job," she murmured to herself. "I sure hope I don't get too froze up with arthritis to climb these hateful chairs before I retire cause I sure do like working for Mr. P."

Finished, she stepped down and seated herself for a moment's rest. With head lowered, she surveyed the green shag carpet for litter and made a mental note that the ash tray on the table next to the wood carved, Tiki god lamp with the fake fur shade, had overflowed, spilling several wood tipped, El Producto Atlas cigar butts onto the rug.

Wonder the man don't burn the house down around him, she thought as she looked up at the pheasant feather framed mirror, searching for hand prints or smears of the like. The green shag rug on the ceiling provided the perfect reflection from which she could gauge the cleanliness of the mirror.

Nancy Rooks, the day maid, was indeed fortunate. Her employer's vampire like habits restricted her cleaning to a few rooms. The jungle room, or the den as the master called it, rocked with night time frivolity but usually was abandoned during the day. So too the kitchen, music room, parlor and dining room as the residents of the main house escaped the probing sunlight.

Deep within the bowels of the mansion, owner, employees and guests were either in various states of alcohol and drug induced sleep or in unnatural states of awareness. It was during just such moments as these that the owner worried about the possibility of a break in by gangsters, or a lone psychotic on a mission only his demonic mind understood, that would result in his death by assassination. He shared his bedroom this lovely summer morning with a stunning woman who had more than assassination on her mind, now that the owner's physical needs and emotional desires had been satisfied. She could barely make out his rough hewn, swarthy face in a room in which all was black except the white shag rug on the floor and the white, leather trim on the furniture. The black velvet shades were drawn closed. Not even a pinpoint of natural light ever fell in this room. The flickering ceiling lights provided the only means of contrast. His lustrous brown eyes seemed to sparkle in response to the twinkling artificial stars.

The King and his bed mate, engaged in some after sex pillow talk, are discussing with morbid fascination, the assassination of JFK.

"Why did they do it, Fire Eyes?"

"I don't really know, Baby Doll, but I think it may have something to do with his being famous like me," he responded.

"Oh, I don't know what I would do without you."

"Don't worry, honey. My bodyguards will take care of me," he said to assure her, but did not fully believe his own response. *He would need to talk to the boys,* he thought, *find out their values. Maybe he needed a professional or two who laid off drugs.*

"But the President had bodyguards and they still shot him."

"But Baby Doll, I ain't going to be riding in no parade."

"You ought to have some of your sperm frozen, you know. Just in case. I so much want to have your son and heir. The world will need him should anything happen to you."

"Well, sugar, then we better get back to doing what we were doing. Remember, even dogs practice all their lives. Ain't no human got it perfect that I know of. But first, I got me a powerful desire for a fried peanut butter and banana sandwich. Back in a minute," he said, as he grabbed his silken robe to cover his nude body from the maid's gaze as he strolled to the kitchen.

"Would you bring me a Pepsi from the fridge?"

"You best lay off the bellywash, Baby Doll, least you won't be able to go to sleep. Cause when I get back, we'll see if I'm up to one more go. Either way, you know where you go when it's beddy-by time," he responded as he let the door close softly behind him.

"Mornin' Nancy, you make sure you do a good job," he said as he smiled that smile that caused a woman to forget her age and her upbringing. " The boys got pretty riled up last night and left quite a mess."

"My, Mister P, you startled me," she responded "But I think I know which boy did the most riling."

"Now who would that be?" he said shyly, hanging his head down in mock injury.

"Better left unsaid, Mr. P. What takes you up this early? You ain't got nothing big on for today that I know of," Nancy Rooks asked.

"That remains to be seen," he responded as he lewdly swept his eyes back to the master suite.

Nancy Rooks blushed.

Mr. P chortled, pleased with himself at having caught her in so simple a verbal trap. Just as he was not a hunter of animals, nor was he so mean spirited as to not let her out of the trap he had sprung. He promptly changed the subject.

"Naw, I'm just hankerin' for a fried peanut butter and banana sandwich. I'm on my way to the kitchen to fix one. Want me to make one up for you?" he said.

"Best not, I've a heap of work to get done. Thanks just the same," she said, turning back to her dusting as Mr. P left the room.

"That boy would have made that sandwich for me, I know. I'm the only one of the hired hands that he'd do for, not ask to do for him. Probably because he misses his mama, Miss Gladys, so bad," she mused. Then she stooped to pick up the paper hamburger wrappings.

"Sure does like his well-done hamburgers from the Gridiron. He better watch out or one day that 'Slim Jim' figure of his is going to be a pork roll."

♪

Baby Doll sat naked in the center of the bed, examining her breasts, deep in thought. She cupped one, then the other, grateful to God that he had invented contact lenses when he discovered his first experiment didn't work. Otherwise, she wouldn't have been able to see the perfect marble, yet unveined luster of her breasts, each with an awesomely developed rose colored nipple.

These little babies are not going to stay this way forever. Mama said that when you have kids, forget it. They sag and the men don't like them any more. Well, when I have a baby, it's going to be his, whether he likes it or not, she thought. *In the meantime, I probably have until I'm twenty-five before the wear and tear on these beauties makes them start to sag and not be perky enough to hypnotize him.*

Baby Doll was sadly aware that she was just one of many in the fight to catch Mr. P. She had the advantage now, being close to hand so to speak. But she was smart enough to know that time was running out. He had a wandering eye and became bored easily. She had to act quickly. If she were going to snag him, it wouldn't be by playing fair. He was making it awful tough on her. Mr. P kept her birth control pills in his medicine chest, which was locked. Only he had a key. Each evening, before the partying began, they conducted a solemn ritual in which he handed her the pill and she had to swallow it with a sip of milk before his very eyes. He wanted iron clad proof that he was protected from becoming a father again.

He never let her sleep with him for fear of her doing something tricky. Bed was for sex at night and sleeping single in the daytime, behind a locked door. Moon, the foreman, had a key, and Mr. P of course, but that was it. Moon had strict instructions to use his key only in case of an emergency, or he would have his butt kicked off the estate by Mr. P personally.

Only once had Mr. P violated his sleep over code. He had risen early, randy as all get out. His lust drove him to her bedroom where he woke her and took her back to his bedroom, locked the door and really laid it on her. Licked her toes, admiring her sooties, his baby talk for her dainty little feet. Then he promptly passed out from the combination of the pills the night before and his powerful, bull like exertions. He had been working very hard the previous two months and he over did the drug thing. He liked the feel of his mind when he was under the influence, but occasionally went too far. That was such an occasion.

And it was her golden opportunity to get what she wanted. All she needed was a little bit of semen and she would be in fat city. She could go have it stored until she came up with a good alibi on why she had to leave him for a while. Then it would be off the pill, artificial insemination, pregnancy and birth to a healthy child before he had a chance to figure out how she did it.

She labored long and hard that night. She used every womanly trick in her bag, and her bag was large, for this was a very experienced woman. Try as she may, she could not overcome the powerful combination of drug remnants that coursed through his veins and kept him comatose through the night. Fearing that he might wake and find her there with him, she left around midnight to join the party.

Now she was reduced to trying to convince him to do the job himself.

The peanut butter was creamy, just right to spread one tablespoon on each slice of bread like his mother had taught him before she died. She wanted her baby to keep on having his favorite snack, made like he liked it, even after she was gone. And so there he stood, in the kitchen by himself, trying to blink away the sunlight, while he went about his cooking

Should have brought my shades, he thought. *Now, mash that 'nana, and spread it on the peanut butter.* He could hear his Satinin's voice telling him to spread the margarine evenly on the outsides of the sandwich while the frying pan was heating, so as to get it uniformly, golden brown without burning it. Cooking for himself in his mother's ghostly presence acted as a balm on his soul. Satinin' had been his only confidant all his life. Her death left a hole in his heart and in his life that would never fill back up again. His mood while cooking was as close as it ever got to what passed for him as introspection, a time without emotional stress. Then he could wonder about his life, his friends and their motivations and ambitions.

He never let his thoughts become so deep as to entrance him, thereby causing the sandwich to burn. That would have been sacrilege, an offense to his dear departed mother's memory.

What is Baby Doll up to? he thought. *She wants me to freeze my juice so in case I get killed, she can continue the family name without me? I don't like the sound of that. What will I care when I'm gone?*

He checked the sandwich by gently stabbing at it around the edges with the Teflon coated flipper. He murmured a sigh of satisfaction at the uniform golden brown color he saw when he flipped it over.

But maybe mama would, he thought.

But thinking about the mechanics of it, the logistics and the storage problems began to make him sick. So he stopped thinking about it and went back to the soothing motions of making his sandwich. When it was done, he ate it warm, with a glass of milk. He was transported back to being ten years old for a moment. It was a pleasant, soothing feeling, kind of like a Valium trip, without taking the pill.

Then he remembered being ten years old and getting that lousy cheap guitar from old Mr. Bobo, the salesman at the Tupelo Hardware Company instead of the .22 rifle he really wanted. His warm, emotional island sank in a resurrected sea of memories of forgotten anger and disappointment.

What a lousy birthday, he thought. The feeling of solitude, like the sandwich and glass of milk, was gone.

♪

The door swung open softly, with Fire Eyes' silhouette backlit by natural light from the hallway window. Baby Doll's juices started to flow. He really was an extraordinarily beautiful specimen.

"Get yourself out a' here, Baby Doll. All that talk about semen freezing has turned me off, big time."

She knew an order when she heard one. Not wanting to risk a display of his monstroustemper over the matter, he had been known to destroy an entire room over less, she gathered her things, held her breath, kissed him on the cheek and retreated to her own bedroom. She wagered to continue the skirmish in the near future, after she got all the facts about the clinics and other medical stuff. Fire Eyes could read and was not stupid. She would come up with a way to convince him.

She never got the chance. When she woke that evening, Fire Eyes was gone. Down to the Delta room at Chenault's in Memphis with Lardass and Billy to sop up sorghum syrup with homemade biscuits. Moon, as the foreman, was left to do the dirty work of telling Baby Doll to pack up and dropping her off at her apartment.

♪

CHAPTER 2   **1996**

THE TRASH

LOS ANGELES, CALIFORNIA

The missile approached its target with unmerciful accuracy. The strike need not be totally destructive, perhaps not even lethal, for the point to be made. As the gold and red, lacquer coated device neared closure, the target moved. Lacking any internal guidance system, the missile continued on course until it crashed harmlessly, destroyed by the energy in its own propulsion system.

I'm getting too old for this, the target thought, as he sought refuge behind a red leather couch, that sat like a blood stain in snow on carpet so white that it dazzled the eyes.

"You low living, cowardly, no good, twerp. What do I pay you for that you can't even talk to the network, let alone negotiate terms? Get up from behind that couch or, so help me, I'm going to break one of these plates over your shiny bald head."

Roxanne was in fine form today, displaying the ugly, a.k.a. real, side of her multi-faceted personality. Her charm, coquettishness, flair for the comedic and overall crudeness had made her a top TV personality with her own show that had been in the top ten for five years. Not bad company, neck to neck with "The Simpsons" and "Seinfeld". No accounting for taste.

But as the show hit the mid-nineties, the ratings had started to slide. Roxanne never looked inward when a failure occurred. She didn't realize that she had the crass attractiveness of the cast of The A-Team, remember Mr. T and all those gold chains, that took a group of writers at the Cheers level to keep her show in the forefront. By the time she had sneered and snarled her way to snare more than 30 million viewers each week, she got what she pleased from the network. She had money, power, the right to choose material, and the authority to hire and fire staff, including the scribes who wrote the show. So when the viewers started to tune out, she started firing writers. At first, the money for replacements was good enough to attract the best writers. They were willing to take the money and her gaff, just for long enough to put a down payment on their dream vacation home. But Roxanne quickly ran through the dream team, began to settle for lesser lights and was now reduced to begging and conniving any wordsmith who could help to relentlessly churn out the weekly scripts for the 18 annual episodes.

"You think I won't do it," she screamed, a grating, scraping, raspy sound that would shrink the gonads of a full grown, silver back mountain gorilla to the size of a couple of ripe olives, hold the pimento.

Her face flushed, engorged with blood, fat and ready to burst like a ripe melon. She picked up another plate and sent it flying toward the couch. "How do you think I got rid of that wimpy, good for nothing that I was stupid enough to marry when I was just looking to get away from my family? Ha, he begged me not to leave him and the kids, actually got down on the floor, in tears, and grabbed hold of my leg like the mutt he was.

Oddly, the sound of her own voice recanting this tale of her triumph over adversity had a calming effect upon her. The color of her face began to pass through various shades of red, from fire engine to flannel shirt and then faded to cotton candy pink as she continued. Her voice modulated in tone. Morphing through one personality type after another, she flowed naturally from outward outrage to a narcissism fed by the memories of past, pyrrhic victories.

Dominic Celio, crouching in terror, trying desperately to maintain his dignity by not wetting his pants, couldn't help but think, *Man, she is good, going from James Earle Jones to Redd Foxx and then into an old smoothie like Harry Belafonte without missing a word. Now I hope the old bitch gets so engrossed in herself that I can sneak out of here. How stupid can I get, thinking I could reason with her better in person? If I ever get out of here alive, I'm going to be a cell phone agent just like all the rest of them.*

Smoothly, in soft, well-structured tones, Roxanne began to speak as she walked toward the couch. In anger, her Rubenesque figure took on the mannerisms of a gutter fighter, aroused and snarling, exerting the sex appeal of a Doberman with flashing teeth trying to rip out your throat. In the calmness of thought, her body softened, her hips rolled when in a full, relaxed stride and she exhibited a sexual aura that was uncommon in a woman of her proportions.

"Come on, Dominic, get up from back there and let me finish telling you the story. I ain't gonna break a plate on your head. These babies are a thousand bucks a setting."

Tentatively he rose upward, eyes closed, judging his position by the feel of his fingers on the couch's soft leather. Released from the tension that kept them squeezed closed, his eyelids opened spontaneously just as they cleared the back of the couch.

"Come on, Dominic, I was just joking you. Park it on the couch and let me tell you the whole story of how I outwitted my ex and got out of that dreary town, and even worse marriage," Roxanne said, in a false, saccharin, shy voice.

Dominic got up on his knees, not to pray, but to think how he was going to get out of there without losing his life, his mind, or his client,

11

not necessarily in that order. Slowly, he stood up and grimaced soundlessly at the pain in his back muscles as he straightened his spine. He was sure this was a sign of advancing age, but now was not the time to dwell on it. He moved around the couch and sat down.

And so she told him.

♀

As she concluded the tale, she spoke, not in triumph, but in a whisper. "Dominic, I'm scared. I don't know what to do, what to change, or how to go about it. Help me."

"Roxie, I'm doing the best I can, but frankly, you've become such a pain in the butt, everybody, including the network guys, is secretly hoping you take the fall. You got pretty uppity when the show was Number 1, you know," he said, not believing he said it.

The nasty, shrieking shrew of a few minutes ago had become a child, tears dribbling down her plump cheeks. "Cheezes, Dominic, I worked so damn hard to get here, I don't want to give it up."

Despite himself, her agent leaned from the couch to pat her on the hand, as she sat there on the recliner, with her legs tucked under her body.

"I can't go back to waitressing or working the clubs anymore. I'm a star, and stars don't do that. How can you put your hand in the wet concrete at Grauman's Chinese one day and be a nobody the next? That ain't fair, is it?" she said, pitifully. Then defiantly, "It isn't going to happen. I'm not going to let it."

She struck a proud pose, then looked at her diminutive white-haired agent and said, "Dominic, sweetie, you were an agent in this town when the talkies took over. You've seen every rise and fall. I knew how to get here, but it looks like I'm not having much luck staying here. How did other stars stop the slide once it started?"

"There's no single or simple formula. And it's tougher with TV than it was with the movies. See, with the movies, you just had to please an audience and be known as a box office draw. With TV, you've also got sponsors to convince," he answered.

"Well what's worked, and what hasn't?" she asked.

"In the movies, sex, a change in the type of roles, you know, breaking the stereotype, going to Europe and making films there, Clint Eastwood. Stuff like that. Sometimes some notoriety on the bad side even helps. Look at Mitchum and that dope deal."

"Well, with my body, I can forget sleeping around. I tried that on the way up and no one was interested. I'm even paunchier now than I was then. And all that other stuff is for men, and movie stars at that. What about TV?" she pleaded, but there was a slight shrillness to her voice.

Dominic Celio caught it. *Overstayed my welcome. Better get out while the getting is good*, he thought.

"About the only thing that I've seen work is a make over in a brand new show. Look at Mary Tyler Moore, Carol Burnett, Lucille Ball. They all managed to do it several times over. And speaking of over, I've got to be cross town in an hour so I'll have to be leaving. Just remember, first you'll have to get them interested in you again, and then the show will come."

With that said, he dashed for the door and was through it as he heard the muffled crash of china against its solid walnut surface.

"That little creep, that's what I'm paying him for, but I'll bet I end up having to do it myself, just like always," she shouted as she turned over the cabinet, smashing the rest of the expensive, Tiffany fine bone china.

13

CHAPTER 3   **1890-1892**

THE DASH

SOUTH DAKOTA

In August 1890, Big Foot's band of Sioux gathered at an encampment on the Cheyenne River to perform a ceremonial dance. The drum beat was soft, deep, but not defiant. The people held hands, man to woman, woman to man as they slowly danced in a circle, chanting:

> The whole world is coming,
> A nation is coming, a nation is coming,
> The eagle has brought the message to the tribe.
> The father says so, the father says so.
> Over the whole earth they are coming.
> The buffalo are coming, the buffalo are coming.
> The Crow has brought the message to the tribe.
> The father says so, the father says so.

The Sioux Ghost Dance Song was repeated throughout the day and into the night. The circle dwindled as one by one, exhaustion took its victims, who simply fell down and slept.

The last person standing was Wolf-Voice, a Hunkpaka Sioux who lived on the Pine River Reservation in South Dakota. He raised his right arm and slowly rotated in a circle as he stared at the hills that surrounded the shallow valley where his people had camped by a small creek.

When the circle was completed, he stopped and raised the other hand. With head uplifted, he spoke these words, "Wovoka, prophet of the Paiute, Big Foot's people have cleansed their spirits and poured the white man's bust head whiskey in the creek that brings us life water from the father. Now let the old ways return, let the white man leave us forever, and the buffalo run wide as a river through these lands once more." Then he fainted and fell onto the dusty earth, worn free of grass by the shuffling feet of the Ghost Dancers.

Running Water, daughter to Wolf-Voice, warned the children in the tepee to be quiet. Her father's tepee was the temporary holding pen for the little band's children who were too young to understand the seriousness of the Dance. Running Water, at 13, was the oldest child in the tent and, thus, was in charge. She was too young to remember a world without white people, or a world alive with buffalo in numbers numerous as the leaves that fall in the autumn.

Her smooth, coppery skinned forehead wrinkled as she thought about the ceremony she had just witnessed. She was worried about the future foretold by the Prophet. But more worrisome still, she did not believe that the medicine was strong. She knew of the muslin shirts that were stored in Big Foot's tent. Her brother had helped fold them neatly, place them in stacks of ten on the sacred white buffalo robe and then cover them with deer hides to protect them from the dust that would be raised by the dance. Wovoka claimed they would stop the blue coats' bullets. Running Water did not believe that the special symbols on the ghost shirts would protect the warriors from harm.

✠

The six horse Overland stage bucked its way closer to its home station. The horses had been changed three times at way stations built at

10 mile intervals along the way. The home station was the first place since the fifty-mile journey started in the morning where a man could eat, get a shot of whiskey and rent a bed to sleep. It was early autumn in Montana. The distant hills undulated in the heat spilled over from summer. There could be a blizzard tomorrow, but right now, the inside of the coach was unbearable. All ten passengers road on the roof where they could at least catch the breeze, hanging on with one hand, holding their hats with the other. A huge plume of dust trailed behind the coach. It hadn't rained in three months.

The home station at Calvin was a two-story log cabin, with a lean-to of the same construction off to the side. It had glass windows front and back, thrown open to catch any errant bit of a breeze. Often as not, they were closed to keep out the mosquitoes and flies. As the driver pulled back the reins on the horses and engaged the big, friction brakes on the rear wheels, the coach slowed enough to allow the dust plume to begin catching up. By the time the coach was stopped, passengers and team were enveloped in what the locals called a Montana summer shower, with dust clinging to clothes and collecting in every orifice that wasn't shut, covered or plugged. The seasoned coach travelers had taken the necessary precautions to protect their breathing apparatus about when the coach had begun to slow. With a hat crushed under the arm, the trick was to maintain your balance so as not to fall off the coach while using both hands, for just a second, to tie a bandana around the face. Passengers that failed to take this elementary precaution, ingested a lung full of dirt and began coughing like they had tuberculosis.

Each man cleaned up to the extent he wanted. No nagging mothers or wives here. Most simply slapped their hats against their trousers, shared a dusting of their backs with one another and walked through the door into the main cabin. All the Overland stage home stations were laid out the same. There were two communal tables with benches to sit at while eating. Up against the blind wall was the bar, consisting of a pair of barrels with two wide planks nailed to them. The only novelty here was the broken backed chair which supported the center of the bar.

Nine of the ten men headed straight for the bar. The tenth was a Methodist teetotaler from back east. The driver would be in after helping get the horses out of their harness. No need to worry about thinking what to order for their meals. They would share from communal bowls whatever the cook had felt like cooking, or whatever he had to hand.

A short, stocky bearded fellow, wearing a dark green woolen shirt with a leather vest, stood at the far end of the bar. He downed his whiskey in one swallow and nodded for another. His hair was white, the beard grey. Two fingers were missing from his left hand, the one that held the glass. He belched, sighed and turned to his neighbor at the bar.

"This place be darker than the inside of a buffalo's butt, hotter than an Arapaho's head when he's been buried in the sand, and has more flies and smells than an Injun pony carcass that 's been boiling and rotting in a Montana summer. But, boys, ain't it just grand, it don't roll and buck like that ass bruising, bone jarring, blister forming, scab ripping piece of transportation that we just spent the last sixteen hours trying to hold on to," he said.

Shifting his weight to respond was a middle sized, slim, almost delicate man, dressed in a dark suit, brown Stetson hat and worn, but polished boots. He wore a gold chain attached to his pocket watch, a holstered colt revolver, tied to his leg with a leather thong and a silk handkerchief in his coat pocket. He dressed the dandy, but didn't talk in a foppish way, and was manly in all other mannerisms as well.

"There's that to be said for it," he responded.

Leather Vest figured him for either a card shark, a hired gun, or a gigolo. In fact, he was neither.

Sipping from the second drink of rye whiskey, Leather Vest continued the conversation, as there was nothing to do but drink, smoke and talk between now and whatever passed for dinner, by saying, "Mong you ever heard of this ghost dancing stuff that's supposed to be floating around among the tribes? I heerd tell it got started by some Payute name of Wavokie, or some such thing, whatever that's supposed to mean. The way Injun names seem to go, it could be Eats With the Ducks for

17

all I know."

The Dandy smiled, and responded, "As a matter of fact, the ghost dancing is why I'm here. I'm from back in Washington, here to investigate the claims we've been getting from the local citizenry."

Leather Vest asked, "Don't you trust your soljer boys? They got eyes and ears, ain't they?"

"That they do, but there are also reputations and promotions to be made out here. This is, after all, the only place the soldiers have to play at the moment," the Dandy smiled as he took another sip of his bourbon.

"You best tell them fellows in Washington to let the blue bellies have at it. These injuns are ready to go. Here tell they's intending to drive us all out so the buffler can come back," Leather Vest responded with some fire, the whiskey beginning to spark an already belligerent personality.

"They've held us off for forty years but it's been costly for them. Surely, even the most poorly informed Sioux warrior must know by now that we out man and outgun them. Do they want to commit mass suicide?" the Dandy asked.

"Wouldn't know about that? I just hear tell they've been cast'n spells and such. Believe they've got something called a ghost shirt that will protect them from a white man's rifle bullets."

The Dandy dribbled bourbon down his chin as he started to chuckle at the comment in mid drink. He put down his glass, removed an inside handkerchief made of cotton, and daubed his chin, while saying with a smile, "Sir, that is a preposterous tale. No such body armor exists in the world, and no one would be fool enough to believe it."

Grabbing his drinking hand and looking the Dandy straight in the eye, Leather Vest spoke evenly, but firmly, "Your missing the point, mister. You know it and I know it but them bucks don't. I've fought them bucks from Bear River to the Big Dry Wash. They can come at you at a

18

full gallop, kill you, scalp you and steal your equipment without slowing down. Now that's when they have some limited thought that they may not come out alive on the other side. I am not interested in meeting up with no Sioux warrior who *knows* it ain't his day to die."

✠

General Nelson Miles, who had stayed in the field during the winter of 1876-77 seeking to avenge the death of Colonel Custer, was ordered by headquarters to the Pine Ridge reservation late in the year of 1891. It had been fifteen years since he had fought Crazy Horse to a standstill at Wolf Mountain, the year Sitting Bull had led his people into Canada, fleeing the reservation that was killing their spirits. Now he had been ordered to Wounded Knee to round up a band of Hunkpaka Sioux who had been said to be causing trouble, or were, perhaps, about to. He found mostly women and children, but herded them together nonetheless. They were surrounded by five hundred soldiers armed with Springfield carbines and complimented by four Hotchkiss guns

With the dawn came the coldest part of the day, just before sunrise. A blizzard was building off to the northwest so there was no weather to speak of, it was just bitterly cold, as it gets in late December in this part of the world. The soldiers began going about their job, which was to separate the men, line them up and disarm them. For the moment, the cold seemed an even fiercer adversary than the four ghost shirted, Hunkpapa Sioux warriors, members of Big Foot's band, who stood before them, apparently warm and content in the trade blankets which were draped around their shoulders and over their arms. The Seventh Cavalry had come to Wounded Knee ready for business if need be, complete with the battery of Hotchkiss guns commanded by old Captain Capron. What happened next has been the subject of many accounts. They vary from teller to teller. Much as the blankets from native Peruvian looms, there are no two tales alike. No one disputes the outcome, the slaughter of sixty-two Indian women and children. The Seventh sustained twenty-nine soldiers dead.

The artist Frederick Remington's account, paraphrased here, was gleaned from his discussions the day after with the men who saw action.

19

Remington had ridden and fought with these same men so he must have valued their integrity. According to him, all was going well until an old medicine man leaned over, picked up a handful of dirt and flung it in the air as a sign of defiance. The four bucks, taking that as a signal - it is not clear that it was - threw down their robes, thereby revealing their hidden Winchester rifles. They raised these rifles toward heaven and then the melee began. It was short, bloody work, with the Hotchkiss battery carrying the day despite the fact that the Indians centered what little firepower they had on the crews of these little cannons.

There was no moon that night. The wounded soldiers had already been carried from the field. Red Cross ambulances were waiting to take them to the main encampment of the Seventh Cavalry for treatment. A guard had been posted that evening to keep the remaining Sioux inside their tents. They had been fully disarmed and the men retained separately. The sky was overcast with moisture laden clouds, the heralds of the pending blizzard. Fires were lit around the tepees in which the warriors were being held to better see that they didn't try to escape. This cut the night vision of any guard who looked in the fire's direction, and who would not, even if only longingly, as the mercury plunged and the winds howled.

By nightfall, snow had begun falling. It became almost impossible to see beyond the length of a rifle. Running Water was crawling through the bodies on the field, searching for weapons, food and her brother's body. She found only her brother. He had stayed alive by disemboweling a dead horse and crawling inside, concealing as much of his torso as possible. A dead trooper's decapitated torso lay over his legs, dragged there by her brother to further conceal himself. He had held onto his knife, and life, in the hope of getting away to fight another day.

His sister found him only by crawling through the snow, using her hands to feel the look of each male Indian face by its contours and shapes. When she didn't find him, she looked for camouflage, for it would have been impossible for anyone to have escaped through the ring of fire.

The trooper was frozen by rigor-mortis. His body slid through the snow rather easily. Rather than pull Stump-Horn out, she shoved her head inside the horse's belly. She could hear his faint breath.

"Stump-Horn. It is I, your younger sister, here to help you. Can you walk?"

"No," he whispered softly. "I am about to die. I am gut shot, so there is nothing that can keep my spirit from leaving my body. The stench of my shit has entered my blood. Its offending odor will drive my spirit away. Do for me this one thing that I may die avenged. Here is my knife, the only weapon I now have. Take it! When you find the body of High-Walking, stick it in that lying medicine man's heart. Surely it is his lie about the shirt, that it would shield us from the power of the white man's bullets, that has killed me and my people." With that said, he died.

✠

Satisfied that this put an end to it, General Nelson Miles wheeled his mount, a brown gelding with black mane and tail, to face the northeast. The low lying hills that form the valley where Sioux women and children had been massacred just nineteen days before, were just beginning to flush with the bright rays of the rising sun. It was a cold day in mid January 1892. Smoke rose from most of the tepees down by the creek. Breakfast for the Seventh Cavalry had consisted of a speck of bacon, a cup of coffee so strong and black that you could almost see it silhouetted against the early morning darkness, and some of those Army biscuits, which wouldn't absorb liquid and were considered interchangeable with grape shot for the cannons. Grub on board, the fires in the Sibley camp stoves were dowsed. The white men's war tents, as the Indians called them, were struck, blankets rolled, saddles and gear adjusted and then the troops, calvary and scouts alike, stood around waiting for the General to make his move.

The column set out for the rail depot in Montana, a trek of 248 miles that would take them through the Crow reservation, the railhead being 60 miles west of the reservation. As was his style, General Miles began to distance himself from his staff, and his visitor, Frederic Remington, the writer, artist and sculptor, who had joined the General for what was to be the last significant campaign of the Indian wars. The General's hell bent for election, flat out gallop, would go on all day, and sometimes all night. The relentless way in which he drove his mounts was the purest form of flattery for the Cheyenne, Crow and Sioux he counted among his former adversaries. When he saw how they rode, he figured that there wasn't any man on earth who was going to outride him. And that was the Genesis of his riding style.

They did the entire trip in thirty-six and one-half hours.

CHAPTER 4   1996

THE FLASH

WILMINGTON, DELAWARE

I was taking the brown paper off the June issue of "Americans in History," when my heartbeat escalated to that of a trapped rabbit. In a flash, I nearly fainted. Not only had I never fainted in my life, I had never before in my life even felt faint. It was the sight of my father, back from his death of more than ten years past, staring at me with his right eye squinted, looking like the toughest SOB that ever lived. So he may have been. I do know that he was willing to take on anyone at the slightest ruffling of his pride.

I sat quickly to recover from my shock. There was his picture on the front cover, staring at me as I vaguely remember him looking when I was very young. He was dressed in the uniform of a cavalry officer, long mustaches drooping below his goateed chin. My father died in 1980 at the age of 120, leathery skin, teeth and hair intact. As far as I knew, I was his only issue, at least the only one he favored with his surname. My name is John L. Bunting.

My breathing and heartbeat began to ease as I sat there in the kitchen, contemplating the picture of a man I dearly loved, somewhat feared and greatly admired. He was the only person I had ever been close to whom I would call a real piss cutter. Dad turned eighty-one the day I was born. Mom could economize, which Mom always did, from that day on with one cake to celebrate both of our birthdays. I was curious, yet apprehensive, about opening the pages of this June issue. I had my own memories. Did I want to add to the baggage? Let's cut to reality. In a maudlin way, I feared the verification of oft told stories of heroism and daring do that I had dismissed all my life as fables made up like bedtime stories to pacify a young child. How much, really, does a man-child believe the stories told by his father, unless reinforced by his mother or by paternal uncles or aunts. My father had no siblings and he married my mother when he was 80 and she was but 28. How could she ever validate the truth of these stories as she was not even born, or was a mere youth, when most of them were presumed to have happened. My Dad did enough from the time he was 80 until he died to make me feel like an irrelevant spec upon this earth. If the stories he told of his previous exploits were more than just fables, if they were indeed true, then I was nothing more than a wisp in the cosmos, perhaps not an offense, but certainly not an addition to, the history of mankind.

His deeds, while I have been on this earth, were more than the average young man could truthfully include in his portfolio. Consider his reaction to a passing rake's flirtatious glances at my mother. He took the act as an affront and caned the ill-beguided flirt into unconsciousness. Yes, caned, for my father still sported one. Not that he walked with a limp or anything. He carried it for the protection afforded by the sword concealed within its wooden exterior. On this occasion, he felt the sword was unnecessary to subdue the six foot four, two hundred pound muscular Lothario. The man had good reason to ogle, as my mother was quite handsome even into her seventies, when her lustrous dark hair began to be shot with gray. Even then, the gray panthers would give her the once over. By the way, my father had reached the century mark the very year that this took place.

James Robert Bunting was an imposing figure of a man until his last year on this earth. He was fairly tall for his era, standing about six feet with broad shoulders that helped to carry the belly which burgeoned to greater dimensions with each passing decade. He was not fat, mind you, just one of those fellows who are well built but not flabby. His mustache resembled a pair of Beagle's ears, drooping down well past his chin and even below the goatee which it framed. Amazingly enough, it was as black as coal, just like his wavy hair which he always wore brushed back and a little longer than was popular in the first sixty years of the twentieth century. Given his contrariness, I'm surprised he didn't get it cut when the Beatles re-popularized the style.

He was a study in contrasts. When raging against some misfortune that had befallen him, he could string curses together that were almost lyrical in style. To the hammer which had the effrontery to bruise the thumb which held the nail that he had been attempting to drive, "You no good, low living, rotten, scum sucking, dung eating, son of a b......" The "You" always came out with a howl, followed by a crescendo that concluded with a deafening roar. He wanted the hammer, which he had flung mightily and was now sailing through the air, to hear his last utterance. On the other hand, I never heard him utter an oath until I was sixteen. That had to have been out of deference to my youth. And I never heard any profanity in front of my Mother. That in itself was an oddity, for Mother, whom I dearly loved, was known to express her self profanely from time to time. Maybe not so odd. For now that I think on it, never in front of Pop.

He was as smart a man as I think I ever met. Yet when I asked why he always squinted his left eye when doing close work, he said the retina in the center of that eye were burnt out one time when he was watching an eclipse of the sun. Squinting helped him to see better with the right eye. He hadn't used smoked glass or any other form of protection because he thought all that talk about hurting your eyes was hog wash.

He gave up smoking cigarettes at the age of 95, for health reasons. Yet he took up cigars on the same day. While he was smoking cigarettes, his brand was Wings. They don't make them any more. I think I can tell you why. During my smoking days, I was a Lucky Strike man. They were unfiltered and pretty potent. One day, when I was out with a survey party near Grandview, Missouri, I stopped at a little country store for a fresh pack of Luckies. It was an old place run by an old man. The old man's face had a faint shadow of handsomer days. Picture Tom Cruise at eighty, with a fringe of white hair and three teeth. Like his store, he was run down and dirty. It gave me pause, but not for very long before the nicotine fit was upon me. I think the reason there was no artificial light in the place was not out of thriftiness. The proprietor didn't want the customer to get a good look at the goods until he had paid his money and left. When I stepped up to the glass candy/tobacco/sundries counter, what should I spy but a carton of Wings. I had to have them. Now being a connoisseur of smokes, I knew that these treasures would require a bit of a stay in my humidor before they were smokable, so I bought a pack of Luckies to get me through the day. After about a week, I thought the Wings would be humidified back to normal, which judging by their texture they were. So, I took a pack with me to work. I lit up with my morning coffee. MMMMMMMMMMMMMMMM. Being a Lucky man in the era of the unfiltered, I thought I was prepared for anything. I wasn't. Within seconds of that first drag I got so dizzy I thought I was going to lose it. No wonder Pop dropped them at 95. Although why they hadn't already killed him, I'll never know.

But once you are hooked on tobacco, it is very easy to rationalize a substitute. Drugs, alcohol, food, sex. Pop stuck with tobacco. He switched to cigars, Marsh Wheeling Stogies from Wheeling, West Virginia. Had them mailed to him once per month. Those suckers were a good ten inches long. In an economy move as he began to age and his income started to go down, he would cut them in half and smoke one half in the morning, chew on the other the rest of the day. That was when he was 110 years of age.

I opened the magazine, thumbing through, searching for the table of contents to find why my father's picture was on the cover.

CHAPTER 5   **1969**

THE STASH

FROM MEMPHIS, TENNESSEE TO

WILMINGTON, DELAWARE AND BACK

The smoke from the cheap cigars drifted through the jungle room, simulating the velvety ribbons of vented steam and fog that the King remembered from the Islands. Of all the low budget, money making films that the Colonel loved so well, that was among his favorites. Not that he got to act, not that the songs were any good now that Jerry Leiber and Mike Stoller had got fed up with the Colonel and quit. Thinking about it, he muttered, somewhat slurring his words, "Bull!" Then he thought, *"Hound Dog" and "Jail House Rock". How could he be so stupid as to tick those two boys off.?*

"What's that, El?"responded Billy, as his head involuntarily jerked at the unexpected, unarticulate utterance.

The King had been sitting on the floor in the center of the room, head drooped, staring at the throw rug on which he sat. It was an animal hide of some kind, white with brown spots. Sometimes, when El was all stoked up like this, the conversation, if there was to be one, started with a question about what kind of animal it came from. They never reached a conclusion, but inevitably narrowed down to two choices, appaloosa or cow. He had an unopened book in his hand, *Profiles in Courage.* The early stage euphoria brought on by drinking always made him conscious of his lack of education. He would boast that tonight he was going to stay up until dawn, reading about his hero, John F. Kennedy. He always meant what he said, but he died with the book unopened, the edge of the pages worn by the touch of his fingers, soiled by grease and sweat. If he had only kept the book in the bathroom, instead of the jungle room, it would have been finished in quick order. Chronic constipation made the bathroom the reading room for the mansion's owner.

There having been no response solicited, the King continued his thoughts. *I know they wrote "Hound Dog" for 'Big Mama' Thornton, but that was just the point. They knew how to write music steeped in gospel and rhythm and blues. If he's not careful, I'll be back driving a truck in no time. I can't sing just anything, it's gotta be right.*

Billy watched carefully, saw the King's condition and decided Billy better get hisself off to bed before Mr. P's volcanic temper blew. There was always the risk of that happening, but when he was talking directly at you, at least sometimes you could see it coming. When he was all doped up like this, he was walking shadowy pathways, talking with his favorite companion, his other self, The Dark One. No one, but no one could track any sign down those murky lanes. The King had been known to pass out under these conditions. Then it was the Mafia's job to cart him off to bed, making sure to pull off his belt and his boots, and then to remember to lock the room on the way out. That's why Moon's job was the hardest. He had to stay up every night, and be reasonably sober, 'cause he was the only one with a key to the bedroom.

Old El could also snap out of one of these drug induced seances, bright eyed and ready to roll. That's why they had standing orders to keep all of his cars in the driveway, full of gas and with the keys in them.

And then there were the uneventful nights, for which they were always grateful, when he simply got up, said good night and went off to bed. But none of these made up for the terror of the arousal of The Dark One, the King's vain, bad tempered, mama's boy, spoiled brat side of his personality. That was the one he carefully chose to never allow his fans to see.

Old Billy didn't want to risk it. "Good night, y'all. It's going to be a long trip tomorrow night. I'm going to get some shuteye," he said. He stood up and eased his way out of the room, mercifully glad that he hadn't disturbed old El.

Unh, the King thought, *If it hadn't been for the Colonel, I wouldn't be makin' that long, sorry, borin' trip. That old hustler even wants to skin me out of my sperm. I could see it in his eyes when I asked him about whether there was places like what Baby Doll had said. Got rid of her sorry ass in a hurry.* At the thought, he smiled the smile that drove women crazy.

Moon was watching him carefully. "Oh, no, "he grimaced, "I hope this isn't going to turn sour on me."

The man thinks I'm stupid. But the money is good, even though the movies are bad. Plenty of women. But he ain't getting his hands on the King's juice, Mr. P thought as he started to get up from the floor. "Whoa, I ain't got my legs tonight. Moon!"

"Yeah, Boss," relieved that El could still talk.

"Make sure Fike has my necessaries packed for the trip."

"Got the list right here. Lardass'll be out first thing in the morning, buying fresh."

The list consisted of items that Mr. P absolutely had to have when he was on the road. They were his touch of home in a foreign land. They helped him doctor a sore throat, blood shot eyes and a cold. Included were cures for bad breath, chapped lips and constipation. Little aids for relaxation completed the bundle, which included the following, by brand name where important, and it was important to the King.

MUST HAVE AT ALL TIMES

Wood tipped cigars (El Producto Atlas or Diamond Tips), Blistex, Tareyton cigarettes, bottles of Dristan and Super Anahist, one card package of Contac, Sucrets in the antibiotic red box, eye drops, emery boards, matches, one jar of Occuline eye pads, Spearmint, Doublemint, Feenamint and Juicy Fruit gum, sour balls, gloves and sunglasses.

"Tell him to put them in a box this time, sitting next to me. That attache case was a pain. It squashed my cigarettes and Contac. I had the little colored balls all over creation."

"I'll get the box myself and do an inventory as soon as he gets in so there'll be time to send him out again if he comes up short."

"And don't forget to tell him to get the burgers from the Gridiron just before we leave. I don't want to stop for anything but gas and to use the restrooms," said the King.

"Big E, are you sure you don't want to reconsider driving the Silver Cloud. It's going to be awful conspicuous on those back roads in Virginia," Moon asked, risking the King's wrath because he knew the Boss was trying to do this in secret. Riding to Wilmington, Delaware in a Rolls Royce was not exactly going incognito. Once they got into the chateau country where the DuPonts lived, they'd be all right. It was getting there that worried him.

"Moon," the King exploded as he threw the book across the room at Marty Lacker, "I said we're taking it and the subject is closed. I didn't pay Michael Landon all that money to let it sit in the driveway. I wish that book had taken your fool head off."

That night, twenty minutes after the sun went down, the white

Cadillac swung through the iron gates that kept the fans and gawkers off the King's property. They headed east out of Memphis toward Pulaski, looking to bypass Nashville. The King had on a cowboy hat, a blond wig and a fake mustache, just enough that a quick look through the car window wouldn't give him away. He had awakened late that afternoon, groggy from the pills and alcohol, and deeply apologetic. Sober, he knew Moon had been right about not taking the Rolls.

Lamar Fike was driving, his great bulk hunkered over the wheel like he was squinting to see where he was going. Mr.P wasn't worried, that's the way he always drove. Said it made him feel the car's grip on the road. His cousin Billy was already asleep in the front passenger seat, getting rested so he could take over from Lard Ass at midnight. Billy had become the King's confidant since his mother had died. It was the blood which gave him a feeling he could trust old Billy. Moon sat in the back with the King on the other side of the box with his sundries and the two small coolers which held the next four hours worth of soda and well-done burgers. Well done was the way the King liked them. No booze or pills on this long ride. The king wanted his sperm to be as healthy as it could be. He didn't want any freaks in his family tree. He was especially worried about having a still born like his twin brother, Jesse Garon.

"How bout turning up the music. Moon done fell asleep and I'm getting lonesome back here."

"All we'll get is Nashville. What do you want, country, gospel or R and B?"

"Try some country. Maybe we can catch Johnny Cash's 'A Boy Named Sue'. He's probably the only singer going who has the right singing style to make that get on the charts. I like it, but I sure couldn't carry it off."

Shortly before midnight, they stopped at a Gulf station where the attendant was going about his closing up ritual. They drained their lizards, filled the tank with gas and moved the rest of the sodas and burgers from the trunk to the backseat. Billy took the wheel and drove northeast, paralleling the Tennessee River, then past the Cumberland

Gap through the Appalachian Mountains. By then the burgers were gone. Billy turned to check his passengers. Everyone but Billy was asleep.

Bless the Lord for that, he thought. *Even old El went to sleep with no pills that I noticed. That'll be good for him.* he thought, then shivered. *Wonder what's wrong with him that he has to go to a Yankee doctor? Old El's been taking a lot of pills lately. Hope they haven't given him cancer or anything.*

They were in Marion, Virginia at daybreak, having crossed the mountains through Stone Gap. Elvis had slept through the night for the first time in more than a year.

"My this is pretty country," Mr. P commented as he stretched and looked out the windows at the rolling hills. "Where we at?"

"About three hours from Richmond. I figure we can make better time to D.C. by going that way."

"Best wake up Lamar. No, hold that. See if you can make it to some place where we can get something to eat, use the bathroom and gas up."

They hit Newark, Delaware at dusk, tired but glad to have arrived close to their destination. They could have afforded to stay in the posh Hotel DuPont in downtown Wilmington. El preferred the anonymity afforded by the Howard Johnson Motel and Restaurant on the southern edge of this college town, home of theUniversity of Delaware's Fighting Blue Hens.

"Explain to me again how a bank got into this business," the King asked.

The Doctor/Banker/Curator was a distinguished looking, grey haired gentleman, with the looks of an aging movie star, picture Robert Wagner. He was seated behind a large, cherry desk that had been burnished and polished to a mirror like sheen. No object spoiled its visage. The phone sat on the credenza behind him. His dark blue suit was in perfect contrast to the gun steel grey of his hair. The plain, dark rum colored tie served as a transition point between his jacket's blue color and his shirt's brown egg complexion. The King would have been impressed, if not intimidated by this man back in his truck driving days. Now he was secure in the knowledge that he could buy and sell guys like this a million times over.

Doctor Winston B. Trader, after much careful thought, responded, "I have to be rather circumspect in how I answer that. Allow me to try by the use of analogy so as not to offend our sponsors. You are aware that there are certain families who live in Appalachia that have developed some rather peculiar offspring, are you not?"

"Yeah, like having seven toes, crowing like a rooster or being born without a nose. Is that what your talking about?" said the King.

"Precisely. Now the cause of that is inbreeding brought about by long isolation of those people who live in the hills and hollows. They have not benefitted from good roads to get them out where they can bring fresh blood into the gene pool."

"I get it. That's why the old folks caution you not to marry your first cousin, even if she's pretty.."

" Aptly put."

The King looked puzzled. "Then why ain't this place down in the hill country where it could do some good?" he asked.

"It is in a manner of speaking. Only hereabouts the hills are made of money," said Dr. Trader.

"I still don't get it," said the King. His expression began to change from bewilderment to the early flushes of anger.

"The gene pool in this area has been closely knit because money marries money. Marriageable people from outside the local aristocracy need not apply. As more and more loons began to show up in respectable families, rapid action was needed to prevent further embarrassment. A group of elders got the idea of enriching their bloodlines by adding carefully selected donated semen to artificially inseminate some of the younger married women who have yet to become pregnant. All of this is without the knowledge of the younger husbands whose wives withdraw assets from time to time," explained the Doctor in very hushed tones.

The clouds lifted from the King's brow. "Now wait a moment, you're not...,"

Dr. Trader cut him off in mid-sentence, "Rest assured, we are not going to use your deposit for that purpose. Absolutely not," he exclaimed. "The Board of Directors wanted two things from the Bank, secrecy and a source of income to make the operation self sustaining with no more influx of funds from the founders. Donors such as yourself are afforded the privilege and privacy of the service for which you pay generously. Thus, the bank, and your presence here today."

The King smiled, "Let's get on with it."

Billy was asleep in the back seat of the Caddy. Moon and Lard Ass were playing black jack on the hood when the King came traipsing down the steps of the Wilmington Trust building, a magnificent granite edifice flanked by bronze eagles. He was humming to himself when he broke into a smile and said, "Let's get the hell back to Memphis, boys."

They were out of Wilmington and whistling down Route 40 toward Baltimore within the hour. Lamar Fike was hunched over the wheel, fiddling with the radio and looking for a place to get some gas. Mr.P was tapping his fingers in time to an imaginary tune in his head.

Moon leaned over, speaking softly, "Boss, if you don't mind my asking, what's a doctor doing setting up an office in a bank?"

"It's some kind of big secret, hush, hush stuff."

"You going to be all right, El?" Moon asked.

The King smacked him on the shoulder like a playful kid rough housing, let out a whoop and shouted, "Marty Lacker, I'm going to be immortal."

CHAPTER 6   **1996**

FAT CHANCE

CANNES FILM FESTIVAL, FRANCE

I could kill that Celio, she thought. *I hope he was right about a little bit of notoriety helping a girl's career. There's no doubt that my little escapade today is going to be front page news in the National Enquirer, The Star and every other grocery store rag. This might even make the New York Times.*

Roxanne sat quietly, for the moment, buck naked except for a threadbare woolen blanket which she placed on the damp stone slab to keep her buttocks from freezing. The rest of it she wore draped around her shoulders and across her lap. Humped over in thought, all she needed was a derby hat and a wad of cocoa leaves in her cheek to perfectly emulate an Andes Indian woman.

Familiar with the fame of their captive, the Cannes police had placed her in a holding cell in the old part of the jail. This section of the jail had been built before the modern age of enlightenment. Centuries before, the dungeon served as permanent housing for political enemies.

Its only refinements were for punishing, not reforming, unruly inmates. No indoor plumbing adorned any of the cells. Pale natural light danced with the dust motes in the interior cell. It entered from a small atrium through a gun slit set in the upper part of the cell wall. The gun slit was not placed there for the prisoner's comfort. The slit allowed a guard to shoot the occupant in case of a riot.

Roxanne's temporary quarters hid her from the voracious paparazzi, who even then surrounded the jail. Several had been caught scaling the walls. Another had to be tied up to safely lower him from the roof of the jail, where he had secreted himself awaiting a photo op. These alleged news reporters coursed piranha like through the streets in schools during the annual film festival. Oblivious of the harm to their victims, they voraciously stripped news, swallowed rumors and spat out their putrid prose to fill the void of the daily entertainment shows and weekly publications.

The cell had a battered, unpainted chamber pot with two, drooping rope handles on the side. An oak top, cut as a cross section from the trunk of a young tree, had been carved to loosely fit the top of the vessel. This sop to human function was the single adornment in this dreary place of confinement.

Maybe I should have told someone what I was going to do, she thought. *I knew I was going to end up in jail. I should have thought this one entirely through. I don't speak French, have no idea what laws I may have broken or how long they have the right to hold me. Crap, I could be in here forever. How am I going to capitalize on this if I'm stuck in here? Can't even talk to the paparazzi.*

The day had started well enough. The sun broke over a cloudless Mediterranean sky, promising both a warm, but not hot, day and photogenic light. It was quiet, the only sounds coming from the bicycles and cars of people on their way to work. Cannes in the spring, which is when the annual film festival is held, is one of a string of opulent resorts along the Cote d' Azur. Shopkeepers and restaurant owners from Monte

Carlo to Menton, were just beginning to prepare for the onslaught of tourists. The first of the private yachts was already moored in the harbor. Their owners would take up permanent occupancy for the summer in the Gare Maritime, sailing from one source of pleasure to another through the Golfe de Napoule and around Pointe de la Croisette. It was just a bit early in the year for the cruise ships which made Cannes one of their favorite ports of call.

Cannes is the southernmost city of the Riviera, whose rugged, irregular coastline, lush vegetation and mild climate attract hordes of sun seeking visitors from northern Europe. Whereas in historical times the monks of Lerin fortified the city against Muslims marauding from the sea, the 70,000 residents now welcome one and all. Tourism is THE local industry, urbanization having smothered the traditional occupations of harvesting from the sea and the land.

Thus the film festival was started in 1946 to focus attention on the city, launching each tourist season in exuberant fashion. Thrill seekers, aspiring actors, directors, producers and fans all flock to the festival to be seen, to see who is there and, almost as an after thought, to be there when the Palms d'or is awarded for the best film. This vast, heaving throng of the beautiful people, perhaps the largest convention of narcissists ever assembled in one place, little suspected the events that would temporarily interrupt their Saturnalia.

The caper Roxanne had devised to bring her back into the public eye was fool proof in its simplicity. What she had in mind was a mad, naked, jiggling dash across the Alées de la Liberate, or whatever those Frenchies called it, after the March aux Flours, the flower market, had closed. Her starting point would be near the Hôtel de Vile, the town hall, on the west side of the Alées, closer to the Gare Maritime to the south than to Rue Felix Faire that bordered it on the north. The finish line would take her through the potre d'le poeta into the Place du General de Gaulle. All she had to do was take off her raincoat as the door to her limo was opened, zig zag through the square, being careful not to drop too many people on their butts, and exit to another open door in a second waiting limousine on the Place.

♀

A light-blue Volkswagen van was parked in a mimosa tree's shade at the northwest corner of the Market, near the intersection of Rue Felix Faure and Rues Luis Blanc. Beside it, two men, arms flailing, were having a heated discussion. The short, fat one, who was sweating profusely although the temperature had not yet reached 70 degrees, kept gesturing over his shoulder. He repeatedly wiped his scalp with a red silk cloth between gestures. Like many men with the same problem, he attempted to compensate for his male pattern baldness with a full, neatly trimmed short beard. It was shot through with white, as if he had just finished a sugar doughnut, and failed to wipe his otherwise jet black beard. In contrast to his scarf, he wore a white silk shirt, already grey around the armpits from nervous sweat, and black, denim trousers. Black, $150 untied Nikes completed his wardrobe.

His companion, whose face was distorted in agony, was an enormous man, truly Bunyanesque in height and physique. He had wavy steel gray hair. His matching, bushy eyebrows would have been the envy of John L. Lewis, the old labor leader from the forties who had led the coal miner strikes in Appalachia. Schuler by name, he had the mannerisms of a man's man. Around everyone but Alf. Alf who was just a little better than half Schuler's height but weighed about the same.

"Alf, are you sure about them dogs?" Schuler said, pointing in the direction of the van. It came out almost as a whine.

The van was full of barking, snarling dogs, soundless despite their ferociousness. They were a substantial breed. Whatever they had been before their owner had shorn their fur and dyed what was left, they now looked like dingoes, the wild dogs of Australia. Standing about two feet tall at the shoulder, they had broad muzzles, long sturdy legs and large paws. Each charge of the tawny brown animals, with white underparts, resulted in a slight rocking of the van, which caused Alf to bob back and forth as he responded, "I've told you a thousand times, Victor. They just look like dingoes. A real dingo will chase an animal or man, bite off its nose first and then one part after another to see how far it can run. These pussies don't know how to bite anything but canned liver."

"It's just that I don't want anything to happen...,"

Alf interrupted, "Then why did you hire me? Sure you do, you want to scare the living crap out of the people in the square to get some major, but cheap, publicity for your movie. And believe me, any movie with a name like *Dingo* is sure going to need all the help it can get. I'm glad I ain't got none of my money in it," he snarled, bringing his arms up in the pose of victory Rocky made on the stairs of the Philadelphia Art Museum.

"Let's go over the plan again, Alf," Victor Schuler pleaded, "I'm scared witless."

"You were born scared witless," Alf shot back.

"Just go over it again with me how you'll keep them from biting anybody when they're let loose," asked Schuler. He thought he might be going to pee on himself. He was that nervous. But he had bet his life's fortune on this movie. It simply had to be a hit at the box office. With the pittance he had left for publicizing his film, he had hired Alf and his imitation dingoes, who also were featured in the film. The plan was to run them through the crowd, snarling and growling, and let the paparazzi take care of the rest. They figured the resulting film and photographs would make every newspaper and TV news show in the world.

"I keep forgetting that you are a big, dumb kraut. How many times I got to tell you. I feed them before I let them loose. They're too full to want to eat anything else."

"And they'll head straight for the center of the Alées before they veer to the west, I remember. But how do they know to do that?" Schuler continued.

"Cause I've put the same scent at that spot as I trained them with

40

t'home. I put a lump of fake dog poop over it so people wouldn't step on the spot and carry the scent away on their shoes. If that happened, we'd lose control in a hurry. And before you ask, they'll head for the other van in the Place because I'll have a loudspeaker of a dog whistle tape blaring." said Alf.

"Better get ready, then. The flower market is starting to close," ordered Schuler.

♀

One week before the Film Festival, the Cannes police were told by an informant that members of the Fraternity Opposed to Nudity, Depravity, Lewdness and Eroticism, FONDLE, were planning a major demonstration at the Festival. This bit of information was all the police had to go on. Captain Fosse Arrét sat in his brightly lit office in the Cannes gendarmeries pondering how best to prepare for this assault on the gaiety of the event. The room was devoid of any personal items. For that matter, it was absent any article not supplied by the government. The walls were painted that ghastly apple green which must have been the universal color of choice of every government in the world. Where the paint was not flaking, it was either stained by contact with dirty clothes and sweat, or yellowed by nicotine. Arrét's predecessor had been a chain smoker who died of lung cancer before emphysema snuffed out his life. That had been over three years ago. Captain Arrét, a nonsmoker himself, was repulsed each morning by the smell of stale cigarette smoke which still clung to the drapes, the cloth fabric of his chair, and was exuded by the walls.

Although he himself was a closet FONDLEr, he would not allow his passions to over rule his responsibilities as a policeman. He was deep in thought on how best to control any mischief that FONDLE might be planning.

They have never used guns, explosives, arson or any other forms of terrorism which could injure people, and thus their cause, he thought. *Their forte is to ridicule, impede or stop a planned event, not to terrify or maim,* he reasoned.

41

Three years ago they had hung a huge brassiere from underneath the clock of the Hôtel de Ville, with one naked breast hanging uncovered. The nipple was emblazoned with a huge dollar sign. Their point made, there had been no demonstration, nor other outward sign of their presence.

I believe they will strike either at the Alées de la Liberté before the awards, or at the Palais des Festivals, during the ceremony. Those two places will draw the most celebrities, the most fans and, therefore, the biggest concentration of paparazzi, thought Captain Arrét. *I will need mounted men both for mobility and to see over the crowds. The horses will also be useful in controlling the mobs of curiosity seekers,* he concluded.

The Captain picked up the phone as he rotated his chair to look out the window, *I shall call my friend, Charles Mistral, Captain of the Nice police. Surely he will lend me a company of mounted gendarmes for a week if we pay their salaries and expenses.*

The light coming through the gun slit was noticeably fainter than it had been when Roxanne was first put in the cell.

"I've got to get out of here before nightfall. If I have to sleep on this stone bunk, I won't be able to roll over in the morning," she murmured to herself. *I hope Dominic got my fax and has a contact over here with some pull. The publicity I can use. Arthritis I don't need,* she thought as she began going over the day's fiasco in the Alées de la Liberté.

Roxanne had done an excellent job of planning her caper. The receptor limousine had parked in the Place du General De Gaulle in the wee hours of the morning, finding space among the tradesmen's trucks. The trucks were overflow from the Alées de la Liberté, where they were already busy unloading flowers and other greenery and crafts for that day's market. By early morning, these trucks would be replaced by others and the automobiles of the sundry patrons of the market. Best to have the get away vehicle in place when the opportunity existed. If it meant a few thousand francs for the local foot patrol, so be it. Nothing had been left to chance.

At precisely 12:59 p.m., the limousine driver opened her door. She popped out, barefoot, her naked body clad in a green Burberry trench coat.

"Ouch, the pavement is hotter than I thought it was going to be," she remarked to the driver as she hopped up and down to reduce the pain signals being sent to her brain. She had thought about sneakers, but hadn't wanted to spoil the Godiva like look of her streak across the Alées. For that matter, she had thought about riding in on a horse but had given that up when she realized that the size of her buttocks would equal those of a Percheron. Not a flattering picture, but surely one some unprincipled paparazzi would eagerly seek the angle for.

As the town hall clock struck one, Roxanne untied the belt, threw her coat in the car, and turned to face an unsuspecting crowd of Cannes tourists who were about to become unwitting, and unwilling, voyeurs. Her 5'-6" frame was carrying 250 pounds of milk colored flesh. Sagging breasts the size of honey dew melons began to flop wildly as she broke into a sprint. She raised her hands from her crotch to encase them lest one of them knock a pedestrian unconscious as she passed by. She revealed a bristling patch of auburn pubic hair that matched the color of the hair on her head.

As she gained momentum, the crowd began to notice her and moved out of the way. She was fortunate that her only language of fluency was English. She was unable to understand the catcalls that were hurled at her as she ran through the gauntlet.

"What a disgusting lump of flesh."

"Throw a blanket over that bitch."

"What an offense to my eyes. Grab her and cover her up."

"Who let the hairless pig out of the pen?"

She was having an effect on the crowd, and that was what she was here for. Soon the paparazzi would be clicking their cameras and running their video cameras to get the best shots they could to please their voracious customers, the mass media.

People were parting before her as did the Red Sea before Moses. As they did, she spied the milestone that marked her halfway point, a plaster-of-paris lump, sculpted and painted brown. Roxanne had found it during her nocturnal, barefoot reconnoitering of her proposed pathway across the Alées, testing the cobblestone for holes, lumps and jagged edges that might bruise or cut her tender feet. The lump only had to be moved a few feet to put it approximately at the mid point of her run. Slipping in the wet spot where it had lain, she had mentally praised the perpetrator for having the presence of mind to leave this fetid bit of liquid to give passing authenticity to the crudely manufactured fake.

"Get on with it, man. We're going to lose the crowd, and with it the publicity," Victor Schuler shouted. Inextricably, the crowd surged away from the Alées at a time when they should have been gathering in greater numbers to ogle the second rate stars who frequented places like this to be admired by the public.

Alf mumbled back, not an apology, but his attempt at a reasoned statement of why things hadn't gone the way they had planned. "How was I to know that my key to the van would break in the lock at exactly the moment when I went to open the door to let the dogs out?"

"I don't care, just get the dogs out," Schuler shrieked. When Alf took no measures to respond to his request, Schuler took a Luger Model Number 1908 from a holster concealed by his sport coat and fired two rounds through the side window of the van. He carefully aimed his pistol to miss the startled dogs. The window was still in the process of shattering into shards as the enraged dogs burst through it. The time was 1:05 p.m.. Roxanne had just past her midway milestone.

♀

Roxanne was heading northeast, sweating profusely and feeling glad that her run to fame and fortune was more than half way over. She had been in training for this for over three months. Yet her heart felt like it was going to jump from her chest. Ludicrous though it was, she had a mental image of her being the white Florence Griffith Joyner.

The dingoes created a sensation when they came coursing through the crowd. People screamed, fainted and ran to get away from the snarling, foaming muzzles of these creatures from Hell. They started, paws slipping on the cobblestone paving in their frantic efforts to immediately run at full speed now that they were released from the hot, stinking van. They headed on a straight line to the south east, directly toward the former location of the scent that Alf had placed to keep them on track. Now, with the wind uncharacteristically blowing to the west, they picked up the scent from Roxanne's heel and veered sharply from their intended route. They bayed, a long mournful croon, as they began to descend on their prey.

♀

Captain Fosse Arrét was at his command post when he heard the shots. He immediately ordered his lieutenants in the field to marshall the mounted police.

Wise of me, he thought, *to have stationed my mounted forces along the Boulevard de la Croisette, between the Alées de la Liberte and the Palais des Festivals. Now they are in a good position to catch the FONDLErs and put them away where they can do no more mischief.*

The mounted police were directed to enter the crowd at the nearest point, which happened to be the southeast corner of the Alées de la Liberte. At 1:07 p.m., they penetrated en masse, presenting a solid wall of slowly moving horse flesh that proved to be an irresistible force. They breached the flood of people just as the prow of a boat pushes a wave of water before it. About 20 meters into the mass of people, the crowd began reacting to the other forces motivating their movement, Roxanne and the dingoes.

$$♀$$

Roxanne was thirty seconds from her destination when events over took her. The crowd, which had been dutifully parting before her, suddenly became a heaving mass of hysterical, frightened people, careening past her as they tried to get away from the baying dingoes. Roxanne turned to see what had provoked them. As she did, her unshod heel hit a discarded snow cone. She lost her footing while at full gallop, slipped, careened forward, flipped and landed on her massive rump. And then the dogs were upon her.

Truth be known, the dogs saved her end, or in the end, from being trampled by the crowd, which was now so far out of control that many unfortunates were being physically mashed against the horses who were now totally enveloped, like hot dogs in a bun. Not liking the press of flesh any better than the people, the horses began to buck and shy away to the side. As the horsemen began to further lose control, their mounts began to rear and whinny frantically. Mounted policemen were suddenly air born, their landings cushioned by the frenzied crowd. At that juncture, the crowd began to disperse, making it easy for the few gendarmes who had retained their seats, to see the writhing pack of dogs who had begun to lick the sweaty parts of Roxanne's exposed flesh. Those who weren't licking, were sniffing her nether parts.

The cameras were clicking and the camcorders whirring by the time the police came to the rescue. None of the paparazzi had even considered coming to Roxanne's aid. Who would be foolish enough to disturb a scene that could make any one of them a year's income in one brief moment?

The police finally beat and battered the dogs from Roxanne's nude figure that lay bruised and whimpering, in a fetal position on the smooth cobble stone. They arrested her, accusing her of instigating the entire affair. Vic and Alf left the dogs, the other van and snuck out of town.

ROMANCE

GREAT SIOUX RESERVATION, MONTANA

The 25th U.S. Infantry Bicycle Corps was made up entirely of black enlisted men, save their white commander, Lieutenant James Ray Bunting. The troopers called the boss man Lieutenant Jimmy behind his back, sir to his face. They liked Jimmy because he was tough, fair and most of all, treated them like men. Lieutenant Bunting's command was quite small. Sergeant Mose Miller was responsible for Corporal Jackson Brown, musician "Taps" Bloodworth and five privates. Among the latter was a bicycle mechanic who had learned his trade as a boy growing up in the Bowery section of New York. His name was Elijah Winter. Everybody, including Lt. Jimmy, called him "Tools."

Bunting's chiseled face, with the aquiline nose, was a study in strength and focus. With his curly black hair and square, slightly jutting chin, he was a ruggedly handsome man. But the rest of his body made him look like he had been built from spare parts. He was just shy of six feet tall, had a powerful barrel of a chest whose bottom ribs, the floaters, rested just an inch above his hip bones. Being so short waisted, he always wore his trousers just a little bit low, a kind of subconscious compensation to make him look better. This strong torso rested upon a pair of skinny legs, substantially out of proportion to the mass they supported. The thigh bone was abnormally longer than the shin bone. As a result, people were often taken aback when this low rider suddenly towered above them when he dismounted. As appendages to these heron like legs, his feet were large in mass, but short and very wide, with extremely high arches. His boots had to be custom made, with a slit on the inside, from the boot's top to within an inch of the sole. The rawhide laces that he used to lace the leather together had been died black.

His arms and hands were out of proportion to the same degree as his legs and feet. The humerus was disproportionately longer than the forearm, to which was attached a broad, flat hand made up of digits as thick as Italian sausages.

The long bones attached to his powerful but short torso made him an outstanding horseman. When in the saddle, his low center of gravity made him one with his mount. It is as if he were genetically bred to be a horseman. Perhaps those high cheekbones belied ancestral Mongol blood in his veins. The same gifts which favored him in controlling and staying with a horse also gave him monstrous lifting strength. He had once been seen to raise a foundered mule, arguably stripped of its baggage, by knotting its harness, grabbing same and then lifting the dead weight from a crouch. The weight of his hands and feet, attached to those long members, also carried a monstrous wallop. The mule he had put back on its feet had been felled by him with one hammer like blow in a fit of rage when it balked on the trail. No soldier in the 25th ever had even a moment's thought of disobeying orders after witnessing that feat of strength. As sergeant Miller observed, "Wouldn't do no good to get on Lt. Jimmy's bad side. Might end up like that mule, down and out."

Despite his legendary skills on horseback, Bunting was inspired to lead the first U.S. Army corps of soldier cyclists. His inspiration came from a magazine article he read about Italian sharpshooters on wheels. Bicycling soldiers had been a part of the Italian Army since 1870, more than a quarter of a century ago. In fact, all the European armies were so equipped. He was personally embarrassed that the largest army in the Americas was so woefully behind the times.

The bicycle was the hoola hoop of the 1890's. People went absolutely nuts over them. The safety bike of 1884 had led to the rapid replacement of the models that had gone before it. The bike had almost all the features of a modern bicycle, from adjustable handlebars and cushioned seat, right down to the equal diameter pneumatic tires which gave a comfortable ride. By 1895, they were selling at a ten million a year clip, which made them a billion-dollar industry. Costing between $50 and $150 each, they were where the average man and women were now putting their luxury money. Lieutenant Bunting had read in a Scientific American journal that "The tailor, the hatter, the bookseller, the shoemaker, the horse dealer, and the riding master were going out of business throughout the nation because of the fierce competition for the average man's dollar."

Popular songs of the era inspired by the safety bike were *A Bicycle Built for Two, The Cycle Man* and *The March of the Bloomers.* Bloomers,of course, were the cycling attire designed by women's activist Amelia Jenks Bloomer. The Saturday matinee at local entertainment houses was no longer being offered due to the sparse attendance. Church attendance was down as couples cycled all day Sunday, getting exercise, fresh air and pleasure all from the same activity. The clergy blasted the infernal machine as the work of the Devil and an invitation to sin. The *Georgia Journal of Medicine and Surgery* reported on the gynecological aspects of the pastime. The bicycling maiden's "body is thrown forward, causing the clothing to press against the clitoris, thereby eliciting and arousing feelings hitherto unknown and unrealized by the young maidens." How blasphemous. No wonder the preachers railed from their pulpits. Oh, shades of Rock & Roll.

The lieutenant had been instrumental in persuading the commander in chief of the Army, who at the time was none other than General Nelson A. Miles, the victorious commander at Wounded Knee, about the merits of a corps of wheelmen. Arguing that they were cheaper than a horse, required little care and no provisions, Bunting had won the day. His argument required little persuasion on the part of the General, who was an ardent cyclist himself. Miles had been experimenting with bicycles since 1892, when he had sent a message by bicycle relay from his Chicago headquarters to General O. O. Howard in New York. It worked kind of like the Pony Express, with the cyclists working in relays. Kind of an odd experiment for the time as the message took more than four days, through heavy rains, to arrive. A telegraph would have gotten it to Howard almost instantaneously. But it demonstrated the prowess of the bicycle in traversing all kinds of terrain in all kinds of weather.

Yes, the General was a fanatic over the fad which continued to sweep the nation's middle class. Was it not he who had taught Fahreda Mahzar how to ride one when she was appearing at the Chicago World's Fair as a Midway attraction? Little Egypt, her stage name, far outshone Edison's light bulb, which was introduced to the world at the same time. Dancing the hootchy kootchy in a semi-transparent skirt, the lithe beauty had driven men wild. The General, who had met her at a party given by the Mayor of Chicago, feigned surprise when told that his student was indeed the woman who appeared seminude as she performed the Oriental danse du ventre to the delight of millions.

The 25th had been organized in July 1896 at Fort Missoula, Montana. Lieutenant Bunting wasted no time in whipping his charges into shape. By October, the troopers stood for a tableau photograph in Yellowstone National Park to memorialize their 791-mile ride from Missoula. Burdened with 80 pounds of gear, they had clocked better than six miles per hour over bad roads despite heavy rains and high winds. The lieutenant was greatly pleased. His goal was to beat the horseback record set by his commander in chief on that wild ride back from Wounded Knee in '92.

✠

It was mid-May, 1897, a Sunday. Bunting spent his free time that day lying on his bunk finalizing the route that he and his men would take on the 3800-mile round trip from Missoula to St. Louis and back. General Miles' petition to Secretary of War Lamont the previous year had been successful. The 25th had been expanded to include a white surgeon, a black corporal and eleven more privates.

Proving that the bicyclist could deal successfully with a variety of terrain was a critical element of trail selection. As the day wore on, he became convinced that he was as close to the optimum as he was going to get. When they departed, they would strike due east through the mountains to Helena. From there, they would head southeast over rocky terrain until they struck the still distinguishable wagon ruts of the old Bozeman trail. This is the portion of the run where he would try to break the General's record on his wild dash from Wounded Knee, 248 miles in thirty-six and a half hours. That would mean maintaining a speed of almost 7 miles per hour, including breaks for resting the men as well as performing their daily ablutions. He had thought of having his men urinate while riding but thought better of it. Mounted defecation had been out of the question from the start, of course.

Following the Yellowstone River as they went east, he then intended to ford the river, coming into the Sioux Reservation where they would cross the Bighorn River on their way southeast toward the Platte River. The stretch between where they intercepted the Bozeman trail and Fort Phil Kearny, to the south of the reservation was about the right distance. Conditions between the Bighorn and Fort Kearny, where they would be the most tired, were the best they would encounter in the first half of the trip. The worst would be 170 miles in the sand hills of Nebraska, just before they hit the Platte. Then the ferry across the Missouri to St. Joe and on to St. Louis.

✠

Running Water brushed the mosquito from her sweating brow as she tended the fire. She was boiling the two prairie chickens that her younger brother Laughs No More had killed with stones he had gathered on a hunting trip to the Powder River. As she added another knot of wood to the fire, she recalled her mother saying how easy it had been in the old days to gather buffalo dung to fuel the fire. Her memory drifted back to the time, before she had been sent to the white man's school, when she would sit with her mother and listen to her tell of the way things were before the white man came. Back then, the bois de

51

vache, meadow muffins as the French traders had called them, were as plentiful as the prairie grass that was their origin. She would listen to the legend of how the Great Spirit had heard the People's plea for food, fuel and shelter in the cold times when there was ice upon the land, even in the summer. The Great Spirit thought long and hard. The People despaired, for they were hungry and cold. It was after the pleading time that the buffalo was created to be the source of all the People's needs. While this creature lived, he transformed the bountiful prairie grass into fuel to be gathered as they followed the migrating herds of these brown behemoths. The hot, clear, nearly odorless flame produced just enough smoke to keep the mosquitoes away.

When the buffalo fell in the hunt, the hide became both clothing and shelter. The meat was food for all the People. Internal organs that were not eaten became containers for water and grain. Bladders were made into playthings for children and adults alike. Bones and horns were used for tools, fuel, weapons and ornaments. Fat was used as the base for paint, as an ointment and to keep pesky insects at bay. The buffalo was the source of all things necessary in the people's lives. Even the horse, a highly prized animal, was not as absolutely necessary to the People's lives for they had lived quite well for many generations before its arrival. Some said that the horse, unlike the buffalo, was not a gift from the Great Spirit, but was brought here by the white man. Running Water thought that this was probably the case. It was like the word of the white man. What was said was not what was meant. The horse had made it easier for the People to hunt the buffalo. However, the horse's presence in their lives was shortly followed by the white man, and then came the end of the buffalo and the Indian way of life on the plains.

As much as she admired and envied some of the white man's culture and material things, she thought their chiefs to be stone stupid to have slaughtered the herds for short term wealth. How could they fail to see the endless bounty that had been provided by the Creator? Being a pragmatist, however, she had gone to the white man's school to learn his tongue and his ways. She was nothing, if not a survivor. She viewed the white man as being no different than a Crow or Shawnee. Had they not killed each other in the past in fights over the best hunting grounds? This latest war was more of the same, just different human beings.

"When will supper be ready, my sister, for my belly growls at me and I can't drink enough water to drown out its voice?" Laughs No More asked as he approached the fire.

"Oh, you startled me, my brother for I was deep in thought," Running Water responded. "It will not be long now. But you must be patient. The cooking time depends solely on the size of the birds. You have brought me such big fellows, that the boiling water takes much time to do its job."

Laughs No More smiled with pride at her comment. He sat on the buffalo robe beside her. Running Water had spread the robe to keep her deerskin dress clean when she knelt to mix the wheat flour and water into dumplings for the pot. Now, as she began to drop them into the boiling water of the cast iron pot, she spoke quietly to her brother. "I have been thinking here of late that we have to have a new vision if we are to live in this white man's world."

Her brother frowned, turned his head from the fire and spit onto the dirt, "You have been too long at the white man's school. Do you not remember that you are a Hunkpaka Sioux whose brother was killed by the blue bellies?"

She understood her brother's hatred, but knew of his cunning as well. Could he not see that they were going to have to adapt to this new culture that surrounded them? "Brother," she said, "we are a generation in transition. The old ways that our people followed so well are no longer available to us. The white man's buffalo, the longhorn cattle, have replaced our beloved bison."

"Huh," he snorted, "you would have me, a warrior, become a tender of cattle, like a boy?"

"Ah, my brother, although you are strong, swift and brave, these are manly things that need an outlet for there is no longer a warrior's path. Do you not see?" she asked.

"Yes, my sister, my ears here what you say, but my heart does not want to listen."

"Well, each of us is young and must think to the future. We are not foolish enough to believe like the Ghost Dancers that the white man will be driven from the land and the buffalo will return. You and I must adapt to the white man's ways," she counseled.

Laughs No More rose in disgust, picking up a handful of dust as he stood, flinging it in the air defiantly. "You sound like a woman with á la faÁon du pays on her mind," he said harshly. "Who did you meet at that school?"

His sister's blush was a combination of anger and embarrassment. "Brother, do not go away in anger. I do not have any marriage prospects in mind, white or of the People. Sit down, these dumplings are almost ready. Then I want to talk with you while we eat about going over to the Bozeman trail tomorrow, to see the white man's new invention, the bicycle."

Laughs No More was kind and gentle by nature, When it came to his sister, he would always do her bidding, he could not hold a grudge against her for even a moment. Sitting, he waited for her to remove the dumplings, which had been seasoned with pepper provided with the white man's monthly rations. He liked pepper, the way it bit your tongue and made your nose run.

"What is this thing you call bicycle, and how did you come to learn of it?" he asked as he began to drool in reaction to the aroma of the boiled chickens as she removed them from the water and placed them on the metal plates to cool. He did not like the taste the metal imparted to the food, but his sister persisted in using them, saying they were much easier to clean, would not break like clay ones and were light to carry when they shifted camp sites.

"You'll burn your mouth if you eat that now," she said, as she gently slapped the hand reaching out for the food. "Let us talk while the food cools. I saw one of these devices at school. It sits on two wheels and has a saddle like a horse. You mount it, push your feet against two flat slabs they call pedals, and the bicycle moves forward, carrying you just like a horse."

"That is stupid. Why make something to replace the horse?"

"Many people live in big cities where there is no grass to feed a horse. This is a way for them to travel that requires no food or water," she explained.

Now reaching for a prairie hen, and biting into its succulent flesh, juice dribbling down his chin, Laughs No More responded, "But we have grass, and the water runs free for the taking. Why is this thing out here?"

"I have heard that the Army has planned a long trek from the shining mountains to the mother of waters. They plan to use the Bozeman Trail for part of it because they say it is easier for them to travel in the wagon ruts," said Running Water.

"I will carry you there on my horse for I do not wish you to take such a long walk by yourself," he offered.

She smiled inwardly as she accepted his offer. She knew she had aroused his curiosity.

✠

They had left Fort Missoula at 5:40 A.M. on Sunday, June 14, 1897 just as the sun hit the face of the mountain with the curious stripes that overlooked the fort. It would be 100 years before the scientific community accepted geologist J. Harlen Bretz's theory that the stripes were the high water marks of a succession of lakes formed by dams created by glaciers during the ice age. These natural dams failed periodically, releasing billions of gallons of water. The attendant force and velocity scoured and scarred the shape and contours of the land from the Continental Divide westward through the Columbia River watershed to the Pacific Coast as tons of soil were swept to the sea.

The Spalding Company furnished the custom-made bicycles, outfitted to Bunting's specifications. The Corps' exploits were to be recorded by James H. Friess, a Daily Missoulian reporter and biking aficionado. Arrangements had been made by the Department of the Army for his reports to be sent to newspapers all over the country.

By the time they neared the Sioux reservation, Bunting and his men had endured a sleet storm as they crossed the Continental Divide, rain in the lower altitudes, rock strewn roads, swarms of mosquitoes and a populace not overly friendly toward the black troopers. Through it all, they had not lost a man, or reporter, for Friess had trained in 100 mile jaunts on weekends to prepare himself for the rigors of the trip. The rain had stopped by the time they reached the reservation, with 30 hours cycle time in the saddle, riding at a road and man eating clip of 7.5 miles per hour. The rain dampened soil, hungry for water, went from thirsty to dry within the hour, by which time the men in the rear were riding through the dust created by the men who preceded them.

Bunting was sweating, feeling pain in every joint of his body, and desperately wanting to sleep. He had checked his pocket watch at the last break, only 15 minutes ago, and knew they had only thirteen hours to go to break the record. Looking back upon his corps, he could see that sergeant Miller had assigned corporal Brown to the end of the line to bring up stragglers. *Not bad*, he thought, *We're only strung out about a 100 yards. The men are holding up, like I thought they would.* He felt a sense of pride in his men and in himself for having trained them.

✠

"Look, brother, I see signs that the white man approaches on his bicycle," Running Water said as she pointed with the index finger on her left hand toward the dust plume which arose in the west.

Laughs No More dismounted from his appaloosa, knelt to the ground, placed his right ear, the one remaining, to the ground and listened. "I hear nothing," he said.

"Perhaps these bicycles pass by with no sound," Running Water responded.

"You told me not of this yesterday," he said.

"I did not know, for I had never used the warrior's way to listen for my enemy," she blushed, for a woman was not trained in such warrior skills.

"Let them pass by so I can see if they leave sign of their passage, the direction they take and the condition of their mounts, for you yourself have said that they have ridden steady from the Yellowstone. I have done that ride," Laughs No More smiled as he continued, "to save my life. Remember when I crossed the shining mountains to go to the land of the Nez Perce? Although that is where I stole the father of my horse, it is not a ride I would wish to repeat. But I have respect for anyone who can do it straight through, even my enemies."

"But look at the fine horses you now have. You are the envy of our people," Running Water responded.

His chest swelling with pride at her words, her brother commented, "As that may be, I still could have ended up as a slave to the Cut Noses, had I not picked their swiftest stallion."

✠

The Sioux reservation was barren and, according to what the weary troop's bikers could see, without people. Lieutenant Bunting was in the lead as they approached a group of rock strewn hills. His fellow cyclers were strewn out over a quarter of a mile, with reporter Friess, gasping for breath, bringing up the rear by more than ten cycle lengths. The others were strung along in a line according to their stamina and remaining strength. Rank had been shed as dawn broke and the evening chill passed into a blistering hot morning. Rain had dogged their trail every day from Bozeman to Billings. The mud had been unbelievable, in certain passages requiring them to dismount and push their equipment forward at the double.

Nonetheless, they were still averaging just over seven miles an hour, getting closer and closer to their goal. With the recent dry conditions, Bunting had them moving at a reckless pace, even for men who had been properly fed and rested, which they had not been. Their stop at Fort Custer had been but a few minutes, for water, a bite of rations and a brief visit to the latrine. The lieutenant had allowed them one brief luxury, a walk around the parade ground to stretch, dip and otherwise temporarily relieve the soreness in their muscles. Then it was off for the last leg of 90 miles to Fort Kearny.

Sergeant Moses Miller was a proud man, proud of his lofty, enlisted man's status, proud of his physical condition and particularly pleased by his ability to keep up with the pace of the other, much younger, men. From his position directly behind the lieutenant, he was huffing mightily, as he began to ascend the small rise, beyond which Running Water and her brother lay concealed.

I believe if I make it all the way to St. Louis and back, I'm going to consider asking for a transfer. These legs feel like they are on fire and we got nine more hours to go. The sergeant thought. *One of us is going to get kilt amongst these rocks. Bicycles may be better than horses for getting around near prairie dog holes but they don't hold a candle to a horse for maneuvering through this stuff.*

Just then the lieutenant's front tire rolled over the sharp edge of a fractured rock, blew, and sent him sprawling over his canvas pack on the handle bars. He landed flat on his back as his head hit a boulder the size of a watermelon. He was knocked unconscious by the force of the collision. A protruding extension of the same rock that had caused his fall ripped his uniform trouser and caused a deep wound in his leg.

Sergeant Miller was too close behind to avoid the wreckage in his path. Fortunately his spill was onto the other side of the path where the rocks and obstructions were fewer.

✠

"Umph, the blue belly took a bad spill from his mount," observed Laughs No More. "That blow to the head may have killed him. If it didn't, the white man's medicine men will. They are fools who are blind to the healing medicines which the Great Spirit has provided in abundance all around us."

"Let us go see if they need help, my brother," said Running Water as she stood up and beckoned him to his horse. Obviously reluctant to do so, Laughs No More nonetheless straightened from his crouched position, walked to his horse, mounted and held out his hand to his sister. Grabbing his left forearm with her left hand, she leapt up behind him. A soft tap on the horse's belly with his heels was all that was needed to set the appaloosa in motion.

Laughs No More guided him toward the little arroyo that would take them down to where the white man lay among the Buffalo Soldiers, who had dismounted and were crowding around their fallen leader.

✠

"Sergeant Miller, send the men back to their bikes so I have room to work,"ordered the corps surgeon. "Have my bag brought up on the double. I've got to have some way to staunch the flow of blood from his leg."

"Is he still alive, sir?" asked the sergeant, "The blow didn't kill him?"

"No, sergeant. He may have a fractured skull, but his heart is still beating, his pulse is strong. But it won't be if I can't stop the bleeding. Now get your men out of here and get me that bag," surgeon Harris shouted as he knelt with his hand on the lieutenant's wrist.

Surgeon Ross Harris was a stocky man of average height. His dark brown beard was cut short in contrast to his hair, which he wore shoulder length. He had joined the service right out of medical school, looking for adventure in the twilight days of the frontier. The 25th suited him perfectly. He was in excellent physical condition, enjoyed the outdoor life and bore no prejudice against any man based on his color or religion.

Harris decided not to move the injured officer while he remained unconscious. Until he could communicate with him, he had no way of knowing the extent and nature of his injuries.

It is best not to take a chance on aggravating an injury to save a few minutes, Harris thought. *This race, be damned. That's what caused the bloody fall to begin with. We're all so worn out, he got careless.* Harris jumped up, startled by the noise of an unshod hoof on the rocky path behind him.

When he turned around, he was shocked to see a young Sioux warrior, sans paint, astride a beautiful appaloosa mare. The horse was powerfully built, with a massive chest that had black spots splattered upon a soft grey background. The hooves were black with grey stripes. Had he not been concerned for his commander, Harris would like to have known if the horse was available for sale or trade.

"What is the nature of his injury?"

The surgeon, kneeling again by his fallen comrade, was puzzled by the soft, girl like voice that came from the direction of the massive Indian who rode the speckled horse. As he turned again, the appaloosa's hindquarters canted around, by that revealing the partial profile of a very striking Indian woman. High cheekbones, large doe like eyes, a breast the size of an apple thrusting against the deerskin shirt, beautiful white teeth set behind pouty lips were what the good surgeon took in at first glance.

Just then, a private arrived with the doctor's bag. "Thank you, private. That will be all. Send Tools on up in case I need some help."

He opened the bag, removed some cotton bandages and linen swaths. " I've had my belt tightened round his thigh as a tourniquet to stop the bleeding from his leg. The cut is deep, to the bone, and I'm just about to see if this linen, properly applied, will do the trick, " he said in partial response to the woman.

Private Winter arrived, breathing heavily. He had run up the rock strewn path, proud to be asked to assist the doctor, but scared that he might mess up. Harris motioned to him to take the scissors and linen, "Cut me three pieces about as long as that cut with a thumb joint extra all around. I'll apply the linen to the wound so that the fringe will be on undamaged tissue," Harris added as way of explanation. He knew Tools could neither read nor write, but he was a smart enough fellow despite that, and good with his hands, very good with his hands.

"Wait, before you cover that wound, you must treat it. Otherwise, it will putrefy, and then he'll lose the leg, or part of it," the dark eyed beauty said as she slid gracefully from the horse.

"I have nothing more than alcohol, black powder, opium and whiskey. None of those will help to stop the flow of blood in order to allow the wound to heal," the surgeon responded.

"Keep the tourniquet on and wait until I get you what that wound calls for," she directed.

Laughs No More smiled at how the white man and the Buffalo Soldier had so quickly succumbed to his sister. *Some things cut across all races*, he thought. *My sister is one of those things. No man can help but give way to beauty and forthrightness.*

Running Water pulled out a small, obsidian knife and began to cut yellow flowering weeds that grew in splotches all over the reservation. When she had a handful, she put the knife back in the hidden place from which it had come. Then she walked about, staring at the ground, as if she were looking for something. Grunting with satisfaction, she bent and picked up a fist sized rock. Moving swiftly, she found, then knelt by a flat outcropping upon which she began to pound the weed.

When she was satisfied that she had released the healing power of the Yarrow, she handed it to the doctor with instructions to apply it as a poultice, directly onto the wound.

"But what will it do? This is nothing but a common weed," he said while following her instructions to hold it in place with the cotton bandages, which he was now wrapping around the Lieutenant's calf.

"It will stop the bleeding and prevent the wound from swelling shut with inflammation."

As he finished tying off the wrapping, he asked politely, "But are you quite certain?"

She flashed her sparkling smile as she responded, "We have lived in these lands since the beginning of time. We are human beings who also have cuts, bruises, sprains and all the other assorted woes of mankind. The Great Spirit placed our medicine in the plants and animals which surround us. It was then up to us to discover how to match the medicine with the illness. Yarrow's healing properties have been known to us long before the white man came.

The lieutenant groaned with pain as he became conscious. As he opened, his eyes, he saw two pretty women swaying before him, each as slender and beautiful as the other. *Must be twins*, he thought.

"Sir, you've had a spill. With this young lady's help, we have stopped the bleeding from a nasty gash in your right calf. You are also probably sore in your right thigh, from a tourniquet I used to stop the bleeding until we could get a bandage on you. We know you hit your head on a boulder when you landed, so I haven't given you anything for the pain. I need to talk to you while you are lucid so I can make a decision about being able to move you."

Bunting knew the voice was that of surgeon Ross Harris, but it came from outside his vision, which was still filled with two women, not just the one who was standing there that he inferred from the doctor's comments.

"Seeing double," murmured the lieutenant. "That means we are dealing with at least a concussion. I can't tell if the skull's fractured without moving your head. Are you up to telling me where the pain is and then trying to move each of your extremities? I've got to know if there has been any spinal damage.", the doctor said with the loud voice that many people use when dealing with the injured and handicapped, as if they were all hard of hearing.

Softly, the lieutenant answered, "Ross, there is so much pain I can't tell where it's coming from. My head feels like a dead horse is lying on it."

Harris led his patient through range of motion tests over the next half hour. At the conclusion of the tests, he walked away deep in thought, pausing for only a moment in the dappled shade of the yarrow growing above him. His pace back was swift and decisive.

"He can't be moved for at least two weeks, perhaps more, until the trauma recedes," Harris announced when he arrived back at the prostrate form of his commander. "Tools, please ask sergeant Miller to come up here. You may remain with the men."

Tools' brief period in the limelight over, he jogged down to the rest of the troops, shouting the doctor's orders as he neared the reclining men. "Sergeant needed up with doctor."

Then he was swiftly surrounded by the rest of the men, anxious to know about Lieutenant Jimmy's condition.

"Thank God he ain't dead," said corporal Jackson Brown, who preceded to lead his fellow soldiers in an impromptu prayer for their fallen leader's swift recovery.

CHAPTER 8   1996

REMEMBRANCE

DOVER, DELAWARE

I opened the table of contents to 'Americans in History' apprehensively but resolutely. My eyes scanned back and forth, looking for a topic which could be in any way be connected with my father's career. Let me add, his career as I knew it from my childhood through manhood, or as I had learned, with increasing incredulity as I aged, through the telling of stories by my often suspected, but nonetheless revered, Father. I loved him so and hoped that at least some aspect of his tales would be true. The yarn of his I least believed was the story of the Soldiers Who Walk on Air, an apparently fictitious account of the bravado of a bunch of black soldiers in the old west. That's what my father called it, because that is what the Sioux Indians, with whom he had an encounter, called them, the blacks, because they traveled by bicycle, or so he said. I always believed the story to be a fantasy told by him to his only son as a rip roaring tale of adventure. But I always suspected the story line was merely to maintain my interest. The underlying purpose was to teach me respect for an individual's courage and deeds, regardless of race. The yarn had to be a farce, in my opinion, for any number of reasons.

One, I fancied myself somewhat of a historian, and I had never read about a black bicycle corps, or white one for that matter, in the U.S. Army. What good would they do? They had horses, trains and the telegraph to move men, materials and messages. A bicycle would seem not only unnecessary but redundant in that milieux. As a military tool, it was a device invented well after the period when it may have been of use. Or so I thought, and I have always held my opinion in high esteem. For if one does not, who else will.

Second, although my father was literate, read quite a bit and was quick of wit, I never saw him read a book. When, or where, would he have read such a story. We had a single bookcase, scavenged from a lawyer's office in a bank that was being remodeled by Tilghman & Moyer, the construction company my Dad was working for at the time. Pop worked as a carpenter, then a foreman and, finally, a superintendent of building construction. Of course, when he was in his eighties, when I was a boy, he was a superintendent but he still liked to pitch in and help the boys so they could go drinking after the work was done, or leave early on a Friday to get home before dark during the summer. The super got first dibs at anything the client was throwing away. My father had my mother bring the car down town so he could load the bookcase, which came apart as individual shelves, into the back seat and trunk of the car. They were made of oak, had glass panels that one opened with a brass knob thoughtfully placed at the center of the panel. They opened just like an overhead garage door. In any case, those five shelves held all the books in our household, including the Funk & Wagnalls Encyclopedia.

Third, I was quite a motion picture fan, going to my neighborhood theater twice a week, whenever the movie changed. I have a viewing history stretching from Roy Rogers and Trigger at Saturday matinees to Kevin Costner and *Dances with Wolves*. With all this worldly cinematic experience, I had never seen a picture on the subject. Wouldn't Frank Sinatra and Sammy Davis have lunged at a property like that? So it couldn't be true, but it was. How did I know? My Father told me so.

The article was entitled "An Army on Bicycles." The historian who wrote the article did so without benefit of interviewing those with firsthand experience, because they were now all dead. In an instant, I had a revelation that I had been given the privilege of hearing the truth from my Father, first hand, unabridged and for my benefit. I had heard the struggles and triumphs of another generation, unvarnished, raw. It dawned on me that the real reason for telling me about his life was to tell me what is in my genes. In that way, he wanted to help me as I ventured down life's pathway, with all the wonders and perils that I might meet. My father knew he wouldn't be there to counsel me, so he did so indirectly with his stories. I didn't know it at the time, but I was the original boy named Sue.

CHAPTER 9   **AUGUST 16, 1977**

LAST DANCE

MEMPHIS, TENNESSEE

Ginger Snap woke up around two that afternoon, feeling refreshed after less than six hours sleep. The former Watermelon Queen of Dorchester County thought about the pleasant, yet uneventful evening and morning that had preceded her and El going to bed at around six thirty this morning.

El had eaten his dinner about 10:30 P.M. A fried peanut butter and banana sandwich, which he had prepared himself, was the snack he wolfed down with his favorite bellywash, Pepsi Cola, cold from the can, not with ice. That kept the wolf at bay until he had his sit down dinner of chicken fried steak. There followed a trip to the dentist to have a cavity filled.

Amazing, she had thought at the time, *When you are the King, you get service at your convenience. I'm sure that old dentist didn't want to be grinding away in the middle of the night, but grind away he did.*

They had then returned to the mansion, where he had worked on some songs he intended to include in his upcoming concert. At 4:30 or so, before sunrise, even before the false dawn, he was ready to play, not work. Whatever the game you wanted, the mansion would provide the means to frolic. This morning it had been a couple sets of racquetball with his cousin Billy and his wife. Then came the performance, with El at the piano singing as only he could. In shape, or not, he still made the women cry and faint. This morning, it had been a series of ballads, all sad, concluding with Willie Nelson's "Blue Eyes Crying in the Rain."

Then it was off to bed. She was exhausted, as usual. Even though she had been living with Fire Eyes for quite some time, she still wasn't used to calling this fat, past his prime rock and roll singer Fire Eyes. In any case, his nocturnal rhythm was still out of sync with her natural biorhythm. But hey, it wasn't every man that gave a girl a $12,000 Lincoln Continental for a present when it wasn't even her birthday. As she drifted off, she heard him get up, couldn't sleep again, even with the pills.

He's got the pre-concert jitters, she thought. "Don't fall asleep in there again," she had said. He had done so on numerous occasions. She sometimes found him asleep on the floor, naked except for a towel or wash cloth that he had mindlessly grasped for whatever warmth it afforded his shivering body.

"I won't," he had slurred in response, his voice made inarticulate by the ineffective drugs he had taken to bring him some blessed sleep.

The King had walked into the reading room, the bathroom designed in response to the severe constipation that was his bane during his adult life. He had closed the door, probably picked out a book, and hoped to read until he got sleepy or passed last night's meal. He had a full selection of books in the customized, moisture proof glass encased bookcases. Most of them were on religious subjects. Those were the kind he usually was partial to on his sleepless days.

Ginger stretched in feline fashion, rolling from her back to her stomach, then raising her naked buttocks, as she moaned softly. *He may be pudgy, out of shape and getting older, but it's still a kick waking up in the King's bed*, she thought. She picked up the phone to call her friend Melissa. She always liked to call her from the King's bed because it made Melissa outrageously jealous. They chatted for a few minutes. Then Ginger Snap put the phone down on the receiver, and rolled out of bed.

"Funny, the door to the bathroom is still closed. He must have fallen asleep in there again," she sighed. As many times as she had done it, she still hesitated to open the door when she thought he might be in there. It didn't help the romance to see him sitting on the throne, writhing with his constipation. Even though the toilet was in its own compartment in the bathroom, he rarely remembered to close it.

She turned the gold handle, slowly eased the door open and saw that the lights were still on. He lay on the floor, just outside of the compartment, hunched up in a fetal position. His skin was blue and cold to her touch.

The King was pronounced dead at 3:30 p.m. by Shelby County medical examiner Dr. Jerry Francisco. He had passed over when he couldn't pass that fried banana and peanut butter sandwich and chicken fried steak.

The King is dead. Long live the King. And perhaps he would.

CHAPTER 10   1996

LAST CHANCE

HOLLYWOOD, CALIFORNIA

The sign painted on the glass entrance door to the elegantly appointed reception area read "Celio's Stars." Up, and to the right, a twinkling star shone down on the lettering. Some type of glitter had been blended in with the paint to make it wink. Dominic Celio claimed he had industrial grade diamonds included in the specially formulated paint. His competition said they were cubic zirconium, forgetting that this door had been installed back in the forties, when rhinestones were the ersatz diamonds of choice because cubic zirconium hadn't been invented yet.

In any case, the receptionist's desk was vacant, the area dark except for a glimmer of light slipping under a set of mahogany doors. The dim light bled from underneath the doors, staining the dark green, plush hallway carpet with a yellow cast. Behind those doors, Dominic Celio sat at a large desk that consisted of a flat pane of glass, beveled around the edges, and supported by four, marble Corinthian style columns. The desk was bare, as it always was. Not even a telephone marred its surface.

In Celio's opinion, it was the ultimate symbol of power and authority. A physical demonstration that he was no pusher of papers, but a man valued for his power, his vision and his thoughts.

Celio had a problem. Fortunately, over the years he had developed a sure fire method to come up with solutions. Throughout his life, or at least since he started his career as a Hollywood agent at the age of twenty, Celio had developed a consistent way of meditating through his life's dilemmas, with a remarkable degree of success. When he really needed to think aggressively but with creativity and flair, he would wait until evening, when the office was closed, and then begin his routine.

First, he secured his perimeter by verifying that all entry ways-client, preferred client and service-were closed. Then he used his cellular phone to notify security that he would be shutting off all lights, except in his personal office, for the rest of the evening. Ditto the phone and security systems for the same period. This would include turning the cellular phone power off at the conclusion of his call. A small flashlight lit his path down the long corridor to his office. He softly opened and closed the door, locked it and walked behind his desk. A supply of 14" red, cinnamon scented tapers were kept in the credenza there. Celio had withdrawn two, placed them in the silver holders on the small, teak coffee table in the corner opposite his desk. The whispered exhaust from an air-conditioning duct caused the flames to dance, casting shadows of flickering light on the walls and diffusing the scent of cinnamon to the room's sole occupant. The intensity of the aroma was not steady, but pulsed from indistinguishable to a pungency that caused his eyes to tear, just slightly.

Dominic Celio had discovered very early on that more than one soul dwelled within his body. His creative self came out at night, in an environment that he, and only he, could create. He fooled this wonderful creature by satisfying all of the senses except the sixth, which Dominic believed in him was his creative sense. Celio had read Aristotle in his youth. He had found logic in Aristotle's list of the five senses of sight, hearing, smell, taste, and touch. The sixth sense he thought to be legend, or something genetically bred out of the human race. Perhaps it lived on as a vestige, like the human tail, without function or functionality. Or so he had believed until he accidentally discovered his own. It first had come in fits and spurts, like the sperm from an ejaculating dog, unwillingly uncoupled from the focus of his intentions. Only after many years, much reading and a great deal of thought, had he come up with a theory that he called "Satisfy the Five and the Sixth will come alive." It worked on the simple principle that he needed to de-energize the five Aristotle senses in order to bring out, and focus on, that part of his brain in which resided his muse. The energy normally used by the other senses could then be channeled to the sixth. It was this surplus of energy which Celio believed made the process work.

As with anything, he had put his theory to the test using a variety of unrelated happenings and conditions. The flickering candles were from his childhood bedroom. When he was ill, his mother would light two red candles for him to read by. He recalled watching the splendid, sometimes scary, shapes the shadows from those flickering flames made in his dark room. Rare was the night he did any actual reading as he let his imagination run wild.

He recalled the sense of hypnosis that came upon him as the candles flickered in their quiet old house, in which his parents and siblings had long gone off to sleep. That remembrance opened the second lock to his enchained riddle. To induce the silence he had first worn ear muffs, then found the protection worn by competing skeet shooters to provide a better effect. But as he grew older, he was now 86, he found that classical music stimulated his imagination. This night, the strains of Ravel's 1922 transcription of Modest Petrovich's Mussorgsky's Pictures at an Exhibition played to satisfy the sense of hearing. After decades of listening, Celio believed that the Frenchman Ravel had preserved the basic Russianness of the original work for piano. The same CD included Mussorgsky's tone poem, A Night on Bald Mountain by the Philadelphia orchestra under the baton of Eugene Ormandy.

Finding a satisfying smell had been easy. He had eaten a fresh baked cinnamon roll with his black coffee every day of his adult life. The aroma, as the oven was opened, seemed to release a swarm of endorphins that soothed a man's soul.

72

Taste and touch were easy as getting a five-dollar piece of crack in Harlem. One of the constants of the home remedies used on the children in the Celio household was a cold remedy concocted by his father. It consisted of one part each of fresh orange juice, clover leaf honey, and Napoleon cognac. This ghastly mixture was heated to a temperature just below the boiling point, then allowed to cool to slightly above room temperature. It was administered by the teaspoon full, the number of teaspoons being in accordance with your age, weight and illness. Dominic Celio supposed there was a complicated formula, but if there was, it was never passed down from his parents. Once you had managed to swallow the malodorous mixture, its taste lingered through the night. It was not unpleasant, being more of the honey and juice than the cognac. Before each creativitve session, he made the concoction and self administered it. For touch, he simply kept his hands, palms downward on the cool surface of the glass of his desk.

But tonight it wasn't working. At the moment he believed that his batteries had been drained. The convergence of energies was bringing forth no illumination in the darkness of his mind. He fully realized that he no longer represented the creme de la creme of the entertainment industry as he did in the forties and fifties. Back then he could not only shut down a picture in progress but a studio as well. But still, he thought there were a few favors he could call in. He allowed his thoughts to wander to the events of the past week, seeking any type of pathway toward a solution to his current, vexing problem.

"Maybe I really am getting too old for this crap," he sighed as the music swirled around him.

He had been at his desk, ready to call it a day, go to his club, and have a martini while he played gin with the "boys." That's what he called the pensioners, just turned 65. All of his old cronies were dead. Getting up a game of cards was a way to gain new friends. It was easy enough. In the old days, when one of the players died, they asked for applications for a player to fill in the table. They had begun looking for a replacement the same day Abe died, suddenly of a brain aneurysm while he was calling out "Gin." He never got it all the way said so they left his money in the pot. They had the decency to retire to the bar, taking their drinks with them, while the paramedics cleaned up and took Abe to the hospital to be declared dead. Then they chose their new partner and renewed the game.

They had not been a sentimental bunch, those old friends. But they duly attended the services and funerals as the group dwindled down to the last man, Dominic Celio. He didn't believe his new card partners were any more considerate than his previous ones, likely even less. This bunch would probably not see him out of this world into the next. But he was pragmatic about it. It passed the time. He was a widower who had outlived his wife, their children and all of his closest friends. The club was safe, warm and offered companionship and passably good food. By the time they finished with cards and dinner each night, it was out the door to a waiting taxi and time to call it a night.

The call came just as he was walking past Myrna, his receptionist. Myrna was a real find. Slim, good looking, auburn hair that flowed in waves to just above her shoulder blades and smart. Best of all, she was smart. Great, outgoing personality, the type that can soothe the savage beast, even Roxanne. If Celio knew someone was coming in flaming, he'd make them wait fifteen minutes out there with Myrna. Calmed them down and had them smiling by the time she told them to go on into his office. Best paid receptionist in Hollywood. He paid her $150,000 a year and he still felt she was underpaid for services rendered.

"Mr. Celio, I have Roxanne on line one for you. Are you in or out?"

"I'd better take it. She's had a pretty rough time over there at Cannes, even for her," he responded as he turned and walked spryly back to his office. Dominic believed that by walking spryly he could stay one step ahead of the Grim Reaper. So far it had worked.

"Roxanne, my dear," he said after he opened up the credenza and picked up the phone, "how are you and where are you."

"I'm in Pam Harriman's office at the U.S. embassy in Paris. It was the only way I could get the lousy paparazzi off my back. I don't know what my gig in Cannes stirred up stateside, but it's a real gusher over here," she said.

He could hear the satisfaction in her voice. *He had to hand it to her,* he thought. *If it was publicity she wanted, she had truly gotten it.*

"It has stirred up the entire world, Roxanne. That clip of the dogs swarming all over you has been shown on CNN. It's getting more play than Desert Storm," he said, stroking her a bit.

"Yeah, but will it do me any good? I got a bruise on my butt the size of Rhode Island. Had a photographer do some stills of it, just in case. I'm hoping I'm getting some compensation in return for all I've been through," she said, getting to the point of the call. "Look, I'm coming home from west to east trying to shake the press and TV guys. I've got flights to places I never heard of but I should be back to my place by the end of the month. When I get stateside, I'm coming in black face with grey hair and a cane so I don't think I'll be recognized. Here's what I want you to do."

♀

What she had in mind was a welcome home party, Hollywood style, a big glitzy affair held in her honor and, sub rosa, at her expense. Dominic had a little better than three weeks to get it done. He had gone about arranging it in typical Hollywood style. He had called all of his clients, all of the other agents in town and tried pulling in all of his old markers. Thousands of invitations had been mailed because he expected a low percentage of RSVP's. His hunch was right but even he was appalled when he found that Baby Doll, Pee Wee Harman, Mr. Moonbeam himself, ex-Governor of California, and Elvis's ex, Priscilla, were the highest level of luminaries to respond in the affirmative.

Celio had thought at the time, *Roxanne's gonna go ballistic if this is the best I can do. I can fill the place with Rent-a-Guests. But that will be so obvious it will kill any favorable publicity we might hope to garner from the affair.*

As he stared at the two red candles, the flame from which gave off the only light in the room, he sighed, "It's tough getting old. I wish I'd been born a red Indian or a Chinee. Their people respect the elderly. Here in Hollywood, they're like a bunch of hyenas, waiting for anything in the herd to show a sign of weakness. Then, it's goodbye, baby."

He turned and looked at the clock on his credenza. It was a sterling silver statue of a nude woman given to him by a grateful Marilyn Monroe after he had landed her that great spot in *Some Like It Hot* with Tony Curtis and Jack Lemmon. The clock part was a ball she held in her hands as she stood frozen in a permanent pirouette. It was three o'clock in the morning.

"I don't have the energy to stay up this late and think clearly anymore," he said out loud, startling himself at the sound of his voice.

He turned the switch on the gold plated table lamp, called the security people, blew out the candles, and nestled himself on the couch. Sleep came within minutes of his having reached up to turn off the light.

♀

The room was still dark and cool when Dominic Celio woke the next morning. He buzzed Myrna to make him some coffee and bring it in with some fruit and buttered toast. She would do that while he showered and shaved, holding his calls until he was finished with breakfast and was drinking his second cup of coffee.

There weren't usually many incoming calls in the morning. This Friday morning wasn't any different. Myrna opened the door to his office and brought two pink telephone messages, one from his worthless nephew, the other from his friend of many years, Ira Deutsch She also dropped off the morning LA Times.

Myrna spoke, "Did anything come out of last night's session that I can get a jump start on?"

"No, quite frankly, I was so stressed out from worrying about it, I just couldn't get it up."

Myrna smiled at his lame attempt at lasciviousness, and said, "Give yourself the weekend off and try again Monday night. Go play cards with your cronies and get it off your mind."

"I wish I could but I've only got ten days. That's not much time to draw in at least one big name," he responded. "No, I've got to keep plugging. Roxanne is my only big name under the age of seventy. I'd have nothing to keep me active if I lost her."

Myrna sighed, looking at the old man she loved almost like a father. She bent over, kissed him on the forehead, and looked him in the eyes as she murmured, "I've been with you 30 years. You hired me right out of Hollywood High, remember? In all that time, I've never seen you fail. I don't expect you will this time." Smiling, she straightened, turned and left the room, silently closing the door behind her.

The old man smiled, thinking, *She's right. I'm putting the pressure on myself out of fear of losing Roxanne as a client. What I should be doing is putting pressure on someone else to show up at this celebration. Now all I have to do is figure out who and how.* He smiled with satisfaction, the loss of worry more refreshing than the night's sleep and his morning shower.

He began to read the paper, a tried and true way of getting his mind off his problem for a while so his energy reservoir could fill up again. An article in the Times, by a Wall Street Journal staff reporter named Littman, was what gave him the idea. Not an original but a copy cat of a fresh idea that at least Roxanne would not have heard about.

The piece in the paper discussed an upcoming 18th birthday party for Randy, son of Aaron Learned. Not a big deal on the surface, but the way in which the Learneds proposed to use the event to publicize an upcoming Learned soap opera, featuring who else but Randy Learned, was a new wrinkle.

Nifty idea, Dominic thought. *People are going to come to the kid's birthday party because of the publicity the new show is going to draw. Me, I got the notoriety to draw the press, but I got nothing to publicize. Hmm, I think I got the makings of something here.*

He picked up his phone, pressed the button for Myrna and asked her to get Ira Deutsch on the line.

"Ira, I need a favor," he said into the receiver. He rehashed the poor response to his first attempt at drawing some flashy people to the Roxanne do. He then explained that he had avoided the higher level movie crowd on the first go round, holding them in reserve for another try. A good thing, too. Roxanne's TV peers saw no advantage in showing up at her soiree to help her right her dying career. "What I need you to do, Ira, is check around to find out who has a new movie coming out that is a little short for publicity money that might want to use my event for the exposure. Exposure they are going to get, if nothing else. Will you do that for me?"

"Sure enough. I'll call you back at the end of the day to give you a run down on my progress," Ira said. "See ya."

♀

Right at five o'clock, Myrna announced that Mr. Deutsch was on the phone.

"Stay for a bit, Myrna, if you don't mind," said Dominic Celio. "I want you to make dinner reservations for Ira and me, if I can talk him into it."

"Sure, boss. Call me when you're ready."

Ah, what a treasure, he thought as he picked up the phone. "Ira, if you have anything, how 'bout joining me for dinner to discuss it. My treat."

"I've got something but maybe not what'll do you and Roxanne some good."

"Ira, I know you better. What do you say? Name the place"

"OK Dom, any place except that goyem club of yours. Until they have some real Jews as members, I ain't setting foot in the place again. Have Myrna call me with the place and time and I'll meet you in the bar for a drink before dinner," Ira responded.

"Good enough. Just one thing, before we hang up. I want to get started thinking about how to talk the producer into coming in on this. Who is he, and what is the name of the movie?"

"Guy named Vic Schuler, movie called Dingo."

♀

It was loud, it was late, it was lewd, crude and downright rude. Roxanne loved it.

Old Dominic pulled it off, she thought to herself, intoxicated with the publicity her welcome home party had drawn in this jaded old town. *I don't have idea one as to what this is going to mean to my career, but it feels right and I feel right. Something's going to happen tonight.* She was stone sober as she stood talking to as unlikely a trio that even Hollywood could produce; the King's former wife, a mistress who had come after her, and the live-in of record on the night he died.

Priscilla was just as sober as Roxanne, or so she appeared, but Ginger and Baby Doll were plying away at whatever the waiter brought around, attempting the delicate surgery of cutting away their awkwardness in such grand company, while being careful not to stupefy their powers of speech.

Roxanne, remembering her own past feelings of low self esteem, chimed in to help them out, "So, how was the King in the sack. He sure looked like he could have made me howl with delight," she said to no one in particular.

Priscilla recoiled from the crudeness of the question. Ginger Snap smiled pleasantly, trying to maintain some semblance of self control, but Baby Doll jumped eagerly into the conversation, because they were finally talking about something she not only understood, but had experienced first hand.

"Oh, he was just great! My juices started running just from him looking at me. He was so well built, and had as righteous a set of buns as I've ever seen on a man," Baby Doll gushed in fond memory.

"How 'bout you, Ginger. He was yours, and yours alone, at the end when he was a fat slob. Could he still get it on with all them drugs he was taking?" Roxanne posed her question crudely so as to elicit a response from the fog laden maiden.

"What was the query?" Ginger asked as she listed to port.

Realizing that Ginger was loaded, Roxanne ignored her and turned to Priscilla. "You had his kid, what was it like being the mother to his child and lover at the same time?"

"I wasn't," came the somber response.

"You wasn't what?" Roxanne asked.

"After our daughter was born, he wouldn't have anything to do with me," Priscilla responded, afterwards taking a petite sip on her seltzer water.

"Like not have anything to do with you in what way?" Roxanne pushed on aggressively, excited at this bit of gossip.

"Sexually," was the whispered reply.

Roxanne, caught in the process of gulping her Perier, spritzed it involuntarily on her guests, as she shrieked, "That's outrageous"

Priscilla was repelled and appalled at Roxanne's comment on what was her private life. Ginger Snap, still pleased that she hadn't yet passed out, vowed to not accept another drink. Baby Doll's enthusiasm in her newly found ability to talk to a STAR, gushed out, "That's why I used an IUD to prevent conception. He shared that thought with me, one night when he was carried away with whatever he was on, drugs I mean."

Roxanne thought about that for a moment, looked over Baby Doll's trim, but busty figure, mentally smoothing away the wrinkles, strengthening the muscle tone, trying to imagine a Baby Doll from 20 years past. "Honey," she said, "He may have been a good lay at his age, being in prime shapeand all, but you can't tell me, you weren't plotting to marry him. What better way than to get knocked up?"

Baby Doll totally lost her inhibitions with this woman, "That's not the way I saw it. I didn't want to end up like Priscilla. And it worked, for a while."

"What happened?" asked Priscilla and Roxanne simultaneously, their curiosity aroused for disparate reasons.

"I thought the only way to get long term control of him was to have his child, but I knew his feelings about having sex with the mother of that child. So, I suggested that he make a deposit in a sperm bank," Baby Doll responded quietly.

"What happened then?" the intrigued duo asked together.

"He freaked out, threw me out and that was the end of that."

Ginger Snap, having laid off the sauce during the last hour of conversation, interjected "Ha, that explains it."

"Explains what?" shot back Baby Doll, once again intimidated by the surviving mistress.

"Why he asked me all those questions about artificial insemination, freezing sperm and such," Ginger responded, having sobered slightly by laying off the booze.

81

Roxanne's interest peaked. "Did he say he was going to go through the procedure?" she asked.

"No, El was just interested in how long the stuff was good for, and how a woman could use it to get pregnant."

"Sounds to me like he already had done it. Had he?" Roxanne shot back. Eagerly seeking a response, she moved so close to Ginger that their breasts were touching.

"Don't know. I surely never wanted any kids, his or otherwise," Ginger, the faded beauty, said.

Thwarted by Ginger's lack of interest, Roxanne turned to Baby Doll, who was absolutely beaming at the attention she was receiving. "When did he throw you out, Baby Doll?"

"August 12, 1967," came the response.

"Thanks a load," Roxanne said as she turned on her heel to look for Dominic Celio, Agent to the Stars. She had a blockbuster of an idea that couldn't wait for the party to be over.

TWO

GREAT SIOUX RESERVATION, MONTANA

Before they left for Fort Phil Kearny, she had made them gather long green poles from the willows and scrub trees that grew down by the creek. Make them 'three men long' had been her directive. One end should be no bigger round than a man's thumb, to allow the pole to be bent with both ends stuck in the rock. The tops of these poles met in the center, forming a frame that looked like an inverted cup. Where there were no cracks in which to lodge the sharpened ends, Tools had obligingly made them.

A group of privates gathered clumps of man high dried grasses and cattails from the freshwater wetlands that formed in the low spots in southeastern Montana where the Indians loved to hunt for ducks, geese and other fowl. Laughs No More rode back to the main camp to get the rawhide she would need to construct a temporary shelter, similar to the ones she had built in her youth when they were at play. She had been taught to build these hunting shelters by an old Osage woman whose name was Buffalo Bird. "Not a very nice name for a very nice woman," she had thought at the time. Buffalo birds followed in the path of the monsters, dining upon bits of undigested seed they found in the fresh manure that marked the passage of the buffalo.

This type of hut was ideal for sheltering the injured lieutenant for several reasons: it could be built around and over him without having to move him, it was generous enough in proportions to shelter her as well, porous enough to allow the night breezes to enter, and light enough to cause no damage to him or her should it be carried away in a summer thunderstorm. The simple construction made it easy for her to rebuild by herself in the event it was destroyed.

She had built him a nest next to where he had fallen to comfort his body from the rock. Layers of reeds were overlain with grass and then reed and so on until he had a comfortable mattress about six inches thick. She then placed a folded blanket on this nest. Eight hands had ever so gently lifted him onto the blanket. He had been sedated with laudanum, an opium solution in alcohol. They had to wait until the drug wore off to see if they had further damaged his already injured body. From what they could tell at the time, they hadn't.

Surgeon Harris and sergeant Miller had argued with her, unsuccessfully, that staying with him, nursing his crippled body, carrying his wastes, cleaning and feeding him was no job for a pretty young woman. Her counter to that won the day.

"That is what a mother does for her child. In his condition, he is no more than a child. His mother is not here. Even if she were, she could not survive living under these conditions. She would be a burden to him when just the opposite is required."

Lieutenant Bunting came out of his drug induced sleep just before noon. Running Water had made him a portable shelter to shade his face and a portion of his body from the sun, which now stood at its apex. Informed of the extent of his injuries, he ordered the men to proceed with the mission under sergeant Miller's command. The surgeon was to stay at Fort Kearney, making frequent visits to his patient, until he was satisfied with his rate of recovery. Then he too was to go forward, catching up with the group by train.

The Corps was out of food and anxious to get to the fort. A brief nap while the quarreling was going on had left the soldiers groggy and miserable. They were anxious to leave by the time the surgeon was convinced to let her use her natural methods for healing. However, she asked him to give the patient one more dose of laudanum to give her time to gather the raw material she needed to prepare her tonics and ointments

She had slipped off, leaving him alone for a short time in the early afternoon, when the snakes would be sleeping, warming themselves in the sun as they lay coiled on flat rocks throughout the arroyo. She gathered knitbone down in the wetlands. From the leaves, she would make tea which, when taken internally, would, heal any internal trauma. She would grind the root between two rocks, combine the powder, which the whites called comfrey, with some dried wild tobacco and enough honey to make a bruise healing paste. White man's tobacco lacked the spirit to heal. She had traded for her small cache with a Cherokee whose grandmother had brought seed on the long, forced march from Georgia to Indian Territory. She collected more yarrow for a poultice change. Dandelion leaves would be gathered fresh, mashed to a pulp and fed to him at the onset of constipation.

Running Water was greatly pleased as she returned from foraging, having found a stunted prickly ash growing on the side of a hill. She knew the tree from her boarding school in Nebraska. A Shawnee girl had made her a tea from equal parts of fresh bark and water when she had told her of the pain in her lower back that came from sitting in class all day on hard wooden seats.

"Oh, how I sweated after drinking that tea," she recalled. The pain had gone away within a few hours and had never returned. She made a similar tea for the handsome lieutenant, as well as a syrup which she prepared by boiling off almost all of the water. She blended a portion of the residue with honey and stored it in a bark cup. The rest she dried for future use. The prickly ash took away the pain without dilating the eyes and taking away the senses like the white man's medicine did.

She had returned just as he was wakening. The sun had pierced the veil of the temporary shade as it moved across the sky. Bright light, shining on his eyelids, brought him to consciousness. She had then moved the grass and reed shade canopy upon her arrival, started the fire for the prickly ash tea, made a little three pole stand from which to hang her pot and placed the water and shredded bark in the pot to boil.

Not wishing to be idle while waiting for the tea to boil, Running Water began to build bundles of reed and grass using the grass to tie off the bundles. If her brother did not return with the rawhide before dark, she would make do with twine she made from the grass. The grass bundles would go on first to keep the shelter cool and smelling fresh. The reeds would provide a harder exterior shell, to shed the rain, in the unlikely possibility that some should find its way to the reservation at this time of year.

✠

And that is how she remembered the beginning of their relationship. She had nursed him back to health over a two month period, done all the things a mother would do, and through it all their love blossomed. Her brother had been partially right. They had been married, but in a union recognized by both state and church, not ‡ la faÁon du pays as her brother had suggested two years ago. She was now Mrs. James Ray Bunting, the proud mother, this very day, of twin boys. While the boys slept in their individual bassinets, she had day dreamed, waiting for them to wake so the midwife could bring them to her to hold and snuggle.

How proud the lieutenant had been when they were born, healthy, red faced and squalling. How shocked she had been two months before when he told her he intended to name them after the commanding general who had formed his beloved bicycle corps. He was blissfully unaware that this same man had been responsible for the death of her brother and slaughter of many women and children of her people. When she gently told him of this, they swiftly reached a compromise, for this was truly a marriage with a foundation of love, not born out of convenience or sense of duty. The children were named Miles Aaron and

Miles Garon. Thus bestowed with the honorarium to the general, they were to be called by their middle names everlasting, and that was the end of that.

CHAPTER 12   1996

GUMSHOE

DOVER, DELAWARE

The phone rang just as I was heading for the door. Usually, I don't answer it when I am at home. It is just too frustrating trying to find it. My wife successfully lobbied for a cordless Sony Model SPP-A450. It's a good unit, as portables go, without those annoying fade-outs and static accompaniments to conversation that I got with the last two I had tried as I meandered through our house. But it is the very utility of the thing which precipitates its downfall in the Bunting household. For you see, my wife and daughter leave it wherever they are when their chat draws to a close. I do mean wherever, for it has been found in the dirty laundry, the kitchen sink, under a bedroom pillow and, inside the downstairs closet, among other more common places.

But this time I was on a case. In fact I had four in various stages of development. It might be a client, his attorney or one of the other experts involved. My workplace at home is where I do much of my thinking and probing for possible clues and solutions. As a result, I field a lot of calls when I am actively involved in my chosen profession, forensic engineering. In fact, I am a Fellow in the National Academy of Forensic Engineers, of which I was also the youngest past president. I specialize in environmental cases. My area of interest, and expertise to the extent that I have any, is in cases related to water contamination, i.e., keyed legally to the Clean Water Act. My investigative and creative powers have also led to assignments well outside this specific area of interest. I have testified as to ship movement in the Delaware Estuary, docking procedures and raw material off loading techniques. I have investigated the justification for utility rates, and on the basis of my findings, provided testimony in court that lead to my client's relief from an expensive judgement. Mine is an active mind that seeks to create solutions where there is no obvious pathway. The mundane simply bores me. That is why I eventually sold out my interest in the engineering firm that I had co-founded. Thankfully, I am now at the point in my career that personal financial gain is no longer a factor in my accepting an assignment

I pushed the 'find-it' gadget on the phone, in frustration, and jumped when the receiver beep came shrilly from the spot where I was standing. There it was, right on the rug, underneath the bar stool. I picked it up, hit the button and answered, "John Bunting speaking."

"Is Katie there?" squeaked the nasal voice of my daughter's favorite third grade chum, Ashley Winters.

"No, Ashley, she and her mother have gone to the mall. Something about a birthday gift, a party on Saturday."

"Please ask her to call me when she gets home," said Ashley.

"Certainly," I responded. "Goodby."

That little episode illustrates why I don't field many home telephone calls when I am not on a project. I find the interruptions to be somewhat annoying. Had I not picked up, Ashley would eventually have been able to leave her message on the answering machine. My wife, Patricia, once asked me why I don't just use the machine to screen my calls when I'm into a project. My response was that I thought, and still think, the practice to be a display of bad manners. Further, when I'm on the hunt, timing is everything. Sometimes events, and my reasoning, are too singular to be coincidence. In any case, now I had to rummage through drawers looking for a bit of paper to write the note for Katie. Bother!

I believe I am as affable as the next fellow when tossed into social events. I just don't seek them out. My friends apparently have recognized my introspective bent over the years, for they rarely call me at home. Another good reason for not answering the phone.

My current assignment came to me through Jeff Bross, senior partner and seasoned environmental lawyer with the firm of Barros, Truitt and Herman. They have their principal offices in Wilmington in the Brandywine Building at Tenth and King Streets, with satellite sites in Dover, the state capitol, and Georgetown, the County seat in Sussex, the lower of Delaware's three counties. These branches are small offices, two or three attorneys at any given time, each with a secretary, receptionist, mail girl wrapped into one person. These triple duties never warranted much in the way of a salary, as there always seemed to be a surplus of these bright, attractive and charming young ladies in the area. Jeff runs the Dover operation. Although he is a city boy born and bred, he recognized early on that Dover was where his contacts had to be if he was going to get the job done for his clients.

I was on my way to Jeff's office when Ashley had called. I now closed the door behind me, got into my 1970 Chevy pickup, and drove down to his office on the Green. Office space on the Green comes at a premium. Some of the quadrangle of buildings that surround this lush lawn of Kentucky blue grass and towering sycamore trees were built before the Revolutionary War. In fact, Delaware's contribution to the Continental Army, the Blue Hen's Chicks, marched to join their fellow volunteers from this very spot. They had signed on, and then fortified themselves with rum and other spirits, at the Golden Fleece Tavern. The tavern building still stands on the east side of State Street where it enters the Green from the north. Of course, it is no longer a Tavern. Its patrons couldn't possibly consume enough spirits to pay the rent. Only lawyers and state and county offices could afford the premium prices. The more humble law offices and their cast of supporting service providers spill out to the north and south, hemmed in by the state capitol complex on the east and a cemetery and museum to the west.

The Barros et al branch was housed in a former residence on the west side of the square. Built in the latter part of the nineteenth century, it is a sturdy brick building. Although of Victorian style, it is otherwise architecturally nondescript. I parked my truck in a sunny, almost always nearly vacant lot of Stanley Mitchell's State Farm Insurance Building. I don't know how many customers Stan has, but clearly they don't stop in to pay their premiums.

The walk back on the undulating brick sidewalk took less than five minutes. Another of the pleasures of living in Dover. You can get just about anywhere in town within fifteen minutes, except twice per year when the Winston 500 stock car races came to town. That's the NASCAR race they call the Monster Mile because it has the steepest banks on the circuit. Race weekend, you simply avoided the northeast part of town for three days. For those addicted to the slots at the track, that either was a cold turkey weekend, or required a trip to Atlantic City to satisfy their appetite for gambling.

"Good morning, Mr. Bunting," the smiling, red headed woman behind the inlaid teak desk said as I stepped in the door. The desk was an expensive, hand-me down from the main office, a well- built piece which once adorned a senior partner's office in Wilmington. So was Margaret. The desk had been purchased to display the owner's good taste. So had Margaret been. But that was a long time ago and another tale altogether.

"Hi, Margaret, is Jeff in yet?"

"Waiting in his office for you along with your coffee, one third of a spoonful of sugar, no cream."

Lucky man, I thought. *Margaret is half the reason Jeff is so good at what he does. She runs the office, sets the ambience and gives him the time and space he needs to think.*

And he thought well, very well. I had worked with perhaps 50 attorneys in my career. He was in the top three, right up there with Peter Hansen and Tai Lassen. Each shared a common trait, a degree in engineering. Their awareness of technical jargon and theory simplified our working relationship. It allowed us to use our time to the client's advantage, creating winning strategies, while the grinders in our respective offices sifted through the data upon which we would base them.

A smiling Jeff rose from behind his desk as I entered his office. He was a striking man, six feet six, slim as a marathon runner, which he was, and with a shock of brown hair reminiscent of John Kennedy. The women were crazy about him. The young ones thought him cool. He never dated anyone over 29. I can't imagine what his sex life might be like. But then in this age of Aids, I'm glad to be married with one less potential threat to my health and happiness

"Hey, you're looking good, John. Been working out?" he said as he folded his arms across his chest, gazing at me, sizing me up. We were friends, close enough not to need to shake hands. He was wearing a white, oxford cloth button down shirt, blue pin striped trousers held up by bright red suspenders which matched his tie. Oxblood Florsheim's completed his dapper outfit. He always wore a suit to the office, ready for the unexpected client.

"Yeah, had a little bit of blood pressure problem so rather than take the medicine, I do the tread mill every day, weights twice a week."

"Take it from me, it shows. Has it helped your blood pressure any?" Jeff asked.

"Amazingly, yes. After I started eating fresh fruit for snacks and avoided the salt in processed food, I'm back to normal," I responded. "Enough about me, what's up?"

He waved me to the leather sectional sofa in a bright corner of his office, the master's study it was when the building was a private residence. Setting his and my coffee on cork coasters to prevent any stain on his highly prized solid cherry coffee table, he began, "I had a call yesterday from Wesley Townsend. He's an in-house attorney for BCC-NA, British Chemical Company here in the states, actually in North America. You're aware that they have their North American headquarters up on Concord Pike and a major production facility north of the county landfill, up near the Pennsylvania border?"

"Of course," I said, perhaps a little sharply, for I've lived Delaware for more than thirty years.

"John, I don't mean to offend. You of all people should know my style by now. I never assume you know what I know. I always make sure you do. So calm down and bear with me. Because I didn't pick you for this assignment, Wesley Townsend did."

I arched an eyebrow in surprise, saying "Why I don't know the man. How did he hear about me?"

"Man, how often do I have to tell you that you're famous," Jeff Bross laughed as he slammed the coffee table with his open hand. "It's the mystique of the 6 P's. He read that old potboiler of yours, *Global Competition: How your skills at negotiating can effect your ability to survive in the global economy.*"

"Hey," I exclaimed, "I've made more money off cases from the odd business type who's actually read it than I did in royalties. Speaking of which, what's the case?"

Jeff Bross told me what he knew over coffee which he sweetened with brandy as the sun drifted down behind the museum's steeple, which offered a cool, welcome shade to our little retreat in the former study. We left together, to continue our discussion over dinner and a drink at W. T. Smithers, a pleasant little watering hole, a short stroll away on north State Street. If there was anything called action in down town Dover, that's where it is, but not this early. There would be a few people at the bar having an after work drink before they went home. Just the regulars during the week.

CHAPTER 13   1996

PRIVATE EYE

WILMINGTON, DELAWARE

The diminutive woman was no more than a small brown and tan spot on the huge red leather couch. Her saffron hued skin hinted of oriental ancestry. It glowed with vitality, blended well with the athletic litheness of her body, which she elected to camouflage with a muted brown, hound's tooth sport coat over a white silk blouse. Her tan, cotton and wool slacks, had side pockets which completed the slightly mannish look that was hers by choice. She was snuggled in one corner of the couch, her left arm cocked into the arm rest, the fist serving as support for her angular chin. Her dark brown hair was cut short, in a wedge. She was attractive, knew it and never gave a second thought to using her good looks as part of the tools she brought to her trade. Pester Size was a private detective.

"Miss Size, I...," Roxanne began.

"Call me Pester."

Momentarily flustered, Roxanne said, "Why of course, Pester." Having said it, she began to wonder just who was the stinking boss here, but knowing how much this woman's skills might mean to her future, she doused her flaring temper with those good thoughts and went on, "The assignment I have in mind is very delicate in terms of the need for secrecy. That is why I have elected to interview you. You come highly recommended by my agent, Dominic Celio."

Speaking in a low monotone, a trick she used to make sure she had the listener's attention, Pester said, "Look, Roxanne, my reputation has been built on secrecy, so that's not even an issue for discussion. What you don't seem to understand is that you are the one who is being interviewed, not me. I want to find out if your problem has two features that I require in order to take on an assignment."

"You've got a pair of balls on you, kid. Tell me, what are the two requirements?"

Continuing the rasping whisper, Pester said, "Complexity and money. The job has to interest me and pay well. I don't do divorces, blackmail, security and the traditional kind of P.I. work."

Roxanne was dressed in a black, velvet sweat suit, the toenails of her bare feet painted jet black. Her hair was cut short in a bob, just like she wears it on TV. She filled the candy striped recliner like coffee fills a cup, right to the brim. She smiled, a genuine smile which for her was a sneer, then spoke, "I can't make my assignment any more interesting than it is. So let's just say this up front. I'll pay all your expenses and any fee that you stipulate, as long as I can afford it. This is as important to me as my own life."

Pester Size smiled in return, "One down and two to go. Tell me what you need."

Size bent over in a gesture of conspiracy. Her every move was calculated in her business as well as her social life. The raspiness in her voice was a perfect example. Since it gave everyone the impression that she was a Marlboro puffing, Jack Daniel's drinking, hard-boiled dick, she allowed the impression to flourish. No one, except for her Thai mother, knew that it was the result of a childhood accident. As a lackadaisical eight year old, she had been asked to hold the leash of a dog that her Thai aunt was about to slaughter for meat for a family wedding. She was standing with the leash twined around her neck, demonstrating a no hands method of holding the animal for her friends, when her aunt came rushing out the door, knife in hand. The wild-eyed dog took off running with Pester in tow. She had talked hoarsely ever since

Roxanne began, "I heard a fascinating Elvis story at my party last night." Looking at her watch, she continued, "Actually it was this morning. This may take a while. Want to send out for some pizza?"

"Sure," said Pester Size, "I'd like mine with the works. It'll kill me when I'm 60, but that's a long way off. Have them send over some Killian's Red with it."

♀

The grandfather clock in the hall struck one. There were two empty pizza boxes sitting on the white rug, a boorish offense to the expensive statement intended by the equally expensive interior designer who had been hired by Roxanne for that purpose. She had been smart enough not to try to decorate her home with her own taste in colors and furniture. Two empty Killians were strewn absentmindedly in the box by Roxanne. An equal number stood rigidly at attention on two coasters on the glass topped end table next to the couch.

The two women rose in unison. As they shook hands, Pester Size said, "I'll take the job. Rest assured, if it's out there, I'll find it. When I find it, I'll get it for you, even if I have to steal it."

She handed her card to Roxanne who accepted it, saying, "I will open a $100,000 account for you to draw on for expenses at the Wells Fargo Bank in Walnut Creek. It will be under the name Wilma Miller, to make it difficult to trace it back to me. I will also deposit the first installment of your fee. Of course, this will all be done through a third party, to maintain my distance from anything you might do."

"Understood," Size rasped, as she broke the handshake and began to walk toward the door. "My reports will be made in person or over the phone, depending upon the circumstances.

They both parted feeling they were involved in a win-win situation.

When he opened the door, Pester Size began to think she had the wrong man. Hadn't Fike been a huge beefy man? Yes, she remembered from her research through the host of biographies on the King, his nickname had been Lardass. The man who stood before her couldn't weigh more than 150 pounds. He laughed, waived her in saying, "Yeah, I'm Fike. I had an operation to lose some weight. It was too effective, I damn near wasted away to nothing. But I'm better now."

"Thank you for seeing me, Mr. Fike, I know it must seem strange that I'm poking around in the King's business after all these years."

"Honey, with all the stuff that boy stirred, they'll be digging up cadavers in the next century just to settle bets about what he done," he said in a good old boy, swaggering way. But then in a more somber tone, "In fact, Miss..."

"It's Pester, like I said on the phone, Mr. Fike," she smiled demurely. She had dressed the part today, eschewing her slacks for a business suit with a skirt.

"Yeah, well, Pester if you read all them books like you said, I don't know what else I can tell you, other than you missed one, the last one I was involved in with Billy and Marty. The reason I know is I told in that book about getting my intestine tied off to lose weight. You wouldn't have been surprised at my appearance if you had read that 'un, would you?" he asked.

"You've got that right," she responded. "What was the name of it?"

"Don't worry 'bout it. I've got several boxes left out in the garage. I'll get one for you 'fore you leave, " he smiled graciously.

"This is a pleasant home you have," she said falling right in with his hospitable ways.

"Why thank you. Losing El after all those years was a mighty big set back for some, me included. But I finally got my head on straight, began making a few dollars."

"What is it you do?" Pester asked.

"Publishing, here in Nashville, back in the entertainment business. But you didn't come here to talk about me. Just what is it you want to know?"

"My client has come across some information that leads us to believe the King was involved in some kind of secret medical procedure when he was younger," she explained.

"Well, hell missy, you don't need to be talking to me. It's his doctor or old Doc Hoffman, his dentist down to Memphis, that you need to see," Fike said, relaxing a bit now that he thought he was off the hook.

"No, I don't think this is something that he confided to anyone, at least directly," Size went on.

"Shaw, woman, if it's a secret, how would I know about it. I was his driver and all around whipping boy. If he confided in anyone, it would be his cousin Billy. He's here in Nashville too, working in maintenance at some factory or other," Fike said, gesturing with his right hand as if pointing at the factory.

"Like I said, I don't think he told anyone except the ones who performed the procedure, and they most likely were handsomely paid and sworn to keep it to themselves. Let me tell you what little, and it is very little, we know."

"Good, start by telling me what he was supposed to have done," Fike said, interested now in helping in return for something new in the life of the King, after all these years.

"That I cannot do, for I swore a vow of silence on that point when I agreed to take this assignment."

"Pester, it sounds to me like you're like the lady who was ordered by her sultan to get pregnant after being locked up in a harem with only women and eunuchs. You don't appear to have the right equipment to get the job done."

"Oh, but I do Mr. Fike, believe me I do. I'm looking for a memory of an unusual trip that took place after September 1967, destination unknown to us. However, we think wherever it took place, no one who was with him would have recognized it as a medical facility. Most likely, his companions would have not been allowed to enter the premises for fear of revealing his purpose..."

Fike interrupted, "How long would he have been in there?"

"An hour, maybe two, certainly not longer than a half a day."

"Missy, I think you hit pay dirt. You'll need to talk to Marty, he's right here in Nashville too, back in the business. If I'm right, your next stop will be Wilmington, Delaware. Sit tight," he said. " Let me get him on the phone. You tell him what you told me, then ask him what El told him in the back seat of the white Cadillac on the way back from Wilmington."

He was right.

Pester Size flew into Philadelphia wearing a beige jogging suite, a black wig, gold rimmed Ben Franklin glasses with plane glass lenses and a white beret. Her attempt to appear innocuous was successful. She was in and out of the airport without leaving an imprint on anyone's memory. Driving a rented grey Taurus sedan, she drove aggressively onto I-95 South, took the Route 322 exit about fifteen minutes later and then went westward on Route 1. She passed charming Chadds Ford and Longwood before reaching her destination at a bed and breakfast in Kennet Square, Pennsylvania. She had selected this form of lodging because it would be nearly impossible for anyone to discover her whereabouts. Much safer than a hotel or motel for the clandestine operation in which she was involved. If her mission was successful, she doubted anyone would ever be able to recreate her modes of travel, her lodging or her actions. Only fifteen miles from center city Wilmington, Delaware, it was the perfect hideaway.

This idyllic little community of 500 souls, nestled away in the rolling green hills of southeastern Pennsylvania, had become overrun with Spanish speaking people. They were the economic foundation for the local mushroom industry, willing to work for a minimum wage with the raw and composted horse manure. Long hours they labored in the dark, dank mushroom houses that dotted the narrow, two lane roads that meandered from village to village. She wondered how the Wyeth family, whose paintings of the area and its people were famous throughout the world, reacted to this change. Andrew Wyeth was her favorite. A print of his Christina's World was the featured painting in the living room of her apartment. The original hung in the Museum of Modern Art in New York City. Wyeth had shocked the art world, and his neighbors for that matter, when he revealed his years-long affair with his Chadds Ford neighbor Helga Testorf by exhibiting many paintings he had made of her in 1986. That's another reason she admired his work. He was an artist with stones, not some effete, snippy bisexual dilettante.

Andrew Wyeth is getting close to eighty, she mused as she began to unpack her things. *I wonder if he is still getting it on with old Helga?*

Wyeth was the final reason she had selected this particular B&B. She secretly hoped to meet him as she shopped the local stores and ate in the local restaurants. Despite its bucolic appearance, the small Brandywine Creek watershed was home to some of the wealthiest and most influential people in the country. Tucked away in the lush farm country, almost every crossroad yielded a tavern or restaurant with a menu to suit any palette.

Her unpacking complete, Pester Size lay down on the blue and white quilt for an afternoon nap. When she awoke, she planned to take a leisurely shower, get dressed in something casual and have dinner at her favorite restaurant, the Dilworthtown Inn. The inn, a revolutionary style tavern located just west of the Wilmington Pike on a secluded road, was a stone's throw north of the Chester/ Delaware County line. She had made her reservations upon arrival at the airport. She planned to take the back route tonight, looking forward to driving the winding roads that snaked through the hills.

She fell asleep while trying to remember the road names, "North on Wawaset, then east on Street Road, then south on the road that followed Brandywine Creek until I get..."

♀

Pester Size awoke the next morning, showered, dressed and departed for Wilmington. Today she wore a dark green skirt, light green turtle neck sweater and brown pumps. She topped it all with a plaid blazer to cover her prominent breasts. Taken in its entirety, a very bland attire selected so as not to attract attention. The drive down Kennet Pike brought her swiftly into the city on Pennsylvania Avenue. She parked at Ninth and Walnut, walked to the inter-city mall on Market Street and had a breakfast consisting of a cup of Twining's Earl Grey tea, a purple plum and a banana. She took her time, bought a copy of the News Journal and read it cover to cover, wanting to be familiar with local news. The hot topic of the moment had to do with the disappearance of Governor Tom Carper's appointment secretary. Foul play was suspected, a prominent local family was possibly involved, President Clinton had called to offer his help, FBI etc.

This story had completely overshadowed the one which had been national news. An apparent bad seed in the DuPont family had shot and killed one of his employees, a wrestler who lived on DuPont's estate. It appeared to Size that there was just as much business for people in her line of work on the east coast as there was on the west.

She looked at her watch, 10:00 a.m., just the right time. "It's not too early and it's not too late, soon be living in a brand new state." The catchy, closing lyrics from 'Oklahoma' slipped through her thoughts as she left a tip and rose to pay her bill.

Market Street had been closed to traffic since she had last been in Wilmington. It was planted with trees. Statuary and benches to refresh the mind and body of the weary shopper were solitary companions this lovely morning. The mall was virtually empty of pedestrian traffic. Rodney Square, on the other hand, bustled with people, buses and cars, their combined noise producing the caterwauling symphony one expected down town in a small city. She walked around the block, looking for hidden entrances to the Wilmington Trust Building at Ninth and King. There were none, other than a service entrance in an alley. That was hardly a fitting place for the king of rock and roll to be welcomed.

The main entrance doors, glass with brass fittings, were manned by a doorman who doubled as a security officer. Pester Size strode briskly up the granite stair, hesitating momentarily as the black doorman graciously nodded his head and opened the door. She nodded in acknowledgment, somewhat taken aback at this courteous service in the corporate downsizing nineties. Size thought the doorman's maroon uniform, with gold epaulettes, looked as if it had been de rigeur in the roaring twenties. For that matter, so did the doorman. He was one of those fellows of indeterminate age, with the white hair of the elderly, whose sprightly movement and wrinkle free visage painted a perplexing contradiction.

She walked onto the mezzanine's marble floors, slowly scanned the area, then walked slowly to the desks where the deposit slips and other bank paraphernalia were kept. She selected several brochures that described the banks services, information on certificates of deposits, still searching for the transitional passage from financial propagation to human procreation. Nothing appeared obvious. There were no doors marked private, no passage ways guarded by modern plastic ID servers or even old fashion security guards, more in place with the ambience of the bank.

102

Size looked at her watch, noting that she had been in the building for almost seven minutes. She realized a diversion was necessary if she was going to stay in the building without arousing suspicion. She strode over to the customer service representative waiting area, sat down on a leather couch, picked up a Wall Street Journal and began to peer over the top, still searching for Alice's rabbit hole.

"Got it," she thought, "They have a curving stairway to the second floor, but an elevator as well. I've got to find out what services are provided on that floor, then get a look at the elevator compartment. Wouldn't take rocket science to have it open to more than one area."

"You are next, Ma'am."

The statement, coming from the chubby, perky, young lady, startled her. Size jumped in her seat, turned sideways and stared directly into the breast of a short woman, whose attempt to compensate for her lack of height resulted in a six inch tall, moussed wave.

Rising, Pester Size smiled, and in a cultivated voice said, "Good, I'd like to open an account, and there are a few other services I am interested in."

Smiling in return, the customer service rep said, "Step this way. My name is Fonda Wilson. We'll see what I can help you with. Whatever I can't, I'll arrange an appointment with our other account people, suitable to your schedule, of course."

Pester Size had two appointments on the second floor within fifteen minutes. She feigned a slow recovery from a jogging injury as the reason for needing to use the elevator. Wilson went with her, spoiling any attempt to scrutinize the elevator's interior on the excruciatingly slow ride up. The ride down was entirely different. Dazzled by her poise and charm, the middle aged assistant bond account manager walked her back to the elevator, pushed the down button, and held the door open for her. He stood there with a dazed smile as the door closed.

Size immediately dropped down on her hands and knees. She

extracted a magnifying glass from her purse and began examining the carpet where it contacted the rosewood wall on either side of the front door. The frayed edge, not visible to the naked eye, clearly showed that one side of the elevator had a concealed door that opened just like the normal entrance. The dividing line between the two sides of the door was invisible due to good workmanship. Size wasted not a moment trying to find it. She knew it was there. Finding out how to use it was of no concern to her. Pester did not intend to burglarize the place. She had a better idea.

♀

For the occasion, Pester Size wore a matronly outfit, seven sizes larger than her petite size three. Judicious padding added to the dowdy image of a portly, stay at home matron. She had also streaked her hair with gray to round out the disguise. She could not get up from the chair, or her temporary weight gain would droop around her ankles. She had waited for the call, left the door ajar and then arranged herself to greet her guest.

A ruddy faced, middle aged man in a rumpled suit announced his presence as he swung the door open. Of average height, a little on the pudgy side, his facial features and the greying brown fringe of hair around his bald pate gave him a forgettable look that was immediately pleasing to her. The brown colored rims of his glasses added to his Mr. Average appearance.

"Good morning, Mr. Anderson. I'm pleased you could meet with me on such short notice. Have a seat. As I mentioned, my infirmities preclude me from being a more gracious hostess."

"No problem, Mrs. Atterly. My mother has similar problems with mobility," Wayne Anderson responded, thinking that his own mother's infirmities stemmed from a love affair with the bottle, not illness or weight. "How can I be of assistance, Ma'am?"

Pester Size began her well-rehearsed dialog, "Mr. Anderson, this is an extremely personal matter that is of great importance to me. I will tell you what I want to know, and why. I believe I will get better service from a clever fellow who knows the facts. How you obtain the information is immaterial to me, as long as it is done discretely and within the bounds of the law. I am prepared to pay you a $5,000 retainer, in cash, as a demonstration of my good faith. Expenses will be drawn from the retainer. No accounting for them is necessary. If you succeed in this inquiry, I will give you a lump sum of $25,000 as your reward."

Wayne Anderson tried not to appear too eager when he responded, "I trust I can be of service, Ma'am, but that all depends on what you need me to find out. How about you share that with me on this visit and we'll see if I'm your man."

Pester Size proceeded to do so.

After she had retained the private investigator, Pester Size flew back to LA to catch up on her other work. She had asked Anderson for weekly reports by mail. She still didn't trust the Net's security. Weekly reports would come in handy. She could plagiarize them to meet her own schedule with Roxanne.

The story she had given Anderson was the old saw about the other woman, or she had added, somewhat sadly, the other man. She couldn't be sure. He had pumped her for details. She had feigned tears. All she knew was what a friend of hers had told her. She was not at liberty to give the friend's name as it would embarrass Mrs. Atterly to have her friend know that she had followed up her gossip by hiring a detective. The friend was in the process of preparing to divorce her husband. Accordingly, she was spending a great deal of time at the Wilmington Trust bank with her account manager trying to hide, to the extent they could, her various and considerable assets before she filed the action. One day, she had observed Mr. Atterly coming out of the first floor elevator door. He had surveyed the mezzanine before stepping out and walking briskly toward the exit door. Her friend thought that rather suspicious behavior. Having caught her own husband in the midst of an affair, she had given Mrs. Atterly fair warning. She also made sure to position her chair where she could not be seen from the elevator but could clearly observe all arrivals and departures. Mr. Atterly's were frequent and covert. Or so Pester Size had told Wayne Anderson.

Given her lack of mobility, she needed someone to help her. She did not want to alert her husband to the fact that she was on to him. Conversely, she wanted Anderson to see who used the elevator with regularity, at starting and quitting time. She implied that her nemesis was an employee of the bank. In fact, she was only interested in male employees of the sperm bank, for it was through one of them that she would initiate phase two of her plan.

CHAPTER 14   1996

PACIFY

BEVERLY HILLS, CALIFORNIA

Pester Size had purposely dressed in white slacks, a white silk blouse and a black mohair blazer in order to provide a stark contrast to Roxanne's blood red, leather sofa. She hoped to somewhat overcome her Lilliputian feelings when she sat in the Gulliver sized couch. Her black linen pumps lay on the floor, as she sat facing Roxanne, who had dressed in a grey sweat suit for the occasion. She looked like an engorged maggot in the outfit but it went well with her striped recliner.

"Pester, tell me some good news. I've had a really crappy week. It looks like my show is going down the toilet," Roxanne said in a low tone. " Dominic hasn't been able to get them interested in finding me a new project. Looks like they think I'm all washed up."

"Sorry to hear that," Pester said in a perfunctory manner as she withdrew a sheaf of papers from her valise. "I'm making good progress."

Roxanne brightened, saying "Did he do it?"

"Too early in the game to know that," answered Pester. "However, I'm pretty sure I've found the depository."

"Where is it?"

"In a bank in downtown Wilmington, Delaware," Pester replied.

Roxanne's mouth fell open. "In a bank," she screeched, "In fricking Wilmington, Delaware. Where in the hell is Delaware?"

"It's a small state just south of Philadelphia. Wilmington is its largest city."

"Must be some punk place that I never heard of it before. I wonder how Elvis knew about it? He wasn't exactly a scholar," commented Roxanne.

"Whatever," said Pester. "I've hired a local detective to gather the names of all the staff who seem to work in the area where I think the sperm bank is located. There's an elevator with a secret exit. He's photographing everyone who frequents that elevator at closing time."

"Then what?"

"He's showing their faces to people in shops around the bank, trying to get their names."

"What's his cover?" Roxanne asked.

"I don't know. That's his business. I told him I'm a wife who's trying to get the goods on a cheating husband. My story is that I think he's cheating with someone who works on the second floor of the bank. My hubby has been seen coming out of that elevator on several occasions and that's not where we do our banking"

"So your plan is to infiltrate the organization through a male employee," Roxanne concluded.

"Not necessarily," came the response. "I told Anderson, that's the detective, that I suspected my husband might swing both ways."

"What happens after he gets their names? You can't do much with a list of names."

Pester Size's contempt for her client's level of intelligence did not show in her face as she explained, "Once he has their names, he'll build a profile for me, things like income, debt, likes, dislikes. I've brought a sample of one for you to look at. After you read it, I'll take it with me and destroy it. There'll be no paper trail on this job when I get done."

Roxanne took the proffered paper, read it and smiled as she handed it back, saying "Pester, this looks like a script for bribery or blackmail."

"Whatever it takes, Roxanne, whatever it takes."

"How soon before you select your victim?"

"Anderson says he should be able to wrap up this part by the end of next week. It won't take more than a day or two for me to pick the two best candidates for him to follow around. That's Phase 2. I want to know every detail about them before I go to the next stage, what type toothpaste they use, what they drink, their bowel movement habits, the works."

"And once you do, what then?" asked Roxanne.

"That's when I earn my money," Size responded gruffly.

Roxanne flipped back the recliner, grabbed her own crotch in a gross gesture, and shrieked, "Earn your money, Pester baby, and I'm going to be on my way back to the top of the heap."

CHAPTER 15   1915

RED, WHITE AND BLUE

BENECIA, CALIFORNIA

On June 28, 1914, Archduke Franz Ferdinand, the heir to the Austro-Hungarian throne, was murdered along with his wife in Sarajevo, Bosnia. The culprit was a Serbian terrorist. One month later, to the day, having been dissatisfied with Serbia's response to its ultimatum, Austria-Hungary declared war on Serbia. This was the dawn of World War I, as a series of historical military alliances brought the big powers into the fray very quickly. Russia immediately mobilized against Austria causing Germany to declare war against Russia. Like dominoes they fell into the war. France challenged Germany in defense of Russia. Britain came in defense of Belgium when the Germans marched through that tiny country to get to France.

By September, German divisions had reached the outskirts of Paris. The French and British forces then rallied, driving the Germans back across the Aisne River at the first battle of the Marne. The battle line had remained much the same after that, although probe after probe caused staggering casualties, the French suffering losses approaching 400,000 in the first quarter of 1915.

✠

The little village of Benecia, California, nestled in the hills on the northern banks of the Sacramento River, was a quiet, unpretentious town in 1915. In late April, the grass on these hills begins to turn flaxen. The winter rains end in late February. There is no rain again until November.

Benecia's small army post was as satisfying in its solitude as it was boring in the day to day routine. Captain James Ray Bunting sat in an oak rocker on the front porch of the tiny, two bedroom bungalow that he shared with his wife, Running Water, and Aaron, one of their twin sons. Garon had left hearth and family on his seventeenth birthday, claiming he wished to seek his fortune back east, but in reality chasing the daughter of a former noncommissioned officer who had served under his father's command.

Captain Bunting was reading a week old issue of The San Francisco Chronicle while waiting for Running Water to get ready to go into Oakland for a movie. He sipped his coffee, laced with a bit of brandy, as he wondered whether America was ever going to join the rest of the world and go over there to beat the Krauts. From the way the paper read, the Allies were having a rough go of it. Just last week, the Germans had used chlorine gas for the first time in a surprise attack at Ypres. They had followed up with a two-corps attack and nearly pierced the French line.

Good thing they are spread so thin, Bunting thought. *Looks to me like they lacked the reserve troops to take advantage of their surprise. The Kaiser must be wondering if he bit off more than he can chew about now.*

It was early in the morning, the sun had not yet warmed the cool evening air. Steam from his coffee fogged his spectacles as he took another sip. He set the cup down on the railing, reached for his pocket handkerchief and then stopped, smiling. Through the window, he could hear his wife softly singing "Peg O' My Heart." That had been a hit back in 1913, when he had taken the family back east on furlough.

As he listened, he wiped his glasses clear, placed them on his nose, being careful not to bend the gold ear pieces. As he was returning the kerchief to his pocket, her voice faded as she moved to another part of the house. He returned to his paper, interested in reading more about the bombing of London by Zeppelin dirigible airships.

He set the paper down in his lap, reminiscing, *It's been almost twenty years since I took that fall while we were trying to show the Army brass what hot technology the bicycle was. Now they have trucks, airplanes, dirigibles and poison gas. Rumor had it that Winston Churchill, first lord of the Admiralty, was trying to get the Brits to build a land ship, some kind of armored vehicle that could get personnel through the German machine gun fire unharmed.*

Just then, Running Water stepped through the door, a small traveling bag in hand. "I'm ready, Dear," she said with a smile.

Rising, and pitching the residue from his cup across the railing at the same time, her husband returned the smile. His white teeth gleamed beneath the splendid mustache he had grown to compliment his sideburns. "Dear, I was just sitting here thinking, you are the best thing that happened to me in my twenty years in the Army."

She smiled in return, stepped toward him, reached around his neck and gave him a long, warm kiss.

"If you keep that up, we're never going to make it to Oakland in time to check into the hotel and make that movie," he said, grinning widely as he looked down into her soft, doe eyes. He pulled her to him and began to sing, "I want a girl, just like the girl that married dear old Dad. She was..." Running Water put her hand over his open mouth and pulled away from him.

"You win," she said.

He always did. Tools, his corps' bicycle mechanic, had once said to him "Lieutenant Jimmy, if we ever run up against hostile forces, the boys an' me want you to start singing The Star Spangled Banner before we start shooting. We figure then we might not have to even limber up our rifles cuz when the LORD gave you an extra helpin' of brains, he had to scrimp somewheres."

Aaron had once described his father's baritone as the closest thing to a dying bear as he ever wanted to hear.

"Let's get your bag in the Model T, get her cranked up and headed for the ferry across the Carquinez strait."

They could pick up their mail in Martinez and then follow the shoreline to San Pablo Bay. That trip would take them through Pinle, San Pablo and then Richmond. It was a beautiful day, the air was just beginning to warm as they turned onto the dirt road to the ferry.

"What was the name of that movie again?" James Bunting asked as they bumped along the narrow road that began dipping down to the water's edge.

"A Fool There Was, starring Theda Bara."

"The Vamp!", he replied in astonishment. "Why do you want to see her?"

Running Water leaned over, saying "Kiss me my fool," the famous Theda Bara line from the movie that she had read about in Vanity Fair. "I am almost forty, dear. I need all the hints I can get on how to keep my man interested in me."

"Darling, you've got no problem that way," he said, smiling.

"What a sweet thing to say."

They had reached the ramp just as the ferry was heading back from the south shore, the operator having seen the dust drifting behind. James

Bunting busied himself during the wait. He redid his earlier inventory of his Hammacher Schlemmer survival kit of emergency food supplies. Given the precarious road conditions and the propensity of automobiles of the day for mechanical failure, the wise motorist travelled fully prepared for anticipated disasters. The kit included two two-gallon canvas water bags, two tins of fruit, four half-pound cans of salmon and ham, and two pounds of sweet chocolate.

The ride across the ferry was uneventful. In contrast to their playful chatter on the ride to the ferry, the Buntings were quiet, each enjoying being out on the water. The California hills, golden in the midmorning sunlight, served as a perfect backdrop for the acacia trees that dotted the southern shore.

✠

James Bunting let the engine run when he went into the Post Office in Martinez. Built on the North side of the Plaza, the building offered shade to Running Water as she waited patiently for her husband to get the mail from their box. The Plaza was alive with the bustle of people doing their weekly shopping. Entire families came to town to socialize and do their dealing. It was a pleasant atmosphere which Running Water never tired of, an enjoyable place to visit. On the other hand, she wouldn't want to live here, preferring the solitude of a tiny village like Benecia.

James came out of the building reading an official looking document, the rest of the mail bundled under his left arm. He paused on the wooden porch, then smiled as he stepped down onto the brick paved street. As he walked toward her, the smile faded, replaced by a look of bewilderment. As he seated himself in the car, he took the bundle of mail from under his arm and placed it on the seat between them.

She touched his hand as it rested on the mail, softly saying, "James, what's wrong?"

In response, he handed her the document he had been reading.

115

Reading it, she too was now puzzled. Their son Aaron had been accepted at West Point. She would have thought her husband would be both thrilled and proud. It was what every military man wanted for his sons, it was what he had wanted for Garon. He had quietly expressed his dismay to her when Garon had turned his back on the opportunity to go chase that hussy.

"Honey, I just don't know any more. There's too many ways for a man to die in battle nowadays. It doesn't look like this war in Europe is ever going to end. I just know we're going to get drawn into it. I'm fearful for Aaron's future if he attends the Point," he said despondently.

"James, let's work through this before we get back home. It's what Aaron wants. Let's make sure we don't spoil it for him."

"You're right of course. Every young man thinks he's immortal. I've a furlough coming up. Perhaps we'll keep this from him. We'll go down to Frisco for a couple of weeks, take in the Panama- Pacific International Exposition. I'd like to hear that fellow Sousa's marching band. I hear he can make your heart stir with patriotic fever."

Thinking, *That's my old James*, she patted his hand and said, "We can break the news at the Tower of Jewels."

"Good thinking. I wonder if we have enough money set aside to take him back east through the Canal. I've read that is a sight to see."

And so they traveled down the road on the way to see Theda Bara, the Madonna of her generation.

CHAPTER 16   1996

HOW TO

DOVER, DELAWARE

Jeff Bross was delighted when I accepted and took the initiative in the case we had discussed over dinner the night before. I was intrigued by two things, the difficulty of the problem was the primary reason I took it on. That a 10 percent contingency was offered should we succeed was also a great incentive. I was hoping to take my wife and daughter away for the summer, for three to five months on a grand adventure, touring the world. Ten percent of several million dollars ought to allow us to do it in style.

The assignment was for a U.S. subsidiary of the British chemical conglomerate, GBCC-NA. The local plant was facing closure due to a permit driven $6,500,000 expenditure needed for the purchase and installation of additional wastewater treatment equipment. Product manufacturing was to be diverted overseas where this capital investment, and its attendant $800,000 annual operating cost, would not be required. My job was to figure out whether they had to construct and operate the equipment in order to stay in business.

This wasn't about worker productivity. Management had to consider all of the costs of production. Other consulting firms had suggested only costly equipment solutions to the problem. Apprehensive local management retained me to develop a more attractive alternative.

I was fairly confident about our chances for success. I have more than 25 years experience working for, or with, manufacturing companies with world wide operations. Thus, I have observed, first hand, the ever increasing international competition for manufacturing facilities, their associated jobs and other benefits that accrue to the country fortunate enough to woo them. The competition is not limited to external corporate rivals. Competition can be even fiercer within a company, pitting one plant against another.

This was clearly a Clean Water Act issue that fit within my experience. My background in that area would be a great asset to the problem solving team. I am a registered Professional Engineer with a master's degree in Environmental, nee Sanitary, Engineering. Prior to obtaining that degree, I worked at a major oil refinery on the west coast as a wastewater treatment manager. Then it was on to managing all water pollution control and water resource programs for an eastern state regulatory agency. I was fortunate enough to be working in that capacity when the Clean Water Act Amendments were passed by Congress in 1972. Thus I had the opportunity to set up the various programs and become intimately familiar with their requirements. This period of my career also gave me an inside view of the workings and mind set of an EPA regional office I dealt with and with EPA headquarters. Having worked as a consultant prior to the refinery experience and for twenty years since leaving the regulatory position, I have acquaintances and friendships that cross all the boundaries of the environmental world. I have served as a soul source consultant to EPA, am a Diplomate of the American Academy of Engineers and have published and presented many articles on environmental issues.

My method of preparation for an assignment of this type never varies. It evolves around the six **P**'s, **P**roblem identification, **P**reparation, strategic **P**lanning, **P**ursuit, and **P**ersistence to reach the ultimate **P**ayoff. The payoff in this case saved the client more than $8,000,000. Jeff and I pocketed $800,000, which we split right down the middle. That was the job that made my finances comfortable enough to now allow me to pick and choose my clients and projects from then on.

CHAPTER 17   1996

SWITCHAROO

WILMINGTON, DELAWARE

Wayne Anderson had done well, in Pester Size's opinion. Two candidates made the short list after her rigid winnowing process. The woman, a Ms. Tina Hazzard, had chosen a career over marriage and family. She was now a sour, old maid whose dreams were shattered when she had been passed over repeatedly for promotion to Assistant Curator. She clearly held a grudge against the company, and more specifically the presiding Curator, Winston D. Trader. Pester pondered whether the woman's bitterness was deep enough to want to embarrass the old boy.

That could run two ways, she thought. *Reason enough to do the deed. Also, reason enough to 'discover' the loss. Risky business, wouldn't do to have her go public with her find. Roxanne would definitely not like it.*

Pester placed Hazzard's picture back in the manila folder. "She is a handsome woman," remarked Pester to herself, then opened the folder again to check her age. "Hm, over 50 and looking just as good as Linda Evans."

Pester closed the Hazzard folder, retrieved the other candidate's jacket and opened it. Getting up, she stretched, then slipped into the little kitchenette, hidden from view by a tri-panel silk screen divider upon which was painted a copy of a Hudson Valley landscape. Deftly, she poured water into a small electric tea kettle, plugged it in and then walked back to her desk to resume her work. She then picked up the folder and took it to a mahogany lectern that she had found in an antique shop in New York. Standing to read from time to time broke up the tedium and usually refreshed her thinking. She placed her hands on the small of her back, arched into an inverted C, then raised her hands above her head, forming a Y, shook her fingers for a few seconds to let the tension drain, then lowered her arms and went back to the folder.

Lawrence G. Fowler held a doctorate in English literature and a master's degree in computer sciences. Born into a Walnut Creek, California family of moderate income, he headed east to seek fame and fortune immediately after passing his oral exam at Whittaker college, the college which hailed President Nixon as one of its famous, perhaps only famous, alumni. The doctorate was prestigious, the master's, from the University of Delaware night program, purely utilitarian. He didn't deign to have it printed on his business card. It struck him as demeaning

Fowler was the epitome of class, a bachelor by choice, and prissy to a fault. Washed his hands three times in the men's room. Cleaned the eating utensils with his napkin. In the Green Room at the Hotel DuPont, mind you, a four star restaurant famous the world over. All of this was in Anderson's report.

"I wonder if this guy is queer?" she mused, but there had been nothing in the report to show that he was so inclined. In fact, there had been nothing of passion in anything that Anderson had uncovered. In his mid-fifties, Fowler had apparently never been married, nor engaged for that matter. He was ruggedly handsome, with dark black hair, obsidian eyes and a trim, but well shaped figure. Inexplicably, he had boxed while in college. He stayed in shape by performing all the basic

121

exercises that were in your ordinary pug's routine. He dated sporadically, women of his age or slightly younger. Some were pretty, some just well groomed. While under the watchful eye of Anderson, the women seemed to occupy a niche required by Fowler's social fabric. When Johnny Mathis and Deniece Williams appeared at the Playhouse, someone named Linda Poore was available for a chat during the intermission. Same thing at half-time with Wendy Aycoth when the University of Delaware played Navy at Annapolis. Go you fighting Blue Hens! He appeared to be looking for companionship, not sex, although a few times, when under surveillance by Anderson, Lawrence Fowler had dallied long enough for a roll in the sack.

From what Anderson could determine, Fowler had no male friends socially. He rarely played golf, and gave up tennis and racquet ball years ago. He did nothing that would draw him into the social milieu.

There was a bit of mystery about the fellow, though. For the last ten years, his annual income had been in excess of $100,000. He drove a sporty little Conquest, nine years old but holding its age like Sophia Loren. He owned an elegant condominium in trendy Trolley Square. His dress always fit the occasion. A handsome man living a comfortable, boring life, passing on in years, looking forward to replacing Curator Trader upon his retirement and then retiring himself, in another ten years or so. His bank account, securities and other financial interests had been about what one would expect for a single person living the life that he led. That is, up until about a year ago, when a steady decline had begun. Like the drops from a melting icicle, fueled by the rays of the sun, first his checking account, then his savings account balances had rapidly disappeared. The size of the deposits to replenish his dwindling checking account led Anderson to believe that Fowler was selling off stocks and bonds to keep from going Chapter 11. Bankruptcy! Therein lay a scandal, a public revelation, that was the antithesis of what his present position, and that to which he aspired, required.

Pester had caught that at first reading. She had wondered what it could have meant. Drugs? Sex? Blackmail? She had hoped the latter, for it would be fairly easy to track down the blackmailer, purchase his merchandise and then turn it to a more profitable and satisfying use. To

Pester's disappointment, Doctor Fowler's financial distress was caused by the fourth horseman of man's misfortunes, gambling. Anderson was able to find a relationship between the opening of the slot machine casino at Delaware Park and the Doctor's dwindling resources. Hanging around the ten- dollar machine, Anderson had learned that Fowler had developed a 'can't lose' system on his PC and had been losing right along while applying it. Local players had seen him at the machine for Herculean thirty-six hour stints on weekends.

Pester Size closed the folder neatly, having memorized its contents, and placed it in a file drawer in her credenza. The whistling steam kettle brought her back to the real world. She took a bag of Earl Grey from the cabinet and placed it in a chipped mug that she had drunk Ovaltine from in her childhood. While it steeped, she began her plan of assault on an unsuspecting Lawrence G. Fowler, Ph. D.

The flight into Philadelphia had been uneventful. Pester Size was now back at the bed and board, so pretentious that it had no name, just a brass sign, 'BED & BOARD,' on one of the brick columns that guarded the entrance way. She had unpacked, then began numbering each outfit and the accessories that went with it. Pester had planned her campaign as carefully as Genghis Kahn had planned the siege of Zhongdu. Just as Genghis Kahn had marshaled his Chinese bombardiers and catapults capable of hurling hundred-pound stones at gates and walls, so Pester planned to deploy all of her skills, feminine and otherwise. The Kahn had accepted treasure and a Jin princess in return for lifting the siege. He came back later, after an affront by Jin Emperor Xuanzong, raised the city and massacred its citizens. Pester Size hoped to gain her prize by siege and leave with no one the wiser. The continuing threat of exposure of Lawrence's complicity in her plot should be enough to maintain his silence.

To prepare herself for the campaign ahead she had her hair dyed black, with some grey highlights to make her appear more the age of the women with whom Fowler sought companionship. She had lifted weights and worked on the speed bag in addition to her normal workouts, to become more physical in appearance. She put on an extra, hard body, fifteen pounds. Out of necessity, she required, and acquired, an entirely new wardrobe. While in California, she had written a book and personality profile for her new persona, Melanie Buckley. Melanie was a woman of Oriental and English stock, married to a prig of an American who had threatened her with divorce if she did not bear him a son, and heir, to the family fortune.

Day 1

She launched her attack at the gym where Fowler worked out. Jake's Gym was on the lower east side of the city, scary at best in the daytime, ruled by the jungle at night. Fowler exercised on Monday, Thursday and Saturday. During the week, he went immediately after work, before supper. On Saturday, he was there in the morning. That was when he did his most rigorous bit of training, about two hours. Afterwards, he drove directly home to clean up, carefully placing a plaid blanket over the leather seats of the Conquest to absorb the sweat from his invigorated body. Anderson said he apparently went to extremes not to be naked around other men. Hopefully, from all indications, he had no such aversion with women. The game plan called for this gym to be the place of first approach.

Jake Parkowski, the gym's namesake, sat on a stool behind a plywood counter, once stained brown, now with portions of the exterior skin peeling upward, giving it a brown and blond streaked women's hairdo look. He had half an unlit cigar in the corner of the left side of his mouth, the left eye closed out of habit to protect it from the curling smoke that was now nonexistent. He had a blade-like nose on a sharp featured face, slightly gone to seed with age. There was no missing the fact that the vestiges of a powerful physique remained in his body.

This guy was one tough monkey in his day, Pester Size thought.

"Whatcha doing here, miss? This ain't exactly Gold's Gym," he spit out, obviously surprised at the appearance of a luscious babe amongst his lascivious clients, covering his embarrassment with a display of gruffness.

"I'm just looking for a no frills place to work out. I'm not into looking for Mr. Right, I just need a place with a speed bag and free weights," she retorted, rather coldly.

Surprised by the huskiness of her voice, Parkowski cocked his head to the side to hear her better, revealing a cauliflower ear that looked like it had been bitten off and reattached. At first it did not appear that he had understood what she had said. A full minute passed before he responded.

"Look, lady, I don't need your money or the trouble you'll bring. Body like yours, every man in here will be trying to put the make on you."

"Let's settle it right up front Jake. Tell them that I'm your granddaughter and that you'll beat the shit out of anyone who lays a hand on me. What do you say?"

Parkowski, who turned his head back to face her directly, was grinning from ear to stogie. "That'll be seventy-five bucks a week, payable in advance, grandchild of mine. By the way, what's your name? I'll need to take you around to introduce you."

She handed him three twenties, a ten and a five as she responded in her gruff voice, "Melanie Buckley."

Day 2
She had hit pay dirt that first day at the gym, for she had been introduced to Mr. Fowler, himself. Jake had preceded the introduction by saying that Fowler wouldn't give her no trouble cause he was the only gent in the gym, other than himself. Everyone gave Jake a little bit of razzing for never telling anyone he had such a good-looking grandkid. Jake took it in stride, but let every sweaty soul know full well what would happen to them if they so much as used foul language in her presence.

Perhaps it had not even been necessary. When she had gone to work on the speed bag, the whole gym went silent, as everyone turned to watch. She made her bones that very instant. Everyone went back to work knowing that she wasn't in there just to wiggle her splendidly proportioned buttocks in their faces. She clearly knew her way around. She also knew that she had piqued the curiosity of one Lawrence G. Fowler, for he was one of the men who had paused in his exercise regimen, to watch her speed and agility.

This day, Sunday, was to be devoted to rest and relaxation. Having made contact on the first try, she intended not to rush the process. Pester Size slept in, showering and slipping into a pair of jeans and a Penn State sweat shirt just in time to meet the last call for breakfast. She intended to spend the entire afternoon at Longwood Gardens, the lovely old DuPont Estate. A dinner at the Dilworthtown Inn would be followed by a leisurely drive back to her lodgings. Then it would be pajama time, with a good book. *The Quest for Love, Sensual Poetry by Patricia* sat on her night stand, awaiting her attention.

Day 30

Progress toward her goal had been steady, with no real surprises along the way. Within a week, Fowler had asked her out for a drink, outside the gym, of course, not wanting to risk Jake's wrath. She had demurred.

His next move came about a week later, on a Saturday morning. This time she accepted his offer of a Sunday afternoon visit to the Hagley Museum and an early dinner. She had moved into the Hotel Dupont for this phase of the operation, not wanting to lose her safe haven back in the rolling hills of Pennsylvania. He arrived in his red Conquest at precisely 1:30, dressed in a white and pale blue striped shirt, a white mock turtle neck sweater, cotton worn inside the shirt, beltless chino trousers and L.L. Bean leather dock shoes. She, in anticipation, wore a plaid skirt, wool pullover, panty hose the color of merlot wine and ox blood penny loafers. Quite the trendy pair.

The museum tour with Fowler was just as she expected. He was quiet, introspective and reserved. Although these were all qualities she respected, it made for a dull afternoon and the prospect of a tedious dining experience. She assumed the Green Room at the Hotel DuPont. Au contraire! What she got was the Queen Bean Café in Claymont, a gritty, blue collar town on the Philadelphia Pike. The ambience was a step down from a truck stop, with tables, chairs and flatware equally mismatched. She couldn't remember ever seeing a conical, plastic white lamp shade on top of a pink plastic lamp. Did anyone really like seasoning their food with ceramic salt and pepper shakers shaped and painted to resemble Poland China pigs, black with a white band around the middle? The menu was equally eclectic. One quick scan precipitated a giggle, then a laugh, and, finally a guffaw.

"Excuse me," Pester mumbled, her mouth covered as she attempted to stifle her uncontrollable laughter.

He bent forward, puzzled, offering assistance by placing his hand on her shoulder. She leapt like a young colt at the unexpected hand of an equally young owner and dashed in the direction of what she hoped would be the lady's room.

After fifteen minutes of regular breathing, murmured chanting and removal of one layer of makeup and replacement with another, she returned to the table as serene as she had been at the museum.

"I'm sorry, have I done something to offend you?" Fowler asked as he rose from his chair at her approach.

"No," she murmured demurely as she accepted his gentlemanly act of placing the chair under her as she moved forward in her seated position. *Perfect*, she thought. *He's mistaken my amusement with the menu as a tearful breakdown. Now I've got him.*

The incongruity of pierogies sharing menu space with sesame-crusted pan-seared tuna with a side dish of wasabi horseradish obviously did not appear abnormal to the average diner at the Queen Bean. Coupled with the funky Formica atmosphere, she had thought it hilarious. Certainly, it was unlike anything she had seen on the west coast. But she puzzled over his concern that he had in some way hurt her. What it could be was beyond her understanding. Therefore, she went on the offensive and tried to draw it out of him.

Placing her hand over his, she said, "Please, Larry, don't allow my little outburst to take away from an otherwise pleasurable day."

He brightened, "I am certainly pleased to hear that. I thought you were upset by the contrast between the visual richness of the treasures at the Hagley Museum and the apparent seediness of the Bean."

Sensitive guy, she thought. *Must have lost the charms of some lady friends in the past who he found were only out for his money.*

She said, "Things like that don't bother me. That's not what life's all about. Besides, it's the menu that excites me."

Playing the part, she continued huskily, "I've been under a great deal of stress lately." Then, touching his hand, "But don't let that intrude on our evening." Not wanting to dare the risk of another outburst, she said, "Please, order for me. You obviously have dined here before and are familiar with the items they offer."

Lawrence G. Fowler was in his venue, he positively beamed. Speaking in conspiratorial tones, like a CIA agent selling his country's secrets to the KGB, Fowler whispered, "Melanie, prepare your palate, for you are in for the surprise of your life."

And she was.

For an appetizer, they shared a balsamic shrimp and mozzarella martini. The shrimp was sauted and served with scallions and tomatoes. Marsala wine and balsamic vinegar both deglazed and added a sweet and sour flavor to the mixture. In the appetizer cocktail, cherry tomatoes and small balls of mozzarella shared space with fresh herbs in a martini glass. They munched slowly, washing down the flavors with Perrier.

To save room for dessert, they also elected to apportion a vegetable napoleon between them. The delicious smell wafting from the roasted zucchini, eggplant, porto bella mushrooms and tomatoes made them salivate. Layered with melted mozzarella cheese, the napoleon resembled lasagna.

She opted for the brownie layered with chocolate fudge for dessert, he for the bread pudding made from fruit-studded pumpkin bread. Hot, steaming Kanan Devan tea capped the splendid evening's fare.

Then it was back to her hotel. She leaned over and kissed him on the cheek, whispered her thanks for a lovely evening and dashed from her car to the waiting doorman, turned to waive good bye and then walked through the proffered door opening.

Smiling to herself as she waited for the elevator door to open, she thought, *I've got the poor chump now.*

And she did.

CHAPTER 18   NOVEMBER 28, 1996

SHE DO

A FARM IN RURAL IOWA

Fields surrounding the white clapboard farmhouse were blanketed with snow that continued to fall in ever increasing amounts. A fire, started early that Thanksgiving day morning, burned hot and smokeless, puffing a telltale grey from the brick chimney only when Roxanne added more wood to the cast iron insert. The Alberta clipper that had swooped down from Canada the previous evening brought with it a driving wind that howled as it impaled itself upon the dormers, overhangs and gingerbread of the late nineteenth century Victorian house. The exterior of Roxanne' home, painted ivory white with emerald green trim, normally stood in stark bas-relief to the brilliant-blue Midwestern sky. Today, it virtually disappeared under the recurring white-out conditions.

The farm was northeast of Boone, a small community of 5,000 souls, nestled on the east bank of the Des Moines River. Most people thought Roxanne to be not only rude and crude, but stupid as well. This farm spoke well against the latter for it was located in the Des Moines Lobe, a flat area in central Iowa with dark, deep, prairie soils, rich in organic content. Her purchase had not merely been a hideaway for her and her former husband, but it was actually a wise investment. Paid for in full, it gave her the secure feeling that she would always have a home and a steady income, regardless of how low her fortunes might sink in show business. Her prenuptial agreement with her current husband, Ken, specifically identified the farm as her property, inaccessible to him in the event things didn't work out.

What a holiday for Roxanne. The house was a warm shelter against the storm. The stove would keep them cozy even if the power went off and the generator ran out of fuel. The fragrant aroma of stuffing and turkey in the oven permeated the entire first floor. She and her husband were laying back on the leather couch in the living room, watching the Detroit Lions and Forty Niners. A smile lifted the corner of her mouth as she thought, *Little does he know, nor will he ever unless he ticks me off, what other use the turkey baster had been put to that very day.*

Her package had arrived by Federal Express, late in the afternoon the previous day, just as it began to get dark. She had secreted it into the kitchen, removed its frozen contents from the freezer bag, and cut the whitish grey wad in half. One piece went in a plastic bag, which she labeled Urine Sample - DO NOT USE and placed carefully in the freezer. The other half she put in an empty, sterilized jar, which she put in the refrigerator. She was up before sunrise this Thanksgiving Day, gently warming half her stash in a teacup to 98.6 degrees Fahrenheit. One big squirt was all it took after she got herself lubricated. She didn't look forward to carrying the baby through the summer and had given a surrogate mother some really intense thought. She finally decided that going through the entire maternity thing was the only way her public would believe that she was the mother of Liza's half-brother.

CHAPTER 19   1919

I DO

BENICIA, CALIFORNIA

Captain Bunting was relaxing on the shady front porch of their small bungalow. The day was northern California bright. Running Water was in the tiny house, performing the spring cleaning ritual. All of the windows were open. Smoke from the burning aromatic wild grasses and herbs that she gathered, and dried each fall, wafted from the down wind side of the house. He likened it to a spring tonic, purging all the musty smells from a house sealed up against the winter's chill and rain. She was humming Irving Berlin's *A Pretty Girl is Like a Melody* as she brought a throw rug out to hang in the little tree in the yard. The little willow served as an extra pair of hands when she wanted to attack the rug with her compact wire dust buster. He thought it ironic that just over 20 years ago he had met her on the reservation, and here she was a thousand miles away from her home, singing a showstopper from the Ziegfield Follies of 1919. He smiled at the thought.

The novel he was reading lay pages down in his lap. He had paid $1.90 for *The Four Horsemen of the Apacolypse*, the year's apparent runaway best seller, and was determined to read it, if only to satisfy his conscience that he hadn't wasted his money. But he found it terminally boring. At this stage in life, he couldn't get himself worked up about wealthy Argentine ranch owners traveling through the art studios of Paris. Not much excitement there compared to the backdrop of what had been happening in Europe. The old oak rocker squeaked as he rocked back and forth, remembering how pleased he was that his son had made it safely through the winding down of World War I.

Second Lieutenant Miles A. Bunting had graduated with his class just in time to ship over. He was with Pershing in the closing days as the Americans swept through Vauquois and Montfaucon on September 26 and 27. After that, things slowed drastically, the American offensive serving as a magnet for every German reserve unit on the western front. The Germans were forced to retreat all along the line as the American army pressed on in the Meuse-Argonne. Then the British cracked through the German defense on the Selle River. On the same day, October 17, King Albert of Belgium got the combined Belgian and British army moving in Flanders. Within a month, it was over. A German delegation, led by civilian Matthias Erzberger, reached an armistice agreement with Marshall Ferdinand Foch at 5:00 a.m. on November 11, 1918 in Foch's railway-coach headquarters on a siding at Compiegne. The scene was to be reenacted on June 22, 1940. This time, however, the fortunes were reversed.

Bunting's revery was broken by the appearance of a uniformed cyclist, sternly pumping to navigate the little hill up to the cottage to avoid the juvenile embarrassment of having to step off the bike and walk. The appearance of the Western Union delivery boy brought a chill to Bunting's heart. In his trade, they were invariably the bearers of bad news. He had only the short letter from Aaron just after the Armistice. Nothing since then. He didn't know if he was still over there, or state side. Hadn't heard from Garon in more than two years, either.

Then he noticed the U.S. postal delivery man, Rich Gallo, astride a sturdy mule named Sara, slightly behind the messenger, and gaining. Sara strode up this hill every day at the same pace. She seemed to give a side wise snicker as she passed the boy, who now was shamefacedly walking his bicycle the remaining 20 yards to the house.

"Morning, Capitan," the mail man said as he jumped from the mule's back. "I think you have news from MG. Been a long time," he smiled as he handed the single letter over. "More than two years, I betcha."

Bunting smiled as he leaned on the railing, "Don't take any foolish bets, Rich."

Rich Gallo smiled broadly, turned to return to Sara, then shouted as he mounted, "I hope it's good news, Capitan." He urged the mule on with his heels. She stepped out, without a bridle, but knowing the way to the next stop as well as her master.

"Care for a drink of water? You look right peaked, son," Captain Bunting said, addressing the young man with the sweat stained uniform, who was just now leaning his bike against the little tree.

"That would be awfully nice. Could I sit a spell in the shade while I drink it?"

"Sure," Bunting responded cheerfully, "Join me on the porch. You're coming up here with that telegram anyway, aren't you."

The boy took his cap off, wiped his brow with his uniform sleeve, and smiled as he gestured with the envelope in his left hand, "Yes, sir, I sure am. Plumb near forgot about it." Then he loped up the stairs and placed it in the chair. Bunting had disappeared into the house to get a cup of cool well water from the hand pump by the sink.

✠

The Western Union boy had disappeared down the hill by the time Running Water had come out on the porch. She sat in the rocker while her husband fussed with the letter from Garon and the telegram from Aaron.

134

"Which one first, Mother, your choice," James Bunting asked his wife, knowing it would be the letter. She feared, just like him, that the telegraph brought bad news. She nodded.

He pulled out his pocket knife, carefully slit the top of the envelope, and removed the letter. He read as follows:

March 15, 1919

Dear Mom and Dad,

I've been meaning to write but I just haven't seemed to find the time for it. Am working hard at two jobs, and am making ends meet. I married Gladys Miller in 1915, shortly after I left home. Know that makes things awkward between us, but I love her, she loves me, so we think that's what counts. Have two little girls, one almost four and the other just a year old. Rose and Clara. I will try to write more often. Hope this finds you well.

Your loving son,

Garon

Running Water spoke first, "That will be tough for them, won't it?"

"Yes, my dear. Probably ten times worse than it has been for us. At least out of respect for my position in the Army, most people have kept their opinions to themselves."

She sighed in response, and with head lowered, murmured, "And for that I am grateful."

"Nonsense, sweetheart. This entire race thing is born out of ignorance and stupidity. I'd not willingly abide their opinions to begin with." He moved toward her, lifted her gently by the chin to stare in his loving eyes. "We have had the best of times."

She smiled as her sadness lifted, "Would that Garon and Gladys can say the same thing at our age."

"Come," she pointed, "Now open the telegram and let's get it over with."

He repeated the process he had done with the letter, but unfolded the telegram with a slight hesitation. He read,

MARCH 25, 1919

ARRIVED IN NYC 3/20. POPPED ? TRUDY JOHNSON, GEN B.'S ELDEST. OK. WEDDING @ NANTUCKET 5/25/19. PLS COME. WILL WRITE. LOVE AARON. AM OK 2.

Bunting folded the telegram, placed it in his trouser pocket, removed his glasses, being careful to hang them on the railing just so. He walked over to his seated wife, grasped her hands and gently pulled her to him. As she rose, he drew her to his bosom, and encircled her waist with his arms.

"Ah, my dearest. We are growing old," he said softly, his face nestled in her still black, bountiful hair.

"That we are," she responded. "Shall we go?"

"That we shall. I've never been to Nantucket. Never been to my son's wedding. And I never want to miss a chance to show off my beautiful bride."

CHAPTER 20   JANUARY 13, 1997

BOOHOO

WILMINGTON, DELAWARE

The elderly, white haired man sat in the soft cone of light that shone from the single bulb in the old-fashioned banker's lamp. The emerald green glass of the lamp cast a ghoulish light upon his already pallid skin. His right hand, peppered with liver spots, trembled as it held a single page of the leather bound book closer to his gold rimmed spectacles.

"My God," he muttered to himself, "How could this have happened?"

Dr. Winston D. Trader, curator of Brandywine Valley Frozen Assets Trust, already beside himself with grief, was fighting off a rising anger as he reviewed the results of the annual inventory. Deposits on hand, withdrawals and specimens unaccounted for were set forth clearly on the page. During his tenure of thirty years as curator, there had never been a last column entry.

137

Trader was once again reviewing the findings of the Packer, Picker and Pucker audit. He thought, *If word got out, this could be the end of his clients' trust in the Trust. This could mean his job.*

✠

By examining the leather bound audit report, he had confirmed with his own eyes the statements made in a personal call from Mr. Borden at Packer, Picker and Pucker's. Trader then went to the depository to examine the supposedly purloined specimen himself, by himself. He had carefully withdrawn a stainless steel vial, encrypted with # BVFAT/32@MGB, placed it in a Thinsulate carrier and gone to his personal room within the freezer vault. This was the room that held the secrets by which he guaranteed the trustees that any pilferage or substitution would not go undetected. This was decades before the advent of DNA testing. He had been in the forefront of the frozen sperm field at the time. That was why he had been retained as curator. His system still worked. Only he and William Bailey Borden from Packer, Picker and Pucker knew how it worked. Bill Bailey Borden had done every audit personally since 1970. Bill Bailey Borden had instantly seen that a substitution had occurred, just as Trader had when doing his own comparative analysis. He had then returned the vial to its current slot in the storage cell.

Borden had recommended that the vial's resident sperm be DNA tested immediately and compared with that of existing male employees, of which there were five, including Trader. Trader ignored the recommendation, quickly reasoning that secrecy, not an opportunity for a leak, was warranted here. He didn't want to be disgraced at the twilight of his career. Further, he knew his employees to be pretty quick witted. Whoever did this knew all about DNA testing. They would never switch their own sperm for the original donor's on the extremely remote chance that the substitution was detected. Finally, he had checked the user's and inquiry log. There had been no entries, despite the age of the specimen. He had decided to take the risk of keeping a lid on the episode, wisely seeing that the odds were in his favor. The Board had suspiciously asked to see the annual audit report in the early years. For the last decade, they ignored the technical inventory, concentrating, to

138

the extent that they did, on the financial aspects alone.

Satisfied that he had made the right decision, Trader had acted upon it immediately. He called his friend, and business acquaintance, Steve Herman at Barros, Truitt and Herman. Trader had said that he needed someone to investigate a problem that had occurred at his place of employment. Not wanting to disclose the nature of the problem, Trader said that he needed someone with forensic skills, a cut above what he believed to be your average private investigator. A great deal of discretion would be required. Steve had allowed that he had a good man, Jeff Bross, in their Dover branch whom they relied upon to maintain close ties with a retinue of private investigators, physicians, scientists, an altogether pot pourri of experts in the many fields that their law practice required. Mr. Bross's people were retained on the basis of their ability to keep their cases confidential. Steve had promised to ask for a minimum of three candidates and to screen the experts himself so as not to let Jeff Bross know who had been selected.

That had been last Friday morning, January 10. Steve Herman had come through. The octogenarian sat at his burnished, cherry desk, nervously awaiting the candidate, a Mr. John Bunting whose credentials had been e-mailed to him an hour before.

✠

Doctor Trader sat sipping a glass of 1993 vintage Pepperwood Grove Pinot Noir, a rather pedestrian wine, but one that pleased his palate. After all it was his club, was it not, and he could stock the type of wines and spirits that pleased him. For instance, although he rarely drank beer, he nonetheless had a case of Killian's Red iced down and ready for delicious consumption on a hot summer's day. Never more than one at a sitting, but greatly preferred over any of the imported stuff offered by his club, the Rodney.

He reflected that he was glad to have been born in a generation where a men's club was something to aspire to. Nowadays, a member under forty was a rarity, and was typically a rich snot who had never worked a day in his life. No stalwart leadership there. The club would be on the wain in the not too distant future. But his future would be over long before that ever happened.

Trader sipped his wine, then took a slice of Edam cheese proffered by a waiter who circulated in the non-smoking members lounge. He realized how fortunate he was that he still had the majority of his teeth, thanks to a dedicated dental technician who, when Trader was in his early fifties, revealed to him the wonders of flosssing. No more bad breath, no gingivitis to cause his otherwise pearly white teeth to fall out.

Trader was finally relaxed after a four-day ordeal that had caused him more anxiety than he ever had in his entire adult life. He liked this John Bunting immediately. After two hours of discussion, and disclosure, for he thought the man trustworthy from the outset, Trader had offered the assignment, and was greatly relieved at Bunting's acceptance. Now there were four who new the secret, including the switcharoo.

CHAPTER 21   1996

UNDO

WALNUT CREEK, CALIFORNIA

The air inside the Wells Fargo bank immediately had a cooling effect on Pester Size's sweaty neck. Her disguise as the victim of an automobile accident consisted of a black, shoulder length wig, accompanied by a neck brace, carefully applied makeup on the right cheekbone to simulate a bruise, and a bandage wrapped over her left ear and around part of her face. When on surveillance assignments, Pester chose to conceal herself by blending into the background. When she had to be seen to accomplish her goal, she faced the choice of dressing for anonymity, hoping to be faceless enough not to be remembered, or dressing in outrageous costume, to achieve the opposite effect. Remembered, but not as herself. She normally opted for the former, even though her lush, brown oriental eyes made it difficult to pass herself off as anything but unless she wore sunglasses. Sunglasses inside a bank would be too much of a giveaway that she was trying to hide her identity. That would make the teller remember her every feature.

The auto accident victim was one she had used successfully in the past. Mentally, she went through her checklist while standing in line. She had paid out almost $70,000.00 to five credit card companies over the last six months for charges she had made. Then she had canceled her orders, or returned her purchases. The net result was she now had $70,000 worth of credit against which she could draw, with no tax obligation. Further, she had drawn down her checking account balance to a low enough amount that closing the account with a cashier's check would not draw undo attention. Her cover story was just icing on the cake.

She was confident as she stood in the roped off line, waiting for the next available teller.

I hope I get the mousy little woman with the half pound of mousse in her hair, Pester mused. *Looks so distracted she probably will miss her money count for at least an hour at the end of the day. She looks like a migraine sandwiched between a fight with her meaningful mortal and the onslaught of her period, or ditto except she missed her period.*

Luck of the draw, the moussed mouse motioned for the next customer, even as Pester gazed at her. She limped slightly as she approached the teller's work station.

"My name is Wilma Miller," she said in her normal hoarse voice, while handing the teller a slip of paper. "That's my checking account number. I'd like to close the account. I'd prefer a cashier's check. I can't wait to get the hell out of this town. Crummy drivers. The freeway is like a demolition derby"

Pester needn't have launched into her well-rehearsed act. The teller dully surveyed the account on her monitor, squinting her eyes to gauge the rate of recent activity.

Lost her contacts on top of whatever else is depressing her, thought Pester. *She'll pop enough Valium when she gets home that she'll be lucky to remember what day it is tomorrow, let alone who she serviced today.*

"For that amount of withdrawal, you'll have to see a customer service representative and get an authorization and check from them," murmured the moussed mouse, obviously already self sedated down to a thinking level one step up from a rock.

Motioning for her slip, and receiving it after a long, befuddled pause on the part of the teller, Pester limped slowly toward the powder blue, leather covered, Queen Anne style chairs. There she sat, a new member of the customer service representatives' clientele. No matter the bank, these reps always appeared to have a full dance card.

She attempted to read the Wall Street Journal with her single exposed eye, but gave up, overwhelmed by the dullness of the articles on the front page. She really didn't care to know the intimate details regarding the sale of some of Coca-Cola's non-performing, non-carbonated beverage plants. Sounded vaguely sexual, but a little too complex to grasp while performing her act.

It took another half-hour, but she got her check, got out of the Wells Fargo Bank, got out of her disguise, and got the hell out of town. There would be no eulogy for the recently departed Wilma Miller.

CHAPTER 22   **JANUARY 6, 1997**

REDO

BEVERLY HILLS, CALIFORNIA

Just after New Year's, Roxanne had come to the realization that she was definitely not pregnant. Desperate, knowing she had only one more shot, as it were, at rekindling her faltering career, she had made an appointment with a fertility doctor. She had asked him about all the procedures, including the one with frozen sperm, and had been surprised and shocked to learn that you were supposed to allow the frozen sperm to melt right there in the vagina. So here she was on this bright winter day in early February, locked in the master bathroom of her Beverly Hills home, with a cube full of ice trays, practicing her technique. She was trying to develop the correct muscle control to make sure she could hold that precious wad long enough for it to melt.

On March 17, 1997, the rabbit died. Roxanne swore off alcohol and over the counter drugs. This kid was going to be perfect.

CHAPTER 23   **SEPTEMBER 9, 1956**

DEBUT

MELFA, VIRGINIA

The woman standing in the yard with her back to the highway was a blur to the driver of the light blue and white Crown Victoria who was racing the departure of the Cape Charles Ferry. If he was late, it was a two-hour wait. The road was sparsely traveled. He had never seen a highway patrolman, so he blasted down the road at 90 miles per hour. He had to slow down for each one of the little towns, strung out like knots in a piece of twine, placed there to measure the distance from the Maryland state line, about five miles between them. A traveling salesman, he didn't want to be trapped on the Eastern Shore in one of those pitiful hovels that passed for motels in this part of the country. He wanted to get over to Virginia Beach, to an air-conditioned room in a big hotel with a friendly bar and room service. To his mind, the eastern shore of Virginia was a desolate place, populated by a few well-to-do farmers, all of them white, a bleak middle class of shop keepers, all of them white, and a poor, landless underclass who worked the land in the summer, most of them black, or the water in all seasons, most of them white. It was a flat, sparsely populated, peninsula that split the Delaware and Chesapeake Bays before spanning out to the Atlantic Ocean. He firmly believed that only fools, and those too poor to leave, lived there. If in the summer it was hot, humid and with mosquitoes in unbearable numbers after nightfall, in the winter it was a featureless landscape whose inhabitants appeared to be in hibernation. One year, as Christmas approached, he had driven the entire distance from the Maryland line to Cape Charles, about 60 miles, without seeing another car.

The tall, slender Negress was surrounded by children, five boys and one girl, rising like steps, starting with one little fellow about three years old in a physical display of the annual celebration that preceded effective application of birth control practices. One step was missing.

"Clearance, y'all get out here now. Leastwise, we gonna miss the show at your grandaddy's. C'mon now, the mosquitoes is startin to swarm," the woman called in a sweet, but insistent voice. "Your brothers and sister did'n do nut'n they deserve to miss that show."

"Mama, I don't want to go. I'se tired from workn' in the field yesterday. I'se gotta work for Mister Walsh again at sunup. I needs to be home here resting," a whining voice responded, sing song fashion.

A little firmer now, "Clearance, I ain't let'n no chile of mine stay home alone at night. Now get yourself out here, fore I got to come in dere and whup your skinny behind."

"Yes, Mama, I'm coming, but I sure don't relish the walk to get there," the skinny, little boy answered as he flung the screen door open and stepped slowly down the single step onto the bare dirt of the yard. He filled in the gap in the stair steps of his siblings, proving to the casual observer that this was a healthy family with no stillborn children and no losses during their infancy. They were all barefooted, as was their mother.

The mother's physical appearance was stunning, worthy of a super model. Tall, with a slender figure, with prominent breasts, somewhat enlarged by childbearing and nursing, she caused men of all ages and races, to give a second look as she walked past them, with hips gently swaying. Her aquiline nose, with high cheekbones, thin lips and wide smile were exceptionally alluring. All of her children seemed to be miraculously cloned from her body. More than her obvious good looks, Clearance's mother treasured her long black tresses, which tonight she had swept up in a bun, held in place by a snood, to keep her lustrous hair from becoming damp when the sweat rolled down her neck, her spine and into the small of her back. For it was unbearably hot, on this September evening, the sun just beginning its slow descent into the Loblolly pine forest that paralleled the road for miles.

"All right, you young'ns, we're gonna walk down a side of the railroad tracks. Train's already been through. Less dangerous than walking 'longside the highway. Come along now, we still got time to get there."

The three-year old walked about 100 yards before declaring that he could walk no further. The oldest boy picked him up without instruction from his mother, but not without a chiding comment, leavened with a smile, which seemed to be a permanent feature, stamped at birth, on all the clan.

"Robert, I ain't always gonna be able to carry you. Tha's why the Lord gave you them feet. They's not just for tickling you know," said the oldest boy, Charles, to his brother.

The brother responded softly, shyly burying his head into Charles' shoulder, "Tha's why the Lord made older brothers, for to carry the little ones when they gets tired, don't you think, big brother?"

"Is Daddy going to be at Grandpa's when we get there?" Charles asked his mother.

"No, he's likely at the packin house by now. Working a double shift today, in the field at sunup, in the packin house 'til long about midnight," she answered.

"On Sunday, Mama? That's the Lord's Day. He shouldn't be work' on the Sabbath."

She softly rubbed little Robert's hair while speaking in response to his question, "You're right little man. I don't like it but I got to 'bide by your Daddy's think'n. Roun' here, you got to take your work when it's to hand. Otherwise, we be starv'n in the winter, with no cash and no possibles."

Clearance tugged at his mother's worn cotton dress, "Mama, Grandpa had work year round before he retired. He never worked a Sunday, as I remember."

"You're right. Think on it, and I believe you'll come to reason out just why that is," His mother responded as she popped him playfully with a knuckle on his forehead.

The little family shuffled slowly beside the railroad, now more than halfway toward their destination, Grandma and Grandpa's three bedroom shotgun cabin, with its silver grey, unpainted clapboard siding.

"Mama, think we ever gonna have a television, like Grandpa?" came a query from the pack of children that encircled their mother like a litter of puppies.

"Lord, chile, there's a mess of things standing in line before a TV. You all need shoes, clothes and coats afore winter sets in. We got taters, flour, beans and other necessaries to stock up on before the work runs out. No, honey, don't see no TV in my future. Jes' be happy someone in the family has one."

"But we only get to see it once a month. And it's such a long walk."

"That's why we only get to see it once a month, babies," declared the mother.

"Leastwise we got the radio, and our imaginations," piped up Charles.

"Thank the Lord for that kindness," his mother said, putting her typically optimistic spin on what was an otherwise hard life.

♀

"Come along now, you hea'h, time for the little ones to be in bed," the woman said to the little brood, the youngest two of which were already asleep. Little Robert cuddled safely in a sling made from an old cotton feed sack, which freed his mother's hands to carry the kerosene lantern which dimly lit their way back home.

Charles, and his brother Edward, took turns carrying little Doris, their four-year old sister.

Clearance had been chattering, excitedly all during the trek back home. "Mama, did you ever see such a thing in your life?" continuing without giving pause for an answer. "That white boy sure had some moves. It sure was a really, great 'shuu', just like Mr. Sullivan said it was gonna be."

"Well, I am sure I didn't much care for them moves, as you call them. They were vulgar to me, offensive to anyone with a Christian upbringing," his mother replied.

Clearance switched directions, "But Mama, didn't you like his voice?" he asked shrilly.

She had never seen this normally shy, retiring boy, so wound up. "Well, yes, I do believe we could find a spot for him right next to you in the Holy Trinity Baptist Church choir."

Clearance grinned even wider at the thought.

"But, I think he's sold out to the Devil already. Wouldn't be fitten to have him in the choir at no respectable church," the mother commented further.

"How's that, Mama?" the boy shot back, a puzzled look on his face.

"Why he's sing'n that rock n' roll music. That truly be the work of the Devil."

149

"Oh, Mama, you don't believe that. You've always said that music helped purify the soul," he reasoned.

"Not that kind of music. Take care now, I won't have it on the radio in my house."

♀

The heat that had soaked into the spine of the Delmarva peninsula began to give way as the leaves changed into their autumn dress. The prevailing wind shifted from the southwest to the northwest, bringing cool Canadian air with it. Hog killing time wouldn't be far off. School had started for colored and white children alike. Clearance and Charles checked their trap lines immediately after school so their mother could begin to plan what to have for supper. Rabbit was a welcome alternative to fat back and beans. Then there was wood to be chopped and brought in for the cook stove. The tin stove in the parlor had not yet been started, so there was still a little daylight after chores were done to satisfy the boys' wishes. Then it would be dark, homework, supper, a little bit of whatever comedy was on the radio, and then off to the bed that they shared with younger brother Edward.

Clearance spent that free time fashioning himself a guitar from the slats of an old peach basket, some fishing line and a scrap of two-by-four that had blown from the bed of a passing pickup truck. Clearance believed that the Lord, hearing his nightly prayers and seeing his need, had simply taken that piece of wood from the truck, and laid it on the road for him to find. He was sitting now, on a piece of unsplit oak, whittling the neck from that divinely provided board as his mother watched. He knew as well as she that it wouldn't make a musical sound from its peach basket sound box. But it would allow him to more closely resemble his new found idol, the one who, in his mind, had replaced Muddy Waters, the legendary blues guitarist and composer.

His mother assumed he had learned the words and melody to Heartbreak Hotel, Don't Be Cruel and those other tunes by listening to the family radio when she wasn't around. There seemed to be no controlling it. All the kids in Virginia seemed to like this new music.

Although it had the scent of sacrilege, she wondered if rock and roll was not the Lord's response to her prayers to find something to pull her son out of the shroud of overwhelming shyness that had surrounded him. She smiled at the thinking of such a wicked thought.

CHAPTER 24   **JANUARY 14, 1997**

CLUE

DOVER, DELAWARE

I don't have what one would call a bona fide study, more like a spot in the southwest corner of the living room of our home. My home office is a roll top desk, purchased 25 years, and one marriage, ago at an unfinished furniture store. The working surface of the desk is scarred by the initials and notes of my first daughter and her friends, also from one marriage ago. They had used my previous spot, in my previous workshop, as a clubhouse when I wasn't there to interfere with their activities. Just like the expensive antiques, mine has the requisite pigeon holes and compartments, but the real work and filing get done elsewhere in my spot.

I think on a notebook computer which fits conveniently on the open, top left-hand drawer of the desk. The notebook's dimensions are a tad short of bridging the gap between the drawer's sides. Volume. 6 of the Woman's Day Encyclopedia of Cookery, HADDOCK TO KETCHUP, spans the breach nicely. I bought the computer with a monochrome screen but soon tired of that. Fortunately, it came with a

VGA card. A 14-inch Gold Star color monitor now allows me to think in color. It is perched upon a two-file drawer, oak finished cabinet to my left beyond which is a view of the neighboring woods through a large plate glass window. The filing cabinet clashes significantly with the dark cherry tables in the room, which had been carefully, and artistically, selected by my wife to set off the expensive light green and beige oriental rug which is the center piece of this rarely used room. Patricia no longer had the will nor the energy to fight for the ambience of the room, being in the midst of starting a publishing company from the ground up. So I was allowed to drag in my oak cabinet.

My chair is vintage 1920's, rescued from a bank by my father, who was in the construction business at one time. He was a superintendent for a bank remodeling job in Allentown, Pennsylvania and rescued this sturdy wooden office chair, with a spring back, four arched legs, and a seat somewhat made to conform to the shape of the human buttocks. Somewhat means that you can sit in it for about two hours before a certain derriere deadness drives one to get up for a walk, or other form of exercise, to stimulate the flow of blood.

Filling out my small work space are a light to read by, which is brass and sits on the top shelf of the desk, and a light to read the keyboard by, which sits over daughter number one's initials, FLB, crudely engraved into the wood when she was in grade school. Now that she is the mother of two of my grandchildren, may a similar plight be brought to her favorite furniture.

The spot is where I'm currently sitting, pondering yesterday's meeting. The house is quiet, except for the ticking of the wall clock, a hand wound Regulator, also a refugee from my father's bank job. It had been built by the E. Ingraham Company in Bristol, Connecticut. I don't really know how old it is, but would guess its age to be ninety years or so. I had painted it with red enamel as a teenager, to go with the colors of my bedroom. Having come to my senses as an adult, I stripped the enamel down to bare wood, and finished it with tung oil.

Things had gone well with Dr. Trader. We discussed my background at length, particularly my reputation as a problem solver. The old man caught on very quickly to my method of the six P's. Nothing unique about the method other than the hard work it takes to make it a success. The first step in the process, as the reader may recall, is to identify the problem. Once he had decided I was his man, the good doctor had shared with me his perspective of the problem. Specifically, he perceived the theft of a client's deposit by substitution as the problem. The possibility of word getting out to the Board of Directors and the public at large was viewed as slim, given the age of the specimen and the fact that only four persons, including the thief, were aware of the larceny. However, he did not want a recurrence. Therefore, I was retained to prevent that from happening again. If I could catch the thief as well he might reward me for this dividend from my efforts.

I had arisen with the dawn on this wintry day. Breakfast aromas linger in the house. The scrambled egg was laced with raw onion and red bell pepper. On the side I prepared a fried mashed potato into which I had blended left over corn kernels from last night's meal. When sprinkled with hot Hungarian paprika, it was a most satisfying complement to the egg.

Second cup of coffee in hand, I had started work at about seven fifteen. Unlike Dr. Trader, I believed there were a host of problems, and was well on the way to compiling them. It had begun snowing the previous evening, just as I left Wilmington after my meeting with Dr. Trader. By the time I reached Smyrna, it was drifting heavily across Route 13. Many cars were stranded, scattered like a children's toys after play, in both the median and alongside the four lane highway, which is the major north south artery in the state. I dismissed any thoughts of taking my usual scenic, no stop lights Route 9 cut off through Leipsic. I decided against the Route 1 bypass, even though DelDOT gave it highest snow clearing priority. The normal twenty minute ride to my home took more than two hours. Nonetheless I was pleased that the Aurora was equal to the task. My wife, Patricia was stranded with our daughter at her friend Wendy's home near Killen's Pond State Park. They could be there a week before they got plowed out, given the three foot drifts that were being reported over the radio.

In my wife's absence, I have started a fire going in the cast iron insert using back issues of the National Enquirer and Star magazines. I see Roxanne's marriage to Ken is in jeopardy and that JFK Jr. is cracking up. Who are they kidding? Hunks don't crack up, they do the cracking. The fire also serves as a precaution against a power loss, which occur frequently in our area when we have snow and strong winds in combination. Either the wires snap, or some slackerdly simpleton in an SUV is out clipping off power poles. My notes are being copied to the disk in the 'a' drive about every ten minutes. Both batteries for the computer have been charged so I could continue to work for a few hours if the electric goes out. Ditto the batteries for my snake flashlight to provide keyboard light.

The beginnings of hunger pangs direct my attention to the Regulator clock. It is noon already. I had been steady at it for almost five hours. Time to throw some more wood on the fire, have a light lunch of a couple of nectarines, a handful of shelled, unsalted peanuts and a small glass of milk.

R

After lunch, I read my notes to summarize in my own mind what I thought were the broad set of issues that I would have to deal with to succeed in my assignment. It was not as simple as Trader thought when he retained me to devise an improved security system. First off, I had to figure out how the theft had been done. Then, who did it, from which I hoped to be able to deduce the why of it all. This last mentioned part of the puzzle, the motive, was what bothered me the most. I had asked Trader not to tell me any of the details of the case. I did not even want to know the name of the donor. Whether he was famous, or a nobody, it would bias my thinking. Better for me not to know at the outset. That way I wouldn't allow details of the case to force a presumption that something is a given, without first validating it myself.

There appeared to me to be more than a few reasons why an employee would steal one of the deposits. I looked at my screen, where I had listed my questions on the subject.

MOTIVATION?
Hypotheses - Inside job for personal reasons

- Passed over for promotion, seeks to embarrass Trader or member of the board

- Offended by amount of last raise, motivation as above

- Secretly harboring a grudge for a long forgotten snub by Trader or a member of the board, motivation as above

- Stress related change in personality drives the person to self destruct, no real motive

- Addiction of some sort, needs the money from selling the sperm

- Romantic involvement, needs the money from selling the sperm

- Medical problem, personal or family, needs the money from selling the sperm

- Mid-life crisis creates need for money, sells purloined deposit

The last four bullets are symptomatic of the real puzzler in this case. There is only one use for the stolen goods. I don't feature someone buying the frozen material to cool a fuzzy navel. Sperm is only good for impregnating. Therefore, an outside buyer's motives, I had reasoned this morning, were severely limited.

MOTIVATION?
Hypotheses - Inside job for sale to other(s)

- So someone could get pregnant
- To prevent someone from getting pregnant

Now why would someone want to prevent some other person from

156

getting pregnant. If this were back in the days of old, the royal crown might be at stake. However, it seemed to me a trifle doubtful that European royalty was storing their precious cargo in Wilmington, DE. Possibly the control of a family fortune or business hinged on the continued barrenness of a sibling's wife. Was the husband impotent, sterile, or dead? Endless possibilities, endless pathways, and so I continued until a casual glance out the picture window told me it was evening, time to add more wood to the fire, and prepare my dinner.

℞

Federal Express made it to my home a little after ten in the morning of the very next day, Wednesday, despite the fact that our no-outlet lane has not yet seen the business end of a snow plow. Immediately sorted and stacked the material according to subject. I am now in the midst of the preparation phase of my assignment. It has taken me the better part of four, twelve hour working days just to enter the sperm deposit and withdrawal data into my computer. The only item of interest that I picked up while performing this menial chore was the fact that some depositors took advantage of an anonymity feature that allowed the account to be registered under a fictitious name. The vial that had been tampered with was one of about four hundred that had elected to use this feature. Doctor Trader had not sent along the table in which the actual depositors list of names was cross indexed against the fictional in code. This set of papers represented the Rosetta Stone of the Brandywine Valley Frozen Assets Trust. He had told me in advance that he would not trust Federal Express, not even a bonded courier, with the document needed to decipher the code. It could be used in his office, where I could analyze the names in his presence. However, I would not be allowed to memorialize the deciphered list on paper or in my computer. Access to the document was a moot point. There was a lot more information to be gathered until I wanted to see it. I had neglected to ask him who else had access to the list. That question was added to the file I was formulating for incorporation into the planning phase of the work.

℞

Today, Sunday, January 18, continues to be bitterly cold. I had

157

decided to take the day off to spend with my family, but the case keeps poking its way back into my thoughts, like an errant song that refuses to go away. While listening to the minister's sermon, my mind refused to absorb it, preferring the spicier work of sorting the order in which the remaining information that Trader had sent should be reviewed. Employee files of those who had access to the depository would be next. That would take a day or two. The next several steps would be delicate ones. In order to winnow down the list of suspects, I would need to know more about them than what I could glean from their files. Background checks on each of these employees would be necessary for all are suspect now. I need to know about any new cars, fancy vacations, gambling or drug addictions, all those myriad pieces of information that metamorphose into clues and then suspects. Motives must be determined on the basis of this information.

Who to use for this work to me is critical. I can't do it personally because tailing the employees will be part of the information gathering phase. I don't have the time to do it expeditiously. There are just too many people, twenty-two in all. Also, since I'll be taking a tour of the facility as a precursor to interviewing the suspects, it wouldn't do to have one of them associate my face with someone who's been following them around. But who to hire? Private detective and security agencies are out of the question. If the snatch was motivated by an outsider, he or she would have had to go through some of the same investigative steps I was contemplating in order to see who had an exploitable weakness. It was just too risky for me to tempt fate by going back into the same pool of investigators.

"Praise God from whom all blessings come, praise Him all..." The singing that preceded the Offering broke into my thoughts as Patricia dragged me to my feet. The service was over shortly thereafter. After shaking hands with the minister, Patricia and I walked with our fellow worshipers down the corridor toward Fellowship Hall where coffee, punch and cookies are served up to all who wish to socialize before leaving. I veered off before getting there, venturing down into the basement to fetch Kate from Sunday school. The three of us rejoined, we munched, sipped and talked with friends we rarely saw elsewhere. The balance of the day was already planned. An early lunch at the Bluecoat

Pancake House was to be followed by play practice at Well's Theater at Wesley College in downtown Dover. Then home to make and bake cookies and pumpernickel bread. After dinner at home we would play Monopoly until Katie's bedtime at eight thirty. I vowed not to brood on the case the balance of the day.

I succeeded.

CHAPTER 25   MARCH 1997

OVERDUE

WILMINGTON, DELAWARE

"Had you a rough day at work, Doc?" Jake Parkowski asked in a rough voice, spoken over and around the cigar fixed permanently in the left corner of his mouth. "Don't often see you in here on Friday nights."

Larry Fowler stepped off the belt of the treadmill, straddling it with both feet, turned the switch to the off position, and jumped off. He grabbed the club towel from the railing, wiping the sweat from his brow as he responded, "Yeah, a good workout is better for the nerves than single malt scotch."

Parkowski smiled, "Women trouble, is it? Don't see that feisty, foxy granddaughter of mine around no more."

Fowler returned the grin, "If she really was your granddaughter, I'd be hanging out here every night, just trying to catch up with her again."

"You and her have a falling out?" Jake asked, curious

despite himself.

"Not one that I noticed. One day she was here. The next she was gone," he answered, noticeably despondent.

"Hey Doc, she was only a woman," Jake said. "Man like you could have his pick." Jake gave him a light tap with his clenched fist to emphasize the point.

"Yeah, but what a woman," turning to walk to the Nautilus as he responded.

He began to reminisce as he started his first set.

Larry Fowler's life bubbled over with pleasure after that kiss goodnight when he dropped her off at the hotel. The next weekend, on Saturday, they had played 18 holes at Delcastle, a gem of a public course west of the city, nicely tucked into the rolling Piedmont hills. It was an absolutely gorgeous day, one of those rare east coast knockouts. A herd of flat bottomed, round topped cumulus clouds grazed slowly aloft at two thousand feet, their puffy, cotton whiteness contrasting sharply with the brilliant, ultramarine blue sky. They cast wide shadows across the course as they passed, like a flotilla of nature's hot air balloons.

Pester wore a white, cotton blouse, tucked in at the waist, with flared shoulders that gave her freedom of movement. Her loose fitting, royal blue trousers, failed to conceal her well shaped, firm round buttocks. The white visor, with PING written in royal blue letters, complemented her stylish, conservative outfit.

Fowler hadn't played in over a year, and was immensely pleased with the 89 he brought to the clubhouse. This was despite the fact that the grip on his driver had split on the fifth tee. He had played the rest of the course with a five wood.

Pester shot an amazing 78, using a very accurate, compact swing.

That stroke didn't give her tremendous distance off the tee, but her ball never went off the fairway. She lost a stroke on each of the 500 yard plus holes, had a ball roll back off the green into a sand trap on the seventeenth and missed two putts when she rimmed the holes.

On the drive to her new residence, he recalled feeling a bit foolish that her mixed bag of clubs hadn't tipped him off to the strength of her game. They were her own, not something borrowed, or bought, just for the occasion. They looked like they had been selected from the barrel of lost and used clubs in a pro shop. The seven wood had been made out of wood. Her sand wedge looked like it had been manufactured before the World War, and not necessarily WWII. She played like a pro, because she knew each club's idiosyncracies. It was like putting a scalpel in the hand of a surgeon. She cut through that course like she had played it every day for the past twenty years.

They had left the course, dashed over to a sporting goods store on Limestone Road, and dropped off his clubs to have new grips put on the lot. They planned a leisurely evening of entertainment at a local night spot near her newly leased condominium in newly fashionable center city. They left the shop, beginning the drive back to Wilmington on a series of roads that had once been cart and cattle paths. A few dated back to the seventeenth century when the state had been part of William Penn's colony. Fowler loved maneuvering his old red Conquest up and down the crooked, two lane roads. The route he took was one of his favorite ways back to the city. Turning left onto Mermaid Stoney Batter Road, the car swiftly dropped to the narrow bridge over Balls Run, then they shot up, and down again, within a distance of less than a mile, to ford Mill Creek. The road was wooded on both sides, absolutely exhilarating in the fall, when the maples were painted red, orange and yellow. Turning right on Mill Creek Road took them past Delcastle, the public course which had been built on the old County Workhouse Farms. Highland West and Crossgates flashed by alternately on the left and right. The light had been green at the Newport Gap Pike. He flashed through the intersection, over Hyde Run, then slowed as they entered the Hercules Country Club, a magnificent company owned golf course that Fowler longed to play. Had he elected to stay on the Lancaster Pike after they made a right as they exited the club grounds, the scenic part of the ride would have been over. But shortly after crossing the bridge over Red Clay Creek, he turned and drove north along the eastern shoreline of Hoopes Reservoir. The Conquest slowed as they entered Valley Garden Park. Then he drove east to Lancaster Pike, on which he turned and raced toward the City, where Lancaster Pike became Pennsylvania Avenue.

Fowler parked the car in one of the three visitors' spots allotted the condominium building in which she had sublet a furnished, one bedroom place on the first floor. The former Rodney Arms apartment house was a three-story affair on the north side of Pennsylvania Avenue between Rodney and Clayton streets. Built just after the Great Depression, it had served the well to do into the early sixties. Then age, white flight and changing lifestyles brought the old dowager down to her knees. Sold and reformulated as professional office space, it served the next generation of Wilmingtonians in that capacity for three more decades. When she had given him the address on the phone the day before, that had been his first clue that her assets might be more than just physical. After more than a half century of service, the building's architecture was still stylish, exterior brick as good as new, and the structure fundamentally sound. Location being what it is in the real estate business, the property had been snapped up before its availabilty was even publicized. The interior had been gutted once again, and then totally redone to be leased as one and two bedroom condominiums, with leases that would all expire on January 1, 2045. Parking was at a premium, so the visitors got short shrift. Rodney Manor, as it was now dubbed, was only a few blocks from the City's thriving downtown business center.

She had gone upstairs to change while he was parking the Conquest, an aged, but well kept steed when compared to the new Volvos, Porsches, BMWs and Lexus (Lexi?) that made up the majority of the tenants' vehicles. The doorman acknowledged him as Ms. Size's friend when he mentioned his name. She opened promptly at the bell, already dressed down in a Fighting Blue Hens sweatshirt, denims and L.L. Bean moccasins.

"We were a long time on the course. Care to freshen up?" she asked, pointing down the hall in the direction of what he hoped was the bathroom.

Gratefully, Fowler started down the hall, knowing that his strained bladder would soon be put to ease. Relieved, hands washed, hair wetted down and combed meticulously, and in that order, Fowler eagerly asked, "Where do you want to go for dinner?"

"How 'bout the Charcoal Pit for burgers and Cokes " came the reply.

"And then what?"

"We'll see," she said, smiling seductively.

CHAPTER 26   **APRIL 1996**

CAN IT BE TRUE?

BEVERLY HILLS, CALIFORNIA

"Smartest thing I ever did was hire that little old squirt," Roxanne spoke softly to herself, the self that most of the world knew, as she placed the tabloid down on the blood red leather couch. She was pleased with the publicity campaign that they had finally agreed upon. It hadn't come easy, but she finally gave in to his idea of starting it with a whisper, softly, so faint as to be lost to the memory of those who read it. No **Hard Copy** or **Entertainment Tonight** for starters. Drop a rumor on the tabloid with the largest circulation in America, the one with a reputation for honesty that weighed in at an ounce more than its weightless competition.

In the Behind the Screens section, just before the classifieds, the article headline asked "Could It Be True?". The last thing anyone would read, the dump for stuff people cared little about. A filler area, where an agent could point to show he had gotten his client something for the money they were paying him/her. She picked it up again, just to savor the moment with one more reading. Dominic Celio cleverly had suggested that they run a picture of Ken and her with her kids from previous marriages. The article was as wide as the photo. Therefore, it was only about four rows deep.

Rumor has it that the aging former TV superstar is pregnant again in an attempt to save her failing marriage to her husband, ten years her junior. "They don't..."

She placed the tabloid back on the couch, still smiling. She didn't need to read the rest. It was all in the first line, pregnant again. The plan was to have the rumor, and the crescendo of publicity, grow in direct proportion to the development of the fetus that was safely floating in her womb.

Roxanne sat with her legs propped on the couch. The midnight blackness of her velour sweat suit contrasted nicely with the red color of the couch that glowed with the light from the late afternoon sun. She was alone. Ken had riled up all her kids from her former marriages. They all had finally left in a huff. Then he left to drive up to their ranch, which he had bought with her money as a place to play with his toys. Stillness replaced the normal, in your face racket of her household. It fit her current mood. Now that she had agreed upon a publicity plan with Celio, she was out of the loop. Her only role was to let nature take its course in growing the baby. That gave her time to put together her personal plan, which was what she had been doing before being diverted by the article in the National Enquirer.

Roaring around in that gas-sucking, $125,000 Humvee up there at the ranch, she thought. *Having a grand old time drinking my beer with his good-old-boy buddies. He wouldn't be whooping it up, if he knew what I had in mind. I know what I want to do, now all I have to do is figure out how to get it done.*

She swung her legs off the couch, and rose quickly, daintily, thinking that six months from now, that same action would be as dainty as a tow truck getting a fully loaded eighteen wheeler moving from a dead start. She walked into the kitchen, grabbing two yellow Number Two Ticonderoga pencils and a yellow legal pad from the antique, roll

166

top desk in her study as she went. She always thought better seated at the kitchen table with pad and pencil at hand.

Before starting to write, she poured a cup of coffee in a chipped blue cup, a souvenir from her waitressing days, and permanent prod to keep her focussed on her career, and herself. She knew that, other than Dominic, nobody cared about her. They were only interested in her money. That went for her husband, her kids, and her so-called friends. This is what she wrote:

I'M GETTING EVEN !!!!!!!!!!

GOAL – GET RID OF KEN BEFORE THE BABY IS BORN

- He's got to be out before he figures out the publicity campaign is going to work. (Warn Celio not to tell him anything.)

- Figure out a way to trash his toys before or after he leaves(Talk to Pester)

- Tape his voice when he refuses to have sex

- Sell the ranch before he leaves and hide the $ (Check with Pester on how to do)

- *Interview after little El is born, saying I had to get rid of Ken for the sake of the baby. Hint around that Ken is queer. That'll make him look good in front of his boozing buddies*

Roxanne laid the pencil down in mid-sentence, suddenly aware that darkness had descended upon the house. The garden lights had come on. She had them programmed to diminish in luminescence as the night wore on to sooth her into drowsiness. She dozed off smiling at how she had begun planning her future.

CHAPTER 27   DECEMBER 24, 1956

WHOOP-DE-DO

MELFA, VIRGINIA

The sky was overcast, the wind blowing in icy gusts from the northwest, bringing the chill of the Chesapeake, along with occasional spurts of snow. It raced across eastern shore Virginia, the flat terrain and dormant fields offering no resistance, other than an occasional stand of trees preserved as a woodlot. Here in the southeastern part of Accomac County, the highest land has to stand on tippie-toe to be as much as twenty feet above sea level. Called Accowmack, "The place on the other side of the water" by the Indians of the western shore who were contemporaries of Captain John Smith, the eastern shore of Virginia remained isolated and remote in the mid-twentieth century.

A flock of Canadian geese fleeing the storm flew over two boys dressed warmly in surplus pea coats. They trudged through the late afternoon, a dozen furry mammals hanging by their tails from a pole carried between them. The boys looked upward the instant they heard honking. Such was the flock's speed as they surfed on the cusp of the fast-moving storm, the geese were almost past them by the time the boys

168

spied the stragglers in the low flying, ragged V-formation. The geese had left the open waters of the Chesapeake Bay at the mouth of Pungateague Creek only minutes before. Flying low over Frogstool, a tiny dot of a few scattered homes, some of the birds began to set their wings to begin landing as they shot over the Machipongo River. They would land in Bradford Bay's marshy shelter on the Atlantic Ocean side of the Delmarva Peninsula before the boys had lowered their eyes, completing the seven and one-half mile, wind driven flight in under 10 minutes.

"Mama sure goin' to be happy when she sees how many muskrats we bringin' home, won't she Charles?", said Clearance, smiling happily. He pictured in his mind how his mother would make such a fuss over the splendid catches the boys had gotten with their traps over in the ocean side marshes near Wachapreague. His father had told him the Machinpungo Indians gave it that name, meaning "little city by the sea."

They were still on Bradford Neck Road, about midway between Quimby and Wachapreague, walking northeasterly, with the gusting winds causing them to lean into them slightly to their left to maintain their balance. There were seven small cemeteries strung along the road, on the marsh side, from Haul Over Light all the way down to the northern most extension of Upshur Bay. The boys had bartered permission from the owners to use the lanes that led to the cemeteries. Every year they clipped and cleaned the grave sites for the right of entry to their trap lines. They were all owned by white folks who had to keep up appearances, but who were either too rich to bother with the work, too poor to pay for it, or too enfeebled to do it themselves. All in all it was a good deal for everyone. The grave sites all received the same degree of care, in that way keeping the seeds of jealousy from sprouting like the jimson weed that had to be ripped out every year.

Charles, a tall, lanky teenager, flashed a smile in return, then quickly regretted opening his mouth to the chilling wind. "Aw, sweet peas in the springtime, that wind sent a spark down through my toof' cavity, liked to electrify my poor old bones."

"We's lucky there's no snow on the ground today," came Clearance's muffled voice from behind the blue, upturned collar, which he held close to his mouth with his gloved left hand. They were sharing the pair of raggedy, red knit gloves. Each boy had his other hand, the bare one, snugly stuffed in a pocket of the sturdy coats they wore. The ends of the muskrat pole were lodged in the crooks thus formed by their arms. Every half mile or so, they switched gloves, and then carrying sides. To keep the muskrats from getting dirty, they were obliged to delay the switch until they found a convenient dogwood tree, or other small tree or bush, to place one end of the pole on while they traded places.

"Yeah, Mama and the kids couldn't ask for better weather for finding collard greens. No snow on the ground, and it ain't but slightly froze on top," Charles responded, his teeth clenched tightly while he spoke as he vividly remembered the shock of the cold air on his now aching tooth.

"Oh, I hope they got at least two bushel baskets. If they did, we're gonna have one fine Christmas dinner. Muskrat, yams, and greens on the side. Can't beat that for good eatn', brother," Clearance said. He was tiring, and they hadn't even reached the outskirts of Wachapreague.

"Charles, how much you think these rats weigh?"

Figuring, Charles walked on another 100 yards before answering, "They about four pounds apiece," imparting knowledge with his response, "So I reckon, between them, and the pole, we carrying about 60 pounds. All together, not apiece."

Hearing his brother's voice, feeling his end of the pole begin to lag behind, Charles regretted his decision earlier in the day. His Daddy always said to start to check the lines down near Quimby, then move north, toward home, with your catch growin' as you got closer to home. In his eagerness to see how they had done, Charles had ignored his father's teachings, and had led his younger brother down the lane just south of Wachapreague, before you get to Herbert Church. Because of that, the load was building as they moved south, and when they made the turn for home, they had nearly four miles to go with the full weight of their entire catch, before they reached the spot where they first started to empty traps.

"It's about three miles to home down this dirt road. If we cut across this field," Clearance said, pointing with his gloved hand, "We..."

"Could either get shot for trespassing, never you mind it's Christmas Eve, or sink up to our ankles, carrying all this weight. Boy, if youse tard, we'll take turns holdn' it up at yonder dogwood," Charles said helpfully, sympathizing with his younger brother, who was even more frail than himself. Looking skyward, he judged the time of day, then said, "We got time to rest 'fore dark. Maybe someone else will help Mama with the wood, in the spirit of the season, so to speak. Sides, we can always use the cull oil lantern if need be."

They trudged on down the road, a little slower now that manly pride had been set aside when they both had confessed to how tired they were. The dogwood tree was on the Grangeville Road, just outside of Wachapreague.

✠

"My forearms is so sore from being a pole rest, I don't know if I can carry the darn thing that way anymore, Charles," Clearance moaned

He straightened his right arm to take the smooth piece of oak from his brother, who was hefting it gently from his shoulder to Clearance's.

"Darn," Clearance yipped as the full weight of the muskrat laden pole sat on his collar bone.

"Here, baby brother, let me put my bandana under there for a cushion," Charles said as he pulled a large red and white kerchief from the left hip pocket of his Levi coveralls. "That better?"

"You better believe it. Man, did that hurt. I thought it was going to break me."

While the two boys were resting by the side of the road, snow began

171

to arrive not as before, as a part of the next gust of wind, but lightly, consistently. The unpaved, sandy back road was deeply rutted from mule drawn wagons, which even in the fifties was a preferred mode of transportation for the poor rural farmers. Plow and plant with a fine pair Monday through Friday, take you town to do your dealing on Saturday, and a reliable way to get to church every Sunday, regardless of the weather, or the condition of the road. The snow began to stick to the unpaved road immediately. Charles looked to the northwest and saw a clearly defined snow line in the direction of the family shack, that stood in a patch of woods near the headwaters of Nickawampus Creek, east of Seaside Road.

Grunting as he hefted the other end from the fork of the little dogwood, Charles bent a little as he placed the pole end on his own shoulder.

"We'll try it like this a little ways. My bending will help to equalize the load. Take some of it off you," said Charles. "Don't like the looks of this. If it gets deep enough so's we can't see them ruts, one or both of us is liable to step in one, 'n take a fall. Likely break something, or leastwise spoil Christmas dinner. We'll take a break at Locust Mount. Let's move"

Marching along in column fashion, one behind the other, the two boys walked straight into what would go down in history as the Christmas blizzard of 1956. Two miles to go and visibility went down to ten feet. Life on the Shore was about to come to a standstill.

✠

"Baby brother, can you hear me?" Charles shouted over the keening wind.

"Yeah, Charles. I can. Where are we Charles? Are we getting close to home yet? I'm gettin' scared. I'm so froze up, they'll have to prop me up against the stove for a hour to warm my blood," Clearance shouted back. His voice was muffled by the snow, and blown away on the wind.

Three hours had passed since the boys had picked up their load of muskrats from the dogwood tree crotch. The snow was blowing off the bare farm fields, unchecked by any winter cover crop, and onto the road. Already there were drifts of up to two feet in depth. The rubber boots each boy wore were open at the top, typical in an area where they needed to be emptied quickly if over topped by water when out tonging oysters, crabbing or seine fishing. Designed for quick removal so that a man could get his feet dry again when on the water, they were deadly on land under conditions like this. Snow, overtopping the boots, quickly became ice water as it melted around the feet.

"We on the road to home, I knows that cause we passed the Oak Grove Church as we turned north. I recognized the features of that stump, about 100 feet back yonder. Daddy and I got the crosscut saw started badly on that one. It was a red oak that Mr. Eichelberger wanted back at the mill that day. It was late, hot, and Daddy said t' hell with it, let's get it done. Funny angle to what we left behind," Charles shouted back. "Best of my recollection is that it was about a three, fo' hunnerd feet from the house, straight down this road, if we still on the road."

"I don't knows if I can make it, Charles. My feet so froze, I can't feel nuttn' below my knees," Clearance responded.

"Can't hear you, boy. Listen hear, you start shoutn' to me as loud as you can. Any thing that comes to mind. We gonna make it, heah?"
"Let's put this pole down, I'll watch it, 'n you go find the house, fetch Daddy to come help me. I ain't goin' to do no 300 feet," Clearance whined, obviously exhausted, delirious and ready to give up. "Cain't go no mo'."

"Clearance, it's Christmas Eve. I ain't comin' home wit' no Christmas Day dinner and no Clearance to boot. Mama and Daddy'd beat me wit' da strop. You listen to me. Talk to me. Scream at the top of your lungs. Anything that comes into your head. Anything."

Charles heard nothing, but he felt Clearance stagger as the pole on his shoulder shifted, then dipped. "Clearance, get your scrawny ass up.

Think about tomorrow, git you smellin' those greens, tastin' the juices from these here rats we carryin'. Come on, boy, it's just a little way. Think about tomorrow." Fear was in his voice. Fear that he'd lose his younger brother, fear that he himself would die this close to home, fear that he didn't know where he was any more.

He could feel Clearance rise up by the elevation in the pole. They continued to walk, slowly, feet dragging, unwittingly still on the road and staggering due north, with the wind about fifteen degrees to the west of the direction in which they were walking. Snow and ice encased that third of their bodies. Clearance's right hand was frozen to the pole that weighed upon his shoulder. The snow had melted slightly, encasing glove, pole, and coat in a ball of ice.

"Clearance, talk to me," Charles shrieked

Howling again, when there was no response, "Clearance, think about tomorrow, with Daddy and Mama, we sittin' there with all the chillen, eatin' them greens, the smell of them cookin' just a fillin' the house. Think of that. Don't it make you hungry, don't it make you warm?"

"Daddy's worked right up to Christmas, Charles. Do you think, maybe, there will be some Christmas gifts for us?" shouted Clearance.

Surprised at hearing a response, Charles yelled into the howling wind, "Don't know. Daddy's never had this much work before cause he never had us kids freeing up so much of his time. He never had so many chances, neither, but now Mama says he has built up a reputation over the years as a solid worker. We ain't never, none of us, had a Christmas present afore," Charles paused. "I wouldn't want to miss the feeling. How 'bout you?"

"No, suh. Not me, either," Clearance replied. "What kind 'a things you 'spect youngn's get for Christmas, Charles?"

"Whatever youse a wantin', I guess, as long as it's not too much," came the answer.

"The only thing I want, the only thing I dream of is a real guitar, so'se I can learn to play like that white boy we saw on TV," Clearance shouted back, his body warming again by the excitement of the conversation.

"You mean Elvis, that rock n' roller you been listenin' to on Mama's radio when she ain't aroun'," Charles warming too, there being no better brother baiter born on the eastern shore of the Commonwealth of Virginia in the last century.

✠

The adrenaline pulse that had caused the boys' euphoria was soon spent. The shouting became more subdued. Clearance's slim body began to quiver, the cold and physical exertions combining to cause complete exhaustion. He staggered hesitantly, following a brother he could no longer see, the muskrat pole his only connection with another human being.

"Charles, I..." was all the spent little boy was able to get out before he fainted, collapsing in the snow, pulling the muskrat pole down with him. Tears began to stream down Charles' cheeks as he dropped to all fours and felt his way along the pole to his unconscious brother. Unable to separate Clearance's ice encased hand from the pole, the older boy crawled around the prone body, using his bare fingers to search for his brother's head. When he found it, he rose, beat the snow from the legs of his coveralls, then knelt down, and placed Clearance's head on his lap. Then he began to scream.

"Daddeeee, Daddeeee, Daddeeee," he shouted, over and over, his high-pitched wails in perfect harmony with the whistling sounds the wind made as it rushed through the trees that lined the west side of the road. Charles vowed to keep on shouting for help until someone came to the rescue, or he too passed out.

✠

"Davis, you hear that? Listen!" The boys' mother turned, looked

175

sternly at her children, saying, "Hush, now. I think I heard something."

Voices stilled, the only noise in the unpainted, clapboard shack came from the keening of the wind, as it whistled through the trees across the road. Brought back to the reality of their missing brothers, the other children stared wide-eyed at their parents.

"There it is again. Don't you hear it?" she asked, grasping her husband's forearm, seeking confirmation.

"Edward, get me the lantern, and that box of kitchen matches," Davis whispered to his son. The lanky boy, a cookie cutter copy of his brothers, raced to the metal cabinet with the broken hinges, doing as he was told.

Shouting now, smiling, his wife exclaimed, "You heard it, too?"

"Din't hear nuttin'. You know I cain't hear them high pitched sounds since I started workin' at the saw mill," Davis responded slowly. "But I'm goin' out there. You, or Edward is gonna have to come wid me. I can fetch and carry, but I'll never hear'em."

"Edward, you're gonna have to do it," his mother said. "Somebody has to be here to add wood to the fire, and keep these babies warm. Let's get you dressed up warm," she continued as she got his red wool sweater, his blue wool coat, red scarf, blue knit cap, and frayed pair of gloves.

Meanwhile, Davis lifted the glass globe, lit the wick, and lowered the glass of the coal oil lamp. He put on his worn, brown corduroy coat, and his brown, felt fedora. Picking up the lamp with his bare, weather cracked hands, for he had no gloves, he kissed his wife, motioned to his son, and opened the door. Snow blew half way across the living room as they passed into the night, closing the door behind them.

Davis bent over, shouting in Edward's ear, "Edward, we gonna stand right here by the house until you hears somethin'. If'n you don't, we'll have to get your mother. Them boys been gone since sunup. It's pretty near eight o'clock. They ain't gonna last much longer out'n this mess."

They stood there as the wind and snow howled and rushed around and by them. Edward didn't dare tell his father that he was both scared and cold, colder than he had ever been in his short stay on this earth. He stood alongside his father, staring into the night, sometimes at shadows cast by the lantern's light, then at total whiteness, as the storm's fresh snow was joined by wind whipped snow from the ground. His keen ears heard an awful lot of shrieking, but he could sort out nothing of human origin. In a matter of minutes, he was shaking and crying. Then the quirky wind began to gust. In a pause, he heard it. His teeth chattered so badly, he could not speak. He yanked his father's hand, and pointed in the direction from which the sound came.

✠

"Lord, my God, Davis, if they hadn't been a shoutin', an' the wind hadn't died, we'd never had known they was out there. My two babies would have froze to death on Christmas Eve," Clearance's mother said to her husband, tears rimming her eyes.

He touched her shoulder, she twisted around, and allowed him to caress her. Her face fell on his shoulder, the tears began to flow. He shook her gently, love in his eyes, for to him she was still in the image of the woman he had taken as his bride when he had returned from the hell of World War II. He had the military life in his genes, but regretted ever having enlisted.

"Darlin'. Those two boys are safe in this house. The best Christmas dinner we ever had is gonna be on that table in a matter of hours, and we got Christmas presents to open for all of our kids for the first time since we been married. There's a fire in the stove, wood on the porch, and a storm ragin' outside. But we're snug and warm inside. Cain't you please cheer up?"

"I cain't but worry that Clearance won't wake up to see that fine guitar that you bought him up to the general store in Parksley," She said to him in return.

But he did.

CHAPTER 28   MAY 1996

WHO?

WILMINGTON, DELAWARE

For May, it was an unseasonably warm day. The humidity, a constant factor in Delaware weather, is bordering on 90 percent. I had been working in the yard all morning.

Weighing the benefits of continued yard work under sweltering conditions versus putting in some billable time on one of my cases in the coolness of the living room, I opted for a quick shower, a change of clothes and a sit down at my spot. The BVFAT case continues to be my number one priority of the several assignments in which I am currently involved. While opening the bvfat2p.wpd file, I felt some degree of satisfaction to have progressed this far in such a short time. The preparation phase was nearly done. It wanted my tweaking the data, which I probably would start and finish today.

My planning notes are filed away in bvfat3p.wpd, awaiting my attention. I am already pretty sure of my approach, but I wanted a little bit more personal employee information first. I had considered, and then dropped the idea of hiring a local private investigator. Then, it had dawned on me that the job didn't require a licensed investigator. This wasn't a movie. The job spec was pretty simple. It required intelligence, patience, and maturity. Most of all, I wanted someone, some ones as it turned out, that I could trust implicitly.

Then it came to me, one of those spectacularly simple ideas that embarrass me when I wonder why I hadn't had the intelligence to grasp them from the outset. In my previous capacity as president of my old firm, I had developed working relationships with men and women with the qualities I sought. Some of these ties spanned the entire three decades I was in the business. I had many friends older than I, or perhaps more financially successful than I, who were in various forms of semi or full retirement. I had a buffet of scientists and other professionals from whom to select my operatives.

I wanted them to inspect property records in the recorder of deeds' office in all three counties, and to check out their residences to find out the year and model of any cars. Go through the trash that they could steal from the curb. See who they do business with, then call around as if they were checking their credit. Check out their credit through Equifax down in Atlanta. Who has maxed out their credit cards, how many, and at what limit. In today's world of easy credit, someone with a good credit rating was bombarded with offers through the mail. A cunning person would have no problem running a Ponzi scheme, paying off one company's card with money secured from another. My instructions were to follow some of the more likely candidates through the weekend. If a guy spends it playing roulette at the Sands in Atlantic City, or yanking the slots at Delaware Park, that's good to know. Sleeping in with a mistress, or mister, is food for my interview table.

Jim Duffield, Tuck Mooreshead and Gerry Esposito made up the investigative team. They were all retired now. Each eagerly accepted the chance to use their skills in a totally different venue. Duffield, a civil engineer, was a career geo-technical specialist whose firm designed earthworks and did foundation analyses for everything from high rises to elevated storage tanks. He had a set of stones to do that kind of work. A mistake could have catastrophic results. Picture a building collapse, a water tower falling on a house. The derring-do of his career was at odds with his demeanor. He is a soft spoken, outwardly pleasant person. On the other hand, he reveals his passion for thrills by racing in the same circuit that Paul Newman did. He's a stand up a guy. About my size, just under six feet, balding, face creased a little like Clint Eastwood, without the wrinkles, he's an average looking man. Just right for the job.

Completely at the opposite end of the spectrum, Tuck Mooreshead stands 6'-5" tall with a graying shock of wavy hair. His bushy eyebrows could serve as a nesting place for a pair of swallows. In flannel shirt and corduroy pants, he looks woodsy enough to be the champion trap shooter that he was in his younger days. Put him in a suit, and he could pass for a diplomat, a banker or college professor. An actor, either self taught or born that way, he can play the situation couth or uncouth. These attributes made him an obvious selection for my new investigative team. I first met Tuck when he joined a team that I headed. A nationally known aquatic biologist before retirement, he now works in a gun shop in Smyrna to fend off the retirement blues. For all that Jim is the mild mannered man, Tuck is bluff and blustery. He brooks no oafish remarks in his presence and is quick to slay a loutish remark with well thought prose. Gruff and blunt with others, he takes exception to my mistakes and simply offers satiric, slightly comedic, comments.

Rounding out the trio is Jerry Esposito, an Italian who would have been called the runt of the litter twenty years ago. Not that he's short. Let's just say, even a white man could jump over Jerry. He is a slightly pudgy, mustachioed mechanical engineer. In retirement, he pursues his lifelong musical passion by building custom banjoes. He wouldn't get the information by blowing someone away, but he'd get it nonetheless, with subtlety, style, a joke, and a ready smile. Jerry's nickname has been Louie since 1978, the year Danny DeVito created the dispatcher from Hell, Louis DePalma, in the hit TV series, *Taxi*.

℞

Based on the verbal and written feedback of the team, nestled secretly among the staff were a gambler, a doper, a male homosexual, and a disgruntled employee who had been passed over for promotion.

Interesting how many of the small staff had a weakness that could be exploited by either an outsider, or a good reason to cause embarrassment to the presiding curator.

I smiled as I recalled Jerry's story about how he had first picked up the scent on the gambler. I could literally picture the scene in my mind, a small vignette, a Technicolor short starring the engaging, disarming little fellow at work.

R

He sure wasn't in there very long, Jerry Esposito thought. *I'm glad to drop the tail, get in some place where it's warm to see what he's been up to.*

Espisito pretended to be buying a magazine from a vendor with a kiosk on the pedestrian only mall. A plume of condensed vapor rose from his mouth as he exhaled, watching as Larry Fowler walked down a side street toward his office at Wilmington Trust. A plume of smoke rose from the one legged owner's cigarette. Clad in an army issue fatigue jacket, his unused prosthesis, with a flaming red garter nattily blending with the duck tape bandages that kept the rain out of the hollow leg, was propped in a corner of the kiosk. He peered at the man who was looking, but not buying. He had been there a good ten minutes. Cursing, the owner pulled his sweatshirt hood up in preparation for exiting the kiosk, which was warmed somewhat by a battered, code breaking, propane heater. The Vietnam vet picked up an aluminum Little League bat with his left hand, a scarred wooden crutch with the right. Placing the bat under the hinged part of the peeling, grey, composite counter top, he swiftly raised it as if bringing an ax handle up for another chop. The counter top slammed into the bare, fixed portion of the counter, with a crack like a shot from a .45 magnum.

Somewhat uneasy in his new found profession, Jerry Esposito jumped at the bang, then simultaneously turned and ducked away from the noise. "Are you looking or buying?" cried the kiosk owner as he crabbed his way through the narrow exit, "This ain't the public library, you know."

Esposito nodded and moved quickly away, stopping when he reached the corner around which Fowler had disappeared. He didn't need to look at his watch to know the lunch hour was coming to a close, as heavily clad business types, in topcoats from three hundred dollars and up, scurried past him on their way back to work. The kiosk owner, having made his point, made a hasty retreat to his warm shop. His protagonist remaining in view, he carefully placed the bat in the corner by the artificial leg, then continued to keep an eye on him.

Esposito waited to make sure that Fowler wasn't coming back for a forgotten parcel. The suspect had carried something in, but left the store unencumbered, with his hands in his pockets. Fowler continued to walk into the chilly wind that swept up the hill from Brandywine Creek, driving a few orphaned, McDonald's bags before it, the ubiquitous leaves of the inner city. Esposito shrugged, then made his way toward Men's Classics, the haberdashery recently exited by Mr. Fowler.

It was a small shop, tony enough to be a shoppe, judging by the prices of the jackets, trousers and other male apparel. Real Harris tweed. Esposito had never seen anything quite like it. The shop keeper was a neatly coifed, sharply dressed, large busted woman in her late forties. She wore a white silk blouse, which accented her well-developed cleavage, over a flared, black flannel skirt. Flanking her, behind what appeared to have been a teller's cage at one time, was a twentyish lovely, obviously cast from the same mold. Just as the older woman cleared the counter, her breasts jiggling with effort as she bounced toward him on three inch heels, Esposito felt some discomfort inside his trousers. He feigned interest in a $700.00 black leather jacket, cut in the Nazi U-boat fashion, turning his back to her to examine the liner. Sickeningly he felt his condition worsen. Then she was upon him. He sighed softly at the fleeting loss of opportunity to hide his ignoble state as he heard her soft, clear, cultured voice.

"May I be of service, Sir?"

"Not just now, I think, "he replied.

"I don't recall that I've seen you in here before. If you haven't been, you are perhaps unaware of the variety of services we offer. We are not simply a retailer. We...," she paused in mid sentence as she saw the discomfort in the small man's eyes as he turned his torso toward her.

"I'm sorry if I've offended you in some way. Let me take my leave and allow you to continue your solitary browsing," she said gracefully, smiling as she was about to turn away.

What the hell? he thought, *If she's got a sense of humor, this may be the opening I need.*

He touched her arm softly, "No, it's not you. It's me. Allow me to explain," he smiled as he looked directly in her eyes. "When I got up this morning, I made a conscious decision to dress smartly. I knew I was coming here to shop, so I didn't want to look too much out of place my first time here."

"Well, you certainly look very charming. I compliment you on your sartorial tastes. The red tie goes very nicely with your charcoal grey suit."

"That's not the problem either. You see, this is the best suit I have. It's the one I wore before my retirement, when calling upon my best clients. So I knew it was in good taste. The problem is with the suspenders."

Taken aback, the woman gestured toward his open overcoat, and said, "May I."

"Of course," he responded softly.

Having done the same thing thousands of times before, she deftly opened his suit jacket to observe the braces. She was surprised to see that they were properly attached to the trousers with leather straps and buttons, not the rude, brass clips of the K Mart shopper.

As she buttoned him back up, she congratulated him on an excellent choice, noting as well that he was not a belt and suspenders man.

He brightened, saying as he smiled a smile that was sincerity itself, "The color of my suspenders is not the problem, as you clearly observed. You seem like a woman of maturity that greatly exceeds your relatively brief time on this earth. Perhaps I can share the source of my discomfort with you."

The shop keeper smiled so broadly it stressed her troweled on foundation. "Please, my name is Margaret," she said softly, completely enamored of this mannerly gentleman, whose distress greatly concerned her, "come back to the corner of the shop. We'll have some tea, and you can tell me what is troubling you."

As she turned, Esposito smiled, "Margaret, wait. Please call me Walter, but don't make me walk over to the corner of the shop."

Margaret spun round with a start, "Why, my dear man, er... Walter, why on earth not? Are you ill.?" she said, with eyebrows arched in a combination of astonishment and sympathy.

Wanting her at close quarters when he revealed his secret, Espisito leaned slightly toward her, whispering, "Come closer," as he pantomimed what he said with a similar gesture.

His tactic had the desired effect, as she first leaned toward him, then took two strides till she was almost in his face as he continued to whisper, "You see, Margaret, I am somewhat like a woman in my vanity about my appearance. When it comes to spending money on clothes, almost all of my resources go to the spectacle of the outer man. A pittance of my wardrobe budget is left for undergarments and other accessories. When I'm out consulting in my $2,000 suit, there will probably be holes in the socks that are inside my Gucci loafers."He smiled conspiratorially as his eyes beseeched the question that had to follow.

Curious, Margaret bought into the false aura of secrecy, whispering back, "But, Walter what do holes in your socks have to do with your current state of immobility?"

"Well, you see madam, my undershorts suffer even more greatly than do my socks. Some of my boxers have been laundered so many times, they are translucent." Pausing for effect, he then muttered, "The strength of the elasticity in some has withered away to the point where they need assistance from a belt to keep them in place. Alas, this morning, I overslept. In my haste to get ready, I made a poor choice." Esposito lowered his eyes, then his face, looking as forlorn as a kindergartner caught short of time in a race to the little boys' room.

The shop keeper began to tremble. She leaned on Walter for support. Tears began to well in her eyes, then slowly slid down each cheek, when the capacity to retain them was spent. She spurted, in sobs, "Walter, you don't mean...?"

Knowing at this rate she would never get it out, Esposito looked up, beaming with an off center smile. "That's right, Margaret, you've got the picture," he said. "If I take one step toward that corner without making some unseemly internal adjustments, my shorts are going to drop down each of my trouser legs. When they do, I'll be forced to waddle over there like a duck."

The stately shop keeper completely lost control, collapsing to the floor in laughter that sounded like the braying of an ass, her bountiful black skirt becoming a puddle that surrounded her. That's when Esposito knew he had her.

And he did.

CHAPTER 29   MAY 1997

RUE

ATLANTIC CITY, NEW JERSEY

Larry Fowler knew the Atlantic City Expressway would get him there quicker, but he liked the pace, the rural scenery, and the quaintness of the little towns that stretched out along Route 40. It was only an hour and a half's drive anyway. Why not make it pleasurable? The little red Conquest swept along through Sharptown, Woodstown, Pole Tavern, and then Malaga, town's that modern transportation was driving out of the evolutionary gene pool. He would bet that Buena, Mizpah, and Mays Landing would fare no better. Buena, population 4,441, looked like it might be surviving because it was close to Vineland, and jobs. That was the good news.

The same proximity brought competition for local stores from the major chains. As a result, Buena's main street evolution showed a clear trend to professional office buildings. As he drove on through, Fowler wondered about the few retail survivors. The Dollar Store, with its ugly yellow sign with black, block lettering, was on the corner, its flyers taped to the widow, describing all the bargains inside the store. This was a chain store, admittedly, but downtown was a good location in small towns throughout the northeast and mid-Atlantic states. Downtown was close to their customer base, the poor, retired and hard luck folks in town. Buena Hardware was on the right-hand side, a little further down the street. The local owner began opening on Sunday about a year back, scrabbling to stay alive by providing more service and longer hours. There were two bars, and then a newsstand that sold a little bit of everything. Fowler stopped there from time to time, more often when he used to smoke, when he would make sure he had three packs of Winstons for the weekend and the first day back at work. Those packs were his insurance, in case he lost all his money gambling. The store also sold paperback books from a rack, magazines, candy, greeting cards, hot dogs, soup, ice cream, popcorn, coffee, and almost anything else one could buy for under ten dollars, consume or use once and then throw it away, except for condoms. That was it for the retail crowd, unless you counted the delicatessen, pizza shop, Chinese restaurant, and the place that offered mom's good eats. Lawyers, accountants, insurance agents, and money lenders had moved into the rest of the shops after the clothes store, sporting goods, drugstore, and jewelry store had succumbed to competition from the Vineland malls. Fowler couldn't understand how small town people allowed a part of the fabric of the community to unravel just so they could save $1.99 by buying a shirt at Walmart's. You could bet that Walmart wouldn't let you have the shirt if you left your wallet at home, as Sam Miller, proprietor of the defunct Miller's Fashions was want to do.

By the time he made the right hand turn onto Route 322 at McKee City, the land was flat, the shrubs reminiscent of the coastal plain. Route 322 became Verone Avenue. The casinos were now visible on the horizon, off to his left. He turned, and drove in that direction, driving until he reached the Bally Grand above ground parking. He parked the Conquest and pulled out the leather briefcase he used as an overnight bag. It was an old-fashioned bellows type, a Double Happiness model, made in Shanghai before World War II, picked up for $5.00 at a flea market. It had probably sold for $100 when new back in the thirties. The leather looked brand new. The brass lock face was worn where the catch action had grooved it over the years.

Fowler walked to the elevator whose open doors beckoned him to come join the fun. He smiled at the good omen, entered, and selected the correct floor without looking at the keypad. On exiting, he went immediately to get another comp card before checking in.

Fowler inserted the keyless entry card, opened the door, and turned on the entry light. Closing the door behind him, he placed the briefcase on the dresser, popped the catch, withdrew a pair of olive hued socks, and placed them in the jaws of the open briefcase. He did this as a precaution against some hopped up hotel thief cutting into the leather looking for valuables. He left it on the dresser, opened the door and left, leaving the light on to welcome him upon his solitary return. In all the years he had been coming here, he had never brought a woman back to his room. Gambling was a serious avocation. It required that he remained focussed for his entire stay. There was no room for sexual diversions. Until he met Melanie, winning at craps or roulette had given him an even greater high than the best sex he had ever enjoyed.

Fowler felt the surge in his nervous system, the signal that his brain wanted a nicotine hit. The last stand in his fight to quit smoking cigarettes had been right here on the gambling casino floor. The brain signaled his heart, which in turn increased his blood pressure, setting his finger tips tingling, just as if he had taken a drag from a Winston.

His bet on red was $500, the maximum allowed at this table. He was using the Martingale system, doubling his wager on red each time the ball fell in the black. He figured that eventually, red would come up, and he'd be ahead of the game. Now with the table limit at $500, he was unable to double his previous bet. Even if he won now, he'd be out of pocket twelve bucks. That didn't worry Fowler. He knew he could make it up. Had to, for that matter. He had maxed his credit cards again to build his stake to the $12,000 he had brought with him. If the ball dropped in the red for the tenth time in a row, he'd be out $1,011, almost 10 percent of his stake. And he hadn't been on the floor an hour yet.

As the croupier spun the wheel, Fowler said a silent prayer, beseeching the gods of gambling to let the ball fall to zero or double zero, if not to the red. That way he'd get to keep half his bet. He liked the way this improved the odds on his winning, whereas in effect it really only reduced the house edge on even money bets. However, it beat the way the game was played in Las Vegas, where they took it all. The house edge on even money bets in Vegas is 5.26 percent, in Atlantic City, 2.63, and in Europe a low 1.35 percent. The European gambit when the zero comes up (they have no double zero) is to take your bet prisoner. If you bet red, let's say, and the next spin of the wheel yields a red, you are free to bet your entire wager on the next spin of the wheel. On the other hand, if the outcome is black, your wager is forfeited. Regardless of where you played the game, they get your money. In Europe, it just takes the house a little longer.

Fowler closed his eyes and waited for the croupier to announce his fate. It was red. An elated Fowler took this as an omen of good fortune. This was going to be his weekend. He started the Martingale all over again. A single white chip was placed on the red half of the diamond at center table. He was into the game. The betting sequence would be $1, $2, $4, $8, $16, $32, $64, $128, and so on through the night and into the morning hours.

Fowler had started playing roulette at 7:00 p.m. on Friday. When he next checked his watch, it was 4:00 a.m. the next morning. He looked at his chips, estimated his winnings at about $40,000. It was time to call it a day. He was drenched in sweat. His lungs ached from the second hand smoke he had been breathing for the last nine hours. He was tired. The sustained highs he got from his winning streak had now taken their toll on his nervous system. Handing a stack of ten $100 chips to the croupier, he asked to be cashed in, assigning the money to his room account. Turning from the table, he shuffled bleary eyed down the aisle, passing the craps table, sparsely attended at this late hour. Black jack was down to one table of five players, with a cute, slender aerobicized dealer, blond, emerald green eyes, and tits enough to smother a grown man. He smiled as he passed her. She didn't notice him, or his smile. Her focus was on the game.

Then into the maw of the slots, where he hung a left toward the exit.

As he entered the hotel lobby, he had a sudden urge to go out on the boardwalk, to get some fresh air, to see the sun rise over the Atlantic rim. Then he remembered where he was, thought better of the idea, and turned back to catch the elevator. He pushed the UP button. The elevator door opened immediately. He smiled. Another good omen. This was going to be a killer weekend, he thought, as he entered the elevator, pushing the five button as he turned.

1. Do you lose time from work because of gambling? **Yes**

2. Is gambling making your home life unhappy? **I have none**

3. Is gambling affecting your reputation? **Soon**

4. Have you ever felt remorse after gambling? **Now**

5. Do you ever gamble to get money to pay debts or otherwise solve financial difficulties? **Yes, just did**

6. Does gambling ever cause a decrease in your ambition or efficiency? **Not yet**

7. After losing, do you feel you must return as soon as possible to win back your losses? **Yes, but I have no $**

8. After you win, do you have a strong urge to return to win more? **Always**

9. Do you often gamble until your last dollar is gone? **Yes, just did**

10. Do you ever borrow money to finance gambling? **Just did**

Fowler dropped the pen in despair before completing the Gambler's

Anonymous '20 Questions.' He had picked up the form during those exhilarating days with Melanie, the days when his life was so full that gambling had temporarily lost its appeal. That is why he had not bothered to fill it out. He had simply put it in a drawer in his desk, and promptly forgotten about it. Until now.

The top of the solid cherry desk at which he sat was clear, save for the form and the ceramic tipped pen. The orderly fashion in which he maintained his desk bespoke the very nature of the man. Clothes in his walk in closet were systematically clustered by group. He could enter, select a shirt, then a pair of trousers, a belt, the sport coat to go with them, and thence the tie. Suits, of course, were sorted by color, with braces already attached. Underwear and socks were kept on shelves to the right of the shirts. Halogen lights could be turned on to make sure that the socks matched the colors of the selected outfit. The socks were grouped by color, of course. Shoes, sneakers, and boots were stored in individual, velvet lined drawers that formed the base of the backless settee in the center of the closet. That is where he usually sat while putting on his socks and shoes.

The desk sat in the center of the living room of his one bedroom condominium. Larry Fowler watched television from the desk chair while he sat working. He had a burgundy hued recliner with an adjacent brass floor lamp. That was his reading chair. At night, he would read by the light cast by the lamp that set the warm colors of the oriental rug glowing. The eight by ten rug was garnet colored, with scroll work and flowers sculpted into its surface in contrasting rose, mauve, red-browns and wheat yellow. The rug was by far the most expensive thing in his condominium. It had set him back $5,000 ten years ago, and was the principal reason why he never wore shoes at home until the moment he was set to leave. The only other furniture in the room was a small Sony portable CD/Cassette/Radio. The radio sat on the matching cherry cabinet which housed his television, a 27- inch model which was more than adequately sized for the twenty by 12 foot room. He had bought the cabinet on a whim at The Bombay Company store at the Christiana Mall two years ago. He had been fascinated by the solid cabinet doors. In his opinion, they added a touch of class to his surroundings. He always closed them when leaving, and promptly opened them upon returning.

The Cyclopean eye that peered at him as he opened the doors to reveal the television screen was the only form of welcome he ever received. This morning, as the first rays of the sun began to pour through the living room windows, the doors remained closed.

The condominium had a small utilitarian, but rarely used, kitchen. A table, and two chairs, purchased at a used furniture place during his college days gathered dust in the room. They sufficed to this day, because he rarely ate in and had never entertained company, that is until last year's glorious summer with Melanie Buckley.

The bedroom was the reason Fowler had selected the condominium. It featured a working fireplace, wall length built-in bookshelves, direct access to the bathroom, and a small sitting area, that had a pair of large casement windows. On spring and fall weekends, he relished making a small fire, then opening the windows to let in the chill. A bright red wool blanket lay on the back of a battered Windsor style chair. On those occasions, he would sit with his feet propped on a matching ottoman, snugly wrapped in his blanket, taking in the view. The blanket had been purchased at a Hudson's Bay store somewhere in the Finger Lakes area in Canada. It had been a gift for his father, inherited upon his death. It was one of the few of his father's things that he had kept, the other's being a walnut bookcase and a gold, antique pocket watch. The bookcase, kept in the bathroom for lack of any other space, forced him to take baths rather than showers to protect the wood veneer.

The watch, with its richly scrolled cover, had been manufactured by the American Watch Company in Waltham, Massachusetts in 1898. His father had purchased it not only to subtly display his financial status but also to hand down to his only son. Larry Fowler had been eager to display his unique possession twenty years ago. He bought a hand braided leather fob with a golden ball fastened to the end. It was always there attached to the watch, when he wore the piece with the vests that were in style back then. He had even had small watch pockets sewn into his chino's. The change pocket in blue jeans was a perfect fit for the watch. Its jeweled mechanism kept perfect time. It hung in a bell jar with a mahogany base at night.

The clock on the wall chimed seven times as Fowler walked to the hall closet. From it he extracted a bundle of split wood, shrink wrapped with plastic. The bundle was part of a $30.00 purchase at the local Acme in the winter past. Ritualistically, Fowler stored the wood for his spring and fall interludes. He made up his mind to call in sick by leaving voice mail with Dr. Trader. This problem had to be sorted out immediately. His financial prospects had never been so bleak.

Using kitchen shears, he cut the plastic. Back to the closet, he returned with a starter log, some newspaper, and a propane lighter. Fifteen minutes later, the sick call had been made, the fire was crackling and warm, the windows were thrown open, and he was bundled in the frayed red blanket. He began to make a mental inventory of what he owned that could be pawned, or sold. The list was short, the car, furniture, TV, CD player, the rug. He set priorities, with the first thing on the list being the first he would get rid of. He took a pencil, and a yellow, ruled pad from under the chair and wrote it down, with an estimate of the value of each.

Television & cabinet	**$200**
Desk & chair	**$1500**
Kitchen table & chairs	**$50**
Recliner	**$100**
Bookcase	**$200**
CD player	**$50**
Clock	**$50**
Rug	**$7500 ?**
Watch	**$500**
Car	**$2500**

The brightness of the day filtered indirectly into the room It was accompanied by the chirping of birds and flashes of color from pansies in the neighbor's yard. They combined to exude a charm that kept bubbling through his gloom, not unlike spaghetti sauce simmering on the back of the stove, releasing moisture with each pop as it thickens.

This is a hell of a mess. Here I am, fifty-four years old, and I'm down to my last twelve thousand bucks. If Trader finds out what I've been up to, I'll be out of a job, with no prospects, I might add, Fowler was thinking. *Who do I know that I can borrow from?*

It didn't take long to figure out that there was not a soul. His close family members were all dead. He had no real friends, merely business and social acquaintances. You don't hit people like that up for big money. He thought about a scam, raising money on false pretenses. Nothing, he didn't have the brains to think of one that might work. Sadly, he thought, he didn't have the talent to carry one through either. He lacked both the persuasive skills and the courage to do it.

Fowler sighed, flipped off the blanket, replenished the wood on the fire, then went to the kitchen to start a pot of coffee. Maybe the caffeine would stimulate an idea. While the water dripped through the coffee in the filter, he strolled back through the living room to use the bathroom. After washing and drying his hands, he returned to the kitchen, grabbed a cup from the cupboard, put a minuscule amount of sugar in, then poured, and stirred. He was thinking about what opportunity there might be to steal something as he settled in the chair again. Even though it was early May, the temperature was still in the forties, thanks to a massive blast from Vancouver that had ripped through Atlantic City the night he had won big. The fire felt good, as did the blanket. He had to turn the thermostat down to keep the heater from kicking on.

He rationalized that he was not a common thief, just a gambler in need of a stake. In fact, he was not a thief at all, just an opportunist who had taken advantage of the single break that had ever come his way. As he sipped the coffee, he remembered last summer. He mused about the passionate sex, the laughs, the thrills, the feeling of being more alive than he ever had in his life.

That night, after they had dinner at the Charcoal Pit, she begged to skip the movie afterward, she had something better in mind. She had. Riotous sex. Melanie Buckley demolished walls of inhibitions that had taken decades to build. He writhed and grunted in response to a thorough and complete lesson in all conceivable positions. A final exam in giving and taking the pleasures of the flesh was what she had in mind.

When he awoke the next morning, in her bed, he had felt purified. He then had a vague understanding of the physical importance of the Native American sweat lodge ritual. He was as calm as a baby, as refreshed as he ever remembered feeling in his adult life. The shower had been running but it hadn't registered on him until the bathroom door opened, and she stepped out of a puff of steam, clad in a large navy blue towel. Her hair was wrapped in another towel of the same color. She had told him the shower was left on for him. Pointing her finger at the bathroom door, she then admonished him to give warning when he was ready to come out. She didn't want him to see her unless she was fully dressed. This had seemed utterly at odds with her behavior the previous night, but a man in lust gracefully ignores such dichotomies. And he had been in such a way for the first time in his life.

In retrospect, their brief affair had been in four parts, just like life. Childhood was for learning, wondering, trying to learn how to relate to other beings. That had been the first thirty days after he had met her at Jake's Gym. The teenage years through young adulthood had begun on that night of sexual indulgence, lasting just four weeks. The gambling fever had subsided then, purged from his system by the giddy days, and sweaty nights. They had made love at least twice a night, every night until she revealed the underlying purpose behind their relationship. She was trying to get pregnant. Indeed, she had hired a private detective to help her find a man who fit her specifications, intelligent, handsome, well built and unmarried. Fowler fit the bill.

She, on the other hand, was married to the oldest son of a wealthy, Italian grain dealer. The inherited machismo of her husband demanded that she produce a male heir. Indeed, it was part of their marriage contract. If she had been unable to give birth to a son within three years of their wedding vows, a divorce was inevitable. The annual post marriage income would be a paltry $250,000. She had sobbed, when she told him this.

He didn't believe a word of it. But the sex continued unabated, so he had acted as if he did. When she failed her pregnancy test the

195

following month, she fell in to despair, saying she might kill herself if she could not become pregnant. And the sex continued, unabated. He attempted to counsel her, suggesting a test tube baby, or perhaps artificial insemination. She appeared to think this over for several days, then again became despondent, saying she lacked a donor. He offered a specimen of his own, but she turned it down. Faulty goods, she had said. However, the sex continued, unabated. She was adamant about two things. It must be a donor who would not know her identity, and he must meet the criteria by which he had been selected.

When his addiction for recreational sex had supplanted his need to gamble, Fowler became aware of the precarious state of his financial affairs. He was nearly $100,000 in the hole, most of that being high interest credit card debt, with no significant assets to his name. Reacting to the sorry state of his financial affairs, he had concocted a scheme that could lead to a conclusion of their affair to their mutual satisfaction. He offered the sperm of someone who met her qualifications. The donor was intelligent in an artistic sense and handsome without question. His muscular, athletic physique when he was young could have laid the foundation for a great appearance even in old age, and he was definitely unmarried, since he was dead. All of this for a price. He had to explain how he had access to the material, the personal risks involved, his tenure and reputation, everything, including the price for his involvement. Then he told her the depositor's name. That clinched it.

She shook hands on the deal. The sex turbo charged to hyper speed. All was right with the world. Except he had to remember which vial contained the sperm in question.

CHAPTER 30   JUNE 1997

THREW

BEVERLY HILLS, CALIFORNIA

"Pester, you did such a great job for me on that little assignment last year, I'd like to retain your services again," said Roxanne, raising her hand politely, anticipating Pester. "I remember your requirements from the last time. The job has to interest you first. If it does, the pay has to be worth your while."

Pester smiled, leaning forward slightly from her sitting position on the blood red couch. She rested her jaw in the palm of her hand, patiently waiting for Roxanne to continue.

"For personal reasons, I've decided to get rid of Ken."

She began waving her hand wildly, "Hold on, I know you don't do divorces, and I surely ain't talking murder here. My problem is the last one, Tom, cost me $16,000,000. I've got a better lawyer this time, so I think I'll do better from that standpoint. The last one, it just wasn't working, but it wasn't because he didn't try. I'm the one who pretty well screwed it up."

Roxanne paused, then continued, "I sent out for pizza, and there's some Killians in the fridge. Pizza 'll be here in about twenty minutes. Want a beer now?"

"Sure," Pester responded. She watched as Roxanne exited the room, noting that she was holding her weight quite well, for a pregnant woman in her early forties.

Roxanne returned with an open bottle of Killian's Red, which she handed to her guest, and a can of Dr. Pepper, which opened with a fizz as she popped the tab while siting back in the recliner. She took a sip of the soda, then put it on the oak table next to the chair.

"Where was I? Oh yeah. Ken, on the other hand, hasn't been right almost from the get-go. It finally dawned on me that he married me for my money. There's no love, no sex, not even companionship. There aren't even any fond memories. I got a lump where my heart's supposed to be."

Impatiently, Pester rasped, "So what did you want done?"

"I'm getting to that. I'm also getting hungry," Roxanne said, glancing at her watch. "I hope that pizza man is on time. I've instructed my lawyer to give Ken as many of his toys as he wants as part of the settlement. My motto is, *toys in lieu of cash*."

"What are we talking about in the way of playthings? Big stuff. Jewels, women, what?" Pester asked.

"Big ticket items that he bought with my money. Things that he, and his drinking buddies, occupy their time with, things that keep him with them, instead of me."

"Such as?" Pester croaked, then took a sip of beer as she awaited the response.

"Well, the jerk bought a Humvee. Then he had it customized with two TVs, and a stereo. Set me back 125 thou. Didn't have any place to play with it. You know, rugged terrain where they could shoot off their guns as they drank beer, and tried to climb a mountain with it. So he bought us a ranch, fronts right on Lake Kaweah. Nice cabin, too. Sleeps eight in individual bedrooms, gathering room with a walk in fireplace, in case they want to roast a whole deer that they shot. Two big screen TVs, fridge by each, always stocked. Real macho stuff. Ruffin' it. No sense having waterfront property unless you have a big boat for water skiing and putzing around. Cost me another $100,000. A customized Blazer, an RV so they can have their cold ones right in the fridge on the way up there, don't have to stop to take a leak, it all adds up."

The door bell rang. Roxanne got up, made her way through the house, grabbed a twenty from her purse, told the pizza boy to keep the change, and brought the box back to her perch. She had a little table set up by Pester for her convenience. She placed the box on the table, opened the lid, and handed Esther a porcelain dinner plate.

"Help yourself. It's got everything on it, just like you like, whatever," said Roxanne, annoyed at how dumb the double like sounded.

They ate and drank, in relative silence. Pester ate four slices to Roxanne's two.

"If you're done, put the top back on, and please take it with you. At my age, if you eat for two, after the baby's born, there'll be three. The baby, and two of me." Roxanne commented. "Back to business. It won't hit Ken that he's got more toys than money until after the settlement. He'll just be focussing on keeping all those things that he and the gang have been having such a good time with. You know, so the partying can keep going right on."

She paused, drained the Dr. Pepper, crushed the aluminum can in her hand, and tossed it on her empty plate. Turning back to Pester with a gleam in her eye, and a smirk on her face, she went on.

"The first thing the cheap son of a bitch is going to do when he realizes that he's got to buy the beer and groceries, gas for the boat and the vehicles, and pay all the regular bills, he's going to look for ways to chintz. And I know what his first cost cutting measure is going to be."

"Go ahead," Pester said, "are we getting close to the point?"

"Yeah, yeah, yeah," responded Roxanne with a smile, waving her hands to silence Pester, "it took me a hell of a long time to think this through. Give a lady her due. Let me lay it all out."

"All right," Pester consented, looking at her watch. "I'll give you the rest of the afternoon. But this better be good."

"Dearie, the money's right, and I'm sure you'll like the job. Like your last caper, I know what I want done. I need you to figure out how to do it," Roxane leered, taking Pester's hands in hers in a show of comradery. "Now Ken's just like a lady going to a grand affair, or to church on Sunday for that matter. She wants to show herself off. If she's a little short on cash, underneath that beautiful gown or dress will be torn underwear and a ripped bra. She's all show, and so is Ken. So I figure he's going to dump any insurance he absolutely doesn't have to have. Then he'll max the deductible on things like the Blazer, where he has to have the insurance. After he's standing out there bare nekked, I want you to destroy it all."

♀

Pester was frowning as she drove north on Interstate 5. She planned to open up checking accounts using false business names at a string of Wells Fargo banks. Starting in Modesto, she then would head west to Livermore, Fremont, San Jose and then to each of the towns in the string that grew together along the western shore of San Francisco Bay; Sunny Vale, Mountain View, Palo Alto, Redwood City and so on right up to San Francisco where, on the seventh day she would rest.

She wished that Roxanne hadn't presumed that she was going to take the job. Having all that money deposited in Wilma's name at the

200

Walnut Creek branch, after she gave them that story about moving back east, was not a good thing. Now she had to piss away a week riding up and down the state, spreading it around. Then she'd have to consolidate it all over again. At least she could do that electronically.

She smiled at the thought of consolidation. A $150,000 fee, and a $350,000 budget to get the job done. This was by far her biggest assignment ever. Then there was the incentive program, another $150,000 if he lost the ranch, and $250,000 on top of that if she could figure out a way for Ken to be thrown in the pokey. $550,000 tax-free dollars in all, if she could pull it off. Three years of easy living if she took on no more assignments. Her retirement package, if she invested it wisely, which she could do with the several aliases she had developed over the years. But first the drudgery of getting the money moved. Then she was going to fly to Honolulu, rent a car, and go to her tiny, inland house in Pomoho, where she could plan her attack in peace and isolation. The divorce was some time off, but the stakes were high.

CHAPTER 31   AUGUST 1960

UNDERGROUND

ONANCOCK, VIRGINIA

Clearance could feel the sweat dribbling down his spine, disappearing between his cheeks, then sliding down the inside of his legs, and into his socks. His new white shirt was soaked through. The cotton fibers had absorbed all the moisture they could. Now it was up to his socks. He began to raise his arm to wipe the moisture from his forehead. His mother smacked it back down.

"Don' you be showin' no disrespec' fo' yo' Grandpa, youngun," his mother whispered.

"But Ma, I'm...."

"Hush, now. The service is almost over, then we'll be goin' back to Grandma's for some refreshments. Get out a' this here sun," she continued, bending over so as not to be heard by the group of friends and family gathered for the services and interment of the recently departed.

The cemetery sat forlornly near Mount Nebob, Virginia, about three miles southwest of Onancock, down a dusty, dirt road. At ten feet above sea level, it caught the westerly winds off the Chesapeake Bay. It was the highest ground between the adjacent Pungoteauge Creek, and Onancock Creek to the north. The mosquitoes rising out of the nearby marshes were feasting on the blood of a gathering that was predominantly black. Clearance looked over the fat preacher's head at the seagulls, gliding in the blue sky, seeking an opportunity for lunch. His stomach began growling. His mother gave him a look, but he wisely kept his gaze straight ahead.

"Ashes to ashes, dust to dust...," the Preacher droned on, finally concluding with a communal recital of the Lord's prayer.

Edward, who had remained silent, and rigid, throughout the ceremony, touched his mother's arm and said, "Mama, can we go now?"

"In a moment, Edward. It ain't seemly to rush away. I want to go give Mama a hug, an' tell her we'll see her back to the house."

Edward whined in response, "But Mama, Grandma knows we're going back to the house."

"Hush, boy. You ain't old enough to understan' about showin' respect through your manners, I guess," said the boy's father sternly. "We be there in jes a few minutes, thanks to your brother Charles' automobile. Couple minutes more here ain't goin' to do you and your brothers an' sister any harm."

✠

As soon as they had reached their Grandmother's home, Mrs. Giddens was out of the car like a flash. She dashed into the house, flinging the screen door as she went in, banging it loudly as she came out with a stack of frayed white towels.

"Charles, you come over here and work the pump for me," she said to her oldest as she strode toward the old pitcher top pump by the shed where her parents used to raise their hogs. "You younguns line up behind your Daddy. We're goin' to be cool in a minute."

Charles had blessedly cool, splashes of ground water gushing from the pump in short order. "Davis, you first, get your head under there, then we'll give you a towel to dry off."

By the time they were through cooling down, Grandma's car came slowly up the lane, driven by Uncle Robert, Davis Gidden's brother. Davis rushed over to open the door for her, when the old Chevrolet came to a halt. She needed some assistance getting out of the car as well. Arthritis had stiffened her joints, bent her spine forward, a combination that made ordinary walking both painful and difficult. Even so, their remained obvious traces of her once beautiful features. The high cheekbones and delicate features of her face had not been erased with time. She was a tall woman, even bent over with age and arthritis. Her breeding ran true for these same features could be seen in her daughters, and their children. She always told Clearance, her favorite, that he was so tall and good looking, she was going to have to buy him a broom to keep all the girls away. But not today, for today was a day when family and friends gathered in her tiny house, and spilled over in the yard, to mourn her husband's passing, and to rejoice his entrance into the kingdom of the Lord.

Even with his family, Clearance sometimes reverted to shyness and reticence. He sat alone in the shade under the big willow tree that his grandfather had planted as a switch in the spring of 1925. A plate of chicken bones, and a smear of mayonnaise were all that were left of his lunch. He half dozed in the shimmering heat, feeling calm and secure in the presence of the human voices that washed around him. Then he felt a tap on his shoulder, like a biddy checking for some scratch. He opened his eyes.

"Oh, it's you Mama. I thought it was a baby chick had lighted on my shoulder," he said as he smiled up at her.

"What you doin' out here all alone, chile?", she asked, already knowing the answer.

Clearance hung his head, "You know me, Mama."

She smiled, kneeling down beside her handsome son, "That I do. That I do. Could you stand some company, or are you off a dreamin'?"

"Please, Mama, do stay. Seein' the family together, and all the other folks has got me to thinking."

"What about?"

"Grandpa's family. Didn't he have any?" Clearance asked.

"He and Mama swear he had a brother who got killed in the last war. But I've never seen him, nor a picture of him for that matter."

"Didn't this brother have no wife or children, Mama?"

"I truly couldn' say, boy. Doesn't matter, though. If they amounted to anythin', they'd been here to pay their respects. They didn't, so they is trash, if there is any of them," she responded.

"But Mama, maybe they're like us, they just don't know."

His mother smiled at him before answering, "Clearance, you may be right. I never thought of it in that way." She bent over and kissed him on his forehead. "You are the thinker in this family, all right. You be stayin' in that school. You'll make us proud, you'll see."

"Oh, hush Mama, you're making me blush."

"Son," she repeated somberly. "I mean what I say. You are the smartest of all my boys when it comes to books. And now that pretty little Stackhouse girl has got you finally learnin' how to play that guitar. Must be some powerful potion she's usin' to get you to strum your fingers raw."

Clearance stood up, then bent over to kiss his mother. "I've got to leave this space, you are embarrassing me to tears," he said. Then he lithely walked into the house to kiss his grandmother goodbye. It was time he walked on back home. He had enough socializing to keep him for a week.

CHAPTER 32   **JUNE 1997**

FOUND

WILMINGTON, DELAWARE

While my set of snoops were busy finding rips in the fabric of individual lives, yours truly was engrossed in other aspects of the case. The lists of questions I had developed when I began this assignment went far beyond the motivational ones. For instance, I had an entire set of questions that related to the sperm bank structure and operations. I developed answers to the ones dealing with the physical facilities while touring with Dr. Trader, under the guise of being a potential depositor. I wonder if Adolf Hitler would have used the service had it been available while he still was alive? Scarey thinking there. Really could have been a bunch of Hitler look alikes stomping around. *The Boys from Brazil* come true. Thank goodness there was no cloning science back then.

Since the sperm bank was a bank, located in a bank, my biggest question was why security hadn't been patterned after a traditional bank's safety deposit system. Seems to me, the two key system would have prevented the pilferage. After all, one key would have been in the depositor's care. Despite the many Elvis sightings over the years, it is unlikely that the King's ghost would show up to make a withdrawal. Absent that, one of the staff would either have to know the locksmith trade, or be able to sneak one in. Not likely on both counts.

But once I had seen the facility, it became clear to me that the two key system was physically impossible. All of the stainless steel vials were suspended in a large vat of liquid nitrogen. This place may have been built thirty years ago, but that part of the technology hasn't changed a lot. Trader said he had considered a dual entry system, but had dismissed it due to the costs of materials that can withstand a temperature of -196 C. In the alternative, he had dealt ingeniously with the security aspects of the project.

℞

The vault was an immense stainless steel tank filled with liquid nitrogen that allowed for cryo- preservation of more than 10,000 specimens. I was dressed in bright red coveralls. My garb sent a clear signal to all bank employees that I was permitted in this area only if accompanied by either Dr. Trader, or a Dr. Fowler, the assistant Curator. Fowler's name had a whiff of familiarity, but I couldn't track the scent. Everyone else who had access to the sperm bank vault wore white.

As we walked, Dr. Trader described the secrecy that surrounded the construction and installation of the tank. Using the DuPont family influence, Air Products thought the DuPont Company was the tank purchaser. Indeed, the tank was shipped to a pigment manufacturing facility in Newport, Delaware, only to be diverted by a purchasing agent upon arrival. DuPont Environmental Services, a company construction department, installed the unit and its accessories at the bank.

Trader paused, interrupting our tour, to make several points, "Now you see, my security system relies on four different but, to some extent, interrelated features. First, by choice, only highly paid professionals on staff have access to the vault. I have been very careful in my hiring practices. A private security firm has done a security check on each candidate before a position was offered."

"That's a good starting point, with a Super Bowl record up until last year," I commented

"Secondly, there is the matter of the uniforms. In the early days, this was a very effective way of spotting someone who was where he, or she, shouldn't be. I had a security guard posted three shifts, seven days a week."
"You said the early days, what..."

Trader anticipated the question, "I've replaced the guards with a computer that inspects the garment color. Supposed to sound an alarm, if anything other than white tries to open the door to the vault room."

"Obviously it didn't," I said, saying the obvious.

"That is puzzling to me, and somewhat disheartening as it points toward a theft by someone I trust," the doctor said softly, obviously saddened by the recurring thought.

He went on, in a stronger voice, displaying the spirit and pride shared by those of his generation. They fought, and won World War II with that same set of values. I've admired them since I was a kid, watching the patriotic newsreel records of the action taking place in Iwo Jima, Sicily and Normandy.

"At your feet, is one of four enclosed transducers which serve as weight cells for the vault. They can measure the weight of the tank, and its contents, within 0.3 ounces. This third measure prevents someone from removing a vial without first having shut off the alarm."

"Doctor, what happens if someone figured a way out to either fool or bypass the system, make the switch, and then turn it back on?"

"The replacement would have to be the same weight, within the tolerance I just told you," Trader answered, "Or the alarm would sound."

"Wait, I don't understand. There must be some way to adjust the weight the transducer is being checked against. Otherwise, you couldn't have any new depositors after the day the bank first opened." I said.

"Just so. I neglected to tell you that we weigh any deposit or withdrawal, and then readjust it accordingly," he added. Then he turned without further comment, and walked toward the exit from the vault room. It was clear the tour was over.

℞

We got out of our coveralls, walked briskly back to his office, and were settled, quite comfortable and warm. Trader was standing with his back turned, saying something unintelligible to me as his high-pitched voice was in the range where I have nerve damage. Too many years working around heavy machinery and equipment before auditory protection was made mandatory. I can make out the vowels, but am a hearing dyslexic with the consonants. Bought could just as well be cop or cot or caught. You get my meaning. It makes for some interesting conversations with those near and dear, unless I can see their lips. I am a pretty fair lip reader.

As the old man droned on, I considered what a comfortable office he had. With its dark cherry furniture, hunters' green plush rug, real cherry paneling up to the chair rail, then wallpaper upon which the fox was dashing for cover as the hounds bore down with hunters in pursuit. His chateau country clientele must have loved it. Made me want to dress in a three-piece suit with a gold pocket watch and chain.

When he turned with glass in hand, I knew what he had been asking all along. I accepted the brandy with a smile, knowing that to not have done so would have been seen as rude. Rude I did not want to be to this fine old gentleman.

I allowed him a sip, then interrupted, "Before you tell me the fourth protection system, let me ask a few questions about your vault operations. How many people have access to the vault room?"

"Ten, for a variety of services including the annual inventory which is very labor intensive." he responded.

"And they are all professionals?"

"Yes."

"Your professional staff maintains the vault, and all its associated paraphernalia?" I asked, a bit unsure at what I was hearing.

"Absolutely," he responded proudly, "and are paid handsomely to do so."

"Even the janitorial work?"

"Quite so." He positively beamed.

I made notes in my stenographer's pad. The use of a steno pad was a habit picked up from my firm where every meeting note and every telephone conversation was recorded in one of these handy, quite portable pads. We never lost any notes. Because each conversation had an associated time and date, these logs ended up as trustworthy evidence in many disputes. Kind of like the Nixon tapes, in a way. I had completed 82 telephone logs by the time I retired.

"OK. That gets us down to the playoffs. Let's see if we can get on to the conference contenders. How many people have keys and access to the terminal where you change the monitoring range of the weight cells?" I probed, willing the answer to be one that reduced the number of potential suspects.

I was amused by his response. The pupils in his eyes took on the manic glow of the predator, he drained his shot glass down an upturned neck, with an Adam's apple the size of a golf ball, then slammed it down on the desk. "John," he exclaimed, "I believe we may be closer to the Super Bowl."

And we were.

CHAPTER 33   JUNE 15, 1997

TERRIFY

WILMINGTON, DELAWARE

The atmosphere in the dining room reminded Larry Fowler of the Rodney, Dr. Trader's club in Wilmington, complete with two billiardtables in the adjoining room. Dark, walnut panels were broken every eight feet or so by lancet windows, whose narrowness gave a sense of privacy to diners within. The hardwood floor planks, varying in width from four to ten inches, were pine with a polyurethane finish. The sun reflecting off the floor and onto the wall paneling was the only light in the room, save from the two candles which provided intimacy to each table. Fowler sipped his pint of Ore House Amber, one of six splendid beverages served up from the on-site micro brewery. He was dining alone tonight, as he had most nights since Melanie Buckley, or whoever she was, had disappeared. The chicken gumbo appetizer had been most satisfying. He was now waiting for his entree, grilled pork chops, marinated in jerk seasoning, and served with a salsa of fresh pineapple and red bell peppers. Despite himself, the glow of the room, the taste of the ale, and the low murmur of the thirtyish crowd, buoyed his spirits.

Since he was as nervous as the owner of a 10-year-old claimer chasing a $1,000 purse, Fowler decided a good meal at the Iron Hill Brewery would serve him well. Just like the horse, tomorrow might find him meeting his maker, not at the slaughter house, but at some equally unpleasant alternative. He hadn't looked forward to driving down the Kirkwood Highway to get here, but here he was. When his meal arrived, he ordered another pint of ale, and decided to ponder his fate after dining.

Fowler chose a Gran Marnier to round out his evening, even though he knew coffee would have been the safer choice. He had achieved a level of calm approaching Nirvana this evening, and he was loathe to dispel it. Contrary to the reasonable man's belief, a good night's sleep was not going to make the world look bright and shiny to him in the morning. Therefore, he vowed to have one more evening of quiet serenity before he took on the devils that had been tormenting him. As it always had, the first sip of his drink sent a shot to his kidneys as if he had been rabbit punched in the ring. That's why Gran Mariner was a good closer on a night when he didn't want a hangover in the morning. One shot of this liqueur was all his body was able to stand. It was tasty, but it made his kidneys throb like a toothache. He sipped the last few drops, rolled them around on his tongue to feel that last tingling sensation, then lowered his glass. The bill and tip previously arranged for, Fowler rose and walked back into the foyer to retrieve his coat. Then he was out the door, walking leisurely to his Conquest. He never spotted the man who had spent the evening slumped in a battered, blue rental van, waiting to tail Doctor Lawrence G. Fowler to his next destination.

The thermostat was purposely set on 65 degrees. The resulting artificial chill in the house required the owner to complement the ordinary bed cover with a somewhat threadbare red wool blanket. It was 9:00 a.m., the Braun coffee maker had just snorted and huffed its way to eight cups of brew, and the apartment's air was pungent with the aroma of Maxwell House's finest. Sunlight filled the bedroom. Fowler opened one eye, then the other. His nose was cold, but his body warm under the blanket.

The feeling of coziness was short lived. As he threw off the bed covers, and swung out of bed, reality hit Larry Fowler like a $10,000 credit card invoice at 16.95% interest. This Saturday was the day he had decided to deal with the two problems that had been giving him sleepless nights for the last two weeks. One was real and had to do with his continuing gambling compulsion. He had maxed out all of seven credit cards again, in a demonic attempt to get back on top without selling all of his possessions. His salary was just enough to pay the minimum payments on his staggering $140,000 debt, buy groceries, pay the utility bills and taxes, and buy gas for the car. By paying out $3500 a month, he figured he could be in the clear in five years.

The shower felt good on his chilled body, but it held no restorative powers for his mind.

I have no choice, he thought, *I've got to give it up. I'll be nearly 60 years old by the time I can afford working out at Jake's again. I feel like a kid who can't control his appetite for chocolate bit cookies, and eats himself sick. And how the hell am I going to pass my credit clearance check this year? If it hadn't been for the money I got from stealing that sperm, Trader would have busted me last year.*

His other problem was perhaps more imagined than real. He knew that the old man had given someone a tour of the place. That had been passed on by Marilyn Rossi, the Sunday skeleton crew shift supervisor. It was not unusual for a potential client who sought relative anonymity to get the tour after hours or on the weekend. Marilyn said he didn't look the type, also that Trader had spent an enormous amount of time with him in the vault.

He had almost forgotten his brief conversation with Margaret when he had gone to retrieve the damaged sport coat he had dropped off for repair last month. Something about a little bald Italian friend of his. At least he had known Fowler's name. Had stopped at the shop because he thought Fowler a snappy dresser, conservatively elegant was her exact recall. Puzzling but not disturbing at the time. But now, with this new event at the office, Fowler had begun to wonder if they were on to him.

He started at the ringing of the telephone. He would have had it taken out of service years ago. What did he need it for? He rarely received any calls, and had an office phone that was perfectly adequate for conducting what little personal business he had. But Trader insisted that all employees have a telephone to insure there was a way to contact them in case of an emergency.

Curious now, he quickly shut off the water, slipped into a terry cloth robe, and strode to his desk.

"Hello, Fowler speaking," he said tersely into the mouthpiece.

A smile cracked the tenseness of his face as he sat, instinctively reaching for a cigarette from the top drawer of the desk, even though he had stopped smoking many years ago. He listened, responding occasionally with a Spartan yes, or no. The call lasted nearly two hours. When it concluded, Fowler gently cradled the phone, then slowly raised his arms to form a V. He was Rocky Balboa, standing triumphantly on the steps of the Philadelphia Art Museum.

"Yes," he shouted in the empty room, "I am going to win. I am going to pay off my gambling debts, and I swear on the grave of my dearly departed mother, that I will never gamble again."

And he didn't. Not with money anyway.

CHAPTER 34   **JULY 1997**

SIGNIFY

LOS ANGELES, CALIFORNIA

When Roxanne finished her appearance on the Larry King show, she had her driver take her directly to the airport. She zoned out until they arrived in Denver. The past several months had been hectic as she continued her public relations campaign while at the same time negotiating the terms of her divorce. That was going in her direction, thank goodness. She couldn't wait until the divorce was final, so she could embarrass Ken publicly by issuing a statement that he was not the father of her child.

During the hour layover, she went to the airport bar for a root beer. With her blond wig and glasses, she was just another middle aged, overweight, nondescript woman, enjoying her draft alone in a dimly lit corner of the room. She was pleased with the way the interview went. King was good at what he did. That was why her agent, Dominic Celio, suggested the show for letting the world know that she was definitely pregnant, not just off her diet. Under his probing, she was able to dismiss the network dropping her show as part of her plan to take some time off to carry the baby to term. Then she wanted to be a full time mom for a while. After that she would come back refreshed, ready to resume her career in new directions. When he asked if she would share with him and his audience, what she had in mind, she had demurred as planned. No amount of skilled questioning had gotten even as much as a hint of her future show business plans. In exasperation, King had invited her back to the show, when she was ready to reveal them. She accepted the invitation, which was exactly how Celio had said it would play out.

"Sly old fox," she thought as she took another swallow of soda. "I sure hope the old fart doesn't die on me until I've seen this thing all the way through."

Mark Downs, her neighbor, met her at the airport. He was standing at the off ramp, knowing it was unlikely she had anything but a carry on bag. Even driving at a sedate 55 miles per hour in his 1984 Chevrolet Cavalier, with its unglued and drooping head liner, she was home within an hour after landing at Des Moines. There was not even enough time to complain that the radio only played one station, with a golden oldies format. The tuning knob was broken.

Downs drove the car down the newly paved macadam lane which Roxanne had installed to keep the dust off her car, and the dirt out of her house. The corn stalks that lined each side of the road were about six feet tall. Given adequate moisture, they would tassel in another few weeks, and then the kernels would begin to grow on the cobs. She absolutely loved the sense of privacy, and security, that this lush vegetation provided. As it came into sight, she viewed the wide front porch with satisfaction, thanked her neighbor for the ride, turned down his offer to carry her one piece of luggage, and walked up the brick steps to the porch. She didn't even bother going in, dropping her bag at the front door, she walked over to the wicker rocker, sat down, propped up her feet, breathed a sigh of contentment and waved to Mark as he drove off.

"I may be a Jew from the home of the Latter-day Saints, but this is where I belong when I need to restore my soul, and my drive," she thought as she heaved herself out of the rocker, and made her way over to the door. The inside of the house offered a cool respite from the humid heat of an Iowa summer. Roxanne dropped her flight bag on the sofa, went into the kitchen, poured and drank a glass of tap water, then went up to bed and slept for 26 hours.

♀

Pester Size was exuberant, as she placed the telephone back on the receiver. She was standing in the lobby of the Sheraton, in Salinas, where she had driven to insure that the call could never be traced back to her. She trusted Wags to do the dirty part of the job, but he was into so many shady activities that she was concerned that his phone might be tapped. Well aware that the Fibbies could also have him under electronic surveillance, and be wiretapping his phone as well, the conversation had been short, and circumspect.

"Deal?" she asked.

"Deal," he had responded.

Click went the phone, all done in less than three seconds. She was now driving south, going home on the coastal highway, Route 1, the scenic route, that would take her forever, but would give her time to relax. Time was what she needed to think through the final plot that would make her enough money to free her from work for quite a few years.

Doctor Lawrence G. Fowler had run true to form. No sooner had he paid off his gambling debts with the bribe she had given him last year, then he was up to his neck in credit card debt again. She had counted on that. He was the perfect foil, to be used over, and over again, with the threat of losing his lucrative job looming over him if she blew the whistle on the Elvis caper. His gambling problem left him forever vulnerable to offers from outsiders.

What a putz when it comes to running his life, Pester thought, *But the guy is a freaking genius when it comes to books, science, government regulations and that kind of thing. Just the man I need to dig up the kind of information I'll need to get this job done.*

Pester picked up the plastic sports bottle, tilted her head, and squirted the spring water into her mouth. As she returned it to the holder, she continued thinking about Fowler's potential on this job, *Larry could take care of the anonymous phone calls, the allegations, with an untraceable, cultured, Sierra Club, environmental alarmist voice. Maybe he should do it from a California club member's home, one who happened to be on vacation at the time. She could see to that. A little breaking and entering was justifiable in her mind, if it was for a worthy cause. Five-hundred and fifty thousand was such a cause.*

Wags, on the other hand, would take care of the dirty tricks. John Andrew Wagenhoffer, Jr., was an ex-cop from back east somewhere, or so he said. His 6'-3", powerful frame had earned him a black belt in Tae Kwan Do when he was in his mid-twenties. He was smart, said to have placed second in his class at the police academy, hard, and loyal to his limited clientele. Pester felt herself fortunate to have used him once early in his career, otherwise he would have been unavailable to her. He was booked, or so he would tell anyone who contacted him who was not on his list.

Wags's stated goal in life was retirement by the age of forty with a ten million-dollar stake. He figured he could get a safe return on his investment of at least 10 percent. That would be enough to carry him. Having quit the force when he was thirty, Wags was now more than half way to his goal, and he was only thirty-four. The fees were getting bigger now that his reputation had been established. Setting aside rape, harming children, and homosexual acts, there were few assignments he would not at least consider to achieve his goal, as long as the fee was large enough. For certain types of projects, Wags had an unwritten code that required him to agree, in principle, on the underlying reason for the job. Terrorism and murder were among them. Pester's job fell into that category. She had convinced him a week ago when they had met at the Musso and Frank Grill on Hollywood Boulevard.

♀

Pester's long, beige wool pants covered the five and a half inch heels she wore to alter her height to that of an average woman. They were cuffed to give them weight enough so as not to flip up with each step. They were literally cleaning the floor as she was led to a booth in the back where there was minimal chance of her being seen in her disguise. She wore a long, baggy white knit jacket that was flecked with golden metallic strands. The jacket cinched her legs just above the knees, about where the bottom of the buttocks would have been for a woman of the height she was pretending to be. Her coat made it virtually impossible for the casual observer to see how disproportionately long her artificially elongated legs were in comparison with her short torso. Mincing steps added to the deception by causing the jacket to sway slightly, back and forth, mimicking the sway of a woman's hips and derriere.

Pester Size wore a black wig with long, straight hair, with two-inch bangs over her forehead, Vietnamese style. Her face was severely made up, altered to make her appear much more oriental than her half-Thai countenance. Hers was a disguise of anonymity. Anyone who did recall her being there, would remember a tall, slender Chinese, or Vietnamese woman. The Kato Kalin look alike sitting at the bar, for instance, assuming he had an operative long term memory function. He had been seated at the bar in a loud, goldenrod yellow sport jacket when she entered the dining area.

The high paneled, private booth she had reserved was empty. She ordered a drink, a Fuzzy Navel, which she would sip delicately, drawing in just enough liquid to coat the tongue, not enough to swallow. Her friends said she drank by osmosis, not by swallowing. By consuming her drink in this fashion, she enjoyed the taste, but not the relaxing, but brain dulling effects of the alcohol.

Her drink arrived, but Wags did not. She checked her Gucci watch. He was uncharacteristically fifteen minutes late. She leaned and peered down the narrow pathway between the booths and the tables. There was no sign of her dinner companion, just that fellow in the loud jacket, sweeping down the aisle as if he were Fabio on a bad hair day. She retreated to the privacy of her booth, looking down to guide her hand to her Fuzzy Navel.

"Sorry I'm late," Wags said, as she looked up to see the flamboyant figure sliding into her booth.

"Now wait a minute, this booth is reserved for me and my date," she said huskily, with a slight bit of menace in her voice.

"I'd like to be your date," the man responded, his voice low, his manner cloying.

She picked up a fork from the table service, and spat back, "If you aren't out of here by the time I finish telling you what I'm going to do, you'll have a fork in your eye to bedazzle the crowd."

"And then who'd ye be hiring to do your grunt work, Pest," he whispered in response, leaning low over the table. "Here, let me get closer so you don't miss." He actually made his right eye glint. His grin was maniacal.

"Hey Wags, it's you. What a rig. Won't be a person in the place that won't remember you."

"Yep," he grinned, then mimicking, "Oh, yeah, the blond fellow, with the big hair. Like Fabio, or Kato Kalin."

It clicked, Pester smiled with understanding, saying "I get it. They'll remember you, but what they remember will be as far from the real you as possible."

As Wags smiled and primped in response to her comment, the waiter arrived. He ordered liver and onions and a glass of Turning Leaf Cabernet Sauvignon. Pester selected the veal scaloppine.

They talked while they ate. Pester explained her client's spin on how to approach the job, by waiting until he dropped the insurance, and then destroying everything.

Wags placed the last morsel of calves' liver on his fork, then paused before popping it into his mouth, "But you've got a better way, I'm here to tell you," he said smiling, then slipping the liver from the fork with his teeth.

"Yes, well there is a bonus clause for us both if we can get him to do some time in the slammer as well as losing his toys," Pester responded.

He perked up, "Bonus you say. How much might that be? I mean, you say the project budget, excluding your fee is $200,000. What's this about a bonus for doing time?"

Lying without hesitation, Pester set $50,000 aside for herself, and answered, "$100,000 to be split anyway I want, cause I'm getting the bonus. She doesn't know about you."

Wags' eyelids narrowed, "That's a delightful topping on the fruit salad. What do you have in mind?"

"Here's the deal. I figure we have two ways to get the target in jail, drugs, or a violation of some environmental statute. From what I've been reading, the sentencing laws aren't much different. It boils down to the cost of the evidence, which comes out of both of our pockets. Check around, see what's available. I'll split 60/40, with you on top, for anything under ten grand, 50/50 for under twenty. Get my drift, I don't intend to be greedy," she explained. Then grinned, saying, "Now I see how you did it."

"What's that?" he asked.

"The nose, that big honker of yours. You made it look almost normal with three different shades of makeup."

He beamed, "Ivory down the center, and Tawny Beige on the outside where the nose meets the cheeks. Can't remember what I used in between to bridge the two."

The waiter appeared, asking about dessert. Wagenhoffer gallantly took the check after both declined. He paid in cash, leaving after she had made her exit, neither wanting any casual observer to place them together on this evening. The waiter could be dealt with, if need be. The project budget was adequate for such contingencies.

CHAPTER 35   1969

MORTIFY

COOCHYVILLE, VIRGINIA

"Where did you say you was workin' tomorrow, Clearance?" his Mama asked as she stood by the wood stove, frying chicken with lard in a large cast iron pan. She took her eyes off the chicken long enough to stir the collard greens that were simmering in a two-gallon porcelain pot on the back of the stoves. Their strong aroma filled the house and carried out the screened windows into the yard on a soft April breeze.

"Clearance, git your eyes and ears off'n that TV long enough to answer yo' Mama," she shouted at her son, who lay with his brother Edward on the floor, unable to take his eyes off the beautiful Negress on the screen.

"Just a minute, Mama, 'til the commercial comes on," he answered, totally engrossed in the scene.

JULIA
Didn't they tell you that I'm colored?

DR. CHEGLEY

Oh, what color are you?

JULIA

Well, I'm Negro.

DR. CHEGLEY

Mm. Have you always been a Negro, or are you just attempting to be fashionable?

"Mama, now why did you have to shut the TV off right in the middle of the show?" Clearance complained. "You know that Diahann Carrol is my favorite."

Standing in the living room alongside the nineteen-inch black and white television set with her legs slightly spread and her hands on her hips, his mother stared him in the eye, and said in a stern voice, "Clearance Giddens, I know you paid for this here TV with your hard earned money. But I gonna' tell you right now, if it takes away the respect you chillen has for me an' yo' Daddy, its goin' out in the yard this minute."

"Yes, Mama," Clearance muttered, his eyes on the new living room rug he had bought his parents for Christmas.

"Now that I have your attention, is you gonna answer my question?"

"Don't reckon I heard what you said, Mama," he replied sheepishly.

"I don' reckon you did either. What I asked was where you be workin' tomorrow," she said sharply.

"Down to Willis Wharf, Mama."

"Now thas' mo' like it," she said as she turned and walked back to the kitchen to tend to her cooking. She turned the chicken parts over with a pair of chrome plated tongs, then gave the pot of greens another stir.

"An' what you be doin' down there. Nary a person w' two nickels to rub together down there. Only work I knows of be to the arster shuckn' house, there on Parting Creek. It bein' this time of the year, he should be shet down."she said, smiling now that she could have an ordinary conversation with her boy, without having to compete with the television. Deep down, she thought that talking picture box was the work of the devil.

"White man from up in Maryland, somewhere, opening up a clam processing plant. I'm gonna' be painting for near a month. It's a big place, Mama, gonna be lot's of work for people. Year round, too," Clearance said.

"Who be workin' with you? Not that Jackson Boggs, I hope. He is not good company for you to keep. He's a drinkin' man, a gambler, and I hear he runs women, too," she said with her back to the boys, dinner having reached a critical point.

"No, Mama, Jackson's been fired again. Boss man says Tyrone Craddock 'll be doing the rough work and I'll be the finish man," Clearance said.

"That be the Craddock boy lives w' his Mama in a cabin up on Frogstool Branch jes' east of the railroad tracks. Goes to our church?"

"That be him, Mama."

She was smiling when she turned, "Well, finish man," she said with a hint of pride in her son's progress in the construction trade. "You go ahead and watch the last of your show. Then you and Edward clean up for supper. Your Daddy be here any minute now."

When the show was over, Edward jumped up, turned the set off and started and raced toward the back door, shouting "Beat you to the pump, Clearance."

Clearance wanted to run, but he thought he was too old for such fooling around. As he neared the door, he heard his mother's voice, "I know why you be watchin' that show, son. An' I be tellin Pearl Stackhouse next Sunday after Church."

"Oh, please don't Mama. I'll never hear the end of it. No suh, won't never," he said as he turned to grin at his mother who was grinning right back.

✠

"Now what's that boy doin' home so early on a workin' day," Mrs. Giddens muttered as she peered out the kitchen window at the car pulling up in the yard.

Softly she spoke as she continued her work, "He and Tyrone had a big painting job down Hacks Neck, near Coochyville. They were part of a crew restoring an old seventeenth century mansion for some rich fellow from up north, name of Dumont, or something like that. He was gonna use it during the hunting season only. He would need a caretaker the rest of the year. She had been encouraging Clearance to get cozy with the man, see if he couldn't get the job. Her son, to hear him tell it, and this rich man hit it off right away."

A stack of cucumbers lay draining in a pan on the sink. A five-pound bag of coarse salt sat between a ten-pound bag of sugar and two gallon jugs of apple vinegar on a wooden shelf next to the cucumbers. Mrs. Giddens had intended to spend the entire afternoon putting up pickles. Her mother had told her that people who depended on pork for meat, lard for cooking, and fatback for seasoning, needed tomatoes, onions and pickles to clear the blood of pork fat. Therefore, Mrs. Giddens always planted at least 12 hills of cucumber seed in her garden every year. She used Burpee's Straight Eight variety because it was resistant to the Shore's droughty summers, and the vines bore until frost if you kept them picked.

Curious now, she looked for Clearance to step out of the car, which was parked in the shade of the silver maple next to the hog pen. When the car just sat there, she began to think that something had happened at work that her son didn't want to share with her just yet. She smiled at the thought, knowing that she'd get it out of him eventually. She hoped this didn't mean they had a falling out. With that unpleasant thought, she returned to her work.

She was slicing cucumbers crosswise for bread and butter pickles which the boys always clamored for, eating them like candy with their sugary sweetness, and had just filled the bottom of the small enameled wash tub with half-dollar size slices when she heard the car door slam shut. Shortly after that, there was a knock on the door. She reeled from the punch to her heart thrown by the knowledge that it wasn't her boy knocking at his own door. Something bad must have happened to Clearance was all she could think as she staggered to the door, wringing her hands in her apron as she went.

There on the stoop stood Tyrone Craddock, his baseball hat in his hand, head hanging low, not wanting to fix Clarence's momma in the eye.

"What is it, Tyrone? What's happened to my boy?" she asked, her voice quivering with fear.

"There's been an accident, Mam. Clearance been hurt, I took him to Eastern Shore Medical myself. He's..."

Wailing as she interrupted, "Is he all right, where is he hurt?"

"They've already cleaned and bandaged him, iced him down and left for Norfolk, Mam. I stayed until they said they couldn' do fo' him here, and had to take him to the city. I'm plumb sorry,' Tyrone mumbled, still staring at his feet.

"Get the car started while I get my hat and purse," Mrs. Giddens commanded. Shucking her apron, she came roaring out the door, smacking the downcast Tyrone in the head with the edge, sending him sprawling onto the dirt packed lane.

"Come on, Tyrone, you can tell me what happened when we're in the car. We're wasting time."

Tyrone got up slowly, dusted off his khaki work pants, and said, "Go where, Mrs. Dickens? 'Til today I ain't never been south of Nassawadox. I ain't never been across the bridge-tunnel. Fact is, I ain't never been on a bridge or in a tunnel, let alone drive over or through one," he whined. "Sides, how would we ever find that hospital in Norfolk? You never been off the shore either, has you?"

Fed up with Tyrone's excuses, Mrs. Giddens grabbed him by the arm, and pulled him toward the car.

"Tyrone, shut up your trap. As long as I can talk, I don't need to have been to someplace to find it. Now get in that car and drive."

✠

"Mrs. Giddens, he's going to be fine. We've got the bleeding stopped, the wound cleaned and closed. There is substantial swelling in the groin area, so he's been heavily sedated. There is really nothing you can do at this time. I suggest you go home, and get some rest."

"Dr. Steinmen, it took Tyrone and me four hours to find this place. I don't know if his nerves will hold up long enough to get us back, without his gettin' some rest forehand. How long before I can talk to my baby?"

"I'd say in about three days we can begin to reduce the dosage to where he'll be aware that you are in the room with him. He'll be able to hold a brief conversation in four or five days."

Mrs. Giddens began to weep. "We don't have the money for that kind of stay. How'm I gonna know if my boy takes a turn for the worse? I'd never forgive myself if he died, and I wasn't here to comfort him. I don't know how we's gonna pay for all his medicine, this room and all your doctorin', either."

Dr. Steinmen sympathized with the woman's plight. "Here," he said, handing her a business card, "You call me collect every evening at seven thirty. If I'm not home, my wife will be. I'll leave word with her on your son's progress. Let's get him well, then we'll worry about the rest."

The older woman accepted the card, and turned to the young man, saying "Tyrone, will you be able to take me over to Mama's every night? Otherwise, I'll have to walk."

"Yes, Mam, I'd be proud to do it," Tyrone responded.

"OK, Dr. Steinmen, I'll be a callin'. Thanks for goin' out'n yo' way fo' me. Can I see my boy oncet afore we leave?"

"Certainly," Steinmen responded.

✠

Their smiles lit up the room as Doctor Steinmen opened the door to the men's ward. She walked swiftly over to her son's bed. Steinmen stood courteously at the end of the bed until it became evident that there would be no need for him in the conversation that was to follow. He got her a chair, and left the ward

She held his hand, as tears glistened in her eyes, then traced down her face, spattering on the bed sheets.

"Mama," he said softly, "You're going to drown me if you don't stop crying."

"It's just such a relief to see you, and know you'll be coming home soon."

"Ain't nobody gonna' be gladder to see me out of this place than me. I don't think I've got a spot left on my behind that hasn't had a needle in it," Clarence said.

"Do it still hurt, son?" she asked, hesitantly, for his injury wasn't a proper topic of discussion for a church going woman, even if she was his mother.

"A little, Mama, but I'm ready to come home, as soon as they'll let me."

'"Doctor says they'll keep you over the weekend. Then Tyrone, my chauffeur, and I will be down to fetch you home," she said, grinning.

"Bout the money, Mama..." Tyrone started.

"Hush yourself, my little lamb, we'll worry about that after you is all well," said his mother.

"No, Mama, it's all paid for. Mr. DuMont flew down here as soon as he heard I was conscious. He came in to see me personal, to apologize. He felt so bad about the accident, that he's going to pay for the hospital and doctor bills, and give me my lost wages while I'm recuperatin'."

His mother frowned, "Clearance, I understand that he's a rich man, so he's got the money. I always figgered they stayed rich by not givin' it away, partikly not to some Negro boy. Why is he doin' this?"

"Well, he said something like, cause of the unfortunate part he played in the whole affair," Clearance told his mother.

"Clearance, now look me in the eye, and tell me the truth. What was he doin' that caused you to get hurt? And why does he feel so obligated to pay your bills and your lost wages to boot?"

Her son cleared his throat, "Mama, if I was to use some of his salty language, I mean say it like he kind of said it, would you know I wasn't gettin' rough like that Jackson Boggs?"

"Son, say it like you have to say it, but come on, get it said."

"Well, Mr. DuMont and his cousin were out walking in the field, with their hunting rifles, taking shots at anything that they, and their dog, she's a Chesapeake Retriever, Mama, smartest dog..." he paused when she squeezed his arm, "Ok Mama, I'll get back on track, but she is..." another squeeze, another pause. "Anyway, they had been drinking all morning, starting with breakfast. Something called a Bloody Mary, whatever that is. So they weren't hitting anything much, just having a grand old time anyway."

He paused to pick up the glass of ice water on the night stand by his bed, sipped from the plastic straw, then put it down. "I don't know if it's the medicine, the air conditioning, don't it feel good, Mama, or the talking, but I sure am puckered up."

She squeezed his forearm again, firmly to encourage him to move along, like the light tap with a switch that you give to a mule's hindquarters to accomplish the same thing. The psychology, with boy and mule, required that each had received rougher treatment of the same type, and didn't want it to be repeated.

"Me and Tyrone was up on ladders, paintin' the trim along the eaves, when a flock of quail popped out of the hedgerow, and took off a sailing, as you know they can. Well, one of them guns went off just as the quail got between me and Mr. DuMont and his cousin. Clean cut one of 'em right off. It hurt so bad, I fainted, and fell off the ladder. Mr. DuMont said his cousin fainted as well. Anyhow, the fall knocked me out. Mr. DuMont had a servant bring him a couple of sheets which he proceeded to rip up, and make a turniket, a thing to stop the bleeding. Then he helped Tyrone load me in the car. He went in the house to call the hospital. Then he called the state police to try to arrange for an escort. They told him, there weren't no traffic anyway, so they didn't see a need for it. Let me get a sip a' water."

Mrs. Giddens filled the vacuum, "So Mr. DuMont, or his equally drunken friend was responsible for this," she said bitterly.

"Mama, it was an accident. Anyhow, by the time he had made them calls, washed up, changed and got down to Eastern Shore, I had been repackaged, and sent on to Norfolk. This time the State Police agreed to meet the ambulance the other side of the bridge. He actually had them stop north and south bound traffic so the ambulance could go as fast as it wanted with nothin' in the way. Called the Governor to get it done.

All for me, Mama."

His Mama softened somewhat when she heard that. Truth to tell, civil rights movement or not, it still wasn't easy being black in the Commonwealth of Virginia. "Go on with your tale, son."

"Well, Mama, you asked why he's agreed to pay. He knows he and his'n done wrong. He said he feels a moral obligation to do it," Clearance said, knowing his Mama would like the sound of that.

She did, she smiled her warm, motherly smile. The lucky man who has seen such a smile may realize later in life that it came more from the eyes than the rest of his mother's face. It came from her inner being, and represented a total commitment. The wise man knows that he will see that look from no other person.

"Mama. Here's the part where you have to realize that it's Mr. DuMont doin' the talkin'." He says to me, 'Clearance, it's tough enough getting through this life with a full set of balls. Fate has dropped you down to one. Boy, I feel responsible for seeing that you don't lose any wages over this tragic affair, that your medical expenses are fully paid, and that you get a new guitar, the best that money can buy, and some lessons on how to play the damn thing, cause you are surely in dire need of that," Clearance smiled in anticipation of picking out his gift.

Seeing his excitement, his mama asked, "Clearance, wheresoever you goin' to find a nice guitar on the Shore?"

"No, Mama, he says when the swelling goes down, he's goin' to bring me back down here, something' about insurance."

"My, my, would you listen to that," his Mama said, smiling at her boy. Things were going to turn out all right after all.

CHAPTER 36   JULY 1997

SMALL FRY

DOVER, DELAWARE

A stifling, humid, not a cloud in the sky Delaware day had driven me indoors early. Mosquitoes scoured the neighborhood, on the prowl for blood donors. Kids arrived at friends' homes smelling faintly of pesticides. From my spot, the neighborhood appeared devoid of humans. My wife and daughter had escaped to the Wilmington suburbs, visiting with her sister Linda. The aroma of freshly brewed coffee filled the house. I poured a cup, then walked barefooted into the living room. House rule. No one wears shoes on the expensive, oriental rug. The sweat began to cool, my tee shirt to stick. I pondered a shower, then shrugged off the thought. I sighed as I reached my desk.

Patricia had left the National Enquirer, the portable telephone, my scissors and a clipping from the News Journal which described the egg shell carving expertise of a local celebrity, on the work area of my desk. As I was cleaning up, I couldn't help but notice the headlines, 'ROXANNE PREGNANT AGAIN'. Does anyone, other than Roxanne and the father really care? The answer is probably yes,

12 gazillion readers.

That done, I began the laborious business of trying to understand my notes from yesterday's dinner meeting with Winston Trader. Winston it was now. The old gentlemen had suggested a first name relationship felt more comfortable to him now that we had worked together for so long, and so well. I'm afraid I relied quite heavily upon that trust to convince him to do what I thought best for him and the Trust.

℞

"What do you feel like tonight?" Trader had asked as we stepped off the elevator at his apartment house.

"Italian, but something basic. I don't need a fresh basil leaf hat as an artistic topping to my pasta."

"I've just the place," he responded, smiling the smile of the confidante who is about to share some hidden knowledge. The doorman opened the glass door with the gold lettering, then swiftly strode to my car, actually my wife's, and opened the door for my companion.

"Thank you, Herman."

"You are most welcome, Doctor Trader"

As we pulled away from the curb, Trader told me to head down Pennsylvania Avenue until I got to either Lincoln or Union, then head south until we got to Lancaster Avenue, to a little place called Atillio's Ristorante. That's not quite how we got there, but get there we did, smack in the middle of Little Italy. The small sign as you entered the dark room read "cash only."

We were now seated at a no frill's table, sipping a $10 Chianti, awaiting our orders. The room was dark, dominated by a bar which was fully occupied by middle aged, Mediterranean types of both sexes. The chatter was lively. I was never a tavern type, but I liked the feel of this place. Gave you a sense of security, as if all the men in the room would rise as one to challenge anyone who meant to do you harm.

Trader interrupted my thoughts, "Good place to bring a consultant such as yourself, John. Nothing on the menu over $8.00. You can turn in an expense voucher for this dinner, and it won't embarrass me to authorize payment," he chuckled, lifting his glass for another imperceptibly small sip of the dry red wine.

"If the food is as good as it smells, this one is on me," I said, realizing it was easy to pick up a $20 tab, plus drinks.

"Don't worry about the food. You're going to love it. I've been coming here for fifty years, ever since Massimo Marconi opened it. Back then, there was so much cigarette smoke in the place, you couldn't enjoy the scrumptious aromas until you received your entree." Changing subjects, "When did you want to start talking about business. I'm anxious to get this affair over with."

Our waiter arrived with our orders, thereby providing a silent, but delicious, answer to my friend's question. Business would be deferred until we had enjoyed the pleasure of a well-cooked meal. Trader had the spezzato, a classic veal stew with peppers, as pleasing to the eye as it is to the palate. Going against caution, I had ordered the fried smelts with a side order of sautéed greens with garlic. They both turned out to be excellent choices. The smelts were crisp, like french fries, hot, tasting something like flounder. I commented to the waiter about the spinach when he returned to our table to see if everything was all right.

"It is the best because the cook sautés the garlic in olive oil before adding the spinach. In that way, the garlic caresses the palate instead of overpowering your sense of taste," he confided with us.

When we had finished eating, we each ordered a small glass of port, extending the meal while we talked. While we were eating, the bar trade had cleared of patrons who had stopped in on the way home from work. A few older couples, obviously drinking their dinner, remained behind, watching the nightly news, chain smoking.

"All right, John, I admire your analytical mind and respect your opinion. I never asked that you catch the thief, but you did and in such short order. Now that we have him, why you don't want to move on Fowler immediately. You'll have my complete attention as long as it takes to explain your reasoning," he grinned, tight lipped as an old man is want to be. "As long as you remember that it can't take past 9:30. That is when I must leave for home to get a proper night's rest."

"We have Doctor Fowler dead to rights. Motive. He desperately needed money to get his finances squared away to clear the Trust's annual investigation. Access. He was singularly in a position to do the deed. Method. Other than you, he alone had a key to the weight adjustment terminal. Not enough to go to court, but certainly enough evidence to fire him, which is just what you want to do."

"Damn right I do, the ungrateful wretch," Trader responded with vigor.

"I fully understand your feelings in the matter, but think about why you hired me for a minute," I coached softly, but firmly.

Putting the glass back on the table after taking a small bit of the sweet, plum red wine, he said, "Why, to make sure this never happens again."

"Correct, and at this juncture I can't do that."

"Why not?" Trader asked incredulously.

"For several reasons. One, someone will have to take his place. We all have warts and weaknesses. Your staff isn't any different. I don't know who exploited Fowler's. I know that money played a part. But was there anything else? Who is to say that they won't try again?"

"Confront the man. Brace him and I'll bet he'll spill his guts," Trader huffed.

"Maybe so. But consider whose sperm was stolen. Was that his assignment, to steal that particular deposit? If so, why?"

Winston Trader's face turned ashen as he whispered, "He couldn't have."

"Yes, I know, only you have access to the book of tables that keys the anonymous donors to the vials," I responded quickly.

"No, he couldn't have, even if he did get his hands on it."

Trader readily agreed to continue the investigation. He now understood that there were still too many missing pieces in the puzzle. Fowler would have a tail on him from tomorrow on until this case was resolved.

CHAPTER 37   JULY 1997

TIGHT SPOT

WILMINGTON, DELAWARE

The sun's rays lit up the wall, causing the chair rail to glow. The radio was set on 98.1 FM, golden oldies out of Philadelphia, birthplace of Independence and American Bandstand. Larry Fowler was singing along with an old Everly Brothers refrain. As he sang, he jerked his head and body up and down in rhythm with the music.

It was going to twilight on Friday night. Fowler was in his bedroom, packing an overnight bag, a small carry on no bigger than a woman's purse. He checked the clock on the wall. A cab would be picking him up in a few minutes. The Blue Rocks were playing at Frawley stadium tonight. Fowler had a ticket down front on the third baseline. The SRO crowd, the noise, and a bit of brew would take his mind off his flight tomorrow. Just enough to drink to take the edge off his excitement, so he could get to sleep right away when he got home from the game. The flight to San Francisco was departing Philadelphia International at 7:00 a.m.. He had arranged for the limo service to pick him up at four.

The horn announcing the waiting cabbie sounded just as Fowler threaded the last catch on his worn cloth bag. Leaving a light on in the bedroom, he grabbed his keys from the desk, opened, closed and checked the door to make sure it was locked. He bounced down the stairs, happy in the thought that he had been able to convince Pester that he could be much more effective if he had a $10,000 cash advance to ward off his creditors. She had agreed to give it to him after this first of two get-togethers to rehearse his role in the new adventure.

Tailing Fowler was easy. Once the cab pulled onto I-95, there was only one destination for a man leaving his home at four in the morning with a small bag, hung like a purse from his shoulder. Philadelphia International Airport. He also carried a small, old fashioned brown leather suitcase. Jim Duffield weaved from lane to lane, hiding from his quarry in the light traffic on the way north. The light blue, Ford Crown Victoria was not a memorable car, but he was taking no chances. Easing his right hand into the pocket of his wind breaker, he pulled the cellular phone out, placed it on the seat beside him, dialed in 03, hit the send button, then picked it up, listened for the signal, dialed in his pin number, and then hummed softly as he waited for an answer.

"John? Sorry to... it's a little after 4:30," Duffield said, speaking loudly, as if Bunting were hard of hearing, not just befuddled from having his sleep interrupted. "Yeah, in the morning. Sorry to wake you, but I need your OK to charge airfare to the job. Don't know where to. Could be any place, though. All I can tell you is our boy is on the way to Philadelphia International and he's packed light. Had a suitcase, too. Judging by the way the cabbie handled it, must be filled with feathers. Thanks. I'll call as soon as I find out."

Duffield swung the car down the off ramp that led to the terminal, two cars separating him from Fowler's cab which continued on, coming to a halt at the redcap's stand. Duffield pulled in directly behind him, slid the phone back in his pocket, then closed the zipper. He watched as Fowler paid the cabdriver.

"I am in luck. He must not travel much, or he's old-fashioned," Duffield said to himself as he watched Larry Fowler accept the stub from the redcap. Duffield turned the ignition off, pulled out the key, and exited the light blue Ford. As he rounded the trunk, he pulled a fifty-dollar bill from the fold of money in his hand. As he handed it to the redcap, he said, "Tell the cops that I'm inside picking up my handicapped mother. I won't be over 15 minutes. He checked the flight number on the bright red ticket on Fowler's bag as he swept past the portable luggage rack."

Inside the terminal building, he felt fortunate to buy a first class ticket to Kansas City on a flight that was otherwise booked. Running back to his car, he thanked the redcap, who turned around, looking for someone in a wheelchair.

"Her flight's been delayed. I'll have time to park the car properly now," Duffield said smiling. He called in his report to a wide awake Bunting who was pleased to have his hound running with the scent.

"I lost him, John. The luggage he checked is still going round and round on the baggage handler, all by its lonesome. Pretty clear to me now that it was a ruse. I'm down here waiting for him to pick it up and he's on his way to somewhere. I don't even know if Kansas City was his true destination, or just a layover. Good idea. I'll let you know what I find out." Jim Duffield hung up the phone, feeling a bit stupid. He checked the signs, and began walking toward the Delta Airlines ticket counter. The terminal was not very crowded. Duffield almost jogged, hoping to be able to correct his error by information he would soon be getting. He arrived at the counter, and walked immediately to a customer service representative. She was short, no more than five feet tall and attractively thin in an athletic way. Her face, on the other hand, was almost as thin and sharp as an axe blade. When she spoke, he could see that her teeth were stained yellow from nicotine.

"How may I help you, Sir?" she smiled.

241

"Well, young lady, I was to meet a friend of mine who had a layover here. Just to chat while he waited for his flight."

"Name and flight number, please."

"Name's Dr. Lawrence G. Fowler. Flight number in was 231. Can't help you on the one out. Anyway, you can check," he responded.

"Sure. Just a minute." She typed in the flight number and Fowler's name, then stared vacantly at the screen. "No. It wasn't a layover. Either he's booked another flight, or his destination was Kansas City. Let me check outbound flights for tonight." She went back to her keyboard. "Sorry, sir. No luck. You might want to check with TWA and Southwest," the customer service representative said as she pointed toward her right. With no baggage to contradict his story, Duffield did just as he was told. No luck in Terminal B.

He walked to the International Circle, then flipped a coin. Heads. He turned right, toward Terminal C, which served seven of the major air lines. No dice after two hours. He then walked back down the concourse, turned left on the International Circle, trudged past Concourse B, and onto Terminal A.

The trail led to Los Angeles, but the flight was long gone by the time he made the discovery. He called in his find to John Bunting in hopes that he had some reliable confederate in LA, but that was not the case. Unwilling to engage a private detective without checking his references for fear of frightening the quarry, Bunting told Duffield to consider it a job well done. Duffield left for Philadelphia the next morning after spending the evening in the closest motel, a Holiday Inn that had seen better days.

CHAPTER 38   **AUGUST 1997**

PLOT

A FARM IN RURAL IOWA

It was extremely hot and humid, not a cloud in the sky. The corn was now tall enough to block any breeze that might kick up in central Iowa. Roxanne, heavy with child, dozed on a bamboo hammock on the front porch. Her energy flagged recently, requiring a minimum of 12 hours sleep to be back in form. She was sweating profusely, but felt the natural climate was good for the child. A loose fitting white satin shawl covered her naked body. At the farm, she had no servants to worry about. Her neighbors had grown accustomed to her strange new habit, sleeping nude on the porch. They always called in advance to arrange a visit. Snoops couldn't see her from the road, thanks to the green corn fields surrounding her house.

Mark Downs cared for her cat, Ernest, during her frequent absences from the farm. A short haired tabbie, Earnest had mixed grey and black fur, weighed in at a pudgy 25 pounds, but had the visage and regal bearing of a lion. As a eunuch, he only left the house and porch to attend to business, or to hunt. At the former he always succeeded. At the latter, victory had recently come to be measured in the chase, not the capture. Ernest was nigh on ten years old. His favorite activity now was sleeping for ten hours on his back in the little nest Roxanne had purchased from L.L. Bean. Secure in his surroundings, having been back with Roxanne for over a month, that was where he was when the cordless phone rang. Ernest acknowledged the ring by rolling over on his stomach, then nestled in the shady spot secluded from the sun.

Roxanne awoke, instantly alert, smilingly pleased at how six weeks of devotion to healthy food and a daily one mile walk in the fresh air had made her feel utterly alive again. She swung her legs over the side of the divan, remarking as she did, "Ungh, I am a ball of sweat again. Good thing I bought cloth cushions instead of vinyl. I'd slide off in my sleep and land right on my butt."

She leaned over to the white table beside the divan, picked up the receiver of the telephone and spoke softly, "Yes?"

"Is this Roxanne?"

"Is that who you're calling?"

A stunned silence followed the shrill response, then "Please hold for Mr. Pearlman."

A smooth baritone came on the line, gushing "Roxanne, how are you and the baby today?"

"Nessus, you old fox, how about you tell me. As my lawyer, you're in a better position to know than I am," Roxanne said.

"You will be pleased. He went for the toys and the lump sum, million dollar cash payment at settlement. His imbecile lawyer thinks the long term money is coming out of your production company, Loki Enterprises. They took the 500,000 preferred shares for the five-year term as if they were real."

Roxanne screamed, then guffawed, "Sounds like neither Ken nor that idiot lawyer of his ever read up on Norse mythology."

Puzzled, Nessus Pearlman asked, "Norse mythology?"

Pleased that she knew more about something, anything, than her stuck up lawyer, Roxanne answered, "You didn't know that Loki was the Norse god of strife and the spirit of evil?"

"No, as a matter of fact, I did not."

"Well, he is. I named the company after my opinion of Ken at the time."

"Yes, well," Pearlman continued, "I hope you and your accountant know what you're doing. Loki is committed to two big budget movies a year for five years. If your aim is to lose money for ten films so Ken doesn't get anything, you'll be losing as well."

Roxanne chuckled, "Those two bozos don't know nuthin' about movie accounting and neither do you. But, thanks Pearlie, you did great. When do we wrap it up?"

"It's tentatively set up for September 19. I'll confirm within a day or two."

"Won't drag into October will it?"

"Not a chance."

"Pearlie, thanks again. Hold up on your final bill until after settlement. I want this behind me."

"No problem, Roxanne," Pearlman responded to a dial tone. Roxanne had already hung up.

"It's going down in September, Pester, can you believe it. He'll have that money spent inside a year. Then I can have my sweet revenge," Roxanne shouted into the phone.

"There may be no need to wait. I think I've found a shorter route to a better way," Pester responded.

Roxanne squealed in delight, "Tell me Pester, tell me. I knew I could count on you."

"Better that you don't know. Just keep on reading the *LA Times*. It won't be long after the divorce is final."

"I'll book a flight back tomorrow. I wouldn't want to miss this for the world."

"Roxanne, save yourself the trouble. Buy a computer from a store that will arrange to set it up, get you hooked to the Internet, and give you a little training," Pester suggested. "That way you can save your traveling until after you have the baby."

"I appreciate your thoughtfulness, hon', but I gotta get home to keep that scumbag from stealing me blind. Now that he knows what's his by right, he's gonna try a little raiding to see what he can make his by possession."

"I can make sure that doesn't happen," Pester offered, her voice tight and raspy.

"Thanks, love, but don't take from my pleasures. I can't wait to see him squirm when I catch him trying to break in the house. I had them come out and reprogram the security system, or whatever they do. He'll have to break a window to get in. Then I can have the cops haul him away."

"Good girl," Pester said. "Look, this may be the last contact we're going to have on this project until it's over and he stands accused of violating the law. You need anything else?"

"No, not that I can think of. You take care to hit him where it hurts. If it hurts bad and long enough, I might be even more generous than I said," Roxanne spoke, gleeful at the thought.

"A bit of my fee goes into the action to make sure it works, so I appreciate the thought. Hope things go well for you. Bye." Pester had lied about her fee covering the plan's deficit. Just a little lie as an incentive for Roxanne to give her a bigger bonus when Pester's plan blows her client's pants off.

She kept the telephone receiver in her hand and began making another call, then terminated it, placing the receiver in it's marble and gold plated cradle. She had found the rotary dial phone at an antique shop. There was only one incoming line because she thought it rude to place a client on hold. Thus the phone could be not only decorative, but utilitarian. It also meant she couldn't use another rude service available from her carrier. Call waiting was a great way to let a client know he was second class. Pester's communication system also did not include an answering machine. The prosecutor's's own evidence collector, she called them.

She walked to the closet, opened the door, and peered into the refrigerator. Had to be careful in selecting a beverage to celebrate the occasion. She shunned anything alcoholic, selecting a bottle of Poland Spring Water instead, a plebeian drink that cost only $2.59 for a six pack on the east coast. She had it flown in twice a year, having fell for the name, the source (Poland Spring, Maine), and the look on the faces of friends and clients alike when she served it. Perier it was not. But she liked the fact that it was not yet trendy in California. It added to her mystery, even if it did cost her $2.00 a bottle.

Taking a sip directly from the bottle, she thought about calling Dr. Fowler at his place of employment, but then thought better of it. No sense leaving a hot scent where a cold trail existed. She'd wait another hour, then call him at home. He said he had what she wanted, could fax or E-mail it. Had even asked which she preferred? Pester had forcefully told him that nothing other than hard copy would do, delivered by him personally. She believed that almost every electronic gadget left a recoverable trail. She didn't necessarily understand how, but she had enrolled in the local community college to start the learning process. In any case, Fowler was going to have to fly out again and deliver the goods in person.

Taking another celebratory sip from her water bottle, she picked up the receiver and dialed Wags' number. They would have to be in the air as soon as the leaves were off the trees. Aerial reconnaissance was the least risky way to plan the project. There was a plane and pilot to rent, a believable explanation for the photographs to be developed, a flight plan to be filed under someone else's name, and a host of other things to be done on an accelerated schedule.

"Duffy's tavern, Archie the manager speaking." Wags had picked up a collection of old radio show tapes at a tag sale and had been totally taken by the humor and innocence of the thirties and forties radio programs. He repeated the opening line of one such show. It became a first line of defense in his rather primitive security system. At another time, it would be "Yoo-hoo, Mrs. Bloo-oomm" from the Goldbergs. His favorite, however, was "Who knows what evil lurks in the hearts of men? The Shadow knows!" Then he completed his introductory remarks with the chilling laughter of Lamont Kranston's alter ego to the organ music, playing *Omphale's Spinning Wheel*.

"Wags, cut the crap. Is that you?"

"To who?"

Roxanne took another sip of spring water to sooth her raspy throat. "It's Pester, with a need to talk to you privately."

"Ah-ha, the game's afoot, is it?" Wags asked.

"You might say that, and he's running fast. We have no time to lose. When can we meet?"

"The call is yours. I have no specific assignment at this time. I can fully devote my time to your enterprise. You have the money, I have the resources. Tell me when and where."

She did.

CHAPTER 39   1970

THANKS A LOT

MELFA, VIRGINIA

Fall had descended quickly on the eastern shore of Virginia, arriving overnight with a northwesterly wind, swept in from the Chesapeake Bay. The leaves had already been turning. The temperature dropped below freezing, killing off the mosquitoes, making the shore livable again until spring.

"Mother, we sure is blessed this year. Look at the marblin' in this heah beef," Davis Giddens said to his wife as he slowly placed the hind quarter of beef on the table.

"Lawdy, Lawdy, Davis, when you brought that Holstein bull calf home last year, I was plum worried to death that it would die from lack of somethin' to eat. Din't tell me you swung that deal wit' Mr. Nelson, owns the feed mill down to Exmore. Took you all summer, but that warehouse clapboard sure do shine with that white paint you put on her," Mrs. Giddens smiled as she looked at the beef, and her husband.

"Well, I figured now that Clearance used his sick money to buy us that freezer, we ought to have something tasteful to put in it," Davis remarked as he worked the butcher knife back and forth on the knife sharpener. "I'll be wantin' this heah knife to be extra keen on this rump, cause I wants them round steaks to peel off like I was skinnin' a rabbit. Are you ready, cause I'm a gonna start to cuttin'?"

"Well, I've got my space cleared, five rolls of freezer paper, a bowl of fresh water to rinse my hands, two old kitchen towels to dry them with, three rolls of freezer tape, and two grease pencils to mark the cuts and date on the packages. The wash basin on the floor is for the scraps for hamburger. The coal bucket will do for what's left for the dogs," she answered. "We's ready, I reckon."

An autumn breeze, fired by the warmth of the bright sun, lifted the threadbare pink curtains as it swept through the screens. The last black flies of the season clung to the screens, seeking the warmth inside the little house. The Giddens worked swiftly, effortlessly throughout the morning, hands guided by skills learned in the butchering of countless hogs in winters past. They stopped only for a brief lunch, bologna sandwiches on Wonder bread, spread thickly with brown mustard, and a glass of milk. By supper time, all the main cuts were wrapped and in the freezer.

"Mother, I shoah do hope that Clearance gets home soon. We could use a hand grinding up these two wash basins full a' meat."

"He'll be along when he gets along. Them doctors down to Virginia Beach be busy all the time. He as likely had to wait a couple hours to get his examination. Sure was nice a' Mr. DuMont to have his man take Clearance down there."

"Mother, the man shot one of his balls off. I'd say it's the least he can do," responded Davis Giddens. "Course there was that fancy guitar and the lessons. Nearly forgot 'bout that, since I don't hear him play it none."

"He's been practicin' over to Tyrone's. Wants to surprise Pearl. You ought to be glad, too. That loudness would make you even harder t' hearin' than you already is," Mrs. Giddens said, wearily carrying the bowl of pinkish water over to the sink. "I'll be back to start supper, after I get some fresh water from the pump."

Gesturing, Davis responded, "Give it heah. I don't have nothin' left to do but grind that meat. I'd just soon rest and have supper. Mebee then Clearance'll be home to spell me from time to time."

"Yes'm, this has sure been a heap a' work. Won't need no TV tonight to get me sleepy," his wife commented. As she bent to pick up some kindling wood for the stove she said, "Davis, you don' min', it'll just be a steak, fried onions, and boiled potatoes."

"Sounds good to me. Now mind, start yours fust, cuz I wants the blood gushin' when I starts to cuttin'"

"Davis, ain't you seen enough blood already today?"

She realized she was talking to empty space when she heard the screen door slam shut. The draft needed damping slightly to get the cast iron frying pan to a temperature high enough to sear, but not enough to blacken. Davis was back in the house, rocking in his chair, watching his wife cook dinner, a sight far more interesting to him than television. Davis Giddens loved his wife and family. Sitting there in his little shack, he felt content with his life. The smell of fried onions satisfied him more than the sweetest of perfumes.

☩

"Clearance, I'm glad youse back, boy, and I'm extra glad that the doc says your other side goin' to be a wukkin' part of you body. Now, here, grab holt this handle whilst I does the stuffin'," Davis Giddens said to his son. The sweat beaded on his forehead, making it look dimpled in the reflecting light of the 40 watt bulb that hung naked from the center of the kitchen ceiling.

As Clearance began rotating the handle of the meat grinder,

spaghetti like strands of hamburger meat gushed out the end of the screen. They broke off from time to time, landing with a soft plop in the white enameled wash basin on the floor. When the men took a break from the unnatural labor of rotating the handle, Mrs. Giddens would swap basins, placing the partially full one on the end of the table. She prepared ten squares of wrapping paper at a time, placed individually about the table. She would then dip both hands in the basin, extracting about one pound at a time, judging the weight by the heft of the mound of meat. Then she double checked it by rolling it into a sphere the approximate size of a soft ball. If it was the right size, she would fling it with enough force to flatten it on the paper. When all ten papers were filled, she would dip her hands in the bowl, dry them on a frayed, washed colorless towel, then attend to the wrapping. The content of these packages was evident by their shape, so she gladly skipped the extra step of marking them.

It was a gratifying bit of work to be done at her own rhythm. Her hand speed was far superior to the men in her family, genetically implanted, then honed picking strawberries and other truck crops for the fresh market. The farmers paid by the basket, not the hour. She had bought the pretties that helped attract her man when she was young by working from sunup to sundown in summer fields when the temperatures hovered in the nineties. The humidity had left her sleeping soaked in her bed those hot August nights. She remembered, and felt comforted that she was living the good life as she entered middle age.

"Yassuh, he did, and I am."

His mother awoke from her dreaming, saying, "What's that, Clearance? I wasn't payin' no 'tention. Who did, and what you are?"

"Mr. DuMont did, Mama. He lived up to his promise. I am now insured."

"Well, Lord bless us, you be the first in the family that I knows of whoever got hisself insured. I be right proud of you, son."

"And it's a special kin' of insurance," Clearance beamed. "Even most white folks don't have it. All I gotta' do when I need it is use Grandpa's name."

"That's nice. I's proud of you too, but don't forget to keep on crankin' while youse to talkin', cause it's gettin' close to nine o'clock, and I'm ready for bed," said a weary Davis Giddens.

CHAPTER 40   AUGUST 1997

JACKPOT

PHILADELPHIA, PENNSYLVANIA

"John, the Supershuttle limo service is waiting outside Fowler's place even as we speak," said Jim Duffield quietly into his cellular phone.

"I'll have Tuck Mooreshead meet you at the airport. You have the Grenada combat ribbon and the hundred-dollar bill?" John Bunting asked.

"Sure, all ready to go. Here he comes. Same deal as before, only this time it's a different bag. Small enough to carry on board with his over nighter. Looks full, too. Had some heft to it when the driver put it in back. Here we go. I'll call when I get there to tell you what flight so you can coordinate it with Tuck. Make him dress so he doesn't stick out like a sore thumb, will you?"

"Say what you will, Tuck is a pro. He understands the assignment. Besides, he's a backup with only this single shot in the project. Even if

Fowler picks him up, he'll not see him again, at least until after this is over. Good luck. I'll wait two hours until I alert our LA contact," said Bunting, hanging the receiver up softly in deference to his wife, who softly snored with her back to him.

Bunting got up, walked to the bathroom and performed his morning ritual. No matter at what time his day started, he wanted to be bathed, shaved and dressed for whatever the day might bring. Creeping back into the bedroom by the night light's glow, he was naked beneath his beloved, moth eaten wool bathrobe. Hand made by his wife, the cloth hade molded itself to the shape of his upper torso over the years. He had selected the cloth himself, albeit for the design and colors, if not the feel of the cloth, which had been quite prickly for the first several years. The sepia plaid overlay a buff yellow. The single pocket, knee length robe was modeled after a silk affair worn by James Bond, Sean Connery, in one of the earlier films. Buttonless, it was a wrap affair, designed with a sewn on, tie over sash for modesty. The sash ends dragged the floor, the robe gapped open. No need for modesty when there was no one to see, and almost no light to see by.

Noise from the toilet flushing had awoken Winston, the ancient Maine coon cat, who had been luxuriating on his pillow at the footboard end of the bed. He opened one eye to see quarry flashing by. Reflex action extended the claws in his left paw which flashed out, immediately hooking the unfortunate wretch, which then went on to drag him out of the comfort of his sleeping bag. When his head banged against the bedpost, the cat sank the claws of his right paw into the rug in an attempt to maintain his hold on his prize. Winston is no ordinary house cat. He is 20 pounds of muscle and sinew. With his right paw firmly entrenched in the rug, he set his hind feet claws to anchor his position. Bunting had no idea his ghostly ship in the dim light had acquired a jury rigged sea anchor. When the tension started to pull the robe from his body, he spun slowly to place his left hand on the mattress. The spin accelerated as his forward momentum brought more weight to bear on the already taut sash. His left hand missed the mattress. His right temple did not miss the footboard.

The semi-naked form was still at the bed's base when the telephone rang. Patricia Bunting's body quivered slightly with the noise, then her right foot swung over to nudge her husband into consciousness. As it swung through the space habitually occupied by her husband, she rose with a start.

"John. John. Where are you?" Her question unanswered, Patricia Bunting scrabbled with her left hand on the night stand, urgently searching for her glasses. Without them, she had an ape on Mars chance of finding the phone, which chattered on urgently. Pay dirt. As she reached for the phone, she saw her husband laying prone on the floor, and stifled a scream. The telephone went unanswered.

She rolled over and swung out of bed on her husband's side. Kneeling by his prone figure, she gasped at the swelling on the side of his head. Rising quickly, she bounced toward the bathroom, returning quickly with a folded, cool, damp washcloth. After placing it on the swelling, she felt his pulse, sighing with the normality of the rhythm. Then she was up.

The incessant ringing had stopped. She dialed 911. "This is Patricia Bunting at 1776 Liberty Drive. My husband has had an accident. He's unconscious, but otherwise appears to be OK. Please send an ambulance right away."

℞

Tuck Mooreshead parked his car in the long term lot, figuring to save a few bucks if this became an extended venture. Taking the shuttle in, he got off at Terminal E. John had told him that Fowler, a man he had never seen except in a photograph provided by Bunting, had flown Delta the last time. That was the time he had checked in his bag as the ruse to successfully drop the tail. He quickly spied the Redcap with the Grenada service ribbon.

"Good morning," Mooreshead said genially to the Redcap. "Might you have a message for me from a wizened little man, somewhat short of hair, but long in wit?"

The Redcap looked at him, then broke into a smile, "I believe I do. That is if I knew your name."

"Tuck, like the friar from Robin Hood, my good man."

"Your friend said his momma refused to board when she found out it was Delta. Something about not flying on no damn Confederate airline," the Redcap said. Grinning, he continued, "Know what else? If she was forced on board, he said she would refuse to check her bag because she knew their spies would search it."

Tuck was in professorial dress today, a charcoal tweed jacket over grey chino trousers, with a red tie contrasting with a Dijon mustard (country style) colored shirt. He peered down on the Redcap, who was a mere six footer, and inquired, "Did my friend say that he had a solution to his conundrum?"

"If you're asking what he intends to do about his mother, he said to start looking for other flights at the TWA counter. He'd be at American. If either of you hit pay dirt, use the terminal page system."

Knowing that the man had already been paid handsomely, Mooreshead patted him on the shoulder, saying, "Thank you, good man." Then he strode briskly away. *Not good form, indeed, to lose the trail at the start of the hunt.*

Tuck sauntered through the airport, wisely picking the counters with the shortest lines. Fowler was being more devious this time, but he didn't know that Bunting had a snoop at the other end of the ride. Tuck wasn't all that excited about catching and tailing their man from this end. It was like catching salmon in a Native American fish net at the LA end. They had his picture, and hopefully enough men to cover LA International's seven terminals.

Mooreshead had made it to Terminal C when he heard himself being paged. His lanky frame ate up the distance to Terminal D where he saw Duffield waiting, waving the tickets in his hand.

"Here you go," Said Duffield as he handed a boarding pass to his tall companion. "I have no idea where Fowler's sitting, or even if he's on board. He has a ticket, though. Once you are in, walk all the way to the end. If you don't see him, figure out a reason to get into first class."

"And if I don't see him?"

"Come out to the doorway again. John said we're both to go on if we're still on the trail. As far as I'm concerned, he's going to LA again one way or the other. He did it by way of Kansas City last time. Chances are he's doing it again. I'll board at the last moment, assuming you spot him."

"You're going to be the lead dog if we fly on to LA, right?"

"That's right, Tuck. Once we're on board, we don't know each other. I'll trail him, you follow me."

"If all those fellows from the Paraclete agency pick us up, we're going to look like a team of sled dogs," Mooreshead snorted.

"Bunting sent along some photo's so they'll recognize us. They're to back off, if either of us has him in sight. You're sporting that walking stick as added insurance they know it's you. My red cravat is for the same purpose."

"I wondered about that. You never struck me as the pompous type," Mooreshead said with a smile.

"Get a wiggle on. The flight's supposed to take off in ten minutes."

Mooreshead tipped his stick to his forehead, saying "Paget's Irregular Horse to the charge, sir. Smash them bloody Sikh's, we will."

Half the time Duffield had no idea what Mooreshead was talking about. Sometimes he wondered if the big man did either.

Ten minutes later, TWA Flight 871 was cleared for takeoff with both investigators on board. Neither had spotted Fowler. Nor was there an empty seat. Good enough odds for them to bet he was among the passengers, either overlooked in their haste to spot him, or in disguise.

259

R

Fowler sat second from the window on the right side of the plane, midway between the airplane's tail and the cockpit. He was thinking about a variety of things, secure in the feeling that he was not being followed. *I'm just like Sherlock Holmes,* he mused. *When my life is a bore, I gamble to assuage the monotony. Holmes used cocaine. When something exciting comes along, I set aside my addiction without difficulty, without thought, just as the world's first private detective was wont to do. When a disguise is in order, I, just like Holmes, have one at the ready.*

The plane dipped, then bounced ever so slightly, flying through a bit of turbulence. Fowler's grip tightened on the arm rests. He closed his eyes, willing the brief tumult away. Fowler was not flying by choice. Despite the passenger train's slow, suicidal collapse since World War II, Fowler always paid their exorbitant rates to sleep in a private, half century old compartment, if the train could get him to his destination in a reasonable time period. Fifty four hours was more time than he could rightfully spare. As the plane slipped back into a jet smooth ride, Fowler's reveries continued.

I know Pester will be pleased, he thought. *Pester wanted to know what the most likely route was to a big fine and jail time. The other things she threw into the stew were 1) the time from crime to doing time had to be quick, and 2) the method for staging the crime had to be fairly cheap, but conclusive.* He smiled as he remembered how he went about developing the plan he was flying west to disclose.

R

"Norm, I am really pleased you could join me. I need a little direction. I'm hoping lunch on me you'll consider as payment in kind."

Norman Pencader smiled a warm energetic flash of teeth, the kind you have to be looking for to see. "You don't get much legal help for the price of a pizza and a cold soda, Larry."

Norman Pencader was an average sized man, with a powerful

physique that he hid with tailor made suits. His unblemished mocha colored skin provided perfect contrast to his animated, cinnamon colored eyes. Harvard educated, Pencader had come back to his Wilmington roots to seek his fortune as a corporate lawyer. Just being a lawyer wasn't enough to fill the glass that was his zest for life. He was a state senator, marathon runner, and perennial chairman of the muscular dystrophy fund drive. Fowler met him at Parkowski's gym. He liked him for who he was, not what he was.

Fowler looked at the menu, then placed it on the table, and spoke, "Like I said, it's some help in finding where best to spend my energies profitably. I need some pointers. It's not for defending me, or helping me sue somebody."

Pencader flashed that brief smile again, amused by his friend's uneasiness in asking for a favor. "I have to assume that you are conversant with the pleasures of expending your energies on the ladies?"

Not wishing to continue Fowler's discomfort, Pencader offered, "Come on Larry, I have depositions this afternoon. Spit it out. What do you need to know? I won't even ask why, that is, of course unless you arouse my curiosity."

"Knowing you, that won't be too tough." Fowler sipped cold water from a glass beaded with sweat. "Here's the thing. I was watching the news the other night and couldn't believe what I was hearing. The *News Journal* didn't have anything the next day. So I bought the New York Times. Short article, just enough to pique my curiosity. I want to follow up on it."

"What, Larry?"

"What. Oh, what I saw on TV, you mean," Fowler mumbled sheepishly. "It was this guy out west being taken away in handcuffs. Said he could get five years in jail for taking down a wall in a warehouse. The reporter said he could also be fined $1,500,000 for failing to notify the government."

Pencader looked at his watch, impatient at the slow service today. "So what is your question?"

"Well, the guy's not a murderer, rapist or drug dealer. How could that be, that they could throw him in jail for that long, and fine him to boot?"

"Pretty mild stuff, actually. I know of a case down south where two guys are facing 23 years for burying hazardous waste on their property."

Fowler, who almost never used profanity in social discourse, blurted out, "You gotta be sh...... me!"

"Not so, Larry. It's becoming commonplace."

"But there will be a plea bargain or something, right. If we're letting the really bad guys back on the street, surely these guys aren't going to do hard time."

Pencader looked at his friend, sympathy in his eyes, in false Irish brogue he said, "Me boy, you've not been paying attention to Six Pack Pete DuPont, our former Governor."

Fowler questioned Pencader silently with his eyes.

"Allow me to quote you, because Pete is just as incredulous as you. In a recent syndicated article, he said

'Did anyone ever envision a time when people would go to jail for cleaning out a junk yard? Or when an environmental engineer would be criminally convicted for moving two truck loads of dirt? ...Under the Clean Air Act, you can go to jail for filling out a form incorrectly, and EPA officials think it's wonderful."

Awestruck, Fowler asked, "That's ridiculous. How can that be?"

"Quirk in the law," Pencader responded, looking at his watch with growing anxiety. "Look, I'm going to have to skip lunch. But let me

262

satisfy your curiosity. The standard to prove criminal intent under environmental statutes is lower than that for other crimes. That means a prosecutor can threaten you criminally in an effort to coerce a bigger civil fine to the glory of the agency and the betterment of the Treasury coffers. Not quite cricket, but it's being done because the defendants, and their lawyers, know that the lower standard makes it more likely that the client will be convicted criminally in court.

"But,...."

"Larry, but me no buts. The fact is that environmental law allows everyone and anyone to sue over real, or surreal, violations. When the Department of Justice sues, whether or not to pursue the case criminally is up to the individual prosecutor."

Doctor Lawrence G. Fowler was obviously trying to place this information into some organized, therefore understandable, framework. Struggling, "If the ability to convict is tilted so much, then it must be awfully hard to get caught. Otherwise, the system would self destruct."

"Look, I've got to go. Another time, when there's more time. Let me leave you with this. A lot of violations are documented through self reporting. It's like faxing or phoning in when you're over the speed limit. All of these permits have discharge limits. There's a ton of case law that supports the position that a violation of a permit limit is a technical violation. No discussion of mitigating circumstances."

"Wait, before you go. How about the other stuff?"

Pencader flashed a smile, a compliment to his friend's intelligence, "You mean, if there is no self reporting, what are the chances of getting caught?"

"Yes."

Now it was Pencader's turn to be puzzled. "Larry?"

"No," Fowler smiled sheepishly, "I'm not thinking about doing something like that. I'm finally over my gambling problem. My salary from the trust is more than adequate to meet my needs. I'm just socially and politically curious."

Pencader turned to go, "Congress is trying to tip the scales in favor of justice. The FBI is now involved. The criminal enforcement division has been boosted to two hundred agents. You've got snoopy neighbors, disgruntled employees, firees, retirees, environmentalists, bounty hunters, a whole host of individuals operating on their own agendas out there seeking justice. They have information and disinformation, sometimes not acknowledging, or even understanding, the difference."

"Thanks, Norm. I'll make up for the lunch. Where would you suggest I look to follow up?"

"If you're tapped into the Internet, log onto EPA's Web Site. Check out the 'Summary of Criminal Prosecutions'. That's a good starting point. Feed your gleanings to Rush Limbaugh and Newt Gingrich. Might do some good. Take care." Pencader gathered his coat, placed a dollar on the table, waved and made his way out of the restaurant.

℞

And that is what Fowler had done, plowing through a voluminous document which cited case after case where criminal sanctions were meted out after investigation by the Environmental Protection Agency's Criminal Investigation Division, the FBI, and state and, sometimes, local authorities. Penalties in excess of $1 million and 23 years in prison for burying hazardous wastes in Mississippi given to the owners of the property. In another case out west, the general manager of a warehouse operation was fined $500,000 and given a five-year jail sentence for taking down an asbestos containing wall and disposing of it improperly. He had a suitcase full of EPA press releases for Pester describing similar instances.

Fowler had spent the last two months at the library, on line and winnowing through the EPA PR material evaluating, weighing and selecting the types of cases that fit the three criteria that Pester's client had established. To satisfy her client's passion for revenge, the fine must be large. The 'crime' must carry a strong possibility of criminal conviction, with a long stretch in the pen at sentencing. Pester had added a fourth. She wanted justice to be swift so she could collect her bonus as soon as possible. She had hinted that a sweetener was possible if he found at least three totally different cases that met all four requirements.

A typical press release included everything he needed to decide the merits of a case except the length of time between discovery and conviction. By the time he had 100 single paragraph cases that met the first three criteria, he delved further into the bowels of the Agency's on line services. It was simple, but tedious, to down load the lengthy particulars, searching for dates of discovery, conviction and sentencing. Not knowing how the information would be used made Fowler's work easier. He was simply gathering facts.

His shoulder bag bulged with documents on twelve environmental crimes that met the four standards. Fowler was on his way to a big pay day, with an even bigger one being a likely possibility. The seat belt light went on as the plane approached Kansas City.

℞

Mooreshead disembarked with the first class customers, having feigned an injured leg upon boarding, a falsehood lent credence by the presence of his walking stick. He set up shop at the end of the ramp, directly behind a Mexican holding a handwritten sign identifying the holder as Mister Jesus Hernandez in search of Juanita Martinez. The sign was printed in both English and Spanish. Mooreshead's view was not obstructed. Mr. Hernandez could have had another of similar stature sitting upon his diminutive shoulders and still Mooreshead's view would not have been impaired.

Duffield remained in his seat until the last passenger started down the aisle. He then pulled a ballpoint pen from his jacket, pulled a pack of chewing gum from his trouser pocket, and removed the wrapper. He wrote quickly on the inside of the wrapper, crumpled it into a ball in his hand, rose and began walking down the aisle. This stop was just a layover for passengers going on to LA. Duffield returned the pen to his jacket as he cleared the unloading ramp to divert attention from his left hand as he passed Mooreshead without looking at him. He drew Mooreshead's attention to his left hand by twisting it outward, palm open. Then he dropped the gum wrapper. Mooreshead allowed his off the rack, half lenses to slide off his nose, feigned an attempt to catch them, and then knelt to the floor to gather them up, along with the wrapper.

He retreated to a stall in the men's room to avoid prying eyes. The note read:

Brown rug, fake gold rimmed glasses, reversible jacket (now blue) Seated behind me on plane. I am lkg for him U do same

As he turned, he lifted his foot and pushed the flush handle with his shoe. He stepped out of the stall. Larry Fowler was staring back at him from the mirrored basin before which he stood adjusting his toupee. Mooreshead, avoiding eye contact, walked to a place several basins to the left of Fowler. Whistling as he went through a show of washing his hands, he turned his head and was relieved to see that he had a choice between paper towels and hot air for drying his hands. He could be out quickly, or dawdle, whatever the situation called for. As he turned his head back to look at the mirror, he could see Fowler moving quickly past him toward the door.

As soon as Fowler was gone, Mooreshead made short work of drying his hands and then plunged out the door. He saw Duffield, who was returning to the flight area, pick up the surveillance, allowing him the luxury of dawdling on his way back.

The trio boarded ten minutes before takeoff.

R

Jim Duffield stood in the lobby of the Hotel Excalibur, just off the Ventura Parkway, north of Beverly Hills. He was on the telephone. "Good idea you had, John, to bribe room service, the tradesmen, the maid, the front desk, anyone with a snowball's chance in a sauna of seeing him leave his room. It paid off. The last two days he's had an oriental woman come to call. Nice looker, good bone structure, b.. ," Duffield paused, obviously interrupted by a comment from the other end of the line.

Resuming, "Yeah, well if you could see her, you'd know she was worth commenting on. In any case, she stayed here under the name Anne Kwan. Paid cash but asked for receipts. Left an hour ago. I'm staying on Fowler. Tuck's trailing her in a rental. We'll call as soon as there is a turn in events."

CHAPTER 41

SEPTEMBER 1997

HOT TO TROT

WILMINGTON, DELAWARE

Lawrence Fowler had been seated at the cherry desk in the living room since sunrise. He had taken a bathroom break, and gulped down a hastily prepare boiled egg sandwich along with a bottle of Miller Lite. The room was now dark for the sun had set hours ago. The source of his fascination was a computer monitor connected to the Internet. Shortly after receiving his first draw, Fowler had purchased a 166-MHZ Intel Pentium processor loaded with a whole lot of stuff he didn't understand.

On the same weekend that he purchased the PC, he took two one-day, four hour courses at the Stanton campus of Delaware Technical & Community College. Navigating the Net had been the topic of the first. The second gave him a practical understanding of a rudimentary word processing software system called Professional Write. By Sunday evening of that same weekend, he knew all he wanted to know on either subject, or anything else about the PC. He could gather information from around the world and type reports based on the same.

The trip to the west coast had been hugely successful as a result of his previous efforts to come up with a multitude of scenarios from which Pester could choose. Gazing down into his bag full of hundreds of EPA penalty press releases, she had merely smiled and shook her head from side to side. She feigned interest as he had explained how he had gone about narrowing them down to the dozen clinically specific cases that he offered for her review. That morning she had asked him to order coffee from room service. She hid in the bathroom when there was a knock at the door.

Pester concentrated on his briefs for the rest of the morning, breaking the silence only to ask Fowler to order a tuna on white toast with lettuce, no mayo. Chilled bottled water to drink. She was more than half way through the documents, when she paused and broke the silence to say how impressed and pleased she was with his work.

"There are so many things in here that will do what I want, the difficulty will be in picking the best one," she had remarked. They then ordered a pizza with the works and two Kilian's Reds apiece to celebrate his work product.

The next morning followed the pattern of the previous day. She finished reading by noon. She asked questions while they ate lunch. Afterwards she began to make notes from memory, repeating on the dozen cases what he had done on the hundreds of press releases. After more than twenty pages of notes on the yellow lined legal pad, she looked up.

"Can't do it, Lawrence," she had said. "This is a language and world unto itself. I don't understand enough about what I'm reading to make a reasoned decision. There's too much riding on this to operate on intuition."

"How can I help?" he had offered.

Her barracuda smile challenged him, "You are in the wrong business, Lawrence. You should have been a consultant. What will it cost to give me a readable, working document that explains what I need to know to do my assignment?"

"Which is?"

"You know I can't tell you any more than I have. I need to know where the risks are in the hazardous waste program, where people can consciously or unwittingly violate some sacred regulation or permit term. Cut all the B.S. out of whatever you call it, wreckra. And pare it down to something I can work with."

"How soon do you need it?"

"I've gotten the OK to proceed, or you wouldn't be here. End of the month wouldn't be any too soon."

"Sooner is better?"

"Infinitely so," responded Pester, not wanting to haggle over a few thousand dollars with so much at stake. Let the piker lap up the crumbs while she needed him.

"Ten thousand dollars, delivery in two weeks."

"Deliver," said Pester as she thought, *I'm going straight to Roxanne with this. No details, but it'll pump her up that I've worked it out.*

Fowler's day job had become a boring cycle of inventory reports, customer service and human resource functions. He barely withheld his growing distaste for it from his fellow staff members. The burning desire to become curator had dwindled to a cold ash as his interests were channeled to the exciting and rewarding work with Pester. Sleep now was limited to no more than six hours a night. He worked continuously over the past weekend, reading the statute over and over again, until it finally hit home. As far as the Resource Conservation and Recovery Act was concerned, wreckra as Pester had pronounced the widely known acronym RCRA, it was a one act play, Subtitle C, The national hazardous waste management system. All the rest was filler.

He used every effort to keep it light, readable, and yet informative. Hunger pangs sent signals to his brain that it was time to nourish his physical self. It was time for a break, some French bread, a bit of salami with slivers of Gouda cheese topped with transparently thin slices of onion, a glass of port, and a review of his material. Clicking on the print icon, Fowler rose to make his repast in the kitchen, and returned with a small plate of snacks and a jelly glass half filled with a cheap, sweet, fortified port wine. The bubble jet printer was pumping out the last page. Fowler picked up the short stack of papers and sorted them in numerical order. He was somewhat disappointed at how few pages had resulted from ten days of work. Then he remembered how difficult the stilted language was to comprehend, how agonizingly repetitive, how boring, how stultifying, how beautiful it was to take all of that bureaucratese and put it down into comprehensible English for anyone to read and understand. This is what he wrote.

RCRA SIMPLIFIED

RCRA is fairly simple to understand. It has two primary functions. The first is the tracking of hazardous waste from cradle to grave through a paper trail manifesting system. The second is the prevention of leaks from buried storage tanks.

A waste is hazardous if it is either ignitable, corrosive, reactive or toxic. Some examples:

- **Ignitable**–Matches, oily rags, solvents

- **Corrosive**–Anything with a pH less than 2.0, such as sulfuric acid or vinegar or greater than 12.5, like lime or caustic soda. Corrosiveness is what causes the green stains on the enamel in your sink. Copper is being corroded from the pipes and then precipitated out.

- **Reactive**–Sulfuric acid is a good example for this one also because it reacts violently when mixed with water. Discarded Alka Seltzer also comes to mind.

- **Toxic**–EPA has a test you have to fail to be listed for this characteristic. Some common things that would fail are chlorine-

271

based bleaches and household ammonia.

Oh, lest I forget. A discarded material is also a hazardous waste if EPA says it is. They keep a list, actually three, which identify a whole host of substances which are banned from land disposal. Briefly the lists are:

- **List #1, the 'F' list, has wastes from nonspecific sources.** (I know you like the specificity of the source designation. Only the government...) These wastes have an 'F' in front of their list number.

- **List #2 is made up of wastes from *SPECIFIC* sources.** These wastes are made up from the gunk that our manufacturers have to get rid of, such as sludges from oil refineries and wood preserving facilities. Anyone would recognize that these were hazardous.

- **List #3 wastes are commercial chemical products.** If they are being discarded for inventory reduction purposes, or are released (spilled) accidentally. There are two distinct sublists. The 'U' sublist is made up of toxic materials

If you absolutely want to know what is on these lists, you can find them in Title 40 of the Code of Federal Regulations in Part 261, Subpart C. **(Pester, I know you absolutely want to know so I've attached them.)**

Here is what you have to do to get rid of it legally. The hazardous waste manifest system requires that any hazardous waste must be identified by the generator, transported by a certified hauler using appropriate documents and tracked, using those same documents, to an approved disposal site. It further requires that generators have the appropriate storage facilities for waste containment along with backup containment in the event a leak occurs.

The generator designation is site by site. That is why an individual corporation with many plants must have more than one Identification Number. The generator is the originator of the manifest document, the Uniform Hazardous Waste Manifest. This paper includes:

- Name and ID number of the transporter

- The facility that will receive the waste

- A description of the waste

- Certification of proper packaging and labeling

- Signature of generator

There have to be enough copies of the manifest for everybody; the generator, transporter and disposer. One extra copy goes back to the generator from the disposer to validate its receipt.

A generator can store hazardous waste for up to 90 days without a RCRA permit if certain conditions are met. These rules include secondary containment, safety training and how to plan for and react to an emergency related to the waste material.

I'm trying to get through this as quickly as I can. Let's get close to the end of this part of RCRA by pointing out the need to file reports with either EPA or the delegated state in which the waste is generated. EPA's reporting is biennially on March 1 of even numbered years. Some states require reports every year. If you want the details on what goes in the report ask for Form 8700-13A from EPA or its cousin from the delegated state. **(Pester, I can do that for you.)**

In conclusion, if you generate, transport, store or dispose of a hazardous waste, you better have the paper work to show you are in the system and playing by the rules. If you aren't, the roof falls in. Over simplifying here, penalties can be as high as $25,000 per day per violation. Prison sentences are pretty much what the traffic will bear. The law provides for up to 15 years.

Satisfied with the quality of his work, he pulled a Number 10 envelope from the desk drawer and addressed it to the post office box in Oakland that Pester had rented. She had promised a cashier's check in the mail within two days of receipt, and acceptance.

Lordy, Lordy, he thought, *I'm going to be heading toward solvency within the week. This could be the start of an early retirement for me. Trust to luck that she likes my work.*

CHAPTER 42   OCTOBER 1997

GOOD SHOT

BAKERSFIELD, CALIFORNIA

They were an hour and a half out of Van Nuys Airport. The San Fernando Valley residents were left behind to wake up, get the kids ready for school, get themselves ready, and get on the freeways to scurry about getting to their jobs on the choked freeway system. Wags and Pester had left before dawn, their Cessna Skylane RG lifting off the runway with the lights conveniently on just for them. Wags followed the trucks on Interstate 5 to Bakersfield until dawn. After that, he merely followed the ribbon of the highway as it melted off into the horizon.

"Course correction, old girl," Wags shouted above the engine noise, smiling wickedly as he said, "Going to have to yaw a bit to get my compass pointed north. We're going to follow Route 65 from here on up to Lake Kaweah."

"Yaw, but please don't roll or pitch unless you're going to find some air that feels less like a dirt road with potholes," Pester yelled back, her hands showing white knuckles. This was her first time up in a small,

274

single engine aircraft. It was an altogether frightening experience she vowed not to repeat if they ever made it back safely to Los Angeles. She was totally unprepared for the noise and vibration that accompanied their climb to cruising altitude. Even now, skimming along at 157 knots, the engine roared and vibrated. She checked her watch. *Just a half hour from the airport. The lake can't be any more than that,* she thought, *That means I'll be back on the ground in less than two hours. I can deal with this for that long.*

"Your wig's starting to tilt a little and the glue on the fake mole is coming loose you're sweating so bad, Pest. What say you just close your eyes 'til we get there. We're more than half way. On the way back I'll get her further away from the mountains so we won't bounce around so much."

Eyelids already scrunched tight, Pester smiled ever so slightly at the welcome news. *How in the world am I going to hold the camera when we get there,* she thought to herself, then immediately fell asleep from nervous exhaustion. Her leather coat kept her warm in the frigid cabin air caused by leaking doors and a balky cabin heating system.

Minutes later, "YAHOO, we're here, and the leaves have dropped. We're gonna' have a clear shot at the grounds."

"Oh My God," screamed a startled Pester, awakened from a sound sleep by a raving maniac. Her opening eyes, accustomed to looking at the horizon before she dozed off, now gazed upon terra firma. "We're going down, oh sweet Jesus, I'm too young to die."

Her body stiffened as she arched back against the seat, in a vain attempt to get farther back in the cabin to extend her life on this earth, even if just by a millisecond. Her pulse quickened, her heart slammed against her chest as she felt as if she was going to slide out the nose of the plane in its steep descent.

"Pes, get the camera ready. We'll be there in a few minutes. I don't want to be on the site too long. They might get suspicious."

"Camera, my foot. I'm not moving until you straighten this crate out," she screamed back, her body still arched stiffly in the seat. "I'll never be able to handle the camera anyway. My nerves are shot."

"No probléma, hombre. I'll take the pictures while you fly the plane."

Pester fainted. Wags's teeth flashed as he settled the plane out at 10,000 feet to wait for Pester Size to regain consciousness, which she did in ten minutes. Her body, slumped and relaxed in the seat next to the pilot, began to stiffen as she opened her eyes. Seeing the horizon once again, she sat up straight.

"Wags, get me home as fast as you can. I'll do anything to get back on the ground in one piece."

"Pes, I'm going down again but the pitch will be so slight you'll hardly notice. I've got to have pictures to plan the job. That's what we're here for, remember. I'm going to make a big sweep up to Orange Cove, then back to Hanford, Porterville and up to the Lake. We'll continue to drop and yaw in a twenty-mile circle so you won't be able to tell we're not just flying in a straight line."

"Sounds good to me."

"It'll get bumpy as we go down. Just remember, this plane's only twenty years old. It was built to take that kind of thing."

"Well, I'm over thirty, and I wasn't."

They got down to 500 feet, Pester held the controls while they made a north south pass. Wags took over, came back on a west to east bearing, then picked up the camera. Pester lunged for the controls.

They got their pictures and landed at Van Nuys before ten.

CHAPTER 43   1993

BIG SHOT

MELFA, VIRGINIA

The soft road tar yielded a bit of itself to each car that careened
southward down Route 13, heading for Virginia Beach in an endless
stream of pleasure seeking tourists from out of state who spent not a
dime on the eastern shore. Their hands didn't go near wallet or purse
until they were safely across the Chesapeake Bay Bridge and Tunnel.
There they filled the outreached hand of a toll taker.

Heat waves danced up from the highway, the sun glinted from
poorly placed chrome, and drivers jockeyed for position in the mad dash
to the beach. Robert Giddens regretted his decision to take the short cut
down the main highway on the weekly Sunday visit to his parent's
house. If he had made the right turn at Whispering Pines after he left
their home in Tick Town, he could have driven slow and easy, down to
Tasley, then a little zig, a little zag. Now he'd have been on Church Road,
on the way south to Onley. Due to his poor judgement, his wife Raney
and their two kids were huddled in the backseat, listening to him
muttering as cars passed his slow-moving Toyota. Their horns were

bleating at this wretch who interfered with their swift passage through this flat, ugly terrain.

"What's the matter with the car, Daddy?" wailed the little girl.

"I don't know, honey. I just know it won't go fast."

"Those bad people scare me, Daddy. Why are they hitting their horns? What did you do to them?," came the shrieking voice from the back seat.

"Raney, can't you quiet Shiranda?" he pleaded with his wife. " I'm having a bad enough time here. Should've gotten off this road in Olney."

As it was, he had to battle the car and the traffic until he was able to make a left on the last intersection north of Melfa.

✠

The little cottage stood where it always did, in a Loblolly pine woods, east of Seaside Road, at the headwaters of Nickawampus Creek. White aluminum siding covers the unpainted, silver gray clapboard. Black asphalt shingles replaced the mossy, aged cedar wood roof. A sturdy porch built of pressure treated lumber added a dash of sportiness to the little house, replacing the swaybacked affair that for years put out an aura of benign neglect. Two vacant wooden rockers just fit on the tiny porch floor. Silence reigns in the woods where no animal stirs. Shady nooks have been occupied. A soft hum comes from the house, its monotonous drone unheard twenty feet into the woods.

Inside, the shades are drawn. The old, white haired man snores softly in his recliner, stocking feet resting on the soft, merlot colored velveteen cloth. His tie askew, still knotted, but drawn below the unbuttoned white collar, he is taking his after church nap, building up an energy reserve for the coming Sunday afternoon festivities. The glasses, which had perched precariously close to the tip of his nose, now rested safely on the side table, placed there by his observant wife.

She sat in the floor lamp's amber glow, her Bible turned pages down in her lap, speaking softly as to her husband, knowing that he didn't hear, "Davis, ain't it nice that Robert lives as close as Tick Town and comes to dinner every Sunday, with Raney and the kids? We are blessed that he didn't either move too far away, or get too busy to remember his Mama and Daddy."

She continued to rock back and forth, the cushioned wooden rocking chair giving her comfort and relaxation in her old age, as it had in the past. Her face was unlined, her figure still slender. The only signs of decline were her slightly stooped posture when she was erect, and the hair shot with grey that she now had done up in a bun.

Then she shivered at the air's coolness, thinking and speaking, "That's not fair, really, they've all helped out now that they have good jobs. Charles paid for the siding on the house. Clearance bought the air conditioner. There's the color TV, the porch, all those other things that bring us comfort now. All the kids chipped in, except Robert." She smiled, remembering her youngest's chagrin at being strapped for cash, what with one child, one on the way, and Raney not working. "Peculiar, Davis, that Robert's visits started the year the other kids chipped in for the TV. Peculiar, in...."

She paused in mid-sentence, startled by the telephone's shrill chirping. As she got up to answer it, her husband's head came up. He looked bleary eyed around the room. Divining his whereabouts, he asked "Is it Robert and the kids?" Getting no response, he looked about at the shadows in the room, searching for his wife, whose disembodied voice seemed to be coming out of the corner where the telephone table was.

"Clearance, what a pleasant surprise. We haven't heard from you in so long. You never write."

"I'm sorry, Mama, I know I should, but it's just not my way," Clearance responded shyly.

"I knows you can write right well, son, but I also knows you keep right busy,"his mother said, not wanting her son feeling guilty during this unexpected interruption to their Sunday routine.

"What are you having for dinner today, Mama? Don't tell me Robert's going to be sitting down to fried chicken, mashed potatoes, and gravy. Mama, I haven't had any good fried chicken since I left home."

Mrs. Giddens smiled at the compliment, crooning back, "Well son, there's some things you take for granted growing up, that really are special."

"That's your fried chicken, Mama. When I get home, I want you to teach me how you get that special tangy flavor in the crust."

"Maybe I will, or maybe I'll just teach Pearl Stackhouse," she said, smiling at the easy way they fell into the teasing banter. Clearance was the only one who could give as good as he got, and did.

"Now, Mama, you know old Pearl musta married off by now. She's no spring chicken," Clearance said.

"You couldn't tell it by the way she looks. That girl has good bloodlines. You and her make some fine looking children, you don't wait too long."

"Yes, Mama. Could you put Daddy on for a minute? I don't have too long. Make sure he gives you back the phone. I've got something exciting to tell you."

"Davis, come here to the phone. It's Clearance, want's to talk to you."

Mrs. Giddens stood in the shadows, waiting for Clearance's brief, respectful conversation with his father. She knew that although he deeply loved his father, he never could overcome the admiration for him to the point that their conversation could be an easy one. Just 'How you feeling, Daddy? I'm fine', that kind of thing. Men stuff, she believed.

280

The door burst open, a flash of pink and white came dashing toward her. "Granny Giddens, Granny Giddens, It's me, Shiranda, your favoretest granddaughter."

Mrs. Giddens stepped out of the shadows, bent down and swept her granddaughter off her feet, hugging her, and asking, "Now who tol' you dat, youngun?" Shiranda collapsed against her in a splash of giggles.

Davis interrupted, "Here Mother, Clearance wants to tell you somethin'."

"Is that my skinny brother on the phone?" Robert asked as he came into the living room, a smile on his face anticipating a chance to talk to his favorite sibling.

"Yes it is Robert. I'll let you say hello in a minute. First, he said he had something exciting to tell me. Hold on."

"Is that my ugly little brother, come to eat my fried chicken?" Clearance asked.

"Well, he ain't gettin' it today. Cold ham, potato salad, and cold string beans with sugar and vinegar is today's ' it's too hot to cook' dinner."

"What's the matter, Mama, did my air conditioner break down?"

"No, son, not to worry. I just don' have the energy anymore for church, cooking and entertainin' all in one day. Now tell me about yo' excitement. Robert wants to talk, an' I knows you ain't got much time." She laughed when he told her. "Son, I can't hardly believe it. Wait 'til I tell your Daddy and your brothers and sisters."

She handed the phone to Robert. "Hey brother, what's happening? Where the hell, oops sorry Mama, are you?"

✠

"Robert, we look forward to you and Raney's visits with the kids every Sunday."

"I know you do, Mama. We do too, don't we Raney?"

Raney nodded.

"Mama, how 'bout Clearance, going to be in a movie? Can you believe it?"

"I do believe my chillen can do jus' about anythin'. You all talk so educated, it almos' shames me to open my mouf'."

Robert looked shamefacedly at his mother, "We don't do it to shame you, Mama. We all paid attention to our lessons, like we thought you and Daddy wanted us to."

Robert's mother came to him, put her hands on his shoulders, and said, "Dat is what we wanted. Your Daddy and I is very proud of all of you."

CHAPTER 44   OCTOBER 1997

OH MY!

DOVER, DELAWARE

We had a hard frost last night, bringing with it two forms of glory to our little neighborhood. Through the large window that affords my view of the world from my spot, I can see that the trees are now ablaze with fall crimson red, yellow and buffed orange. Out back, as elsewhere in the yard and general environs, the mosquitoes are dead. Despite an energetic effort of chemical warfare throughout the summer, the mosquito control boys can rarely claim victory until they get help from mother nature.

I've been thinking about the case. I can't say for sure that this oriental woman, Pester Size, was behind the theft at the Trust. But it seems unlikely that Dr. Fowler would have fallen off his lofty perch and into a den of thieves. No, his current involvement with her must be related to the original theft, or perhaps merely a convenience to her on another job. A fair assumption is that she got involved for money, on behalf of a client. After all, Tuck said she was a private eye, and had brought back a photograph of her office door to prove it. What was the client's motive? Was he or she related to the donor? Was it an ex-wife, or new, jealous husband?

With a cup of coffee in hand, I judged it best to get to my spot, turn on my slow but steady (28MHz) notebook, and begin a script. A showdown with Fowler was now a necessity. We had nothing to lose. He may not know the motive of Pester Size's client, but there was a possibility he knew enough to give me a start on figuring out why he took the one he did, how he did it, and why.

℞

"And that's how I recommend we do it," I said to Dr. Trader, who sat smiling in response to my proposal for Fowler's interrogation. His teeth had become gapped with age, giving him a somewhat ghoulish appearance.

Dr. Winston Trader had dressed for the occasion in a dark grey suit with almost imperceptible royal blue pin stripes. His tie may have been a collegiate one, but I had no knowledge of that. In any case, it was equally severe with light grey and black diagonal stripes, each about an inch wide. Combined with his pale complexion, white hair and demonic smile, he could have been Torquemada, the first Grand Inquisitor, ready to mete out torture and death in his quest for heretics.

Trader leaned over, then pressed a worn ivory button on the old fashioned, but elegant, brass intercom unit. "Ask Dr. Fowler to join me in my office, Joan," he said.

"Shall I say what it is in reference to?" came the bodiless response.

"No, just convey the invitation, please. He need not bring any files with him. Oh, Joan, a carafe of coffee and some ice water for my ten o'clock pill would do nicely as well."

"Certainly, Dr. Trader, right away."

Fowler was at the door as Joan opened it on her way out from delivering Trader's order.

"Excuse me," said Joan, backing away from the doorway. "Please come right in," she motioned as she held the door open. Then she swiftly exited, quietly closing the door behind her.

"Come in, Lawrence. Have a seat," motioning him to the red leather chair opposite me. "Help yourself to some coffee. I'll be just a second while I take my medicine."

Fowler had paled visibly when he became aware of my presence. The lack of an introduction to me by his boss was already causing him to twitch nervously in the chair. You'd have thought that Trader had been sweating people for years, so well was he pulling this off.

Trader popped the pill into his mouth, took a sip of water, swallowed, and then continued, "Now, to the purpose of the meeting. First let me introduce my guest. Lawrence, this is John Bunting. John is a security specialist I've retained to modernize our system. Bring us into the computer age in celebration of the next millennium."

I smiled. Fowler's lips cracked slightly as he nodded to acknowledge that he had heard and understood the statement. He now sat as rigidly as an errant schoolboy in the principal's waiting room.

"He has made some interesting observations over the past several months that we would like to share with you this morning. Before we start, please do both of you come share coffee with me. Lawrence, I'll have one spoonful of sugar as usual, if you please," the old man said cheerfully to his soon to be departed subaltern.

Fowler rose as if in a trance, and moved slowly to the table beneath the wall mirror. His hands shook visibly as he prepared Trader's coffee. He brought the cup and saucer, spilling coffee along the way, and placed it on a napkin on Trader's desk. I made a cup to be sociable, took my first and last sip, as Trader pointed a finger toward me, his silent instruction for me to begin.

"It is my method to evaluate an entire system, both physical and managerial, before preparing my recommendations for change. In the process of doing so, it came to my attention that there had been a breach of security, and it was a recent one. This made my assignment altogether more interesting, for I now had an actual theft that any modified security system must be designed to prevent."

Fowler sat woodenly, his eyes focused three feet above my head.

"As in all good detective matters, it fell upon me to establish how it was done, identify the thief, and find the motive. Without knowing all three, I would be unable to plan a successful means of defense against future theft. Understand?"

Fowler nodded affirmatively.

"I know that you did it, I know how it was done, and I believe I know the motive. The purpose of this meeting is to obtain confirmation."

Fowler winced at the accusation, but came alive, ever the opportunist, at the chance to salvage something, anything. "What's in it for me? Why not just deny everything you've said?"

Trader came back into the conversation, speaking in a low, soothing voice, "Lawrence, you've been with me for a long time, many years of faithful service. Clearly, you will be terminated as a result of our findings. Put this right and I'll allow you to resign. You can walk away without a blemish on your employment record."

Fowler lowered his head, cradling it in his hands, lithe fingers coursing through his stately mane. The room was silent for all of five minutes before he looked up, focusing on nothing in particular. "I've not much choice, I guess. Just when things were beginning to turn around. Where do you want to start?"

Much of what he said we already knew. I only interrupted when it was appropriate to seek out an unknown. "Your gambling debts tipped us off. Then they went away. How much were you paid to exchange the deposit?"

"I'd rather not say."

Trader's voice breached my response, "You will say, or you'll not work in a position of responsible charge ever again."

"Eighty thousand," came the mumbled answer.

I was taken aback. That was an enormous sum of money to pay for such a minor deed.

"Why do you suppose your client was willing to spend that kind of money for a random exchange of sperm?"

"I have no idea, but it wasn't a random exchange. She asked for the client by name."

"And you were able to deliver the named deposit?"

Fowler smiled, almost proudly under the circumstances, "I was."

Trader sneered, "Impossible. That is pure braggadocio on your part."

Fowler returned the look, and the remark, like that of a boy who had taught himself to steal from a mother's purse, even while it was under her watchful eye, "Not so."

Trader gleamed back at him, questioning the unbelievable.

"True, I don't have access to the Codex, which you think I know nothing about. But this was an extremely unusual request about an individual I was not likely to forget. Memory may be random, but certain events are burnt into our circuitry."

Trader harumphed, "But there are more than ten thousand deposits. How on earth could you remember a specific individual?"

"Well, that was a relatively slow year. He was not your ordinary

Jake, and I noted that the letters on the deposit were not his initials. I didn't write them down, cause I didn't see the need. But I had partial recall when the time came."

I was mesmerized, having lost control of the interrogation. I was on the sidelines, fascinated by the interplay between the employer, and about to be, former employee.

"Who was this man that he became emblazoned upon your memory?" scoffed Trader.

"Why who else but Elvis, the King himself," came the retort.

Trader slumped in his chair, passed out in shock at the response.

CHAPTER 45 NOVEMBER 10, 1997

FBI

LAKE KENAWAH, CALIFORNIA

Pester lay prone in the woods, binoculars focused on the circular, hot mix asphalt driveway. The sun was going down, the air already beginning to chill. She was glad for the warmth of the forest green sweat suit she wore over her thermal underwear. Earlier in the day, she had planted some battery powered microphones. One was in the shrubbery in the center of the driveway, another under the redwood bench by the front door. A short, potbellied man wearing a red plaid shirt, blue suspenders and khaki pants pulled a large Winnebago recreational vehicle up close to the doorway. He left it running as he stepped down, walked to the log cabin, and entered the front door without knocking. She could hear his cowboy boots clicking on the road surface and the deep rumble of the RV engine as it idled in the late evening twilight. She sighed with relief that the system was working. There had not been a sound or movement around the cabin all day with which to test it.

The door opened inward, and out strode Ken, red faced and staggering as he roared, "No such a way Ike, ain't nobody staying here while I go in to sign them papers. Tomorrow I'm gonna' be a free, white, rich redneck. And we're going to paint the town to celebrate. I already done hired a driver to park this critter outside every bar we choose to bless with our presence. He's even gonna drive us back here while we're sleeping it off. Then we can start all over again."

Ken stood aside, watching as his playmates came single file out of the house, in varying stages of inebriation. Then he marched them, drill instructor style, to the RV, the door of which he opened, and held open, until the last drunk was in the vehicle. Then he put in the cork, and off they went, with a roar of the diesel engine.

In two minutes they dipped out of sight. Silence was restored. The acrid stench of diesel exhaust fumes drifted into the woods. Pester wrinkled her nose as she swept the area with her binoculars, searching for signs of life. She lay there for another hour, repeating her visual surveillance every five minutes, until she was satisfied that it was safe to move in closer.

Rising slowly, she put the binoculars back in a leather case, then brushed the woodland detritus from her clothing. The pine needles clung tenaciously to the sweat suit's cotton weave. Pester muttered, knowing that she was going to look an untidy mess as a result. She failed to consider that the purpose of her mission was to complete it without being seen. Such was her vanity.

She left the security of the woods quickly and silently, having preselected the shortest course to the cabin. She was back in the woods, a cellular phone in hand within the hour.

"Wags, you can get them rolling. It's all clear here."

"You been in the house, I take it," came the flat response in a nasal drawl.

Pester could hear the Ryder tractor trailer idling in the background.

"No, I couldn't disable the inside sentry without doing some physical damage to the system. That would be a direct signal that the whole job was a plant. Didn't want to take that chance. I'll keep an eye on the house while you and your crew are setting things up. That'll have to do. Then I'm out of here"

"Seems like this increases the risk of getting caught some," replied Wags, angling for more money for the job.

"Seems like," Pester said, knowing he was right. She heard the Ryder tractor howl before she pushed the end button.

Good, she thought, *I want them to be away from here before sunrise. I'll dicker on how much more he gets when the job's done and I've been paid. There will be time enough to think on what his added risk is worth between now and then.*

℞

Wags and crew crept into the ranch an hour later. The caravan included two rented tractor trailers, a flatbed carrying a backhoe and a forklift with oversized tires, and two Ford Broncos loaded with men. The exhaust pipes on both the backhoe and the forklift were connected to aluminum beer kegs packed with a muffler mix of SOS pads and fiberglass insulation. Wags was out of the lead tractor before the wheels had stopped rolling. His arms were waving a personal shorthand of silent commands to the roustabouts who already had the vehicles started and moving down the flatbed ramp. Two skinny young black men, right off the streets of Watts, jumped out of the lead Bronco, and ran toward the first truck. They wore only cotton briefs under their black coveralls. When the job was over, they would change back into their street clothes, giving Wags their uniforms to destroy.

The overhead doors of the Ryder trailers slid open and the young men jumped in. They each jumped back out with a back pack worn in reverse on their chest. They reported to Wags who was checking an illuminated wrist compass. He pointed to the woods to his left. As they ran off, two Vietnamese replaced them. Wags shuddered at the sight of them.

"You look like the freaking Cong in those coveralls," he said, flashing a grin. "Now come on, and I'll spot you."

He moved quickly, spacing the two about twenty yards apart. "Now face the woods and set up those tripods so the lasers are three feet off the left and right shoulders of Muhammad and Tyrone. Just like we practiced, nothing fancy."

Wags waited, impatiently checking his watch. They had gotten the setup down to under two minutes. He wanted this done right, the rest of the job's success relied on this first step.

"Set Boss," the two men whispered in unison.

"Turn them on."

The thin red beams pierced the night, penetrating the woods. Wags raced after the twin beams. "Perfect," he said as he looked into the forest, tracing the trail of the one off Muhammad's left shoulder. "Good penetration. Follow the beam and get your lights down as far as the laser can take you. After that, just look back over your shoulder to judge your alignment from what you've laid down. Now hurry," he said as he gave the young black an encouraging pat on the buttocks.

Wags wasted no time getting to Tyrone's starting point."Not so good," he commented. "But look here. The laser will get you about 35 yards in. After that, just use Muhammad's line and yours to keep as straight as you can."

Wags stayed for about five minutes, until he was confident that the nine volt lights, shaded in cheap olive green plastic, were visible and going in reasonably parallel to each other. They illuminated each side of the temporary road. Then he left to join the Vietnamese who had already gone back to start shifting the loads from the pallets to the front end loader.

By now, everyone except the equipment operators was sweating profusely. The fork lift would work continuously until all of the trailers' contents had been removed and staged for the next movements.

Good men for this kind of work, Wags thought. *They can work without supervision once they've been trained and gone through it enough times.*

Unlike his robot charges, Wags now had to deal with the only uncertainty of his entire plan. He had no ground truthing when he and Pester had shot the aerial photo's. He had to make do with Ken's Humvee as the basis for scaling everything else on the photograph. Now in the dark, under the minimal light thrown by the bordering lights, Wags worked his way down a memorized trail, leaving lime dust in his wake from a hole in a cloth sack slung over his shoulder. It was tedious work, walking through the woods, holding a three-foot baton in each hand of his spread eagled arms. His arm spread, plus six feet, was the clearance needed by the front end loader. Depending on the roughness of the terrain, they might also be able to get through with the fork lift. It was narrower, so the path he was taking now would suffice.

The Watts contingent, eager to impress the boss on their first job with him, raced past him so swiftly, they might have been a puff of wind, for when he looked up, they were gone. A few minutes later, he could hear the soft scratching of their rakes, clearing away the detritus of fallen leaves and pine needles from the path he was blazing. Sweat dripped from his soaked headband, stinging his eyes as he crept along in the dim light. He stopped, lowering his arms, listening again for an underlying change in the noises of the night.

He grunted as the blood rushed back into the extremities of his hand. The muffled roar in his ears could be the blood now surging through his system, or, as he hoped, the movement of the front end loader with the first load. He dropped the batons, and slowly massaged his deltoid and biceps muscles. Then it was time to move again. The rakers were now close enough to be clearly audible.

℞

Pester had on white cotton athletic socks, a white cable pointelle pullover and a dark blue striped wrap skirt, which completely covered her legs as she half dozed on the red velour love seat in her office. She had been awake for more than 36 hours, was at the bottom of her biorhythm, and needed the clothes to keep her warm. The phone began the first few notes of Vivaldi, when she picked up, punched the speak button with a short, port colored nail, and said huskily into the phone, "Here."

"We're done. The woods have been restored to their pristine beauty, not a leaf or pine needle out of place. Oh, my achin' arse."

"How's the dirt look?"

"That soil scientist I hired up to Cal Tech sure knew his stuff. Even I couldn't tell what we put down after a few passes with the rototiller and the rakes."

"Get on home after you shed the troops. I'll see you in two days with your stuff."

"Gone to glory."

Pester placed the phone back on the charger, got wearily to her feet, and headed for the door.

Time to find a pay phone and get Larry to bring on the federales.

CHAPTER 46   **NOVEMBER 12, 1997**

TERRIFY

BEVERLY HILLS, CALIFORNIA

The door to the master bedroom in the RV opened, revealing a disheveled fat man in a wrinkled white dress shirt and grey suit trousers in the same condition. Bright red suspenders hung loose by his pants, swaying as the vehicle jostled him back and forth.

"Hey driver," Ken bellowed, "Can't you keep this crate from jumping around. I've got to piss like a steer. I won't be able to hit a thing."

The driver, still dressed in a red plaid shirt and khaki pants, looked back briefly, then shouted, "How 'bout I find a spot to pull over so's you can drain your lizard in comfort."

"Yeah, yeah, do that," Ken said as he disappeared into the bathroom, only to lurch out again with a relieved look on his face. He stumbled forward to the driver, squinting his eyes as he peered out the windshield at the late afternoon sun's piercing brightness.

"What's all them trees doing out there? Where are we? I don't recognize this piece of road."

"Sequoia National Forest. You fellows was in such bad shape this morning, I didn't think I'd see any of you 'til sundown. That's such a boring ass ride up the Interstate, I figured to take the scenic route, enjoy myself while you guys were sleeping it off."

Ken slapped him on the back, "No problem, partner. I'm going right on back to bed." He turned and staggered down the hallway. "See you tonight. I left your pay in the fridge if you get bored and want to leave. Plug us in so the air and electric keep running, if you don't mind."

The driver waited until Ken opened the door to the bedroom, then shouted, "You bet, Cap'n." He then checked the side view mirror, put his foot down on the accelerator pedal, and eased out on the road.

Fifteen minutes later, Ken swung the bedroom door open and lurched out, complaining, "Man, I can't sleep the way this thing keeps moving around. I'm liable to puke." He grabbed a bottle of Jack Daniels from the cupboard, a can of beer from the refrigerator, and made his way to the co-pilot's chair alongside the driver.

Propping his bare feet on the dash, he took a generous swig from the bottle, sighed his satisfaction, wiped his lips with his hairy forearm, capped the bottle, and put it in the nylon mesh bag that hung from the ceiling.

"This is more like it. As long as I can see what's making this baby dance, I'll be all right." Hands freed once more, Ken picked up the can of beer from the cup holder and snapped the tab.

Popping the ring of a Friskies Fancy Feast Seafood Feast cat food can at the local SPCA couldn't have gotten a faster reaction. Men with undeniably fierce hangovers, lusting for a taste of the dog that bit them, swayed, crawled and bounced through the RV in a mad race to the propane powered refrigerator. Within two hours they were all uproariously drunk again. Empty beer cans and bottles of Jack Daniels bourbon and Smirnov Vodka rattled back and forth on the floor. Slurred voices peeled out long forgotten songs from the Four Tops, roaring "Baby I need your loving" as the RV barreled down the road. By the third hour, there was a sloppy chorus attempting to harmonize the Carpenters' *Close to You*. One hour after sunset, the RV was silent as it came up the lane to the ranch. The driver turned off the engine, connected the electric, pocketed his money, and quietly closed the door.

♀

Seven men in black uniforms, armed with shotguns and nine millimeter automatic pistols, walked stealthily through the forest. The murkiness of the false dawn melted into a pleasant yellow glow as the sun rose. Squirrels stopped chattering and fled to the safety of their nests as they heard the faint sound of man in their midst. Birds flew away as rabbits froze in place. The silence which preceded the group now extended to the forest's edge.

The leader, with a mustard yellow arm band distinguishing him from his look alike black faced counterparts, halted in mid step, crouching to the forest floor as his hand signals told the others to do likewise. They had reached their objective. All that remained was to spread out to cut off any attempted escape through these woods. Justice would prevail. The leader, back to his quarry, simply raised his hands, pointing outward with the index finger of each hand. The men swiftly moved to their appointed posts, whispering back their arrival through the microphones on their headsets.

Squirrels, curious at the sudden absence of man sounds, noised their comment to their neighbors as they poked their heads out from their leafy nests to look around. A passing crow dropped down, landing on a needled branch, drawn by all the chatter. Soon the forest was back to normal, abuzz with birds, mammals, insects and reptiles pitted in nature's relentless war of attrition.

One by one, a small armada of grey Chevrolet Corsica's rose over the horizon. They undulated toward the woods, like segments of a caterpillar, on the narrow asphalt road. The front seat passenger in the

297

lead car wore head gear similar to that worn by the men in the woods. Clearly operating at the woodland leader's directions, the cars came in at idle speed. Like Indian hunters of old, their hushed movement did not interrupt the morning cacophony in the forest.

The cars spread out to form a vehicular wall just as they entered the circular part of the driveway. Four men, all dressed in camouflage suits, got out of each car, thirty-six men in all. Each man clipped a wooden clothespin on the edge of each car door to prevent it accidentally closing. The locks on the trunks had been made inoperative with masking tape. Bungee cords were quickly removed to get at the weapons cached there.

Weapons of choice in hand, they fanned out, walking to posts that would bring all remaining points of exit within a firing lane. The leader checked his watch, then smiled.

Everyone should be in place in ten minutes, he thought. *Even the techno nerds, wonder of wonders.*

The techno nerds were easily identified by their lack of weapons, their olive green arm bands, and their collective look of bewilderment. There were ten of them, each partnered with an aggressive looking commando type. They trailed their protectors as they walked to their assigned spots.

"What now," the leader muttered as he saw one after another of his charges stop and look skyward in his direction. Then he heard the roar of a helicopter approaching from the south, from the direction of Los Angeles.

"Get on to your posts, on the double," he shouted into his headset. "Take cover if you can't make it."

Roxanne was sprawled on the recliner, desperately trying to get her swollen body into a comfortable position. She sighed as the control buttons maneuvered her into an almost prone position.

"Crap, who can that be?" she blurted in exasperation, as her right hand searched blindly for the portable phone. Her unlisted number limited her incoming calls to a few. Opening manners were never a problem.

"This better be good. I'm not in the best of moods with this kid jumping around like a finalist in the floor program at the Olympics," she hissed.

"It doesn't get any better," growled Pester. "Turn your TV on to Channel 3. I'll call you in a few months. We can discuss final payment."

Roxanne righted herself, grunting even though the recliner's motor was doing the work. As soon as she was in a position to find the remote, she powered up the television.

"...recently divorced from Roxanne Carr, the television sitcom star. The raid, which took place shortly after dawn, involved more than 30 FBI and EPA agents. All of the occupants of a motor home found at his residence have been placed under arrest. WNBC has learned exclusively that the Department of Justice will enter a three-count indictment charging conspiracy, illegal transportation of hazardous wastes, and illegal storage of hazardous waste at a non-permitted storage facility."

Roxanne bellowed, "Got that bastard down. Now let's skin him and stretch his hide until it won't stretch no more. Pester, you done good."

She clicked the screen off, and brought the recliner up, pushing off to get herself upright, she then proceeded to do a little war dance, shouting at the top of her lungs.

The phone rang again.

"What is it this time? I'm not even finished celebrating the first one." Roxanne shouted into the receiver.

"Pardon me. My name is John Bunting. I don't mean to interrupt your revelry, but I believe I have come upon some information that may be of interest to you."

Roxanne's eyes narrowed. "How did you get this number? Anyway, my agent clears all my communications. Don't call here ever again or I'll have your sorry butt arrested."

Just as she was about to hit the disconnect, Bunting calmly stated his purpose in calling, "This involves Elvis."

CHAPTER 47   **NOVEMBER 13, 1997**

IDENTIFY

LOS ANGELES, CALIFORNIA

Bunting was met at the door by a short white haired man, dressed in a blue blazer, white pants, a light blue shirt and red bow tie.

"Please come in. I'm Dominic Celio, Roxanne's agent. She asked me to be with her today. I'm sure you understand why."

"Certainly, Mr. Celio. I am a stranger to both of you, bearing perhaps even stranger news."

"Join me on the couch, Roxanne will be in shortly. She naps quite often, with the baby due any time now."

"Yes, I would have thought as much," responded Bunting, "as I recall my wife did the same thing."

"So you don't have to rehash it, why don't we wait..., Oh here she is. Come dear, join Mr. Bunting and me. He just got here"

Roxanne waddled in, her gait having nothing to do with her weight. It was an accommodation that millions of pregnant women made to the babies they carried.

"Thank you for seeing me on such short notice. May I call you Roxanne, or do you prefer..."

"Yeah, yeah, yeah. Call me what you want but get on with it. It ain't comfortable even lying down in this recliner. Say what you came to say, and get out."

Bunting smiled, "Well, let's proceed then. I was hired by a bank back east earlier in the year to modernize their security system."

"You're wasting my time. What's that got to do with me?" Roxanne spat out.

"I'll get to that in a moment with your forbearance. The bank in question is a rare establishment, it is a frozen sperm bank."

Bunting took notice that both Roxanne and Celio stiffened for an instant. Continuing, he said, "The impetus for the modernization was the theft of a deposit from the bank. Now, clearly, if I was going to successfully complete my assignment, it was important to figure out the when, why, how and who of it all. Understandable so far?" he asked.

Celio nodded, intrigued. Roxanne nodded, not pleased.

"The who, how and why required a bit of digging but in short order, my associates and I had the thief dead to rights. It was an inside job. His motive was as old as civilization. He was in debt, a gambler he was, and needed money. How he did it required some thought and, quite frankly, corroboration by the thief himself, for the security seemed impregnable. But we convinced the company not to make a move on him right away."

Feigning boredom, Roxanne interrupted, "Interesting story, but so far you are still wasting my time."

"Ah, just so, for you are not yet a player in this little tale of intrigue."

The recliner shot up, as Roxanne fixed Bunting with a melting stare.

"For you see, it wouldn't have done to leave it at that. Firing the employee and possibly charging him with burglary was certainly an option, but that wouldn't tell us who put him up to it. He was only a little man driven by greed. It was important to know the underlying reason for stealing the specimen. We had to know its intended use if we were to protect the bank's depositors against future theft." Bunting paused, and asked, "Any questions.?"

There being no response, he continued, "Then we got a small break. The curator of the bank allowed me to place a 24-hour surveillance on the thief. This led my associates to California, to a private detective named Pester Size, and to an apparent dead end. All I received from the surveillance efforts was a rather large invoice for services rendered, and a list of people contacted by this Size woman. The only name I recognized, other than yours of course, was the thief's. At that point I was stymied."

For the first time, Roxanne could not disguise her interest in Bunting's revelation. She sat forward in the recliner, asking him to go on with the presentation.

"But as far as we were concerned, we were really not any better off than we were before. So the curator and I decided we had no choice but to grill the thief. A general beating of the bushes to see what would fly out. The man broke down, telling us about his gambling debts, fear that he would lose his job if the curator found out. There wasn't much new in his confession, until he said that he was paid $80,000 for the heist. I needn't mind telling you, I was floored by the amount."

"Why was that?" asked a curious Celio."That's a small enough sum in L.A."

"Because we thought it a random theft, the pilferage of something worth nothing on the street," replied Bunting.

"Random? Why go to all the bother if he didn't know the identity of the donor? That wouldn't make sense," said Celio.

"Indeed, why? But you see, we reasoned he couldn't possibly know the identity because the specimen was one for which the donor had anonymity in the storage area. The donor used a different name for the registry, whose initials were then encoded on the specimen container. The actual name was kept in a codex by the curator under lock and key. Only he, and eventually I, was aware of its existence."

"And what did the crook say when you asked him how he knew which vial was the correct one?" Roxanne asked, suddenly curious.

"He said that business had been slow the year the deposit was made. A rumor that there had been a deposit by famous donor from outside the area had swept through the bank that summer of '69. The culprit had been able to confirm the rumor by romancing the nurse who had been the only person, other than the curator, to be involved with the deposit. The donor in question was none other than Elvis Presley. Surprisingly, the thief saw only one new specimen come into the vault over the next several days after the King's visit. As he recalled, and it had been many years, the initials were MAB, not Elvis's. Sure enough, when he was paid to steal it, he found only one vial beginning with M in the year 1969. The vial's encryption was #BVFAT/32 @MGB. As far as he was concerned, it could have been A or G, but he knew the M and B were correct."

"And that was the one he stole," said a relieved Roxanne.

"Yes it was."

"So what's that got to do with me?"

"I think you know. You were the one for whom the sperm was stolen. The result sits there in your womb."

"I don't get it. You've no proof of that. Even if you did, you're not a cop or a lawyer. Even if you were, I can't believe the sperm bank could stand the type of negative publicity an allegation like that would generate," Roxanne gloated.

"I have no definitive evidence," Bunting replied, "simply a strong notion derived from my voyeuristic reading's of my wife's National Enquirer. Your falling star, the timing of the theft and the pregnancy, and the attendant publicity all seemed a little too coincidental for me. As to proof, medical science could help us out a little in determining your child to be's lineage. But I am not here on business."

Celio joined in, "Then why are you here? Blackmail?"

Looking offended, Bunting responded, "How on earth could I extort money from a woman who has been using the entire event as a publicity scheme? I am here to provide a pregnant woman with some information that may be helpful to her in the future when she is raising this child."

"Hell," guffawed Roxanne, "what could you possibly have found out about Elvis that the world doesn't already know four times over?"

"Some facts I discovered out of curiosity, that were not really required by my assignment. There is someone who you need to meet Miss Carr. I have a limo waiting, if you and Mr. Celio would trust my judgement as to the importance of that meeting."

Bunting rose, extended his hand, saying "Come, I will tell you some more of the tale as we drive."

R

Bunting faced his companions, with his back to the driver. His offer of refreshments declined, he continued the story, "I was curious about the name Elvis had used in the registry, and whether it may have been ancestral. My interest caused me to spend an entire Sunday afternoon on the Internet, searching through genealogical records. It was an interesting exercise. The Net is alive with genealogical sites. It turns out that the name that was used was that of his grandfather."

"I shoulda' stayed home. This is boring the hell out of me. Where are we going, anyway?"

"To a place in Glendale. We won't be much longer."

"We better not, or you can turn this rig around and take me back."

"This may interest you. The grandfather had a twin brother named Aaron."

Roxanne perked up at the mention of the name, "Just like Elvis's middle name, right."

Bunting smiled approvingly, "Very good. The grandfather's name was Garon."

"That was Elvis's dead twin brother's name," Roxanne squealed.

"Right once again.

Roxanne pushed, "What else did you find out?"

"The two boys grew up and went their separate ways. I took the opportunity to talk to descendants on both sides of the family. Cousins in Elvis's generation were not aware that their counterparts existed. I'm taking you to meet the cousin that Elvis never knew."

"Is he an entertainer, too?"

"He is, but he never made it to the big time. Here we are."

The limousine drew to a halt in an alley lit by a single dingy light that allowed the passengers to read 'Stage Door' as they departed the vehicle. Celio held the door open for Roxanne who followed Bunting into a dreary corridor, through another door, and into a foyer that was close enough to the stage that crowd noise came filtering back. Bunting knocked on a door with a faded white star, then waited patiently.

The door was opened by a tall handsome black man, dressed in a white jump suit trimmed with gold and sequins. Roxanne could see a cape hanging over a chair as she anxiously looked around the entertainer, looking for Elvis's cousin.

"Roxanne," boomed Bunting, "meet Clearance Giddens, the Black Elvis, grandson of Garon, and the father of your child."

Celio and Bunting were able to break the swooning Roxanne's fall, gently lowering her to the floor. That left no one to help Clearance Giddens, who had passed out, and fallen back into his dressing room.

CHAPTER 48   JANUARY 2, 1998

EPILOGUE

DOVER, DELAWARE

This has been an altogether satisfactory assignment. The astute reader needs a few more details to understand how the two sperm vials became mixed up. It wasn't by accident. You see, after Elvis had departed Wilmington, Doctor Trader became anxious about the impregnability of the Trust's security measures, despite the fact that they were of his own design. He trusted his staff implicitly, yet they had never had a donor who was anything other than an ordinary, albeit rich, man. He began to lose sleep, worried that greed would overcome honesty.

The name of Elvis Aaron Presley appeared only in the codex, where it was cross referenced to Miles A. Bunting in the registry. The codex was kept under lock and key. Trader believed only he knew of its existence. And yet, there had been few deposits that year. How easy would it be for a staff member to deduce that the MAB vial had been falsely encoded since it was one of the few that came in that year around the time of Elvis's appointment. The only thing he could think of to further safeguard the King's deposit was to change the number 32, which represented the year 1969, to 23, or 1965. He doctored the books, and no one was the wiser. The sham was already in place when Trader had authorized the annual audit by Packer, Picker and Pucker.

Was it coincidence or fate that caused Giddens' vial to be encrypted with his grandfather's initials, as were Elvis's? The answer came to me during a long conversation I had with the Black Elvis a month after the stage door episode. I asked him why he had used his grandfather's initials in registering his deposit. It turns out he hadn't. Mr. DuMont was behind that. You see, back in the late sixties, the Brandywine Valley Frozen Assets Trust was an all white fraternity. This was before the civil rights movement made the awesome push toward racial equality. Mr. DuMont, of the Wilmington pork belly fortune DuMont's, did not want to risk the smear on his reputation, however already tarnished, if word got out that the deposit he had sponsored was that of a Negro. The young man's future lay before him. For all anyone knew, Giddens interest in music could carry him far, exposing his name to the world. All it would take was for some snoop on staff to make the connection, and DuMont's name would once again be drug through the mud. DuMont knew that Clearance's grandfather had been white. His mother's fair skin and straight, long hair had aroused DuMont's curiosity to the point where he asked the boy about her parentage. Using the grandfather's initials gave Dumont the perfect, untraceable bit of deception he had sought.

That about puts a wrap on solving this little mystery. One other oddity came out of my inquiry into the ancestry of Clearance and Elvis. As you may have already deduced, my father was James Ray Bunting, the great-grandfather to both, which makes me their great-uncle. I'm all shook up.

R

Roxanne gave birth to a healthy, nine pound baby boy at L.A.'s Cedars-Sinai Medical Center at 7:35 a.m. on Saturday, November 15, 1997. Pester Size's bonus was canceled in the delivery room, where Dominic Celio stood in as the surrogate father.

℞

Clearance Giddens hasn't quit his day job but continues to pursue his dream of being a full time entertainer. Meanwhile, he is still packing them in at the Chincoteague Inn, a restored boathouse on the intercoastal waterway in eastern shore Virginia. This information comes courtesy of George Roache's article in the Sunday issue of *The Daily Times*, the Salisbury, Maryland newspaper.

℞

A three-count indictment against Roxanne's ex was returned by a federal grand jury in Wilmington, Delaware charging felony criminal environmental crimes. It is alleged the defendant conspired to and violated provisions of the Resource Conservation & Recovery Act (RCRA) relating to storage and disposal of hazardous wastes-42 U.S.C. 6928(d)(2)(A) and 6298(d)(4), and 18 U.S.C. 2 and 371.

℞

Pester Size closed her office and moved to Reston, Virginia. She now works as a consultant to the Environmental Protection Agency, Office of Criminal Enforcement, Forensics and Training.

℞

Larry Fowler was allowed to resign without prejudice from Brandywine Valley Frozen Assets Trust. He now works as a black jack dealer at Bally's in Atlantic City, New Jersey.

℞

According to the New Orleans *Times-Picayune*, Elvis was seen in the French Quarter on Rampart Street rollerblading toward Louis Armstrong Park late one evening just before Christmas last. We had a blue Christmas without him.